Island in the Storm

MINDSTIR MEDIA

Published by Mindstir Media, LLC
45 Lafayette Rd | Suite 181| North Hampton, NH 03862 | USA
1.800.767.0531 | www.mindstirmedia.com

ISBN-13: 978-1-7361190-0-6

Island in the Storm

HOW ALBANY, GEORGIA, SURVIVED THE APOCALYPSE

By Jay Beck

Contents

Part I – The Decline

The Snake   1
Bank Job   3
The Road Home   11
Asheville, North Carolina   20
Swamp Refuge   23
Sunday Morning   30
Trouble Begins   34
Sheriff Dozier   36
Message from Iran   38
The Doziers   41
Escape from Dothan   47
Iris   52
Willis Graham   60
Phoebe Putney   64
Henry Graham   83
Julian Cordell   86
Henry, Iris, and Jerico   88
SwiftyMart   99
Six Months Earlier   102
Siphoning   110
Lunch in the Park   112

Part II – The Crisis

Crash   117
Ballard and Dozier   119
Revolt Near Dothan   124
Finding Order   126
Dinner with the Doziers   130
Training   142
Fatherly Advice   146
Near Griffin   150
Neighborhood Managers   151
Swamp People to the Rescue   163
Mental Health   166
Crossing the Georgia Border   169

Energy   171
Interstate 75   179
Challenge from Leesburg   186
Barricades   192
Radium Springs   196
Marine Base   204
Tift Park   212
Lake Blackshear   217
Bad News   223

Part III – The Crunch
Henry Graham Emerges   232
Shopping at the Marine Depot   237
On the Base   247
Bobo   257
The Militia Matures   258
South of Albany   274
Report from Leslie   281

Part IV – The Apocalypse
Marine Base   285
Preacher   287
Conflict   296
Dawson Invades   308
Marine Base   320
Unexpected Trouble   333
Henry's Revenge   337
Double Pronged Attack   344
Marines   360
Dothan Attacks   365
Fight in the Swamp   378
the Beltway Battle Begins   384
Back Door Threat   389
Battle for the Bypass   392
The Marines Have Landed   398
Death   400
Marines   402
Willis Graham   404
Two Years Later   409

NOTE

My latest novel, Island in the Storm, is about surviving an apocalypse set in Albany Georgia. It tells the story of how citizens both black and white come together through the unlikely leadership of a young couple intent on saving their town from an encroaching international crisis, while simultaneously staving off the more immediate threat of armed soldiers planning to surround their town and destroy it.

The starting point for this book came when I learned of the large, mysterious and relatively unknown Chickasawhatchee Swamp located near my hometown of Albany, Georgia. The more I thought about the swamp and its vast, although shrinking land area, the more I became intrigued with the prospect of people living there. People living off the grid led the story into the need for their survival and then to an apocalypse affecting everyone. Survival became about caring and needing to trust and work with others. Nurturing the bonds of a society under stress is the way a culture ultimately endures.

I began to write this book two years before the COVID-19 health emergency. As the crisis became acute in my hometown of Albany, Georgia, I was amazed at the parallels to the world of fiction in my book. As devastating as coronavirus has been, with the conflict and lack of cooperation in the world today a story similar to the one in this book could still happened. It is with a sad heart that I dedicate this book to those healthcare workers who fought the pandemic, the patients who suffered its discomfort and the memory of those who succumbed to the illness. Any income derived from the sales of this book will be donated to the United Way of Southwest Georgia to support the Albany survivors of the coronavirus.

For more information on how to help:

Visit: www.unitedwayswga.org/give -
Text: REIMAGINE to 313131

Of send a check to:
United Way of Southwest Georgia,
P.O. Box 70429, Albany, GA 31708

**United Way of
Southwest Georgia**

In Appreciation

I am grateful for the advice and support of several people in the writing of this book.

Retired U.S. Army Major General Dean G. Sienko, M.D., M.S., and Vice President, Health Programs and P. Craig Withers, M.B.A., M.H.A., Senior Director of International Support at the Carter Center. Both provided helpful direction from their collective 80+ years of experience in public health. I appreciate their reading portions of the book and saving me from some erroneous assumptions about public health in a crisis.

Dr. Jay Hakes, author of two significant books on energy, lecturer, and former assistant to the Secretaries of Interior and Energy and James Marlow, CEO and Founder Clean Energy Advisors, and former CEO, President, and Co-Founder Radiance Solar gave me direction on the energy components of this book.

I'm grateful for Mike Corley for taking me on drives into the Chickasawhatchee Swamp area in a helpful orientation and his wife, Robin Corley, helped me with answers on questions about Phoebe Putney Hospital. Martha Hall drove with me around many of the Albany locations for me to renew my understanding of the terrain. Steve Cross provided information on the history of cypress trees in the swamp.

I reviewed aspects of firearms and hand loading with my cousins Beecher and Buddy DuVall, both expert marksmen. Another cousin, Bill DuVall, also commented on firearms and his personal experiences hunting and camping in the swamp, which plays a large part in the setting of the book. I wish to thank another cousin, Graham DuVall, for suggestions on the terrain around Asheville, North Carolina. Talented graphics artist Alyssa DuVall created the maps used in the book to orient the reader on areas near Albany, Georgia, as well as the cover concept. The graphic design for the chapter dividers and black and white introductory page is taken from a painting made by my mother back in the 1950s. Another cousin, Letty Chapman, gave helpful suggestions for the text. Still another cousin, Henry DuVall, provided guidance on drones and ham radio operations. So, there is something of a family affair in supporting my efforts. Claire May, a friend, found additional errors in my draft.

Once again, I am most grateful to my friend and editor, Rosalind Thomas, for her corrections and direction. Many of the interactions between characters and the flow of the narrative have been rescued by her from my less cogent impulses.

This novel is a work of fiction, and I've taken liberties in the descriptions of some locations, as well as institutions and their abilities to handle a crisis. I've also adopted myths as well as habits of swamp creatures. Although I used several names in the book from my friends and family, there are no character references or relations to the characters based on any persons alive or deceased. All errors or omissions are solely my fault and not based on any advice or direction I received. I invite any readers to visit **jaybeck.net** for information on my other ventures, and other available novels are mentioned at the end of the book. If you like this story, please say so on social media or the comments section of Amazon or Barnes and Noble.

Other Novels by Jay Beck

Treasure Hunt

Panama's Rusty Lock

Casting Stones

Part I – The Decline

The Snake

Iris spotted the rattlesnake when she went to gather the laundry hanging in the sun. She almost missed it with the hoe as it tried to slither away - chop, chop, CHOP. What luck the barking dog drew Iris's attention to it weaving through the grass and grown so fat from the rats that lived in the mass graveyard.

After she cleaned and skinned it, she carefully laid the knife down and then hefted the five-foot carcass across both hands, let it bounce, and calculated how many meals they'd make from it. Snakes were becoming rarer, and one this size was a real treat. Pretty good meat that tasted like a gamey fish, not like chicken, which was what everybody used to say before they had to eat it. She'd save the skin and make something out of it later for the kids at the hospital where she was the administrator.

She wiped her forehead, leaned from the table in the yard, and stretched her back. The flies were all over her. She let the dog out of the house where she had put it and tossed the snake's guts out into the ground for its meal, and also to draw off the flies. She knew it was somehow wrong not to save the entrails for her and Henry to eat, but after all this time, she still could not bring herself to eat animal viscera. She buried the head along with the rattles under a large rock so the dog wouldn't get it and eat the poison sacks and whatever was in those rattles that couldn't be good to eat, even for a dog. Gator, like other dogs that had survived the worst of the famine, were becoming popular again. Not for their meat, but for their protection and companionship.

Then she felt a kick. Oh God, don't let it be a problem with the baby. She rubbed her hand in a circular motion over the round spot on her swollen belly. It was bad enough that she had gotten pregnant. They had been careful, but it happened anyway. Everyone was afraid to have kids now. No medicine and the damn germs. The survival rates for the babies and mothers with all the infections made pregnancy a risky venture. Yet, people had been doing it for thousands of years before somebody pulled the plug. She'd just have to be extra cautious now.

It was true that they'd come a long way… Now almost three years… But she could see over at the side of the yard that the big garden still needed lots of work. Damn weeds. Some things never change. Many did. Most would never be the same.

She washed the snake in a bowl with the same water she had used to bathe that morning. Later she would add their urine and pour it along a line of vegetables, maybe the squash or the string beans. The dog finished the snake guts and barked for more, wagging his tail just as her old dog, Midnight, would have done.

She smiled at him while he looked around and smelled for more to eat, and it made her think of a story Henry had told her just last year. It was about something that happened back at the beginning, when the edges weren't so hard. The world was so different then. Back in those days, there still might have been a chance to save it.

Bank Job

Henry Graham watched the old dog across the town square and imagined what it might be thinking as he waited in the quiet time before the robbery. He guessed the fall chill made the dog's bones ache as the cold of the hard concrete soaked through his thin skin. The mongrel had been looking over at Henry in the truck parked across the way past the bank with its motor running, its exhaust stirring the morning air and giving a murmuring sound to the sleeping town. He thought the dog must be thinking that maybe he had some extra food, and would try to look pitiful as it made the effort to stagger over to him. Once it got closer, it would be able to tell if Henry was friendly or would try to hurt him. Dogs noticed that.

As Henry waited in the stolen pickup truck, he coughed at the smell of exhaust and gasoline from the chug of the un-tuned engine. It was starting to get to him through the faulty heater and rusty floorboards. He felt he should not have to suffer this discomfort after driving all the way up here from a South Georgia swamp in his own clean truck, but the fall weather outside made it too cold to turn off the motor in this crappy ride. To top all that, he couldn't find any open fast food places to grab something for breakfast. Around here, most of them were out of business.

He had left the small motel with the "for sale" sign in front that morning with his buddy Trey, where he had paid in cash the night before. On the way to the bank, he and his friend hot-wired this vehicle they had spotted the day before. Unfortunately, getting these inconspicuous rides usually meant they got one with smelly trash, ratty seats, and a half empty gas tank.

He considered the option of stealing a better-quality vehicle, but as he watched the day brighten, concluded that it was good idea not to be noticed when you were in the bank robbing business. So, he shifted in his seat to avoid the spring poking his back and resigned himself to suffering the dusty smell of crusty cow shit until he could finish this job and get back to his own long-bed, comfortable vehicle with the pine fresh tag hanging from the rearview mirror.

As he looked for potential threats that might interrupt the stick up, the absence of traffic and stillness in this town made him paranoid. His imagination conjured up a picture of police hiding behind one of the empty buildings scattered about, hands on their gun holsters, ready to jump out when he entered the bank.

The only activity on the street was that brown dog with white fur framing his face, now slowly creeping toward him down the sidewalk, side bones showing and looking like he might fall over any minute. The whirling activity from earlier years had slowed down to a trickle compared to the last bank job he had pulled only ten months before. Even though that had been over in South Carolina and this was Tennessee, the look of these small factory towns was the same. There was usually only one main bank near the center of town where they had lots of cash on hand to accommodate the flood of payday checks from the one plant in the area.

Henry rolled down the window to toss out the half-eaten, mostly stale sandwich left over from yesterday to the dog. His arm was almost all the way out when he decided the dog was too far away. It might attract attention to whistle the pooch over. Too bad, he looked like he needed it.

He rolled the widow back up, looked over at his partner in crime, and wondered how Trey was going to feel for the rest of this trip. His buddy was taking medicine for his malaria, but sometimes he still got sick, sort of like he had the flu. Right now, his jaw was slack with his mouth cracked opened while he played with his Nintendo, fingers moving rapidly, aimless concentration on his face containing the sprinkles of an uneven, unsuccessful beard. Henry wondered if the facial hair was to make him look tougher and compensate for Trey's five-foot eight-inch height.

Henry could still hear some of the beeps coming through the cracked plastic around Trey's ears from that clunky headset. Trey was not good at introspection or sitting still, and was only comfortable when he had something that kept him busy. So, based on his being engrossed in the game, Henry guessed he was going to be okay, and then realized he had been staring over at him, which would likely make Trey nervous. He turned his head to scan the town square once again.

Henry knew he was good at this job, even better than his father. He thought through every detail. He was careful. He managed to block out the fear and also the pleading of the bank employees and the occasional customer.

He checked the time and saw only two minutes had passed since he had last looked. Henry shifted in the lumpy seat and drummed his fingers on the steering wheel. About five minutes to go until the fat manager would be arriving and opening the bank for business. He and Trey had watched this pattern for the last two days. Based on yesterday afternoon's Brinks truck delivery, they were sure today was the payday for the big Japanese auto parts factory down the road. Because of the computer failures and all the hacking, people these days were choosing to turn pay checks into cash rather than using electronics to handle their finances. If he and Trey were successful, there wouldn't be any money left when the factory workers carrying those slips of paper reached the bank.

It was a business plan that had been working way before Henry got involved. Always hit a different bank and only do a job a couple of times a year. They never robbed the same one twice, and they moved around the southeast so it would be impossible for the cops to anticipate where they would strike next. Trouble was, the factories in these piddly towns were being bought and moved and the small towns were drying up.

To add to his discomfort, lately Henry felt this job was an obligation he didn't want. He was tired of being the main one to support all those who waited for him to return with the money. The thrill was gone. He needed to break this pattern and live a more conventional life.

He particularly did not like the part of the job that involved having to intimidate people and watching them shrink in fear at what he might do to them. It was becoming harder for him to project his mean bandit character to the bank employees.

Finally, there he came. The fat man parked in a space near the door with his name on a sign by the curb. He arrived with a younger woman, same as yesterday. Still no armed guard with them. Maybe she was a teller or secretary. Maybe she was just someone who he gave a ride to work at the bank, or maybe the young woman was someone he was closer to than he should be. Maybe his wife did not know about the ride to work thing. Maybe. Must be. Those plaid golf pants and pastel coat were signs of the older, fat guy trying to look younger and more appealing. It wasn't working.

He lightly swatted Trey. "Turn off the game. Drop the headset. Let's go to work."

Trey looked up as he slowly as he turned off the game. "She's wearing that long coat again even though it's not even freezing. Damn, look at that crap green coat he's wearing. You're right, Henry, that man's wife must be buying all his ugly-ass clothes thinking it would keep him from running around. Look how she's keeping her distance from him. He's checking out her legs and her butt. When you get in there, point the gun at her to make fat ass get the money quicker."

In doing this job for several years after his father got sick, Henry had never run across anyone who was not fearful of a bank robber with a gun. He checked his gun. It was big and intimidating. Even though any bullet could kill you, people were more afraid of the larger guns. They never looked past the round opening at the end of the barrel where a bullet might come out toward them at any moment. If they had, they would have seen that he was not the kind of man who would hurt an innocent person… Not like some of the people you could see out there roaming around today…still without a job.

At six-foot-two, he was taller than most, but not so much he would stand out from many regular blue-collar workers. He wore cheap Ray Bans to hide what the girls called his dark, bedroom eyes. He dressed like most everyone he saw in khaki work pants, a neutral-color shirt with the sleeves rolled up to show the bands of forearm muscles, dark brown hair growing out from under a baseball cap that said "John Deere," and shit kicker boots. He topped that today with a quilt-lined camo jacket. He checked to make sure he had one of those ski collars down around his neck he could pull up to cover from his nose on down when he entered the bank. Then at the last minute, he decided to leave his jacket in the truck. Nothing to snag.

Once he had the money, they'd switch to their own truck, which was also several years old and painted so it was not noticeable, but would run like a bat out of hell if need be. The bank manager would likely follow directions and not call the law as quickly if they took her along. Henry planned to give the man a don't-you-dare look that would give them the time they needed to get away from some fool sheriff throwing up local checkpoints. Then they could roll onto the interstate and head south where the police never put up roadblocks or chased after someone robbing a podunk bank of a few thousand dollars.

The man was unlocking the door now. Henry nodded to Trey. "Showtime. Drive me over to the front door, and then get ready out the back. Leave the motor running. No game playing while I'm inside." As he got out, he tossed the sandwich bag on the ground for the approaching dog as Trey slid over.

Five minutes later, Henry and the young woman, who had her hands tied and a sack over her head, came out the back door of the bank. He guided her into the truck and Trey drove slowly and carefully out of town. As they pulled away from the bank Henry pointed and said, "Watch the dog!" at Trey, who maneuvered around the brown dog with its head inside the bag, its thin tail wagging.

Henry made the woman scrunch down on the floorboard so she could not be seen by passing cars. She was breathing in heavy, short, scared breaths. As they rolled out of town and picked up speed on the highway, she calmed a little and started to speak. "You ain't gonna hurt me, are you?"

"No, ma'am. Weren't thinking on it."

"But you told Ralph that if he called the cops before two hours passed, you'd kill me first thing."

"We wanted him to hold off on calling them is all."

"Please don't hurt me. I need that job. We're all worried that the plant is gonna close and that will likely finish off the bank. They're down to a skinny shift as it is. It's just Ralph and me now at the bank. Everybody else is laid off. Nobody's doing any business, so you likely didn't get as much money as you hoped."

"Things do look kinda parched around here."

"Not just here. TV says everywhere. They say it's 'cause of those Wall Street bankers buyin' and sellin' things and then layin' people off. Even the dang strip centers are shutting down. Nobody has any money left to buy stuff and people are going broke. Now the computer nerds are wrecking everything. You know about that?"

"I wouldn't know about all that."

"They say it's not just here but all over the world. Nobody's paying their bills and now all those rich people that started it are going belly up." He reached out and touched her on the side of her head through the bag. She jumped.

"Ma'am, listen… We didn't put a rag in your mouth so you could breathe better, but if you keep up that yakking we'll have to change our minds."

"Okay, I'll be quiet. It's just that I talk when I'm nervous, but you don't likely need to worry about running into the police. They rarely patrol anymore 'cause they can't afford the gas. Half the stations around here don't have any gas anyway."

"Okay. Time to be quiet now and stay down on the floor."

They left her tied in the truck with the sack over her head at a roadside park where it looked like kids often came to play. It felt good to get into their own vehicle and head for home. When they drove away, they went one way so she could easily hear them depart, and then made a wide pass around the park to actually drive off in the opposite direction. They had to be careful because there were not as many cars on the road, so that made the chance of them standing out and getting pulled over by the cops more likely.

The Road Home

Back home, they grew some food and could cycle through a few of the older setting hens they had for the eggs to supplement the meat they got from gators, deer, hogs, fish, snakes, turtles, and frogs. Mostly, they were self-sufficient and bought fruits and vegetables from truck farmers on the side of the road for cash. Once in a while, they'd poach a cow or grab some corn from a farmer's land near the swamp, that was bigger than New York City, but they were careful not to do that too often or it might raise suspicion about where exactly they were living on a patch of land over in the dank-water, muck-filled quagmire and woods. However, that was not enough.

Four hours south, Trey spotted a sign for a Big Dollar Store, and when they pulled off the interstate and parked, Henry looked over a long list of materials they had to get for everyone on the island. Because they acquired so much stuff on these trips once or twice a year, it often attracted the attention of people in the store. They were always careful not to set a pattern, and went to different places to do the shopping every time. Lately, they discovered that some of the stores where they had intended to shop were closed or short on merchandise.

With almost twenty-five thousand dollars in fresh money, they entered the Big Dollar Store and Supermarket on the northern outskirts of Columbus, Georgia, to load up on all the staple goods on the list. Henry and Trey each ended up with three carts stacked with cases of canned tuna and chicken, soup mix, big kitchen matches, dried beans, rice, pasta, sugar, salt, flower, toilet paper, batteries, soap, Tampax, creams and salves, socks, medical supplies, every citronella candle or insect spray they could find, and every kind of long-lasting supply they needed to keep the island going for several months.

As Henry and Trey pushed the six baskets of stuff piled high, they got the attention of the other shoppers and the checkout lady. She of the big hair piled on top of her head, reared back and put her hands on her hips. "You boys gonna start a commune or something?"

A cover story they'd discussed in the truck earlier was ready. Trey said, "No ma'am. We picking up this stuff for a week-long revival over near Lake Martin, outside of Dadeville, Alabama."

She sneered. "I ain't heard about that."

"Nomum."

"What?"

"No, ma'am. I understand. Well, we headed over there now."

She started unloading the carts and scanning the enormous pile of merchandise. Still suspicious, she asked, "What's your church?"

Trey was gathering and packing things as fast as she slid them to him, then put the sacks of groceries into another cart. Henry lined up the carts by the door to take them out to the truck. He stammered, "We're a... affiliated with Christ the Redeemer."

"Well I heard of them, seem like."

"Yes'm. Like I say, affiliated. May not be the same ones you know."

Somewhat assuaged and pleased that she had found out

some gossip from the strangers, she said, "Well this pile of stuff ought to take care of whatever you need. We appreciate the business."

"Yes'm. Good that we saw you here. Never know what you gonna find over there in Alabama." He gave a nod over to the west and made a face that said folks over there weren't to be trusted.

She nodded. "Well, you're lucky you came when you did. We got a shipment just two days ago. Sometimes the store looks half empty." She paused to look about. "Delivery trucks don't come by regular and sometimes not at all. Things around here kinda dribbling out."

"Yes'm."

The heavyset woman kept a tight eye on them as she rang the groceries, and Trey continued to work as the bag boy to sack everything and put the bags in the carts. She sniffed as she finished and looked over the long string of items before she punched in the total. Then she stepped back and made a WTF face when Henry came up and counted out the cash.

She continued to watch them with sidelong glances, looking through the discount sales promotions painted on the glass of the outside window as they carefully loaded everything into sturdy plastic crates they had in the back of the truck under the slide in camper shell. She had to shift her heft from one side of the window to the other, past the two-for-one special sign and week-old bread close out attractions. They could feel her eyes on them and never looked back at her, but headed out a few blocks toward Alabama, turned around, and used a side road that took them away from the front of the Big Dollar Store and Supermarket in case the snoopy checkout lady was still looking out toward the street. They figured their shopping trip was likely the highlight of the week for her, and she would wish to exaggerate the story for as long as possible to her friends, relatives, or to anyone who would listen, including the cops. After zig zagging around, they found the U.S. 280 highway that would take them back toward South Georgia.

As he drove through the expansive Fort Benning military base, Henry remembered passing this way several years ago when he had started this job, driving for his father, learning the trade. On that day, there had been tanks rumbling through the woods on maneuverers visible from the highway that cut through the base. Today, there was just the nearly empty Seven-Eleven roadside markets, fields recently cut clean of crops and the graceful trees, peaceful roadside homes, and the grazing livestock of rural Georgia. There was a quiet beauty to an afternoon ride on the slightly hilly roads through the South, and with the first chill the fall, the leaves were beginning to turn colors that Henry enjoyed immensely. The gently undulating countryside made him feel peaceful, reassured, and secure. He was sorry that Trey, now riding shotgun, lost clicking in his Game Boy and cocooned in his earphones, could not enjoy the scenery with him.

South of the massive military base, there was a house on fire by the side of the highway. It had almost burned out, and as the yard around it was mostly dirt, it had not spread to the neighboring grassland and woods. Near the house, there was a ten-year-old car that looked shiny and recently washed with both front doors open. There was a mailbox by the road and other signs that it was not an abandoned property. Two dogs stood vigil by the road watching the smoke. Still, it was strange to see it smoldering alone. As Henry glanced back in the rearview mirror, he wondered where the owners could be and what they would think once they returned.

They looked for a gas station and passed two with signs indicating they were out before they got to Central Georgia, where they stopped at the Merritt Exxon filing station near Weston to fill up and top off all the five-gallon cans they had, as well as the dual saddlebag gas tanks on the truck. This out-of-the-way place in the country was often a sure bet to have fuel. On every trip, they were always careful to come back with the gas cans full so they could replenish the big fuel barrel on stilts they had in the barn. When paying at the checkout counter, they also got a big box of divinity candy and some pralines for the compound.

When they got back to South Georgia, they cut down Tallahassee Road just past Sasser near Albany and on down to Gillionville Road, where every few miles they passed a narrow bridge over a small creek feeding into the swamp.

After checking the traffic to make sure no one was watching, they turned onto Eight Mile Road, drove past existing farms and pastures, then turned again back toward Leary where Eight Mile crossed what used to be called Pretoria. Exiting the two-lane blacktop onto the dirt road on the edge of the swamp, they continued bumping along until they reached the one lane path that only they ever used. There was a grinding sound from the rusty chain when they unhooked the barrier lock with the sign that said "No Trespassing." After driving through, they reconnected it, then continued on the narrow path over tall patches of swamp grass all the way back to the dilapidated barn to hide the truck they were using. The barn also had a rusty sign that said "Trespassers Will Be Shot" punctuated with a few bullet holes.

Trey smiled. "You really think it's necessary to do all this hiding anymore? Most of the people our age we see in town know that we live out here."

"Yeah, but they don't know exactly where it is we live. That's the point. I don't think it is such a chore to keep it up. It's safer if we don't have lots of people knowing how to get to us, particularly the law. Our parents still like to think we're sort of invisible. It's not too much for us to try to keep their secret."

Trey, a little deflated, said, "All right. Let's get to these boxes."

From the barn, it was a short walk to lug the boxes of groceries down a narrow trail to the boats near the water. Sometimes it took several trips to get all the stuff they had crammed into the vehicle from these outings back out to the island.

As Trey and Henry hauled crates down to the flat-bottomed boats, Trey looked around at the moss-covered trees and asked, "Henry, do you know where those Creek Indians hid out back in the 1830s when they had the fight with the settlers?"

Henry also looked around as if getting his bearings. "Nah. I think, maybe, it was somewhere down in here 'cause they snuck away from the soldiers that chased them. My daddy told me the story. The soldiers ran them off their land down in here and had them outmanned and outgunned. They killed a lot of the Indians, and woulda killed more, but they were kinda limited 'cause they were carrying lots of baggage like heavy guns. They'd get their backpacks and guns snagged on the vines and limbs, and just couldn't make it through the thick woods carrying all that heavy stuff and maybe a cannon or two, and they finally gave up. It was more overgrown and humid back then, and all that extra work wore them out. Good thing for the Indians. Remember to look for snakes down here."

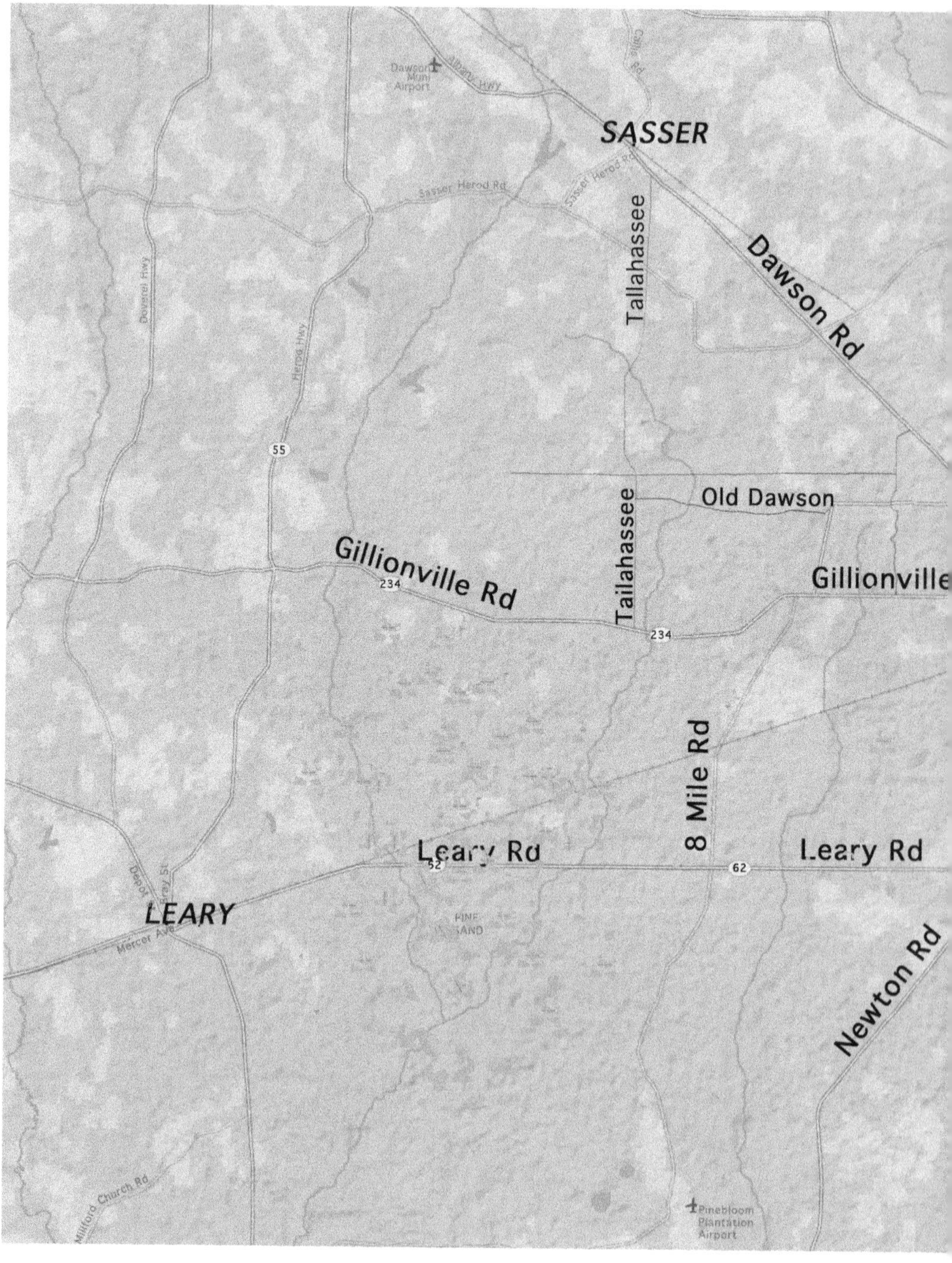
SASSER
Dawson Rd
Tallahassee
Old Dawson
Gillionville Rd
Tallahassee
Gillionville
8 Mile Rd
Leary Rd
Leary Rd
LEARY
Newton Rd
Sasser Herod Rd
Dawson Muni Airport
Herod Hwy
Doverel Hwy
Mercer Ave
Milford Church Rd
Pinebloom Plantation Airport
55
234
234
62
62

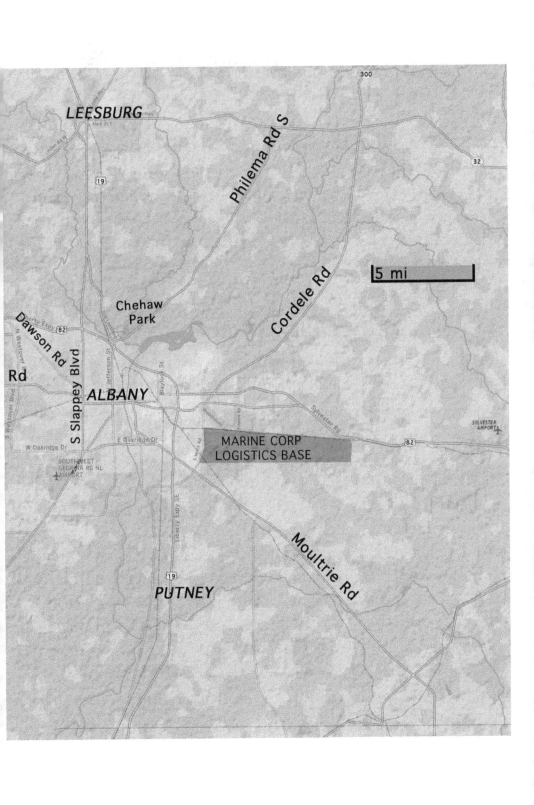

Asheville, North Carolina

Whack! Christy Burdette made a repellant face as the man in front of him doubled over and vomited. "Get him up," he told the two men beating on the other one. He looked over at another man held by two others, wide-eyed and watching his associate being pummeled. He nodded at the quivering man held by his elbows, "You're next."

The man sputtered. "Rowdy, we didn't steal nothin. They were out of gas. We couldn't get to the speed. We got you the money from the other load."

The man called Rowdy turned up his collar to the wind near the top of Mount Mitchell, a mile above sea level on a side road off the Blue Ridge Parkway. He gave the man a condescending look and turned his head to stare down at the spotty lights of motels below on Tunnel Road leading into Asheville. Christy Burdette – he didn't like that name, sounded too sissy. He wanted a name that said "look out," so he got some of the guys he knew to start calling him Rowdy.

Starting in primary school, he had worked to get a stare down that let people know he was not to be crossed. He had to have a look that went with his large size. The look was maybe even more important. So, he practiced it in front of the mirror, then on small kids on the street, and later with guys at the gym. Both his parents were big people and he knew he'd fill out okay, so he lifted weights and found ways to stand with his arms out to the side that made him seem even bigger. Once he got that "don't fuck with me" look to his satisfaction and bulked up, Rowdy Burdette was ready to take on a world that needed someone like him to set it straight.

His full-grown size at six-foot-five and two hundred eighty pounds was usually enough to get what he what he wanted. However, he had a lingering concern from childhood about failure and being shown up in public, so he often got others to do the muscle work. He could blame them if it didn't work out, and once they softened someone up, he'd come in and finish the job. He also found that having a gun and being a big son of a bitch won most arguments before they got too hot.

He left home as soon as he could, just like his old man. His damn mother tried to turn him into a sissy with table manners and always ironing his clothes. Fuck that.

Whack! The man groaned.

"Please, Jesus, you're killing him."

Rowdy gave a sign and the two let go of the man, who then collapsed. He walked confidently over to the one who had spoken, still being held by two larger men. He smelled where the man had wet himself. "You and Punchy over there," he nodded at the lump on the ground, "gonna have to walk back down this mountain in the dark. You be careful not to get snake bit, but first..." he kicked the man in the crotch, grabbed his wrist as he was going down, and efficiently ripped the expensive watch off his arm as he fell. He looked at it in the truck lights and twisted it back and forth. "I've always liked your taste in time pieces." He used his foot to turn the man over, who hung onto his crotch and moaned.

He squatted down near the man and felt a drop in his blood pressure. He always relaxed when the action around him was going his way. He patted the man on the head like a dog, put the watch in a bag with a large wad of money the man had been carrying, and slung it over his shoulder. "I understand business is bad. No gas for running crank from the meth lab. Economy is tanking. Brown out. All that shit. So, you just be glad you got your life left. Now, no talking to anybody. Not to our former friends at the factory and not to the law. You and your buddy need to disappear." He patted him again.

He stood, looked at the other men, and tossed one of them a set of keys. "You boys take that car and go on back to the truck stop to get the delivery van. They're yours. Sell 'em. Divide the money. Our business here is drying up. I'll catch you guys later."

He got into his pickup and the woman slid over quietly, meekly. The former hooker and sometimes stripper had been watching, but looked down at the floorboard when he entered. "Ruthann, I'm gonna give you a ride back to Greenville. There may be some blowback in this dump from those guys making the meth, and I think I'm gonna drop you and head off south." She nodded and pulled the shirt together to cover one of the bruises he had given her the night before. He cranked the truck and headed down the mountain toward the lights on the interstate humming the old Ray Charles tune... "Georgia... Georgia, the whole night through."

Swamp Refuge

As they maneuvered the boats toward the island they called home, Henry and Trey watched for water moccasins limb-lounging in the thick stands of trees that sometimes, even with the slightest disturbance, would drop into passing boats. They gently pushed the gators out of the way, which occasionally snapped at the prodding paddles, but except in their breeding grounds deeper into the swamp, mostly kept to themselves. Mostly.

As they dragged one boat, then the other across a patch of land and back into the water, Trey asked Henry, "When did your old man get the idea to live out here, instead of just coming for hunting and fishing? There is damn little chance anyone will find their way to us through this maze."

Henry grunted as he reloaded a large box into his boat. "It was after the big flood of 1994, I was still young then. I heard later my dad and the other guys say they realized that pushing into the swamp was hard going, but once you got past a certain point, signs of other people dropped off and there was lots of fish and game in those backside virgin areas. They figured that if they moved in here, they would not have to drag their gear back and forth every time they came, like we are doing now."

"Damn good reason. Humpin' this load is getting old."

"Yeah. My dad said they followed the flowing water that was so clear you could see the bottom, and when they kept pushing back further, they found our big island plot on high land. That sealed the deal 'cause it brought them both security and invisibility. He said the whole idea of living off the grid, away from nosey people, prying eyes, and the law, sounded good to his friends and their families. That was about the time they decided to get into the banking business. They found that old dilapidated barn on an abandoned farm out on the edge to keep the cars and trucks and stash extra gas."

Henry blew out of the side of his mouth to shoo the gnats away. "They figured they could just go out to get money when the needed it and come back here to hide. The law would never think to look for them here, and they could cover their tracks so no cop would know how to follow. Best of all, this place is almost unknown outside a handful of hunters and fishermen and timber company folks." He stopped to think as he pushed the boat into the water. "Folks in town do talk about us out here, but they don't actually come looking for us.

"Dad told me that when they checked out the big island, it was well wooded, sturdy ground that stood high out of the water, like it rarely flooded there. Then they split up the jobs, finding how to live without stuff most people needed." He hesitated. "Trey, move that big gator over there out of our way."

Trey slowly pushed the eight-foot alligator floating on the surface out of their way with the boat paddle. The big boy seemed asleep and he never acknowledged Trey's actions, which were practiced and gentle. Trey put the paddle back in the boat and cruised on with the silent, battery-powered motor. "That when they started to build?"

Henry moved his boat past the living log still mostly submerged with its eyes closed. Henry was quieter, speaking slowly, almost whispering. "Yeah. They started to bring in supplies til they were ready to start construction. Made the waterwheels for electricity. They built under the trees, got some camouflage netting from a surplus store near the Marine Base, and stretched that over the houses up in the trees to provide some shade and keep them from being be spotted by airplanes or helicopters. They put fine meshed screens over every opening in the shelters because of the mosquitoes. These battery-powered, flat-bottomed boats don't make any noise to the outside world, where people still fish and hunt around the edges of the swamp."

They had to stop again to portage a patch of dry land, carrying all the supplies and dragging the boats then reloading everything. Afterwards they took a rest. Trey, still mulling over the earlier conversation, got back on his feet and dusted the seat of his pants. "Dragging this stuff back home is too much work. Let's get some help from other folks on the island to come back with us for the other loads."

As Trey repacked the last box into his flat-bottomed boat, he asked, "Phew, that was heavy. It still was a big step for you and everyone to move out here. What tipped the scales?"

Henry checked the balance of the load on his boat before they began the final twisting ride to the island. "I remember my dad saying that the families who moved to the swamp had too many experiences with shiny-shoed bankers that loaned them money for projects that never panned out, and then asked for more money back than they had loaned. That pissed them off, and they decided then that they'd make banking their life's work."

"Okay let's go." To further disguise their passing, Henry tossed bits of food on their trail for the swamp creatures to find and erase evidence of human traffic. He got in the boat, pushed it off into the water, sat down, and switched on the quiet motor.

Trey pulled alongside Henry in the deeper water, near one of the eddies where they threw the animal guts the cats didn't eat into a pond to seed the place for fish. That was where they had stretched nets tied to pullies on shoreline trees. "This here must have been a big change from town. What was it like to be one of the first kids out here?"

"I can't lie. At first, I missed my friends from school and the old neighborhood, but when I snuck out to visit them, it turned out they thought I was cool to live in a swamp. Seems like living out here wasn't as much of a secret as everybody thought. So, things worked out."

Trey used a cypress knee to push his boat away from a spider web attached to the thick- bottomed tree. "Well, this ain't exactly a friendly place to live. In addition to the alligators and snakes, we've got lots of other residents that make living here kind of... interesting." He swatted at an insect on his arm.

"Hell, Trey, that's why they planted peppermint, basil, rosemary, and geraniums. That's why we brought back all these citronella candles and mosquito repellant. That's why we get rid of any standing water and sleep under mosquito nets at night and look out for ticks and scorpions. You know that. It's a full-time job living in a swamp."

"Yeah, but I still got malaria from this damn place. I'm always tired and I still get the night sweats."

"You get the sweats when you don't do your homework. That, or looking at the girls instead of studying."

"I'm still gonna get out of here soon as I can find another place to live and find me a woman."

Several cats ran up to Henry and Trey when they arrived. They rubbed between their legs, weaving in and out. Henry could smell the hot grease where someone was likely frying a large cauldron of fish, so these hungry cats must have been chased away from bothering the cook. The cats just assumed there would be food in all the packages the men brought in, and they were looking for variety from their normal diet of rat and fish entrails. The cats had been brought in to take care of the vermin. They did not bark like dogs to alert someone who might discover the hidden compound by the noise. They could also climb trees in high water from floods or to escape the wild hogs. Henry gave them all a familiar scratch behind the ears as they purred and continued to rub against his legs, weaving in and out, still looking for a treat.

After they finished unloading, he walked to the library past the windmill and several waterwheels tapped into the aquifer flowing below South Georgia that provided water and power to the island. He put the book he had taken to read on this road trip back in the communal library and picked up another. Because there was not much to do on the island, Henry, unlike Trey, loved to read. He often snuggled under his mosquito net with a book to pass the time and imagine life in other places, which included activities unknown to the island culture. From an early age, he had read a book almost every week and made sure to vary the subject matter. Aside from the academics of his youth and his personal reading, Henry's education was largely composed of many courses in the art of swamp living from his daddy, who, in his earlier life, had been a U.S. Marine Corps sniper.

From the library, he went to the home school shelter with the divinity and pralines. He held the package high in the air as dozen young kids climbed on his sturdy frame, grabbing for the candy. As he held them off, he made each one promise to study hard and learn as much as they could before he dropped a piece into each of their waving hands. The teacher admonished him for disrupting the class and giving the kids candy just before their suppertime. He then waved a piece in front of her, with the kids screaming all around, before she just shook her head and took the candy for herself. She gave him an I-can't-deal-with-you look as she popped the divinity into her mouth and closed her eyes in pleasure. Elsewhere, the main camp activities were, as usual, about the acquisition and preparation of food for everyone.

Before returning to the small home he shared with his father, he made a walk around the island. Despite being glad to be back home, over time Henry had begun to feel the island was getting too small. His walk showed it to be the same familiar and boring place. Almost everyone here was content to stay the same and not learn more, develop new interests, or expand their intellectual horizons. Henry felt a creeping lethargy about self-improvement in himself. In the larger society outside the swamp, he was often awkward about what to say or how to behave. He loved the people he had grown up with, but felt his dreams for a larger life were restrained by them and by this place.

The high land area was filling as families on the island grew and kids married the mates they had found out in what they called "public." These new families usually built another house under some more camouflage. This added growth caused the island to seem more crowded, as recently you could see other houses from wherever you were. That meant more mouths to feed and more pressure to pull off more bank jobs to feed them. With the bank robbing profits getting smaller and the island population getting larger, there was a breaking point in there somewhere.

Yet Henry was loyal to his father, Willis Graham, who had been the key leader to start the island. His loyalty put him in the middle between his contemporaries and the older island dwellers, who did not go out as often and did not see the world changing as rapidly as it was. However, both groups depended on Henry to continue the old traditions and to bring in the money.

One of the original goals of swamp living was almost irrelevant now. With the economy in the tank, many people in the United States weren't paying taxes anymore. Some people on the island were beginning to wonder if living here was an idea that had outlived its purpose.

Sunday Morning

One morning, when Henry was barely a teenager, he was stopped by the police along an empty road outside Albany while returning to the swamp from an overnight visit with his old friends in town.

The cops were wondering what a young boy was doing by himself in the middle of nowhere. Since he was in the county jurisdiction, the sheriff was called, and he pulled up on the side of the road in his car along with his wife and daughter. Even though he was not doing anything unlawful, Henry, like most people when confronted by the law, took on the mantle of guilt by trying too hard to look innocent.

He listened to the questions of the tall, fit sheriff while standing off the edge of the two-lane road in a bed of lavender verbena with one leg angled lower and leaning slightly into the ditch. From his position, he could not help himself sneaking glances over at the police cruiser with the writing on the door, the lights strapped on top, and the big spotlight near the front left-side door. What really captured his attention, however, was the head of the young girl in the back seat staring at something in her lap, and then occasionally glancing up to take a look at what her father was doing with the ragged young boy by the side of the road. Henry now had a real motive for his unease as his sneaky, sidelong glances distracted him from following the police officer's flow of inquiry.

However, he politely gave answers to the sheriff's questions, which he had anticipated for just such a moment. He was ready. He told the man where he was going, why was he going there, who he was, and where were his parents were... All manufactured, but with enough facts tossed in to seem real. He could tell that the sheriff only seemed half interested, and was impatient to finish so he could make sure the boy was okay and get on with his day. He was dressed in a suit not a sheriff's uniform, and as it was Sunday, Henry guessed the man and his family were headed to church. Still, it felt to Henry like he was having two conversations in two separate realties. Here was the sheriff talking to him, and over there in the car was this fantasy vision.

The sheriff had to keep regaining Henry's attention from looking over at his daughter while he asked his questions, but Henry's eyes could not help diverting back to the car. He thought the sheriff's daughter was the most beautiful person he had ever seen.

Henry looked down at his scruffy clothes. They were good for rough and tumble with the guys, but they would not impress that dream in the car. He was fit from all the work in the swamp, but muscles were not going to impress her either. Something about her looked like she was about smarts. After exhausting his list of questions, the sheriff looked at his watch and summed up, "So, are you going to be all right out here by yourself?"

"Yes sir. I don't have far to go."

The sheriff looked around at the horizon of the empty highway with not a house in sight, and then shook his head. "Well, I don't know where that is, but you seem like you know what you are doing."

"Yes sir."

"Normally I'd drive you on home, but I'm late to church and I've got my family with me. So, go on along now and be careful. Watch out for any traffic. This is a narrow road."

Henry was glancing at the car again as the sheriff said this, and quickly jerked back to the face of the sheriff, "Yes sir. I will... be careful, sir."

The man shook his head and moved toward the car. The girl looked over at them, and her glance caught Henry's eye. She closed the book she had been reading, and when she put it away on the shelf by the back window, Henry could see that it had a drawing on the front of what looked like a hospital bed with some people standing around wearing white coats. Her eyes passed him over one more time as her head turned to acknowledge her father re-entering the car. Henry appreciated that the sheriff had not been mean to him, but instead seemed genuinely interested in his wellbeing. He was grateful for this attention because it gave him the excuse to be exposed to the perfect face on the perfect head, almost regal, but not arrogant in her quiet confidence and self-containment. He made it a point to find out later that the sheriff's name was Jerico Dozier, and his daughter was Iris.

Henry had never forgotten her face looking up at him out of that book on the side of the road that Sunday morning. Through the years, the memory haunted him as he became a man. He wanted to find her, but he was unsure where to look. When he took on the job supplying the money needed for the swamp, he thought it prudent to stay far away from the sheriff, and that put a damper on finding the sheriff's daughter.

In the years that followed, no matter the girls or women he was with at the time, the memory of her lingered and often pulled him back to that day by the side of the road. His reflections moved slowly, building from the initial fear of being interrogated by the law and knowing he should not divulge the home place of the swamp. Yet, his trepidation had turned into overwhelming calm when he found the face looking up from the book about medicine, through the car window to stare at him right in his eyes. It was a look that did not judge him, but accepted his being there on the side of the road as a natural part of life.

Other people, strangers he had met as he grew older, often looked down on him for his shabby dress, for the feral quality he carried from his life in the swamp. This one in the car had looked at him openly and accepted him as a fellow human being. Nice change. As time passed, however, he feared that he would never see her again.

Trouble Begins

Two rabbits flushed from the brush scampered across the manicured lawn. Soon after, six backwoods men in camouflage clothing carrying hunting rifles and shotguns emerged from the forest near the Gillionville Plantation Lodge.

The exclusive resort catered to the super rich who hunted pen-raised quail while being pampered in horse drawn carriages, traveling through groomed, gently rolling woodlands, resting in five-star accommodations, and eating gourmet meals served by uniformed waiters. Unfortunately, with the economy tanking things had been going slower at the plush resort with the economy tanking. The executives from big corporations came to visit in their private jets less often now. Gone were the ever-alert assistants carrying handmade guns in soft leather pouches, custom-made hunting clothes, monogramed luggage, and laptops held like fragile china.

These rough looking men were definitely not the usual corporate tycoons, but locals who knew the plush facility would be well stocked with all kinds of food, wine, and whiskey. This place had it, and they wanted some. Actually, they wanted all of it.

They quickly overcame the property administrator and his wife, and after raping her, tied them both up in a back room closet with stout rope they found in the kennels. Then they locked the door. Two of the men let the birddogs and horses loose from the stalls and cages, commandeered one of the four-wheel drive hunting vehicles, and pulled the extended-bed truck to the back door for loading. The vehicle was top heavy because it was rigged with custom-fitted, high bench seats for the hunters to perch on the top of the flatbed and observe the dogs working down below, smelling through the groomed forests for birds to shoot. The sides of the truck were sectioned into compartments for drinks, ice, and snacks in case the hunters experienced any hint of fatigue that required refreshments.

The others ransacked the rustic palace, grabbing everything that they could eat, drink, or shoot. This haul included the contents of a large freezer packed with food and several cases of wine and liquor. In addition to the extra guns in the tack room locker, they took all the ammunition from the store room, which they stuffed into the dog cages with the rest of their booty. When they departed, they threw a lit rag tied to a bottle of gasoline into the parlor.

Two of the men sat regally, laughing in the specially designed, high cushioned seats bolted on the rear of the truck. They waved as they passed moss-covered trees like potentates acknowledging their minions gathered for an eighteenth-century review. They ducked under low limbs as the tall vehicle pulled out of the entrance onto Gillionville Road. There, the two men sitting on top transferred back to the modest truck they had used to reach the estate. They drove in tandem calmly and within the speed limit past the Nothin' Fancy Fish House restaurant, Cordrays Mill, and Morgan, Georgia, then south on Williamsburg Road deep into the parts of Southwest Georgia that local people said God had left in an unfinished condition. Their journey then took them off on a dirt path into the woods where they lived alone, and it was unlikely any officials of the law would ever find them - back near the places where, from the beginning of time, no foot had stepped and no eyes had seen.

Sheriff Dozier

The smoke from the burning building, and horses scampering out onto the highway, set off the alarms that brought Sheriff Jerico Dozier and his deputies to the smoldering remains of the plantation house styled into a hunting lodge. Several of the birddogs came out of the woods wagging their tails and looking to be fed. There was a half empty bottle of wine lying in the driveway that circled behind the remains of the smoldering structure.

One of the deputies who had been the first to arrive came over to Dozier. "Sheriff, I've been looking all around and got into some of the house after I put the hose to it. There's two bodies over there about twelve feet inside the walls where the fire caught them."

Jerico looked into the young man's eyes. "I thought I smelled it." He looked over into the remains of the house then back to the deputy. "Take some pictures. Get the bags and some help to move the bodies to the morgue."

"Beg your pardon, Sheriff, but you're not going to do the forensics tests and such?"

He turned to the young deputy. Jerico Dozier was always finding ways to educate his staff. "Well, Bobby, they're dead. They're burned. Somebody... Or several somebodies with bad intentions did this deliberately. This is hard-packed ground and I can't see any tracks that would do us much good. Somebody can look for fingerprints and whatever clues may be on that bottle there, or over in the dog run and horse stables that did not catch in the fire. What's here in this house is burned up along with these bodies. Our supply of forensics stuff is down pretty low. Not sure what else good we can do here just now. Let's get these poor people on the slab and let the medical examiner figure out exactly how they died. That's likely gonna give us more information sooner than poking around here."

The deputy looked crestfallen at the smoking remains of the house. "Damn Sheriff, it looks like America is falling apart."

Dozier swept one foot across the dirt and said sadly. "You may be right, son."

He turned to two other deputies that had gathered to listen to the conversation. "I want each of you to take a different direction on the blacktop out of here. Knock on any doors of people living on Gillionville Road nearby and ask if they saw anything suspicious any time before this fire stared... or after," he looked around, "but first call dispatch and find out who is next of kin. We need to notify the families of these people. It might be the Mansfields, who were looking after the property. See if you can get in touch with any of their family. Don't let on they might be dead, just say that we want to ask them something." He looked around the large yard. "And call someone to come get these dogs and the horses. Times are hard and they won't last long out here by themselves."

Message from Iran

Farook Gilgamesh was past the point of caring. The special medicine his father and wife had needed in the past years had been kept out of Iran by the Americans, and he had watched them both wither and die. He should have been in a position to get what was needed as a scientist in the technology sector of the power grid, but his supervisor said that a level three engineer was not important enough to break the rationing rules. Damn him too. Damn them all.

His section had been working on reverse-engineering the Stuxnet computer worm that had devastated Iran's nuclear industry years before. Now Iran had perfected and enhanced the software's sleeper qualities and awesome destructive capabilities. The super worm would travel undetected, replicating itself from one system to another, infecting them all and then lie in wait until the time planned for it to awaken.

They had used the best artificial intelligence psychology Russia could offer to disguise the attack. That guy Putin had good spies. The new worm would be absorbed into the computer grid systems in the West and wait until the time it would be released. People like Putin and others who paid were supposed to be given protection software at the right time later on. When it came alive, the software would fool the technicians at Western power grids to take exactly the wrong steps to correct problems as they occurred, and only make them worse. Those foolish capitalists would activate a secondary explosion of worms to infect other systems until the viruses caused the entire Western power gird to collapse in a way that would be impossible to repair.

The doomsday computer virus would be so powerful, it would make these small blackouts happening all over the world seem puny by comparison. Those petty computer attacks on each other by the big powers were foolish skirmishes to get attention and make points for their negotiations, and only caused brief panic and discomfort. Even after the drop in trade following COVID 19, the scattered power failures and computer hacking had already disrupted international shipping and cut down cargos by over forty percent more. This new computer infection would be something on a different and much larger scale. The worm was, however, supposed to be just a threat, a key ingredient used to negotiate a settlement to bring Iran back to a world power.

Those same bosses who said he could not get the medicine for his family had told him he was too low level a technician to work in the programming. They said he was only allowed to maintain and test the systems needed to make it work, and to make sure it was secured safely in the special vaults.

The men in suits, who laughed and did not invite him to join them at their dinners, did not know that Farook Gilgamesh was smarter than they thought. He knew how to get into those secure vaults and how to encode the special changes he had devised. Something must be done, and Farook Gilgamesh would do it himself. He knew how to feed it into the system, just as everyone had been planning, except he would feed it into all the systems everywhere… including Russia, including Iran.

Everyone knew the redesigned Stuxnet computer worm was built so that once the system was activated, there would be a time when it was too late to recall the release. Would these men in suits wake up and stop the holocaust or let it all melt? If he couldn't save others with his actions or show the suits that he was their equal, no, their better, then none of them deserved to live. They certainly did not deserve to live in their comfort and privilege.

Time passed. Nothing happened. The men in suits talked and talked. No one agreed. No one was willing to take the first step away from the cliff and agree on anything reasonable. The negotiations kept going on and on. People died. Farook's family died. The men in suits talked. If they didn't solve the problems and agree to stop being petty little boys in a school yard, he'd give them all something to remember. It was past the time delay he had put into system, and the countdown had begun to tick down to doomsday.

Third class engineer Gilgamesh sat in this cubicle alone and neglected. Third class engineer Gilgamesh sat in his cubicle listening to the sound of others elsewhere in the facility talking and laughing in the distance, and a smile crept across his face.

The Doziers

Iris Dozier had always wanted to be a doctor. When she was a child, her playmates imagined marrying a rich and handsome prince charming, becoming Miss America, or raising a flock of exceptionally gifted and grateful children. Fantasy had deep roots in South Georgia and pretending was not limited to the young.

A few wanted professional careers. Some of them left Albany for larger cities and better opportunities, but they were the exceptions. While her friends prattled on, Iris was thinking of bone structure, the time it took to heal a cut, and wondered about the process of food turning into energy. When she heard other girls and boys at her school complain that they did not know what they wanted to be when they grew up, she wondered why not. She had planned her life.

From the time she began to read about medicine, she noticed that most of the doctors she found in her research were men, although she did find two heroines in Florence Nightingale and Madam Curie. Later, she discovered the approachable medicine of Oliver Sachs and the miracle anomalies like Henrietta Lacks. However, local opportunities in medical training were limited.

After starting at Phoebe Putney Memorial Hospital as a volunteer and in doctors' offices as a receptionist and secretary, she began nursing courses at Albany State. She planned a solid foundation in medical science and the practical side of care giving, then she would continue her courses in biology and chemistry toward a degree so she could enter medical school, where her beauty would open the door and her intelligence would secure the invitation to stay.

About that time, her mother started to feel ill and tests showed that she had ovarian cancer. That was the point everything shifted in Iris's life. The Doziers lived off the salary of the sheriff and could not afford sophisticated treatments or round the clock support. Caregiving became Iris's job, and almost constant focus, for six long years. She became a nurse, worked at the hospital part-time, and took care of her mother and father the other part. Iris accepted her duties and the time consuming requirements needed to care for her mother while her burgeoning social life became radically altered.

Attending to the unpleasant tasks normally handled by a hospital orderly, she watched her father as the pain of seeing his wife slowly fade away diminished his otherwise handsome face and left a permanent, sad mask. He was a strong man deep-rooted into a situation where he had no skills. In his hesitant motions and awkward touch, afraid he would injure her further, his clumsy attempts at nurturing his wife broke Iris's heart.

As the months of his wife's illness turned to years, Jerico Dozier became more withdrawn in his frustration to do something, to be of some help, to matter somehow. He started puttering around the small family farm where they lived just outside of town, trying to find something that might bring in more money to help with the increasing medical expenses not covered by insurance. How could he create value from the little he had to invest and find something that he could manage here in Albany, Georgia on his time off? He searched the internet at night, looking for some business venture that would hit pay dirt.

There was a growing problem with trash. Dougherty County was running out of landfill acreage and the county was searching for ways to cut down on what they had to handle.

Recycling as a business had begun to take off about twenty years earlier, and he learned that there was money to be made by the companies that reused junk. Newspapers, glass, copper wire, and other metals had found a home. However, Jerico Dozier noticed a growing business in repurposing plastic into carpets, flooring, and mats. The Dougherty County dump had tons of used plastic, so he decided to become the go-to plastic expert and corner the local market. Through his study every night on the internet, he found the answers, and pretty soon, if there was one thing Iris's father knew, it was the value of used plastic.

He found the that the dump separated the plastic items that could be recycled from the other trash, including all plastic bottles, packaging and cartons, food trays and coffee pods, cling film, wraps, and carrier bags. He cut a deal with the Dougherty County dump that he would take their leftover plastic that was fit for recycling.

Part of the attraction was that, because plastic was almost ten percent of all waste, there was a lot from which Jerico could choose. When that material was recycled, it was not clogging up the dump, and its absence made space in the landfills for other stuff. That extra space extended the life of the landfill and gave Jerico an additional feeling of social and environmental responsibility.

He also felt validated when he learned it took less energy to use recycled plastic than making it fresh, and that conservation reduced dangerous greenhouse gases. With all this going for him, his plan to corner the plastic recycling market could not fail. Once the demand increased, Jerico would have a whole lot of plastic to sell for recycling. Slam dunk. He read that any day now, "green scientists" were going to come up with a machine that would turn all that post-consumer plastic into oil and wax.

He shrewdly got the dump to let him come and haul it off after they had collected it in big piles and removed all the other unusable detritus. With this deal, he got his base product ready to be taken away at almost no initial cost. He purchased a used compactor, and then on his time off and on the weekends, he'd crush and squeeze all the plastic into big bundles the size of a large home freezer. Once these were pressed into rectangular shapes with the hydraulic arms, he'd bind them, naturally, with plastic straps.

His would-be business grew as he stacked the heavy bundles shaped like refrigerators onto pallets, first in backyard sheds, then in abandoned barns and warehouses. Once someone figured out how to repurpose the material, he'd have the market covered and that, according to the articles he was reading, had to be soon.

Sheriff Dozier tried to keep his idea to himself, but the local citizens soon noticed their elected sheriff in close proximity to the growing rectangular stacks of bound, used plastic. Then his wife died, and he was able to see with clearer eyes what had been going on for the past few years and his business obsession slowed to a dribble.

Yet, it wasn't until the economy began to tank even more and new announcements turned pessimistic in the online periodicals he received, such as "New Tech" and "Inventor's Quarterly," and even in "Green Gold," that he began to question his enterprise.

Money was drying up. Then when the magazines folded one by one, he realized he had to reduce his expenses, which had always been a stretch. He became more selective on his trips to the dump and stopped renting any empty spaces. He stopped buying the pallets to stack the bales, and then he stopped buying the plastic straps for the belting machine. They held together fairly well without the straps once he crushed them to death in the press. Then the plastic squeeze press broke.

As the sheriff, he was not criticized openly, but behind his back, people thought he was a little crazy with his dreams of being the plastic trash king. Because he was a nice man and had been an effective sheriff for over twenty years, they kept him on the job, but the growing pile of refuse was becoming a joke that drained his influence and had the potential to get him voted out of office. Jerico's failure with the plastic trash only compounded his feelings from the loss of his wife.

However, Sheriff Dozier was not alone. He was good friends with the mayor. More importantly, his practical daughter, Iris, tried to help her father in his vision, and did her best to support him.

Iris was what most people called a beauty – not self-consciously, but she carried herself with a fresh and wholesome appearance. She was one of those people called by the ladies of the church "beautiful inside and out," which didn't stop teenage boys from grinning and nudging each other with their elbows when she passed.

During her early twenties, when she was of the prime age to be married and having babies, she had been stuck at home. She returned there almost every day after her shift at the hospital to take care of her mother. Earlier, there had been plenty of suitors. She had been called succulent, effervescent, vibrant, luminous, and a goddess by various men, but although attracted to her beauty and intelligence, they became turned off by her sense of duty to a father who was the high sheriff, and by her having to take care of her sick mother. Iris let all the interested men know that she had been brought up to have respect for her parents and her family. When her family needed her, she was going to be there for them.

Now that her mother was gone, she was concerned that she was caught in a codependency with her father, since she still lived at home and looked after him in the same basic ways she always had. She felt it was keeping her single. Now it felt like, even though she was still young, she was becoming… yuck, matronly.

She no longer had the same confidence in her looks, and because she never had the chance to get a full college education, she felt inadequate to assume more complicated medical responsibilities. She was worried about making embarrassing mistakes in areas where she felt underprepared. That was a concern because, with the increasing supply problems at the hospital, she was needed there more and more.

She found the time to stay fit and run almost every day, do her yoga, and keep herself up for the time when she hoped to assume a different life. If that opportunity came, she'd be ready. Still, when she was around her old friends with their kids and their settled lives, she felt like a misfit.

Escape from Dothan

Bubba Gumption had bills to pay. He'd pissed off his papa and the Mills family, and now the rest of the older people on the island were treating him like he was their biggest disappointment. It was not his fault. He could not help being bored out here in the swamp. So, putting those frogs in Linda's bed seemed like a funny thing to do at the time. Bubba was more than a bit overweight and his hair was thinning prematurely. He was not what people would have called handsome, although he had an innocent looking baby face. It was just not that easy for Bubba to get attention from the single women in the camp, or elsewhere for that matter, and he needed to go the extra mile.

He did have what he considered a great sense of humor. Until now, it seemed that everyone else also thought he was funny. That had made him likeable. He was good at playing practical jokes, which went over well most of the time, but with the frogs, not so much. He was so sure she'd see them when she pulled back the bedding, then she would scream, and everyone would laugh. Why couldn't those frogs have hopped out of her bed and gone back to the swamp? The damn things had four legs already. They should have decided to go back to the water rather than settling themselves into the bed. They weren't even croaking.

Bubba had no way of knowing that her dad would decide to take a nap on that same bed, landing on top of it with all of his two hundred-sixty pounds of lard butt. Hell, no frog could have survived that squishy fat ass, and when Linda, a little drunk, went to sleep that night in the same bed her daddy had left earlier, how was he to know she would not feel what was in there?

Bubba remembered what she looked like the next morning coming out to breakfast after wallowing all night in that stew. She was so hungover, she didn't notice her legs until people started shouting at her. Now Bubba's dad had to side with Linda's papa to keep peace in the swamp, and all of them were looking at Bubba 'cause he couldn't stop laughing at Linda as she started to screech and dance around, then ran from her house, past all the other houses in the clearing, and jumped into the swamp water to wash all the dried frog off her. Hell, Bubba still thought it was funny.

Now they were all fussing at him to be the one to go out and get more supplies as punishment for the frogs. It had been five months since Henry and Trey had done the bank job in Tennessee and brought back supplies on the way home. He remembered them saying how scarce things were getting out there. Now it seemed like all the young women were mad at him, particularly the prettier ones, which made Bubba even more uncomfortable around them than usual.

Strange, they had plenty of money from the robberies to buy stuff, but now the problem was finding places that still had the supplies they needed. Looked like people were going back to growing their own food more than shopping at grocery stores. If it weren't for the all the game and fish in the swamp, they'd likely have to find a place to grow their own food as well.

Bubba tried to think of where he would need to go to get the supplies. Maybe over around Dothan, since no one had been over that way to visit a bank or do the mega shopping in more than four years. They had to keep the supply trips spaced out so no one would wonder who was coming into the store and getting such a pile of goods, and what were they doing with all that cash. He'd take the big pickup truck with the small camper cover on the rear end. That way, it would protect the supplies if it rained, or if for any reason he was out on the road for more than a day, he could sleep in the back.

As he cruised along in the truck, he noticed there was not much traffic, which made the drive a little spooky, but he knew he had to get far enough away from Albany to not raise suspicion about where he came from when he bought the supplies. He'd already swapped the tag on the truck with one they had from Macon, Georgia. He passed the bridge over the Chattahoochee river, and was only a few miles outside of Dothan when he noticed that the same truck had been behind him since he entered Alabama. He checked the nine-millimeter pistol on the seat and made sure he had a cartridge in the chamber. He also looked over at the sack of eight thousand dollars he was supposed to use to buy all the stuff on the list he had in his pocket.

Just then, from behind a closed E-Z Mart, a big car pulled out in front of him and slowed down. At the same time, the truck in back of him sped up. He was boxed in by both vehicles. The man riding shotgun in the car in front was pointing for him to pull over to the side. Well, that was not going to happen.

As the three vehicles rolled along at a decreasing speed, he saw a road up ahead, took a quick left at the shuttered Wiregrass Electric Coop onto Hudson Road, and gunned it. Both of the other vehicles came after him, but by then he was flying down the two-lane road that headed straight south. A sign ahead showed that the road was going to dead end just past 2 Bucks Deer Processing. When he saw the T-bone junction, he slammed on the brakes and slid left onto Ebenezer Road. It looked like it would take him back toward Georgia.

It did, but the other two made the turn and came on faster, and one tried to pull alongside of him. He swerved toward the car, almost hitting it. The car dropped back for a while, then came on again. Again, he swerved with the same result. This road was even bumpier than the other. Potholes were everywhere, and he was bouncing around like he was driving over a Chinese checkerboard. He guessed since the budget cuts, there had not been any repairs here for many years. The truck sprung and jiggled as he increased his speed. As he hit potholes, everything was flying up in the air except the pistol he had tucked under one of his legs. It was almost funny to see eight thousand dollars scattered airborne in the truck cab like it was being blown around by a fan.

Ahead, he saw that just past a church, he was about to run into another T-bone intersection. The car was right on his ass. He could see that he had to make his turn at a sharp angle to the left 'cause he was about to run into a dead end on the larger road. They were going over eighty, bumping and bouncing along on the narrow, badly patched two-lane blacktop, and as they reached the dead end, Bubba suddenly jammed on the brakes, causing the other car to rear end him at the bumper hitch. He then hit the gas and took the left turn onto the new road, fishtailing all over the place. White knuckled, he got his truck straight on the new road, and in the rearview, saw the car with a smashed front end wheeling side to side out of control. It zoomed through the intersection and took out a fence, then sailed over a six-foot drop off down into a pasture where it bounced a couple of times, slid sideways, and stopped with a cloud of smoke pouring from the engine.

Meanwhile, the truck chasing him had to jam on its brakes

so as not to sail into the pasture also, and it ended up rocking back and forth on the edge of the drop-off. It looked like those people were done with the chase, and Bubba figured he was done with the shopping trip. He hoped the gas tank, which had been reinforced and was located more in the center of the truck's underside, was okay from the wreck he had caused, and that he could make it home with a banged-up rear end. Not far ahead, he hung a right onto the highway back toward Georgia. If the Alabama cops, usually hard asses, were allowing these kinds of highway outlaws to try to hijack someone in broad daylight, something must be wrong for sure.

He felt the pressure from his shopping trip failure. He sure wanted to bring those fancy cosmetics back to give the pretty young ladies at camp and make up for the frogs. He had even thought about getting Linda a make-up present, some of the fake flowers that kept their color all the time. Well, nothing to do about that now, although maybe he could stop in Blakely on the way home and find a few things in a store there. He sure hated to have the women mad at him, particularly the young ones. He looked in the rearview mirror and hoped the back end of the truck was not too badly damaged. Mmmm, yep, if they were letting people try to hijack cars in broad daylight on the main road leading from Georgia over here to Dothan, something was definitely bad wrong.

Iris

When Iris walked out to the barn early in the morning, she could see the plastic bales pressed, banded, and stacked together. Her father had filled the garage years ago, which had only left her a corner of the barn to park and protect her Prius. With gas availability becoming rarer at the pump, hers was the kind of car that was stolen most often.

She stopped and sat on a bale, petting her big Labrador Retriever, Midnight, while she worried about her father. They got the puppy with the unusually big feet as a comfort dog for the both of them after her mother died of cancer five years ago. He had become her constant companion at home, and she showered him with love while he helped her overcome the sadness she still felt for her mother.

She could tell that Midnight had also helped her father with his depression. Being a typical southern man, he was reticent. Iris had to coax complex feelings and admissions out of him, but he was a kind and good father. It was his failed side venture that bothered her. As she looked around the barn, she could see that it was a good thing he had finally stopped his business. There were still hundreds of thick bales of plastic of no real value stacked on pallets here, and in several abandoned warehouses around town. So, even with no locks and no guards, they were safe from theft.

She felt it was only a matter of time until he would have to begin moving these eyesores someplace else. Maybe he could just haul the stuff from here back to the dump yard. She did feel sorry for him that his dream had not developed. The riches he expected to receive for saving all this stuff had not materialized, and he had wasted money he could not afford. People still talked about him behind his back.

She noticed that folks had started moving back closer to town as the economy began to fail. Some kept houses in the suburbs and used the yards to grow food, but found places closer in to stay so they could get help if it was needed. Safety in numbers.

It was not too long ago when a nearby farm, filled with ripe garden produce, was raided and one of the intruders killed a woman Iris had known all her life. Then several of the neighbors formed a vigilante posse to go after them. She wondered how many of these things were happening, when no one talked about the violence, but just did it.

Her father had to go out to deal with those crimes. He had to talk to the people who had been robbed and convince them to let him find and punish the guilty parties. She knew her father did not have the manpower or resources to control even the beginnings of anarchy. She worried for his safety and the fragile society that was continuing to degrade around them. The crisis of a declining economy and unexpected power outages made her feel insecure – for her and for her father.

Enough worrying about her father. In the early spring light, she saw through barn doors that there was not as much traffic on the road outside the farm, and her watch showed that it was time to get to work. She gave Midnight the rub behind his ears he loved so much and told him to watch over the farm while she and her father were away. He paced back and forth, acting like he wanted to go with her as he always did, but then after some more petting and rubbing of the ears, he backed away to watch her get in the car with his head tilted slightly to the side. She cranked the car, dodged around a stack of plastic, and headed to the hospital where the mounting problems caused by the economy waited for her arrival. She passed a string of comforting day lilies and climbing Cherokee roses on the fence leading to the road that she and her mother had planted years before.

Everyone at Phoebe Putney Regional Hospital recognized that, even though she had not completed a formal medical education, she was smart and capable. In the past few years, she had been promoted up the hospital hierarchy to be a kind of deputy administrative manager with broad authority to make decisions and solve problems, which had recently increased as the economy tanked. As supplies diminished, her job handling the hospital logistics became more complicated. As she parked her Prius in the mostly empty hospital staff parking, put on her badge, and went in to work, she knew that with all these problems at Phoebe, the expectations of the sick being cured was diminishing.

When she arrived, the chief of hospital operations called Iris into his office. After his thorough visual appraisal, he complemented her on her appearance as he usually did, but his face was lined with worry. She could see at a glance that he had not been sleeping well, and that his office was unnaturally untidy. He began by telling her what she already knew.

"Iris, we've got to do something. More of the drug companies and equipment manufacturers are not getting us the supplies we need, even for the basic items like diapers, needles, sanitary products, and bandages. People are at risk from problems that should be easy to fix.

"Because of the power outages and computer bugs, we

can't count on access to the computer records, x-rays, MRIs, and other data, and we don't have the old hard copy records around anymore. So, often we're having to rely on the inaccurate memories of our patients to give direction for treatment. Instead of trying to think outside of the box, our doctors have become more cautious about all our medical procedures."

He rubbed his eyes and shook his head. "The basics of healthcare have now become more basic. I hate that this is happening because this area was hit so hard by the virus. As of today, I've cancelled any elective surgeries and medications are being rationed."

Iris nodded and said, "I know. We've been having to turn people away anyway because of the poor healthcare accounting. Without regular electricity, we can't do decent dialysis and chemo infusions anymore, or use artificial heart machines. They are all too big a risk with the unexpected power failures, and we've been working from paper records. We've been using up a lot of gas to run the generators and can't keep that up forever. Now disease and infections are getting worse. People who come in here unnecessarily are likely to pick up a germ… or drop one off. We need to increase the cleanliness protocol for all of our staff."

The doctor thought while tapping a pen on this desk and nodded. "Yes, that's necessary. Implement it. I like your idea to ask more doctors to move their offices out into the community so they can give practical advice and attention to the early stages of health problems. Out there, they can treat basic injures, teach hygiene and good health habits, and triage cases in the field. I've asked that they recruit all the people in the neighborhoods who had medical care jobs in nursing homes to become lay nurses, for the jobs supporting the weaker people in our community who need help. This place is fast moving from a sophisticated regional medical facility to more of a big clinic.

"I've gotten some of the board members to arrange for us to use those empty bank branches and abandoned fast food places for satellite hospital offices." He gave her one of his longing smiles she felt was too personal. "You know, Iris, I don't know what I'd do without you. You keep making this place function. I know you are continuing to take classes, and see you've put in the paperwork to officially be the administrator. I know you don't have the academic credentials for that, but you certainly have shown you know how to do the job. You have good, practical ideas. I'll put in a good word for you."

Iris nodded and looked at his framed degrees on the wall. School would have helped in medical conversations with complicated terms and Latin phrases. Sometimes she wondered what her life would have been like if her mother had not gotten sick. Would she have gotten married like most of her childhood friends and started having babies? Oh well, she had found a place where she mattered. No. This was where she should be in her life, and she felt she was better off than if she had taken the journey down those other roads.

Iris wondered if it was unethical to promote her career using her boss's attraction to her. Well, she concluded, it did not feel too deceitful as long as she didn't encourage him. She ignored his latest compliment, which made her uneasy, and replied, "Well, doctors and nurses out in the neighborhood clinics can at least take care of basic medicine like broken bones, scrapes, and bruises. We still need to do the procedures we can here at the hospital with limited electric power and the generators like some amputations, appendectomies, and less complicated operations that can still save lives… Even though they are risky and painful without proper meds.

"Here," she handed him several pages stapled together, "I've made a list of all the mental health people in the area. We should ask them to tag team with the medical doctors in the neighborhood doc-in-a-box environments. What's happening has got to be unsettling to many people who may need counseling. We also need to get a list the mental illness patients that could become violent as their meds dry up. It's unpleasant and invasive, but maybe necessary. If that situation gets bad, it could affect everyone."

He frowned. "God I hate all this, but it's good idea. What else?"

Iris now frowned herself. "Some other problems we have are that… without a continuous supply of electricity, oxygen tanks cannot be refilled smoothly, and we can't guarantee a steady inventory to patients. We can't always count on medication that needs refrigeration being kept cool, and changes in temperature might alter their effectiveness.

"One by one, the medical miracles everyone took for granted have stopped. We've moved way past our earlier concern over being sued for erratically operating equipment or spoiled medications. Much of that equipment is hard to clean anyway. Now we have people dying from the lack of medical treatment or spoiled meds, rather than the risk of our treatment being erratic. The lawyers are telling me they are scared of our potential risk."

The doctor nodded. "You need any help deciphering the legal language?"

Iris blushed. "No. I… I can work through that. Also, I've

talked to the funeral homes and the city about setting up larger areas to be used for graves. I asked them to plan to commandeer empty lots, fields, wherever there is a big plot of land."

"Let me know if you need me to weigh in on that."

"Okay. I'm on it. I plan to write them all a note from you on your letterhead. That may help to motivate them." She got up to leave. "I need to go. I'm taking a medical shift later."

He raised his hand. "Wait Just a moment." Her boss liked to reminisce, and noticed her with more than a professional interest. He had only watched, and not said anything remotely suggestive or made any physical advances. Still, she was careful around him to maintain a professional demeanor. Because she was weary, she leaned against the door for support and allowed him the time for his indulgence.

"I know everything's been slowing down in the economy for the last year or two, but here recently, it's just been too quiet. Kinda scary. What does your father say?"

Still leaning against the door, she now crossed her arms. "I remember him talking to me when people started to steal vegetables from yards. That was when Pop organized the neighborhood watches - and that worked, sort of, but people still need food and medicine and other things. He had to get the deputies and the police to increase the patrols. Folks got suspicious of strangers. Everybody hoarded. He doesn't share everything with me. I think he believes it will frighten me too much. Though I bet if he knew the problems we have here at the hospital dealing with the sick and dying, he'd really be scared."

She tapped a knuckle on the door. "You know, we have not even started to talk about the impending crisis in dentistry. I think you should plan how to deal with an outbreak of oral disease in the coming months. Without power to run all the equipment needed for dental hygiene, plus the lack of medication, infection and disease are going to spike. Dentists need to emphasize preventative hygiene now."

"You are right. Can you set that in motion for next week?"

"Yes. I will. Take care, boss. You need to get more rest. You look tired. 'Scuse me, but I've got to see to the families of those three people who died last night."

Later that morning, amid the many disagreeable hospital odors, Iris organized more workarounds, and had to resort to bringing in an old-fashioned diaper and sanitary napkin service and having people wash the foul cloth strips. Yuck. How unsanitary, but how necessary. She wondered what they would do if the packaged bandages, facemasks, and needles ran out. She had to anticipate those needs by investigating how to boil items in scalding water to cleanse them. They had to avoid changing the sheets every day, which increased the risk of disease. Every sanitary problem was exacerbated because the energy shortage had made them cut back on the air conditioning, which until now had helped to keep the bacteria and infections down.

Iris stopped, putting down the schedules and charts that represented the hospital's organization to rub her eyes. She felt that she was handling too much stress and concern for public welfare. The thought of anarchy made her worry about protecting all the institutions that made the country function. The world she knew was slipping away into a situation that was much darker, uncertain, and maybe unrecoverable.

Willis Graham

As he watched his father, Willis, curl into a fetal position, Henry Graham worried that the changes he'd been seeing over the past few years were getting worse. Willis got quieter as the rumors about the economic decline increased and there was more talk about small wars and rioting in other parts of the world. When the gossip began about the United States getting involved in yet another war, he got worse and kept more to himself. That was not like him. Then it became only like him.

As Henry thought about it, he tried to remember exactly when his father began to be so distant and strange. Before this, he had always been a tough guy. After all, he had been to war. Even though he was not big at five-foot-ten, he was wiry, with stringy muscles, and had an intense face that people could read as dangerous. He had seen and done things. To ward off the darkness, he had these talismans he almost always wore: a leather string around his neck with a sea shell on it, a leather bracelet on his left wrist with some bead work and strange writing, and he carried a zippo lighter with some military emblem on one side. He had a habit of clicking it open and shut. Willis had his rituals. He had this way of sometimes looking off for a minute or two, motionless, going somewhere far, a place he had been before where there was no green.

Henry's father, Willis Graham, had taught him almost everything he knew. He had been a sniper in the military and had taught Henry first how to shoot, then how to hunt, then how to be invisible. Henry learned all about camouflage, which paid off

Island in the Storm

when hunting deer, turkey, or hogs. Henry could move without a sound and leave no trace, track, or sign. Whatever happened during the war long ago left a residue inside his dad that had begun to leak out, first at night years ago, and then later it started showing up in the daytime. Henry's mom felt it first, before she left, and then others saw his father slow down and get quiet.

Henry wondered what his father had done that could come back to haunt him like this. He wasn't violent or threatening, he just closed the door to the shop.

So, Henry had to teach himself more about the swamp and the other places he read about and visited when he left the familiarity of home. He learned how to fix mechanical things and how to figure stuff out, how to calculate the intentions of people when they did not tell you the truth. He discovered how basic organizational systems operated. In all that he learned into adulthood, he employed the skills and patterns of how to think things through, and how to use the reasoning that his father had taught him.

As he got old enough and as his father's withdrawal continued, he became the one to lead the efforts to get the money that everyone needed on the island. When he would go away from the island for a day or two, he occasionally saw some of the friends he had as a child. From them, he found out how the world was changing and getting worse all the time. Society was breaking apart.

He trained some of the others on the island, both men and women, in skills he had acquired from his father and those he had taught himself. He was a very accurate shot, and helped the camp set up a reloading stand for ammunition that saved money and trips for more cartridges. He experimented with various charges of powder when he loaded cartridges to find what worked most effectively to cut through the leafy environment of the swamp and still bring down the target.

He and others learned to hunt in teams that could spread out to locate game, and then form into a pincer movement to flush it out toward the waiting marksmen. Although he became skilled in many ways, try as he might, Henry could not figure how to help his father with the problems in his mind, his body, and in his heart. Nonetheless, he still had to step into his shoes and fill in for the man who had made him a man.

Sometimes Willis Graham sat on his cot, watching the movements in the island camp as he reflected on the similar motions of people from long before in a faraway land. He thought about the people he had been sent to protect, to save from terror, and who, from time to time, he had been forced to kill. The women and children here wandered about with the same pace of life as the women and children in that distant place. He reasoned that people everywhere were just trying to get by the best they could, but here in the swamp, they weren't too worried about getting shot going to work.

He lay back and shut his eyes so he wouldn't have to see the people moving about, which brought on the memories from before. He put a towel over his eyes and concentrated on controlling his breath, yet the light was still there. The images were still there.

Sometimes he still smelled the burning gunpowder even in a slight breeze. He could feel the ghost thump on his shoulder of the bullet leaving the chamber, headed toward an unsuspecting person in the distance, usually a man. He felt part of himself fly through the air, felt himself enter and become part of the target, tear into the flesh and destroy the organs, the tissue, the soul of the person. He was there. He was part of it all, the instrument of death. He was Judgement Day.

As Henry watched his father twitch and sweat from the fever in his fitful sleep out here in the woods, he could see his face as the dreams raced through his memory and made his sandy complexion almost white. He knew that he needed professional care, so he half dragged Willis to one of the boats, then to one of the trucks in the barn, and then headed for the Phoebe Putney hospital in town.

Phoebe Putney

Everyone who met Willis Graham described him as tough, and everyone who knew him thought that was an understatement. However, all Henry could see was vulnerability as he watched his father sleeping in the hospital bed from across the room, and he was glad his mother could not see him like this. His father had always prided himself on being virile and manly. Well, he was not like that now.

This was the second night they had been here. He wished he could crack the window open to allow in some fresh, damp air from the evening rain, and let out some of the unpleasant hospital smells collected and hanging in the stale air. At least the blinds were open to give the moonlight a chance to illuminate the otherwise dim space inside the room. Outside, most of the neighborhood was dark and devoid of the electricity that was being rationed by the power company.

As he kept the vigil, Henry remembered when he and his father first bonded before they moved to the swamp, but often visited there to hunt and fish. At eight years old, he first began his lifelong training when he went with his daddy to spot wild hog tracks in preparation for a hunt by his father and several other men.

They were moving slowly through a patch of dry land, and his father was showing him how the tracks of wild hogs left patterns that could be followed by watching the hoof prints and how they rooted. His father was explaining about the hogs, brushing the leaves and swamp grass to look for scat and tracks, when he was bitten by a rattlesnake.

With lightning speed, his father killed the snake, then took the knife, cut his own arm where the snake had bitten him, and sucked out the poison. He then bound his arm with a rag above the bite and let the arm dangle so the blood would run out, carrying the snake poison with it. After a while, he wrapped another bandage over the wound and held the arm up to stop the blood. He had Henry sit in front of him and watch carefully as he doctored himself to learn how it was done.

Once the bandages were tied, his father looked over at him. "I learned in the Marine Sniper School that the world is a hard place, and you've got to be a badass to survive in it. There ain't any place that will make you tougher than this swamp. You got to stay sharp all the time to survive, and I'm bringing you here so you'll learn to handle anything. This snake bite is something I got to grit my teeth and push through. That's the way life is. Now, let's clean this bastard, cook him, and eat him."

After they finished eating the snake, his father checked his arm again, which had swelled to twice its normal size. "I need to sweat the rest of this poison out. We gotta go back to that place that had all the downed trees and build a fire." When they got to the clearing, Willis helped Henry gather a large pile of wood from the remnants of trees downed by a tornado that had swept through South Georgia three years earlier. They found a clear space where Willis made a small tent from his and Henry's ponchos, and gathered several medium sized rocks to heat in a fire. By this time, Willis was sweating and dizzy with fever.

"You got to help me do this thing, son. I need to stay in this little sweat house I made, and you got to keep these rocks hot and keep bringing them to me. Use your gloves and the backpack to grab them so they won't burn you. Put the rocks that have cooled back on the fire to heat again. You got to keep doing this all night. Keep that fire going. Nothing will come up here to try to hurt you as long as you keep that fire goin' hot. Get me more water in this pail when it runs dry. I got to stay in there and sweat. If I pass out, you got to throw water on the hot rocks in the little tent to make the steam. Wake me back up. No sleeping. No slacking off for you. You got to be a man tonight."

Henry kept the fire going, and from time to time, his father would come out of the stench in the shelter to breath clean air and drink water. Henry filtered the swamp water through a cloth before he boiled it and set it aside to cool so there would be a quantity for his father to drink to keep hydrated. That work, keeping the fire and moving the hot rocks, was a lot to do, and although it made Henry tired and the hot rocks hurt his hands through the cloth, he was proud of being dependable in helping his father. He felt that his father was sicker than he let on, and he knew it was up to him to make things better.

To stimulate Henry, keep him awake, and share the time, his father talked through the night about living in the woods and swamp. He explained to Henry what it took to survive and how he needed to adapt himself to the task of becoming like his daddy.

"Henry, I don't have much to give you. We all chose to spend time out here away from other people, and me and the other men do what we do to make money 'cause we didn't like the way the world was going. Nobody hardly knows we come here, so when we come here to hunt and visit, they won't mess with us. Sometimes, when I go off and don't come back home for a few days, I come here. Now, you got every right to choose how you want to live and where.

"The one thing I can show you is how to be smart when you make those choices. I can show you how to survive and be a man. You know I was a U.S. Marine Corps sniper. We were the toughest sons of bitches in the world. I'm gonna show you how to be strong like me, so wherever you go and whatever you do, you will know how to stand on your own two feet and be a somebody that nobody will mess with. Believe me son, if you can make it in this god-awful swamp, you can make it anywhere."

A week later after, Willis's arm had healed and the swelling was down, he started Henry on his training. "First you got to learn how to walk. When you walk, you have to be silent. Look for dry leaves, sticks, or anything that can break and make a noise. Look for frogs, lizards, or any small critters that you might scare and cause them run off in case they'll make noise. Walking is moving your weight through space. Everything counts. Don't lock your knees. Land the heel of your foot soft first, then roll toward the toe as your weight goes forward and shifts smoothly from the other foot. Feel it empty out of one leg and into the other. Always try to keep your weight balanced in your center. Look for branches, vines, or anything that can snag you and cause them move or rustle. Anything you are carrying is an extension of you… backpack, gun, hat… anything. All of it has to come under the same rules of motion. Okay, now walk for me."

Willis corrected Henry, and they practiced until Henry could walk in the woods without making any unnecessary noise. Henry learned to be aware of his surroundings. His father taught him to spot thin spider webs, sticks hidden under dry leaves, rocks next to each other that could make a click or sliding noise if moved by a footstep.

"You gotta not just be in the woods or swamp, you gotta be a part of it. Close your eyes. Stand here and open up all your senses. Smell the rot and decay. Feel the butterflies and mosquitoes and all the crawling insects. Look out there for a sign of anything hidden and waiting for you to come along. There are gators and snakes out there. There are wild boars out there. All of them hide and let their prey approach them. You got to be a part of that. You'll never get a deer or turkey or hog by being clumsy and not knowing where they are… Where they sleep… Where they go for water and to eat. You got to know the rhythms of this place. You got to feel it live, and you got to live with it to feel it. You got to know instinctively if what you are about to step on is a stick or a snake.

"Almost every time I got bit by a snake, I was not thinking about what I was doing. I had my head someplace else besides this swamp and I was out of touch with its rhythms. You got to know what plants are poison and which will stick to your pants. You got to know which vines will not break and might tie you up when you try to push through. You got to know which things out here you can eat, which to use as a medicine, and which can kill you. Now, take your time. Look out there and tell me what's going on in front of you."

Henry learned to move with all his senses. The atmosphere of the space around him became tingling with information, and any element out of place became apparent. In time, he could spot a still squirrel in a tree sixty yards away. He learned to know when something on the ground thirty yards away was a fallen limb half covered by leaves, or a snake waiting for a slow chipmunk. He learned to smell decay, scat, decomposition, and any change that was not the norm. In all the seasons, he knew what to expect, what to watch for, and what to avoid.

As Henry learned more, he and his father moved deeper into the woods and swamp, deeper into the dangerous places. "You got to know what's alive out there and if it is something you can eat, or if it's something you need to be afraid of. That is part of being in touch with the swamp and the woods. All your senses have to be alert at all times, and you've got to develop a sixth sense for danger. There is a lot here that can do you harm. Got to let the hair come up on your arm or the back of your neck. Even if you are sitting still, there are things that can come up on you that are silent and hardly make any movement, but can hurt you. You've got to be able to feel that. Got to let your skin tingle.

"You don't have any excuses for getting hurt. You got to be in control of your life here, or the swamp will take you over and hurt you in a minute. Remember a while back, when I got gored by that pig? I was thinking about something going on with your mother. My mind wasn't here. I was not aware of the danger of that son of a bitch hiding behind a bush. That was my fault. You can't let that happen to you. I should have smelled him. I should have been aware that something was breathing there. I should have felt the menace of that badass wild hog who hated me and wanted to hurt me. That son of a bitch won that day 'cause I was not sharp enough. That is what life is like here, or out there, or anywhere in the rest of the world. You gotta be aware of danger instinctively and you always gotta be ready for it, 'cause it'll come at you when you least expect it. You hearing me boy?"

"Yes sir. How am I gonna know when there is danger if I can't see it or smell it or hear it?" While it sounded like a great adventure, at the same time, life sounded risky and difficult. Henry was thinking that maybe he did not want to be the mean

S.O.B. his father was describing to him. He did not know how to talk to his father about the other side of himself who loved to read, imagine peace and calm, and be with pretty girls. But down deep, he knew that whatever his father wanted him to do or to be, he would work at it and do his best. He knew that his father opened up to him in ways he did not to other people, and that bond was a sacred thing not to be abused or neglected. He felt the vulnerability in his father, how much he cared for Henry and how much he wanted to share everything he valued. He knew, although he could not speak it. That was how his father showed his love.

His father smiled and squatted down. "You're gonna know 'cause there is always danger. This swamp is a place where danger is the only constant thing. Life is a place where danger is a constant thing. You always gotta keep looking out. Under every log in every pool of water, in the bark of every tree, stuck on every vine is danger and something that can hurt or kill you. Never let your guard down."

Now, in the dark hospital room as Henry watched his father sleep, he knew that what got his father hurt, what got anyone hurt, was looking out for others. Caring was a risk that could hurt you.

Willis mumbled again in his sleep. "Get down… Take the one on the left, I've got the other two." His head rocked back and forth. "So much blood… killed, fire." There was again a long sigh and his father was quiet.

Henry looked out the window and checked his watch. It had been a long time since anyone had come to look in on his father. He'd go see what was happening. He stood with no noise.

In the hall, there was the sound of a child crying from a

Island in the Storm

nearby room where a family was visiting. Many families came here to be with sick relatives, and with the hope that there might be food or other comforts available in the hospital they could not find elsewhere. As Henry walked down the hallway, heel to toe, he could see a man ahead of him not quite shouting at a woman in a white doctor's coat. The man was angry and leaning into the woman, who was doing her best to remain calm. She was stunningly beautiful. From a distance, she was of medium height and weight, but carried herself with an erect posture that made her seem taller. As he got closer, he could hear, "You and those other doctors here need to give my momma that medicine right now. We came in here 'cause she was sick and all you do is tell us she's got the cancer but you don't have nothin' to give her for it. She is in PAIN, lady."

Henry stopped a few feet away from the man and the striking woman. He felt a flush of warmth as he recognized the face he had looked for, and could not forget from all those years ago. Her very existence, and her being here now, made him uncomfortable and vulnerable, and he felt the warmth coming up into his cheeks. He stood there and stared at her. The man, noticing him, turned to say, "What you doin' here, big guy?"

"Just waiting for a chance to talk to this nice lady."

The man looked Henry up and down and then turned back to the woman. "So, what you going to do?"

She looked down to her arms filled with a batch of folders and thumbed through them until she found the one with the man's mother's name on it. "Just a minute. She's not my patient, but let me see." She looked down, flipped a page, and nodded to herself. "It's not my place to tell you this, but we are in unusual times here. Mister Morton, you mother unfortunately has the type of cancer that would normally require an operation. We can't do that kind of operation without consistent electrical power, and we don't have strong enough medicine for her in stock. It has not arrived because the transportation industry has just about crashed. Also... The factories that make the particular medicine we need for your mother have shut down."

The man shook his head, trying to find a solution to his panic. "You got some power here. There's lights and fans and such."

"Yes. We have some basic power, but it's limited, and we can't count on enough to run the kinds of machines that would be needed to perform a long and sophisticated procedure. I am terribly sorry to say it, but we can't fix your mother. She is not going to get better." She looked down at the papers and then back up to the man. "I don't know where your doctor is, and I should not be the one telling you this, but there really is nothing we can do to help your mother."

The man, now with his anger subsiding, being replaced with a combination of fear and increasing panic, said more softly, "What about her pain?"

The woman shook her head again. "I'm so sorry, but our supplies are... We don't have the right kind medicine to help with that. We are giving her what we have, but it's not strong enough and she will still likely be in a good bit of discomfort. Perhaps you should take her home and do what you can to keep her as untroubled as possible."

The man turned and fell back against the wall, leaning on it and breathing heavily. His hands balled up onto fists, flexed, and then balled up again. After a few moments, he looked back at the woman, then back over at Henry, and shook his head.

"Hope whatever you are after, you have better luck than I did," he said as he pushed away from the wall and walked down the hall.

The woman looked at Henry, turned, and started to leave when he stopped her. "Ma'am. I came in here a couple of days ago with my dad and he's had a bunch of tests and we haven't heard anything and don't know what to do. I don't think you are our doctor, 'cause I'd have remembered someone as pretty as you are for sure." He hesitated, looking at her with unshielded admiration. "Uh, do you think you could look at one of those charts or folders and see if there is anything you can tell us?"

She looked at him and admired his looks as well, but kept it professional. She got Willis Graham's name and nodded to others in the hall as she walked back to the central desk area and checked a file. She sat down and thumbed through, making some notes, and then checked another file on the computer before looking back up at Henry. "Okay. I'm not your doctor. My name is Iris Dozier, and I'm actually studying to become what they call a physician's assistant." She watched the confusion on his face. "That's kind of a cross between a doctor and a nurse."

He nodded.

"You are in room 436. Is that right?"

"Yes. We've been there for a couple of days and it is a really nice room, but we need to be getting on home if that's all okay. He's… uh… He's kinda down."

She looked again at one of the open folders. "Let me come to see you and your father in about thirty minutes. I have a couple of things I need to do first. I did see your father when he came in and got him started on the tests, so I've got a little idea of who he is and what's been going on with him."

"Thanks. I must have been doing the paperwork when you met him." He paused, unable to avoid staring at her. "Okay... and I'd like to say that you handled that situation about as well as it could have been handled back there." He nodded back down the hall. "I was impressed. And also... I don't mean to be too forward and all, considering where we are and what your job is, but you look about as good as a tapioca puddin'."

She laughed out loud spontaneously, with her head thrown back showing her open mouth. "Well, thanks. This is the first time I've felt good about being here today. Okay. And... Thanks for what I believe was a compliment." She shook her head. "I've been called a lot of things before, but never a lumpy dessert." She laughed again with a welcoming face and penetrating eyes that made contact with Henry's. He could see a vibrant person behind the medical persona. A person he wanted to get to know better.

Then she frowned and looked at him more closely. "Something about you looks vaguely familiar. Have we met before somewhere?"

Henry stammered. "I might... might have seen you with your dad before."

"So, you know my father?"

"I think I may have met him a while back. I hear he is a fair and nice man. And just so you know, I'm not normally... Well, I'm not a bad person who gets in trouble with the law."

She smiled again. "No. I didn't think you were a bad man. Now, I've got to go. See you and your father in a little while."

Back in the room, Willis Graham was still asleep. He'd have to be sick or drugged not to feel the presence of Henry entering the space around him, or of anyone being so close to him.

Island in the Storm

His father had always been aware of his surroundings. Henry sat down and remembered the training he got from a much different man than the one who lay before him now, limp in the bed and snoring slightly.

Henry remembered, as a child still approaching his teen years, how his father had leaned into him with a face that was always intense when imparting his hard-gotten knowledge. "I'm gonna show you what I learned when I was a Marine sniper. The shooting part is the easiest. The part that takes work is being able to sit still for a long period of time.

"You got to learn how to nest yourself so no one can find you, and you also got to leave yourself a way out of the hide so you can't be caught. Like being a part of the woods and swamp, so you blend into it… and it accepts you as part of it. When you are a sniper in hiding, you got to be invisible. Not only in the physical part of not being seen, but you need to be gone in your head too.

"If you are worried about being seen, or even thinking about not being seen, you give off an energy that makes it easier to sense you are there. You got to get it in your head where you are sort of removed from yourself. You can see what is happening, but you don't radiate it. You don't let any energy out. Do you understand what I'm saying?"

"Not really. I'll try to do what you say, but I don't understand how it works."

"That's okay. We'll work on it together. You'll get it over time. When you are in a hide and looking for whatever it is you are after, you can't move. You gotta get in a comfortable place to start with, where you can shoot from that spot if you need to, and then you wait. You got to be where you don't move, even if you have an itch or have ants crawling all over you and stinging you, or even if you feel a damn snake crawl over you. Can't get surprised and jerk. You don't move! You got to practice it to be able to take it. I'll show you, but you need to practice on your own, out there in the woods.

"When you move, you move slowly, so slowly that you can't be seen moving. Always move in the shadows. You got to breathe without your clothes moving. You mostly move squatting or crawling on the ground. Got to be aware of everything in front of you that can give you away, like sticks, bushes, leaves, anything that can move or make a noise when you touch it.

"Snipers are first and foremost scouts. They go out and see and sometimes hear things and report back what they find. It's intelligence gathering. So, a scout has got to be able to concentrate on what they see and hear, and remember it so they can report it back accurately. You got to start to use tricks to remember long lists of things. Starting now. When you go into the woods, pick out ten different things you see at random just when you go in. Remember the size, color, smell, where it was, what direction it was pointed, and all that stuff so you can describe each thing exactly. Do that every day for a couple of weeks. Then start to add two things every time. You need to get to where you can remember very specifically a list, in order, of about thirty or more things. That memory stuff, it's good training for everything you do, not just being a scout."

All those years ago, as Henry sat by the fire next to the tent listening through the night as his father sweated out the snake poison, Henry got a view of the future. He started, for the first time, to see what he would become and how he would live. He learned how to shoot, skin, tan, cook, climb, swim, move silently, and live in the swamp. If he had a pocketknife, he likely could survive anywhere. He thought it would make the rest of his life a piece of cake.

He remembered that long night in the swamp by the fire as his father talked to him and sweated because of Henry's slapping water on the hot rocks. The next morning, Willis was much better, but he was exhausted and dehydrated. They sat by the fire together in the morning sun, drinking water and eating some of the food they had brought in the backpack. After they ate and broke camp, they washed and hiked back to the canoe, paddled back to the truck, and drove back home. Only then did his father go to the hospital to get some antivenom medicine for his still swollen arm.

Now, after sitting quietly in the hospital room with his father, he had gathered their belongings in anticipation of being released soon, sat back down, and had almost fallen asleep when there was a soft knock. Iris entered and filled the room with the kind of light and anticipation that often comes from the presence of a very beautiful woman. Her knocking awakened Willis too. She came into the room thumbing through her stack of folders with the tests and laid the pad on the side table. Her startling presence rendered both men speechless.

She looked up and nodded at both of them. "Mister Graham, how are you feeling this morning?"

Willis rubbed his face to wake up further. "I'm about the same with the headaches and soreness all over, but this room is wonderful. I've never slept in a better bed, and having the bathroom right next to me is, well, it's just incredible." He looked over at Henry. "Even Henry said he slept better in that fold-out chair than he has in a long time. You folks have been taking real good care of us."

She walked over to the foot of the bed and put her hands on the frame. "Mister Graham, when you came in here and started to take these tests, you asked me to give the results to you straight, and I believe you are a man who meant just that." She walked over to the window and looked out onto the nearly empty parking lot at what the rain had left in the moonlight, then turned back to the bed.

"Your record shows that in addition to your war wounds, over the past two decades or more, you have been bitten multiple times by poisonous snakes and other animals in that swamp. They have all injected you with toxins. In almost all of those cases, you did not get to the hospital quickly, but continued normal activity, treated yourself, or had others where you live treat you. Also, based on your medical records, such as they are, you seem to have continued to drink alcohol and caffeine in excess before the meds you were given could complete their work." She gave Henry an accusatory look, then turned back to his father.

"I suspect I have."

"Also, often it looks like…" she walked back to the pad of papers, flipped over to another page, and ran her finger down a list, "you self-medicated or got local treatment, but not from a medical professional. Most of those kinds of treatments, like cutting and suctioning the wound or binding your extremities near to where you were bitten, were ineffective. That treatment is very old school. In some cases, it made the poison entering into your system worse. You also have had several infections from the cuts. Because of your many infections, you are not very responsive to any of the antibiotics we have anymore."

She flipped over to another page and nodded to herself.

"Over the years, your respiratory system and kidneys have sustained a lot of damage. In the past, you have been given antivenom medicine for the bites to counter the harmful components in the venom. However, the administration of the antivenom over multiple instances has been uneven. You have had allergic reactions, leading to excess chemicals in your blood stream that have affected both your central nervous and immune systems. You also didn't get adequate treatment for the infections." She tapped her knuckle on the nearby rolling table that held the folder and looked back at Willis.

"It looks like the treatments did not sufficiently eliminate the bacteria, or the venom that was in your body, and when you voluntarily stopped the treatments early," she looked down to the page, up from the page into his eyes, then back down to the folder, "it resulted in a buildup of the pathogen. Your body's immune system has fought this with some, but not total success.

"That is why you have been having these instances of imbalance, muscle cramps, headaches, and loss of some muscular control. It's the cause of your respiratory issues and now these heart palpitations." She put one hand down on the folder and looked directly at him with a side glace over to Henry.

"I am concerned that given your condition, medical history, and the environment in which you live, you are susceptible to something like meningitis. Not only that, but from what you and your son here told me, you are depressed. Evidently, for the past few years you have been exhibiting signs of lethargy, lack of interest, and other classic signs of depression. That lack of drive and physical activity has also worsened your medical condition.

"Normally, our doctors would recommend, as a precaution, a continued series of antiviral drugs, but the truth is... We do not have enough medicine on hand to treat you, should you develop a serious case of meningitis. Frankly, that illness could be fatal. Our medicine for depression is almost gone, so we will not be able to do much for you chemically.

"These are not normal times, and we are all now unfortunately faced with a situation where we only have a very basic stock of medicines. With a full supply of meds and the fully functioning equipment, your situation would not be such an issue. However, in these times without the medicine or good equipment, many patients here will not make... will continue to have problems. They are working in our lab to create a few of the meds in the greatest demand. Under normal circumstances, we should be getting those from the drug companies, but that is a slow and uncertain process, and unfortunately, those medicines do not include what you need.

"For now, medicine has been put back a hundred years. All I can tell you is to take great care to stay clean and healthy. Don't take any unnecessary risks or do anything that could harm your body. Eat good foods and don't drink alcohol, limit caffeine and do not smoke. Get exercise if you can tolerate it, but watch your balance and don't fall. Unfortunately, that is the best advice I have, and I don't have any miracle medications for you.

"You have to find a way to interest yourself to help with the depression. Find something to get involved in that will get you moving and engaged. Activity can help improve your mood. We are in bad times, and as a former soldier, you have much to offer to help everyone else now. For example, maybe you could help train the militia that my father is going to form. I think that would do your spirits some good. Do you have any questions?"

Willis looked at her with her with a steady gaze from his

bed. "No, ma'am. No questions. I thank you for delivering this report in a straightforward way. I heard what you were saying and what you did not say. It was kind of what I was expecting, and I thank you for doing your job. We're gonna let somebody else have this bed now."

She gathered her papers. "I do wish you and your family the best. I hope you will be careful and avoid circumstances that can make your situation worse. So, you are free to check out." She looked at her watch. "They'll be open downstairs soon."

When she left the room, Henry felt compelled to follow her into the hall. He knew his father would understand, and he called to her as she was walking away, "Puddin'."

She stopped abruptly and turned. Her face was trying not to smile, slightly flushed with restrained approval of the nickname and his attempt at reconnecting with her, particularly after what she had just told them about his father's condition. She managed her composure and said, "Yes?"

Henry could see something else coming from her eyes, something more than medical concern. Now with this perceived encouragement, he continued. "This is not the time or situation, but I'd like to see you again. There is not much of a place around here to take you for coffee, but maybe I could bring some and, you know, we could just sit and talk sometime." The rest of the air he had used in speaking to her came out in a rush, and he quickly took in another breath.

Seeing this, she smiled again, not encouraging him exactly, but also not rejecting him. Here in front of her was this big, strong, handsome puppy dog. "Henry, take your father home now. Look after him and do what I said about keeping clean. Boil the water he drinks, well you too, before you drink it to kill bacteria." She made a move to turn but stopped. "Maybe I'll see you around. A guy like you is bound to be visiting with my father again." He started to protest, but she smiled. Just before she turned to continue on her rounds, he leaned on the wall, looked into her enormous, penetrating eyes, and patted himself with his right hand over his heart.

A voice from the room shouted, "Come on, Spud. Help me get all this stuff together."

She frowned and said, "Spud? I thought you said your name was Henry."

He hung his head. "It's a nickname. Some sort of reference to the family history when we used to eat a lot of potatoes." He rolled his eyes.

"Lord! Mine's 'Tink' for Tinkerbell. My parents liked Peter Pan."

"Yikes. Why do parents do these things to their kids? Scars us for life."

She smiled and turned to go. "Something we have in common. Take care of him. He looks like someone who is not great at following a doctor's orders."

"He's not good at following any orders. I'll do my best... Puddin'."

As she walked away, she said over her shoulder "You're pushing it... Spud."

Henry Graham

Henry felt a lift in his heart as he finished packing his father's meager belongings. He only half listened to his father as he packed the soap, toothbrush, and other toiletries in the bathroom, zipped up the bag, and checked the room halfheartedly for anything left behind.

His father, sick as he was, noticed the change. "You need to get that pretty nurse out of your mind. You're my son and all, but she may be a step ahead of you. She's been to school and done all this doctor stuff." When he saw Henry's face fall, he added, "Mighty pretty though, just the same."

Henry grabbed the two bags with one hand and his father's arm with the other. "We better get on back to home. You know you got to rest more and stay clean."

"Yeah. That's gonna happen."

As they got in the truck and started the drive back toward the swamp, his father's words began to sink in. Henry had just talked to the dream he had since he was a teenager. She didn't exactly say "no" to seeing him again, but like his daddy said… He did not know if he was up to it. She seemed too smart and high class for him.

When he had left the swamp to chase women, his ventures always took him to the seedier places, the dive bars, beer joints, and parties with the friends he had when he was young, before the swamp. In those places, his looks drew women who were more than ready, and there was little conversation resembling something from an earlier age called courtship. Most of his experiences with what might be called "nice women" had been in recent years - when he was taking them hostage from the banks.

However, in his heart and in his soul, he felt compelled to see Iris again… and again. He began to think how he should act and what he should say to someone like Iris. The fact that her father was the high sheriff sent another chill up his back. How would he deal with that? It seemed that everything in his past had been leading him away from the direction he desperately wished to go. How was he going to shake off the attitude, the language, the manners he had been using for the past few years? He had damn sure better clean up his act if he was to have a chance with her. He couldn't become someone else, but he was determined to present the best version of himself to Iris and whoever she was around.

He looked at his father staring ahead. "Maybe you should come into town with me more. You know, be around more people."

"I've been around people. They're overrated."

Henry shrugged as he thought of how he needed to appear and dress around Iris. He began to discard words and acts that had been a part of his life. He realized that he ran the risk of becoming, at least for a short time, a much duller person out of an abundance of caution and the need for self-control. He was fairly well-read, and felt he could speak confidently on basic subjects, but social skills were another story.

"Hey! Keep your eyes on the road and your mind on your driving," his father snapped as Henry ran off on the dirt shoulder and too quickly jerked the truck back onto the two-lane blacktop. "Get your mind off that pretty half-doctor."

As he steadied the truck, Henry thought of what his mother told him when she was leaving his father. She said she had been attracted to his father, in part, as a rebellion from her family. She had grown up with normal traditions, manners, and grace. Even though Willis was a good man, his feral qualities became less attractive over time, and she longed for a life that was not a constant struggle. As she had grown, she felt the need to move past the rough edges of Willis's bad boy charm. This thought caused him to wonder how his father might be seen by Iris or her friends or family, as well as how they would see him.

He pondered the parallels of his mother and Iris. He'd have to work extra hard to show Iris the side of him that was more civilized, like the people in some of the books he had read. He began to have a conversation with Iris in his head, talking to her with the politeness he would have shown his mother.

Julian Cordell

Julian Cordell finished the inventory of the semi-abandoned power plant on Lake Chehaw, northeast of Albany near where the Flint River, Kinchafoonee Creek, and Muckalee Creek came together. He turned to the engineer noting the survey on his iPad for a report. "Make a list of all those missing and damaged parts. Check the warehouse to see if we have enough supplies to fix everything. Go through every storage shed and supply rack to look for parts to keep this place going. Send off to get replacements if we don't. We need to get this plant back to its full potential."

"You think we can?"

"Don't know, but if we keep having those brown outs and power failures like are going on everywhere, we need to be prepared to get more power out of this place here."

The assistant tapped his iPad. "Well, the lines going into town need to be checked also. We need to know they can carry the load and don't have broken parts on the poles."

"You're right. Get a team assigned to check them out when we have time. Get folks up on every pole going to the hospital and city hall, then check the others. No point in fixing this old plant if we can't get the power to where it will do some good"

"I'll get 'em right on it."

Cordell turned his head south toward town. "They need to finish the repairs from that last tornado first." He looked at the interior of the old plant and listened to the roar of water over the dam outside. "Schedule a cleanup crew to come in here also. If we do need to get this thing back up to full capacity, we don't need to be stumbling over all this trash that has accumulated."

The man tapped the iPad. "On the list." The assistant looked around. "Mister Cordell, do you really think you can get this place working full speed?"

"I don't know. The thing was built out of concrete back in 1908 and Georgia Power has been using it until recently, but just for a little bit of backup power. Although, if we can get it running up to full capacity, it will seem like a lot of juice when we have the next power failure."

Henry, Iris, and Jerico

In the next few weeks, Henry found many reasons to ride his bicycle into town and just happen to drop by the hospital for a visit. There were not any restaurants open nearby to take Iris to lunch, so they would go for a walk in the adjacent residential neighborhood or the semi-abandoned Tift Park, carrying a sandwich and reusable water bottles and getting to know each other better.

As they were sitting on a bench in the shade on a warm spring day, Iris remarked, "Man, I miss the air conditioning. We only use it in the hottest days now. Why is it you don't sweat more?"

"I've never had it."

"What?"

Henry laughed. "We don't have air conditioning out where I live. Sometimes we use fans, but the electricity we generate with waterwheels is not enough to power AC. We boil the water we drink from the streams and filter it also. We have a contraption you use with a bicycle that pumps water up into a container where it is heated by the sun. That's our shower. So, I live like most people do when they go camping."

"I could not stand that for long. So, how's your father doing? Is he talking care of himself?"

"He's alright. I'm more interested in what you are doing. Your life and job at the hospital sounds so fascinating."

"It is interesting, but your father needs to be cautious. He should see a doctor regularly and get a better diet recommendation. Bring him in with you some time. I can check his vitals to see if he is looking after himself. Maybe we can all have lunch or dinner with my father."

"Okay. Sure. I'll check with him on that. So, how many people do you have to manage?"

Iris began to invite Henry to visit her family's small farm, where they would walk in the pasture with her ever-attentive dog, Midnight. The big, loveable, black Labrador Retriever was at first protective of Iris and suspicious of Henry, walking back and forth while giving Henry a concerned face. When she brought Henry into the house and treated him like an old friend, the dog calmed down a little, then Henry sat and held his big hands between his knees, palms open like a book, inviting and available. He could relate to dogs. He looked at Midnight directly in the eyes and gave kissing sounds. The tail wagged.

They soon got to know each other, and when Henry played with him endlessly in the game of throw and fetch a tennis ball, Midnight decided that this tall man was his new best buddy. Soon Midnight ran to meet Henry when he came to visit, wheeling his bicycle up the bumpy drive, and often stayed by his side, standing stock still and soaking in the pleasure as Henry rubbed his back, hips, and legs where the beginnings of arthritis were causing the enormous Lab some discomfort. Henry noticed that, after rubbing Midnight for a while, his hands had an old dog odor like a rug than had not been cleaned in a while. He liked that smell, but occasionally bathed the dog with soap and a garden hose.

As Henry and Iris walked around the farm, he used the occasion to kid her. "Iris, I don't know where you got such a funny looking horse. He's like a black Clydesdale."

She looked down at Midnight and scratched his ears, which caused his tail to start wagging furiously. She began in baby-speak. "You don't talk bad about my little Midnight. He's a good doggie."

"Oh! That's a dog! Now I understand. So, you got him from Hagrid. This must be Fang, the old dog I read about in Harry Potter."

Midnight understood he was the subject of the conversation and looked from one to the other.

Back to the baby-talk. "Yesssss. He's such a good puppy. You tell that bad boy you are my favorite, and he can just eat the dog food and you will get his supper instead." Wag. Wag.

"So. You saying I'd like Midnight's dog food over your cooking?"

"Keep that up and you may not have any teeth left to eat with."

"Well, maybe your pony is not so bad after all." Henry squatted down, which caused Midnight to move over to the figure down at his eye level. Henry rubbed the big head behind the ears. "You are just a big baby, aren't you?" Wag. Wag. Wag.

He wondered how he could have passed by the narrow dirt road that served as the entrance to the Dozier place so many times over the years without knowing who lived there. For Henry, walking with Iris and Midnight on the paths around the farm in the afternoon sun, waiting for the sheriff to come home for supper, made him feel like he was in heaven. This was the life that normal people had, and this was the kind of atmosphere that normal people lived in. When he compared it to the life he had known in the swamp, he realized how peaceful being here made him feel. In addition to the graceful and genuine Iris, he acknowledged that the feeling of living this existence was what he had always been missing. He had known instinctively there was more to life, and now he had found it.

Inside the barn, Henry noticed the stacked bales of plastic that reminded him of the critical comments he had heard deriding Sheriff Dozier and his one-time business obsession. As he got to know the sheriff better, he pretended to think Jerico's idea was valid and took care not to offend Iris or her father. He asked questions, and as he listened to what the older man had to say about recycling the plastic, the potential for such a business started to make sense. Too bad there was no place left in the shambles of the American economy to sell what looked to Henry like all the plastic in the world. The sheriff's shoulders were more slumped than Henry remembered and he had begun to develop a bit of a paunch, but the same gentle fairness he had felt on the side of the road many years before was still there.

As they walked the pastures and got to know each other, he slowly began to tell Iris stories of the swamp and about his father's training. He avoided divulging the specific location of the island as he explained tracking animals, how the various seasons changed the colors, reflections in the water, and shading in the woods, which totally altered the look of the swamp. He explained how those changes affected the creatures who lived there.

"I think it's cool how we got a mixture of pine forests and

watery swamps. That's why we've got all the different varieties of animals." He tossed the ball to Midnight.

"There are places where you can see how the timber companies have cruised the tall trees and left the stumps of old cypress down below in the grasses. You can see where they re-planted the pines in rows that are growing back real well. Won't be too many years before they'll come back to hit it again. The rest of it is away from the game trails and roads cut by the timber harvesters. But when we get a good flood, it covers almost everything you can see from the high-water marks. Those grungy cypress and swamp trees and bushes, all packed into a thick, scraggly mass inside the swamp, have got to fight for survival."

Henry took a deep breath and smelled the dry late afternoon air, the mix of something like chlorophyll and something like cut hay. "You know, water finds its level and spreads out to form smaller patches. It stays damp all the time in the lower areas, with all that rot hovering in the deeper pools and spreading all over everything with constant muck. My daddy says it's in those dark places where the deep voices of the swamp whisper, and where there are the real, you know, what he calls 'ghost threats of suctioning earth and murky doom.' He says that's where there are the homes of the residents with teeth. That's why nobody wants to come there much. When we were kids, he used to tell us stories like that at night to scare the hell out of me and the other kids and keep us on high ground. It's those lower places that give city people nightmares. They imagine themselves struggling in quicksand, trying to escape some water moccasin dropping into their boat or around their neck."

Iris waver her arms. "Okay. Okay, I get it. Enough. You'll be scaring Midnight."

He smiled at her. "Still, I like living in a place where things are called by the names the Indians gave them. It ties everything to the earth and the water. The water smells familiar every time I return. It has a mixture of fallen trees, vines, spider webs, and obstacles to be negotiated along with the slithery creatures… newts, salamanders, roaches, turtles, frogs, snakes of all kinds, on up the food chain to the nests of water moccasins, otters, deer, bears, wild hogs, panthers. At the top, alligators sit proud and unafraid… And in the spring courtship, they create a chorus, bellowing in the mid-morning's heat to attract mates. Daddy says it's the big boys staking out their territory."

Iris made a sour face. "Henry, that's icky. It's stuff for you boys. I wouldn't like it."

Henry quickly changed his tune. "It's also a place of real beauty. It's got a big variety of birds like herons, teals, turkeys, ospreys, and vultures. There are also varieties of butterflies, skimmers, beetles, mosquitoes, dragonflies, horseflies, and more mosquitoes."

"Not enticing. You're a terrible salesman."

"Well, we do try to keep it natural. We toss all the entrails from the gators, snakes, and other swamp kills onto foot trails for the critters, or in pools for the fish and turtles. We use everything from the swamp and carry out anything that does not belong there."

"Henry, I get that you like the place, but you need to think that other people living here in town, and more importantly, me, may not be interested in your descriptions of gator guts."

He processed her comments on his descriptions, remembered his mother, and became less graphic with her. He also was careful to leave out the stories of how the swamp people got their main source of revenue, which would have no doubt interested her father. From conversations with her and her father, Henry began to gain confidence regarding how to talk to people like them, and how to act more civilized. His father never made any effort to present himself any better to city folks. He was content to roam the woods and stay in the swamp, and Henry thought that any association with his father would make Iris see him in a more limited way.

Iris was so wrapped up in her work, she mostly talked to him about the current medical dilemma and her frustrations at not being able to help more people. "We had to put many of the doctors out in kind of satellite offices in those empty neighborhood bank buildings with a nurse and some basic medicine. It became harder for people to travel to get to the central hospital without gas for their cars, and we couldn't do much more when they got there than the doctors could do out in those small neighborhood offices. At least with those doc-in-a-box clinics, people could walk to them and didn't have to go far to get some help. In some of those places, they set up neighborhood trading spots to swap food and other essentials in the parking lots. They've become a kind of little neighborhood-based town center.

"We did not get the supplies we needed, and we've had to figure out how to clean needles that were supposed to be thrown away. We're boiling them and using ultraviolent light to reuse for the same patients with the same problems, such as diabetics and insulin, but that is still dangerous.

"We also ran short of regular gauze and had to make bandages and masks out of sheets. We use those homemade bandages for the more minor cuts, and save the remaining sterile cloth for the minor operations and more serious cases. But we can see where, at some point, we will run out of any of the good stuff. We're rapidly moving into Civil War medicine. Am I boring you with all this medical talk?"

Henry nodded. "No. I find it amazing. You are solving problems that affect so many people who need your help. I'm learning things that fascinate me."

"They're prioritizing the more complicated drugs, and that means we have to choose to turn away some patients in order to treat others. Our folks in the lab are using basic chemistry to make medicine like aspirin and coagulates with whatever available chemicals they can lay their hands on. They can't make anything too sophisticated, like what your father needs, but we've got to do something before we run out of even the simplest compounds.

"Somebody rigged up a kind of bellows to pump oxygen, and we're just doing what we can without enough electricity. They do have us tagged for the bigger generators and spare gas when we need it for really big emergencies. I hope they can get steady electricity over to us from the Lake Chehaw power station soon."

As Henry walked with her, he lapped it up. Her culture and caring had softened him from the male-dominated practicality of the swamp. He loved to learn new things and loved to hear Iris talk, to listen to her compassionate mind work.

On Saturdays, people came to sell garden vegetables and handmade trinkets in Tift Park, and Henry and Iris visited there too. He wished that the world could always be like this, calm, peaceful, and full of promise. Everyone seemed to be attempting to hang on to normalcy. The opportunity here, however, was fading as goods to trade or sell became scarcer. Henry remembered two years ago, selling deer meat and wild hog sausages in the same parking lot. The booths diminished as more and more people set up places in their neighborhoods to trade closer to home. The people were still friendly, as they had always been, but now the goods declined and the trash in the park showed signs of taking up residence.

As he watched Iris negotiate the half empty booths with such obvious ease, Henry thought of his mother. He wondered if she was okay, and if she was in a situation where she could survive this crisis. He had stopped by to see her two years ago on the way to a bank robbery in North Carolina. She met him in a restaurant not too far from her home north of Atlanta in Dunwoody, where she lived with her new husband, a young child, Henry's half-sister, and two children from the husband's first marriage. She had left Willis almost eight years ago, and he could not blame her. Willis started his decline years before, characterized by the depression, the drinking, and the dark moods. She tried to nurture his fight against the demons. However, there came a time when she had enough.

She told Henry and Willis that she could not take it anymore, got a no-fault divorce from an attorney in Albany, and moved to Atlanta to live with one of her cousins until she could get on her feet. After a time, she met a man whose wife had died, leaving him with two children. That worked for her. Henry was happy she had found a different life that suited her, and he saw her every year or two. Now he wondered if his mother and her new family could survive in the competition of a large, populated area without enough food or the comforts people were used to in such a big city. He hoped that she was well, but worried about her given the conditions here in the rural area, where growing food was relatively easy and there was less competition for what was produced.

Henry and Iris discovered they had similar tastes in country and western music, and both loved the harmonies of Little Big Town. In the house preparing dinner, they began to sing together over the music coming from an old battery powered CD player. They were getting into the song, with their voices rising ever louder, when Jerico came into the kitchen.

"And I can taste
That honeysuckle and it's still so sweet
When it grows wild
On the banks down at old camp creek
Yeah, and it calls to me like a warm wind blowing…"

"Ahh!" Sheriff Dozier held his hands by the sides of his head. "My ears are bleeding. Neither of you can sing a lick. It's like cats are fighting. Poor Midnight thinks we've got a new pet whose tail is caught in the disposal."

They both laughed. Iris said to her father, "Well, I've heard you at church trying to sing hymns and I can't imagine you are any better."

"At least there I've got the cover of other people who can carry a tune, and know what key it's in."

"Okay, mister grumpy, wash up for supper."

She watched her father and Henry laughing and talking to each other as they passed the soap and towels over the sink. They were alike: smart in subtle ways, inquisitive, and humble. Henry did not try hard to impress her like many of the other men she had been around. She had enough pressure at work. He was steady and capable, and morally strong in his own quiet way, in addition to being handsome and incredibly fit.

Here was a guy who was so easy to be around. She also did not feel intimidated. Because many of the men at work were so much more educated than she was, she felt inadequate around most of them. This man standing in her kitchen with his back to her complemented her life and did not compete with it. As if he was reading her thoughts, Henry laid the towel on the sink and turned to look at her with a grin.

SwiftyMart

Ussief Urangia checked the stock room to make sure last night's clerk had restacked the boxes properly after she had re-supplied the SwiftyMart store. He switched on the electronics that ran the gas tanks outside and made sure the trash cans had been emptied. He prided himself on an orderly presentation.

Shift manager was the best job he could get to support his growing family since arriving from Bangladesh three years ago. He had heard from a cousin who worked in one of the other stores that his big boss, somewhere in North Carolina, owned over a hundred of these combination roadside markets and gas stations.

This one in particular, isolated with no other buildings nearby on the highway east of Albany, was vulnerable to theft. Because it was hard to find managers willing to work there, Ussief, even with his hesitant English, got the job. He tried to be friendly to all the customers and wore a Georgia Bulldog jersey so the locals might think of him as one of them. He kept his hair cut short and had only a thin, trimmed moustache, not a beard. This brought him criticism from some of his relatives and friends, but he felt it important to blend in as much as possible, and not look too much like an **émigré or a potential terrorist.**

Life was hard enough without standing out in a crowd and perhaps inviting ridicule or worse. Lately Ussief's efforts to man-age the store were getting harder as the supplies for the station continued to dwindle. Half the time, they were short of gas. He would often run out of high test unleaded, which was resupplied less frequently. As the year moved on and the days got longer, it seemed the big semi-trucks arriving to refill the underground tanks were slower in coming.

Now even the store merchandise was running out. As he completed his cursory inventory, he was disappointed to see many of the drinks in the cooler were low in stock. The snack food supply trucks were also coming less often, and he had to spread out the cakes, candies, chips, and canned goods on the shelves to make it look like the store was full when too often, it was actually half empty.

If this situation did not get better, he would get more pressure from those people who called him from North Carolina to complain that, because gas sales were dwindling, he needed to sell more food merchandise. He worried that the people in North Carolina did not understand his predicament, and that it was not his fault he had less of everything to sell. He had to have this job to feed his family.

He had begun to wonder when his first customer would arrive when the van pulled in. Four men got out, all dressed in dark clothing and wearing hooded sweatshirts. They were also wearing sunglasses, even though it was still early, and the light was not strong outside. As they entered rapidly, one of them came to the counter, pulled out a gun, and put it right in Ussief's face. He backed up to the counter behind him and raised his hands.

The other three grabbed a box of trash bags, took out all the bags, and began to stuff them with merchandise from the store. They moved quickly down the aisles and went for things that they must have seen before. It seemed as though they knew which items they wanted. Ussief tried not to look at any of the

Island in the Storm

men, but instead stared at a space up on the ceiling at the back of the store. He kept praying that they would hurry up with their business and not shoot him. Losing this job was one thing, his life was another.

The man holding the gun seemed nervous and continued to glance back and forth at the other men ransacking the place. He kept changing his grip on the gun and waving it back and forth when he turned. Ussief hoped that the gun would not go off accidently. Someone outside in the van had turned it around so the back doors now were facing the store. He guessed that meant the driver in the vehicle was ready to drive off quickly if someone else pulled up. When the bags were full, one of the men would put them in the van where the back door was open.

Ussief's arms were getting tired of being in the air. As the blood ran down into his body, he could feel them tingle. There was a final blur of activity that was fast and efficient, and after two of the men took the last of the bags to the van, one of the others came up to the man with the gun and nodded. The two men took Ussief to the back-storage room of the store with the gun pressed to his back. This made him very nervous. One of them opened the cold storage locker, pushed Ussief in, and closed the door. There was a light inside, and he could see the meager sandwiches, baked goods, milk, and other perishables stored there. He heard some faint scraping sounds and distant talking, and then there was a thud against the door that he imagined was something to keep him inside.

Then it was still and quiet and cold. Ussief wondered, when other people came into the SwiftyMart, would they know to look for him in the locker?

Six Months Earlier

Six months earlier, Lamar Ballard, the mayor of Albany, Georgia, called a group of officials, including his old friend Sheriff Dozier and the city and county commissioners, together to discuss a growing concern.

The mayor, a track athlete in high school and college, was of average size and had kept his frame lean. There was a nervous energy about him, held in check by the willpower it had taken to achieve his success. He was measured, thoughtful, precise - traits that showcased his analytical mind. He always dressed as if he expected to be presented to an audience. His friend the sheriff kidded him that he suspected the mayor often looked at himself in a full-length mirror before leaving his bedroom in the morning, and would ask for his wife's approval before exiting the house.

Perhaps being fastidious was in his DNA, encouraged by training from determined parents who carefully coached their children to conform to the manners and appearance needed to achieve their prioritized goals. Perhaps this was a part of what all black men had to consider in gaining the respect and honing the tools needed to be a political leader in a town where the racial divide was roughly fifty-fifty.

Now he stood erect in front of the group with his shoulders back, attempting to disregard the churn in his stomach as he considered the uncertainty of the weeks and months ahead. He paced back and forth near his chair, unable to restrain his nervous energy.

"Folks, for a couple of years now, we all have all seen the

decline in the economy that started with that virus thing, and it seems to be accelerating. We have gone from a recession to what looks more every day like a real and perhaps lasting depression. We've had some instances of civil unrest, and there is a lack of available food and medicine. We all know gasoline is high and hard to come by at any price. We all hope and pray this looming crisis will get resolved soon and everything will be back to normal. However, it's our civic responsibility to think ahead."

He stopped his pacing and looked around the room as he spoke. "We're here today to set up a plan now in case things get a lot worse, and before we get hit in the face with something that may be impossible to handle. I'm calling on all of you to play a leadership role in your districts and neighborhoods."

He unveiled a large map and showed them his idea to divide the areas in and around greater Albany into regions that further subdivided the existing city and county commissioners' election districts. Each of them would be responsible for the area closest to their home. There were, however, more sections on the map than there were commissioners in the room. He said additional leaders would be appointed for the extra sections to have practical control over smaller areas of the town. He explained that if the plan was implemented, in addition to their regular duties on various committees, each of them would have to take a role as the leader of a geographic section composed of units representing several dozen neighborhood blocks, and they all would be called "Block Captains."

The city council president, Larry Godwin, raised his hand and began speaking before he was recognized. "That sounds too much like a military operation. Let's call them... ah... Neighborhood Managers."

Ballard shook his head in the affirmative. "Larry, if that will make you happy, I'm all for it. Your contribution is duly noted."

Godwin smiled and nodded to his left and right and brushed at his cashmere jacket, looking for lint.

Ballard turned his attention back to the meeting. "At least this way the... Neighborhood Managers would be known to the people living in those districts, and the newly designated leaders in charge of those areas would be familiar with a specific system of hierarchy and chain of command." He went on to explain the mayor would be the overall boss, and the county sheriff was to be the military boss. The two men, even separated by a generation, had always worked well together, and under this system, the infrastructure of both city and county governments would have someone over them that they knew from years of service.

"Now that we have seen the geographic areas of your responsibility in the emergency plan, here is what we are asking you to do." He waved some folders and put them on the table. "I have here several reports on our existing resources, and have divided up the information into committees for you to review. There are six major areas we need to consider: nourishment, medicine, sanitation, power, transportation, and security. Your names are on the cover of the envelopes of your assigned area of responsibility. Because this is important, I want you to take the next week and study them. I want your thoughts on how to help resolve any problems and how to implement the plans for each of these areas.

"With some help from our staff, I've studied similar environments in recent history. Those crisis situations happened mostly in wartime, so we looked at those as well as peacetime emergences. Don't share this information broadly, as we don't want people to get in a panic or assume the worst. Come see me if you wish to make an adjustment. We will meet back here this time next week."

One of the county commissioners asked, "Don't you think this is premature and unnecessary?"

"No, Marcelle, I don't. The people in Washington, on both sides of the aisle, have done nothing for years except fuss at each other. It would be nice if they and the other leaders in the world got together and actually solved problems, but I don't see that happening. We have a responsibility to ourselves and the people we represent here to get prepared for what I think are even worse times ahead."

City Council President Larry Godwin stood, pressed down his jacket and trousers, and walked to the front. "Now y'all all known me. I'm just a country boy that gets by with a little charm and a lot of prevarication. Hee, hee. That's a joke. But I got to tell you honestly, this is a crazy idea. It would diminish the system we've had governing here for many years. Our form of govern-ment is established and approved by the State Legislature." He glanced over at Mayor Ballard and smiled. "You can't just wave a wand and change it. We are fine just as we are."

Godwin spread his hands. "Lamar, the mayor's job does not make you God or give you powers to see into the future. This kind of alarmist and frankly… Scaredy cat rhetoric is not worthy of you or the leadership of all of us elected officials here in Alba-ny. We don't need to spend the resources or the time to chase our tails on something that our national leaders will likely resolve soon. We have real work to do here and we need to get back to creating progress and growing our economy."

A supporter of the mayor said, "Like some of our national

leaders have tried to solve our other problems in the past few years?"

There was mumbling around the table. The city and county leadership had been divided into two camps for several years since Ballard's election.

Mayor Ballard let the mumbling quiet, then sighed and tapped his pen on the shiny conference table that Godwin had insisted the city purchase along with other expensive furniture the year he first ran against Ballard for mayor. "Larry, our city and county governments are not segmented enough to handle smaller neighborhood needs in a crisis. We've got to plan now to be able to manage, to use your word, something like a depression or wartime stress, here, where we live. What we have now is fine when everything is going okay. However, we're not organized to MANAGE a severe crisis unless we can communicate down to the neighborhood blocks and individual houses."

Godwin walked back and forth. "That's not true! I can easily handle my responsibilities. My people respect me and will do what I say. The economy has already hurt my real estate business. This crazy idea will put a stop to future development. People will be scared."

"Larry, we've been working on this and studying it for several months. People need to be concerned, if not scared. You chose not to come to the early planning meetings. It's too late now for you to complain. You will still have your authority, but there will be smaller groups below you who will also have authority. Your job will be to coordinate with them and help them."

Godwin stood with his shoulders back. "I damn well know my job! It's you who seems to be exceeding yours." He raised his arm like an orchestra conductor to point at Ballard. "You are taking this economic stress far too seriously in what seems to be to be a grab for power."

"Larry, if we have to implement this plan, and then our problems get resolved, we will revert this new system right back to where we are now. As I've said several times in earlier meetings," he looked around the room, "if you all want to replace me, go for it. However, as long as I'm in charge, this plan is what we will be doing. We're not going to implement it today, but we will get ready and appoint the neighborhood leadership. If things get worse, we will put it in place."

Godwin sputtered, "It's damn tyranny and unnecessary. It's cowardly behavior."

Ballard nodded earnestly. "I hope you are right. I hope I will be incredibly embarrassed and run out of office for what I'm proposing. I have no doubt you will keep close watch and take notes on what is about to happen. However, Larry…"

"What?"

"You can get with the program or get off the city council."

Godwin slammed himself into a chair and folded his arms over his chest.

Ballard ignored Godwin's snit, and pointed around the room. "Now, I don't want you to come back here a week from now with a report that says to study the problems some more. This meeting is to develop a plan of action that will solve problems. Come back with your recommendations for neighborhood leaders. If you don't have any ideas, just say so. Don't BS me." The mayor again looked around the room at the staff and his trusted friends, stopping his gaze at Godwin. Before concluding the meeting, he declared, "We all need to think carefully about who lives in the sections I've shown you today. Your sections.

Your responsibility.

"Take an inventory. Find people who can work with their hands – carpenters, metal workers, farmers. We need people who know how to fix and operate mechanical things. And we're going to need muscle. Think of people who are big and strong but not aggressive. We still have a lot of unemployed, some living in the commercial buildings and strip centers that were converted into public housing. They need something to do. We may need to increase the police force and start an auxiliary military force, like a militia. We need all the help we can get, and need to find us some smart people with a variety of skills to join us. We need to plan how to do this now, and not wait until our problems bite us in the ass."

When everyone left the large board room and it had gotten quiet, the mayor turned to his secretary, who had been taking the minutes, and said, "It feels to me like I'm struggling to hold onto a rope that contains my family dangling off a cliff. Every day the rope slips a bit more and tears into the skin of my hands, still flexing and tugging against the inevitable." He shook his head. "I sure hope I'm wrong about this feeling." He tapped on the big table.

"In any case, get the staff to call the colleges to look for ways to find and store salt. We may need it to preserve food here in South Georgia. Put out a note from me to secure whatever we have in storage. We don't need it to cover the roads in the winter. Oh, and Gladys, don't copy anyone. I don't want that jerk Larry Godwin finding out and making speeches that we are having a meltdown."

The next week's reports from the Neighborhood Managers were spotty, but action was taken to set up the layered extension of the city council and county commissioners for direct communications down to the street level. Although erratically implemented, almost everyone felt the mayor's plan was something they could organize and start to use, and it gave them all specific tasks to do that were at least partially useful. Most of the things they needed were in short supply. However, the planning that started months before gave them the foundation to face the crisis once it hit later.

Siphoning

In the predawn, at a motel outside Atlanta, Rowdy Burdette finished pouring gas from a five-gallon can into the one thousand-gallon tanker truck and handed the man back the empty container. "Hurry your ass up and tell those other guys to get a move on." He looked around the dark parking lot as three other men ran from one car to another, siphoning gas with rubber hoses and five-gallon cans.

The next man wobbled up awkwardly with the heavy can. "That's about it from down there," he nodded back at a row of cars outside the motel. "Most of them weren't full."

Rowdy sneered. "We got to hit one more motel before it starts to get light. Here, pour this in. I can't do all the work. Don't spill any. That is liquid money."

The man gave a grunt as he hefted the can and tipped the spout into the opening. He looked over at the big, tall man as he started to pour. "How'd ya figure this out?"

Rowdy snorted. "With electricity only working half the time, the only gas we can be sure to have is what was already around. You never heard of supply and demand? The more of this stuff we got, the more stuff we can trade it for. Everybody needs gas. With this size tanker," he thumped on the side, making a deep, semi-hollow echo, "we can move quicker in and out, folks won't ask questions, and ain't nobody gonna catch us, just pay up."

The man lifted the now empty can back. "I've only got two more down that way and then we'll be done here. Where to next?"

Rowdy looked out at the road. "We're gonna head south on I-75 toward Florida. What cars are left out there will be on that road, and we can sell or trade to the gas stations on the interstate or in those little towns along the side. Move on now and get those other two cars. Be quiet. We don't want to be shooting anyone and get the law on us."

Lunch in the Park

Tuesday was a bright, sunny day as Henry and Iris walked the two blocks from the hospital to Tift Park to eat lunch on Iris's break. They could see overflowing trashcans. Pickups had become irregular due to a lack of fuel for the trucks.

They walked past the place where people sold or swapped things with each other and socialized at the weekend farmer's market. There were still uncollected horse droppings from wagons used to bring in produce to sell or barter in the parking lots. Horses were becoming more familiar around town as people began finding alternative means of transportation.

Now the lack of sanitation permeated everything, and everyone was trying to get used to the constant odor of excrement and trash. As he steered their walk away from the garbage, Henry noticed that he breathed through his mouth most often now.

As was usual with them, Iris did most of the talking, and as usual, she approached one subject as a way to get to another. "You know, Henry, we are what most folks would call attractive-looking people in a conventional movie-TV kind of way. However, that is not who we are. I'm so sick of people judging me by how I look."

"Well, I've been mostly appreciated by frogs and turtles, so…"

Iris waved her hand to quiet him and continued to lead the discussion, letting Henry's patient listening serve as the release for her frustrations about the medical crisis that was becoming worse every day. Over the past weeks, she had been educating

Island in the Storm

Henry and he found her conclusions frightening. Most of all, he loved just being with Iris, absorbing both her beauty and her knowledge.

"You know I'm being serious here. You try to make a joke out of everything."

"I know. It's just that I love to see the look on your face when you get like this and start to preach back at me. I think everyone needs to have their buttons pushed from time to time. You haven't had that as much as you needed because you are so pretty, and people have always wanted you to like them. I kinda see that as one of my jobs."

"Well, you are fairly good at it."

"Yes, and I understand what you were saying. One of the things I lo... I really like about you is how you see life and how you sincerely want to help other people. What could be a better way to live than that? What could be more attractive than that? Certainly not the way your hair waves and bobs up and down or the way you walk. Well... maybe some of that, but..."

"You're doing it again. Stop it, or I'm going to go back to calling you Spud."

"Okay, Tink... or was it Puddin'?"

"I said..."

"Okay. However, you know, in addition to your good parts, you can also be kind of bossy."

Iris shook her head. She found it reassuring to talk through the important decisions she had to make with Henry. His kidding gave her emotional relief, but it was in his listening as her sounding board that she was able to validate the best choices from a range of bad possibilities. She didn't need his judgement or approval so much as the comfort from his presence and his loyalty.

She needed to talk it out with herself.

She walked with her head down, partially eaten sandwich in one hand, her other arm swinging and pointing to punctuate her monologue. "Before now, we have extended life with the drug companies, nutrition, and medical procedures, and that rug is being yanked out from under those who need it the most. Not only the elderly, but many who are sick and the very young who need supplements because their immune systems are not developed. Once they run out of their supply of meds, many of them are going to die. It's sad and it makes me so angry to see this happening, and there is nothing we can do.

"We forget that in Europe before 1800, the average life expectancy was around forty years. Even by 1900, the life span was only about fifty years. That's when we began to develop medicine and science and found ways through sanitation, immunizations, access to clean running water, better nutrition, and drugs to keep us alive and functioning longer. Without the drugs, we're gonna have to rely on healthy habits, and that's likely to drop our lifespan down from over seventy-eight now to maybe more like sixty years."

"How do you know that?"

"Reading and asking questions. I never went to medical school, so I have to fill in the blanks where I can. Wait. You broke my train of thought. I'm thinking of something I have to say to a bunch of people in a few weeks. You are my practice audience."

"What an honor."

"Quiet and listen. You can critique later."

"Good so far."

"So, now we are placing more emphasis on preventative medicine. Sanitation has become more important. Hand washing and cleanliness. The vast industry that had grown to prolong life and produce miracles in healthcare has diminished. Antibiotics have been overused for a long time and have become less effective in the past few years. We have not had many new antibiotics for some time. All those medicines are now scarce. The idea of keeping people alive for another few months in intensive care or on ventilators, heart machines, or by other artificial means is no longer possible or practical. We've had to make some hard choices.

"And because of the lack of energy… Well, you know hospitals were one of the main public users, but even with what we have from solar, wind, and water-generated power, it is not enough." She stopped, crossed her arms, and shook her head. "I feel so inadequate for this job."

He started to say something soothing, as he often did when she got upset about work, but she held up her hand. "Henry, how could we let this happen? What were our leaders thinking? More importantly, what were they doing over some ego thing, and what the hell are they doing to try to fix this?"

Henry looked down and rubbed his foot in the dirt. He thought what Iris was saying was a lot to digest.

She walked further with her head down, then stopped and looked at him. "Henry, I'm worried about the potential for violence. Everyone today has a gun, and many are carrying them around. People are already taking the law into their own hands. Most people who bluster, swagger, and carry guns don't have any idea what a bullet can do to a person. I know you are a hunter and so is my father. Most of the people we know are responsible with guns, but a lot of people are not. Everyone who carries one should come into the operating room and see the impact of a gunshot. The human body is so fragile, and a bullet just rips it apart.

"We don't have the equipment, supplies, or training to handle large scale injuries from bullets. Staph infections are increasing. If people start shooting each other, it will be like the Civil War, where twice as many died from disease as were killed in combat. I just hate this place where we've come to."

He reached and put a hand on each of her upper arms in a move to calm her. "I don't know, Iris, we've just got to look after each other and hope we can fix all this stuff that's broken in the world. I know that living in the swamp taught me that life is about being aware of everything else around you and how it fits into that space... How each thing functions and how it relates to everything else. That's just how we have to learn to survive... together."

Part II – The Crisis

Crash

Albany Mayor Lamar Ballard checked his cell phone as he came into his office early, but it was dead. Must have forgotten to charge it. He was worried about the lack of gasoline to operate the equipment to pick up all the trash, and as he sat down wearily at his desk and clicked on his computer to look at the supply charts... Nothing. He checked the power to see if it was plugged in. Yes. Click, still nothing. He flicked the light switch. Nada. He thought to himself, "The world crashed on a Wednesday. It died not with a bang, but a whimper." Then as he thought some more, "Actually, after several years of whimpering, this was the final but silent bang."

When he tried to call for help, the line was dead, and when he went into other offices, he found the same. Somebody had finally pulled the plug. Maybe someone would get the power back on and the phones to work again. He was getting so tired of trusting others to make things work, and then being disappointed. He suddenly felt grateful that he and Sheriff Dozier had been planning for something like this.

After confirming his suspicions, he then sent handwritten notices to tell everyone it was time to implement the crisis system they had devised. He had to trust that his Neighborhood Managers were ready to handle the communications in their assigned neighborhoods. Over the past six months, the Managers had trained for how to coordinate their neighborhoods in such an emergency, and they knew to ask for help if it was something that they could not handle. His note told the Managers to use the satellite offices with the medical people as their neighborhood headquarters until they could collectively figure out if separate facilities were needed.

His plan allowed for one emergency radio station, operated with a generator, to broadcast messages at certain times of the day. People would be able to tune in on battery powered radios to get public messages sent to the Managers - and anyone else who wanted to listen. He got one of Dozier's deputies to set up a time to make the first broadcast. He would announce dates and times for several meetings already on tap, beginning in key areas that would need special attention they had identified several months before. The announcement would also call for training in various areas that included volunteers for a broader military and security presence, and taking a fresh inventory of the assets in each neighborhood. It was admittedly hit and miss, but the plan they had devised would begin a pattern of order and give some reassurance to people who suddenly had no internet or regular power. It was time to start living in the 1800s.

Ballard and Dozier

An hour later, Lamar Ballard joined Jerico Dozier on the Riverwalk down by the Flint River waterfront, a place where they met to discuss things they did not want anyone else to overhear. In the open space, they could see anyone coming from at least a hundred yards away. Today, they sat side by side on the inside wall of what used to be a moat surrounding a sculpture of the long-since deceased Albany native and recording superstar, Ray Charles.

Without enough spare electricity to run it, the fountain had been drained of water months ago, and sat as an empty circular moat that surrounded a metal Mister Charles sitting at a metal piano. The music of Ray Charles had greeted visitors from speakers around the statue until that too was cut by the lack of electricity. Mayor Ballard looked over at the solemn sheriff. "Well, Jerico, we're in uncharted waters now. Electricity finally just died. We've got to hold this place together or it could get very bad very quick.

"Albany is the hub, slap in the middle of a quarter of the land area in Georgia. We are the big dog in the yard, and the closest other city of any size is about eighty miles away. We've got supplies of just about everything people will be wanting in this crisis, and we're gonna be a target to everybody who thinks they can just come here and get what they want. We've gotta protect and serve the people who live here, and we likely don't have enough supplies to take care of ourselves."

Dozier moved himself over and squatted down with his

back leaning on the five-foot tall pedestal that supported the bronze piano and the metallic, magnificent, blind singer. From this position, he could look the mayor in the face as they talked. "Yep. We've got to get everyone to work together and conserve everything, like we have been discussing for the past few months. All those lists of people with certain skills we have been collecting and training on a voluntary basis… Well, now we have to put them to use for real. You need to call for meetings of people who can take on jobs in energy and food. I'll make a list of who to invite to meetings on security and transportation. We've got to keep the Neighborhood Managers in the loop. Starting right now, they are going to have to hold the neighborhoods together."

Ballard looked around. "We've mostly got to think about feeding everyone. You know, even though the Roddenberry syrup plant in Cairo closed, I think there is still a lot of the equipment down there that they used to grind sugar cane and make syrup or sugar. Camilla has a big processing plant."

Dozier snapped his fingers. "Yes, and there is lots of truck farming all around here. The ag extension folks would know about that, and where the biggest acreage is for planting various crops, and better still, how to plant more. We're also going to need hothouses. I'll invite those ag people to our next meeting."

Ballard continued, "You're right. We need to be in touch with the other farmer's markets around, bigger than we have in Tift Park. They'll know the local farmers. We've got to agree to raise a variety of food so we will have a balance of nutrition available. If this lasts long, we'll need to plant more fruit trees."

Dozier, with his studies on recycling, had learned a thing or two. "Yes, and some people have been using fewer pesticides

Island in the Storm

and fertilizers that we can't get any more anyway. Organic stuff. They can show others how to do it."

Ballard nodded. "We need to be the sales brokers for all the crops that are grown around here. It will be better if we can be the central point that sets the trades. We're the logical place because all the main roads in Southwest Georgia lead here."

Dozier laughed. "Making all those bargains will give the lawyers something to do."

Ballard said sarcastically, "Yeah. As you know, full employment for the lawyers has certainly been a big goal of mine from the start."

"We also need to get someone to the Miller-Coors bottling plant and the microbrewery over there on Pine Avenue. They can see what kind of energy it might take get that equipment up and running to purify water. We also need to look at all the canning operations within a hundred miles. Not sure how viable they are, but it might give us a way to stretch out the shelf life of our food supply."

As their focus on the food discussion waned, Ballard then coughed and shrugged. "How could those assholes have let it come to this? The screwed up the virus thing and now this. Why the hell couldn't they find a way to work together? Damn them."

Dozier shifted his weight on his sore knees. "Well, Lamar, I don't normally hear you talk like that. I agree with what you say, but that ship has sailed. We've got to keep the violence down and get organized. We're in survival mode now.

"By the way, we've got to take over all the remaining gas for critical needs and lock up the pumps until we can manually pump it out. We're going to need whatever is left out there. I'm going to have to put my deputies on it, or some people from the militias we've been planning to start."

The mayor reached and tapped his knuckle softly on the metal of the sculpture, which made a deep gong. "I'm thinking about your daughter. We need to get more armed guards at the hospitals and places around here that have medical supplies. We need to control everything at the drug stores that is critical to public health."

"That's going to take more manpower than we have right now."

Ballard nodded. "We'll just have to get it with those militias."

Sheriff Dozier also tapped the metal. "We also need to confiscate cartridges and find all the gunpowder we can. I'll call the college chemistry people and ask them to get saltpeter, sulfur, charcoal, and whatever else it takes to make gunpowder. They need to figure how to mix it without blowing themselves up."

Ballard nodded. "Good idea. Another thing… Money will soon be worth nothing. We've got to set up some sort of incentives for people to cooperate… Like food. Everyone is going to have to do their part to get us through this mess. We can't have people just sitting on their ass and complaining."

"Enough of that already."

Ballard looked across the river where Albany State University was located. "I'm going to get with the economics professors at the colleges and come up with a workable barter plan we can use. In the meantime, we need to consider a work-for-food idea where we provide some basic level of food and water for everyone, but reward those who actually do something to help by giving them more. Maybe the workers are the first in line to get

Island in the Storm

some sort of electricity from the batteries. Something like that."

Dozier shook his head. "Well, whatever we come up with, people are gonna complain, so it may as well be something that gets the jobs done. I'll have my deputies and the police ready to tell folks why we have set up such a system to all those people who will no doubt be upset. We need to get the preachers involved for some of this stuff; got to work on how to explain things to calm people down. I'll get any suggestions sorted before we bring them to the Neighborhood Managers."

Ballard looked over. "Some things a committee can handle, but we've got to make most of the decisions ourselves."

The sheriff looked down at his feet. "Yep."

Mayor Ballard nodded again thoughtfully, then looked hard at the sheriff. "These kinds of conditions in other societies have led to war... the Middle East, Europe, Asia. It's changed those cultures. Changed those people, mostly for the worse. You think we'll be attacked?"

Dozier gave his friend a serious look back. "We're the biggest target in a hundred miles... The most likely to have a supply of... whatever... stuff. Once people think about it, they'll realize the Marine Depot or Logistics Command, whatever they are calling it now, is the holy grail of survival. They'll be coming... from far and near."

The mayor said, "I'll start to set up the meetings. Why don't you send a message to get us on out there to see the base commander? We've got to convince him to work with us. We gotta combine forces, but man, I hate to see it come to this."

Dozier slapped his knees and stood. "Me too. Okay. Let's go to work."

Revolt Near Dothan

Walter walked from the barn after feeding the last of the hay to his two remaining cows. There was little left to eat now, except what was in the garden, and he wondered how long his wife and kids could live off that and the meat from the cows. He was almost finished curing the one cow he had killed a few days ago and hoped the other two could live off the grass in the closed pasture - and not get poached. He'd trade most of the fresh meat for canned and dried goods like rice and beans. Some people were still dumb enough to do that. Maybe that would hold his family over until he could come back with more food from the trip he was about to take.

His wife knew how to shoot, and if he had to protect the family, his fourteen-year-old son was man enough to kill. It was a bad situation any way you looked at it.

Without gas for the tractor, he could not plant a crop this year. Without any money, they could not survive. Now the only chance seemed to be throwing in with the bunch mostly from over at Fort Rucker. His cousin who worked on the Army Base said they were putting together a group to scavenge for food supplies, and that there would be enough of them so they could just take most anything they wanted. There were some hard types in the group, but he didn't see any other way to survive. He'd just go and do this thing long enough to get what he needed and get it back to his family. They had to have the means to survive, and there wasn't any other way here in the sawgrass outside of Dothan, Alabama.

Island in the Storm

His cousin told him that the bulk of the Fort Rucker people were going to head over to Dothan and scrounge there. A select group would split off and head over to Georgia. They'd take two mortars and two machine guns, but because there was not enough gas, they would use mostly small arms that could be carried by each person. They'd have two trucks that would be packed to the gills with supplies, plus the heaver ordinance, but he and his cousin and the other foot soldiers would be just that. Walking would make the going slower, but they'd take on more food where they found it on the road and grab more vehicles or get a ride if they found a stash of gas. Walter spent some time thinking how he would get the food and other supplies back to his family. Maybe a cart he could pull? Maybe gas to power a car? A horse? He'd have to do it before his family's supplies ran out.

Hopefully he wouldn't have to do anything too bad to get what they needed. His cousin knew some of the leaders, so that might help. He didn't want to hurt or kill anybody. He didn't want to be mean, but he'd do what he had to do. He and his family would survive no matter what it took. He loaded his gun and readied his backpack. Now he'd finish packing the cured meat from the cow. Trade the meat. Join the gang. Hit the road.

Finding Order

Henry entered the Albany City Hall feeling nervous and out of place. Sheriff Dozier had told him about the meeting to organize efforts that would counter the new crisis, and Henry wanted to see what they were proposing. He was only familiar with the decision-making of the swamp families, which had become predictable. Here in these halls were people he did not know, some in white shirts and ties. They all looked like they had been to college, and were rich by Henry's standards.

He moved from room to room, standing in the back and listening. In most rooms, there were up to two dozen people talking, writing on blackboards or big pieces of paper, and discussing different issues. There in the first room was the mayor with the people from the electrical company, and those few people who had solar panels on their roofs to generate electricity. They had invited folks from the farms that still had windmills standing on the property (that had not been taken down as an eyesore), and even invited that crazy inventor from out on the Kinchafoonee Creek who thought he could run a generator off a floating, spinning water wheel.

He listened as they all got their heads together, then got some help from others coming into the room who worked for plumbing, roofing, automotive supplies, construction companies, and even the family that had the main bicycle store.

They split into subgroups and developed various ways to use wind, solar, water, and human power to generate energy... Not in an abundance like there was before, but enough to charge some batteries or run a generator for short periods of time, and to recharge batteries for continued use. As Henry listened, a plan emerged to provide some basic electricity for lights, fans, heaters, and other simple needs, and that put everyone in a better mood. Some of what they were planning sounded like the water-wheels they had been using in the swamp.

In the hallway, a man was urgently saying to another, "We've got to get electricity to the pumps. Without electricity, we can't get water to any houses or faucets anywhere."

He went further down the hall to a meeting of the school systems. Someone there was talking about how their kids were complaining about not enough electricity to watch celebrity videos, charge cellphones, or personal grooming. As he listened, the group quickly lost the meaning of why that was important.

The superintendent of the schools suggested, "We should continue providing education to our community and parents should encourage attendance. School happens in the daylight, and it doesn't take much to read a book and put a chalk mark on a blackboard. Our kids need something to do and the parents want them to learn something useful. We plan to supplement our normal curriculum with practical survival knowledge, and to explain the decisions the local managers are trying to implement. We want students to get involved by giving them the knowledge needed to solve current problems and anticipate others. We've got the Albany Technical College's professors and students pulling textbooks from the back of the library to find out how to get some of the old equipment around town working manually, without electricity.

"We've been working with the college professors at the west campus of Albany State to develop teaching manuals for apprenticeships in all key functions of society. It's a practical substitute for being in college, and offers full employment for the students in medicine, legal, anything mechanical, building trades, farmers, city and county workers, whatever. We might as well train our children to do something useful. There's gonna be new jobs in repurposing old equipment into parts and replacing worn out parts. There is a huge need for parts inventory."

City Councilman Larry Godwin stood. "That sounds like a waste of time. We may get the electricity back any day now. The superintendent is talking about dumbing down our education. It's likely to change our economy for the worse. When the power comes on, we'll have to retrain our students back up to where they were before."

The superintendent countered. "I believe doing nothing would waste time. Better they learn something than sit and wait for the internet to reappear. I recommend we set up a suggestion box at every neighborhood center for anyone with a good idea about how to make things better. I'll assign teachers living nearby to read the suggestions and put them in different piles according to what has been suggested. We can discuss the practical ideas at town meetings and assign people to work on implementing them. Whatever happens, we'll be trying to improve where we are right now. It'll teach our children practical things about how democracy can work."

Henry began to feel invested in what was happening in the room. He felt the energy of their discussions, and he was learning a new way to do things with people, with strangers, through discussion and goodwill toward a common purpose. This situation was new for him, and he felt that these people, whom he had formerly considered as just unknowns who lived nearby, were a part of his world and he was part of theirs. He began to go to more of these meetings, and smiled a few days later when he heard someone say that one person who came to visit from the next town over said, "We could see you all out there glowing in the night."

Dinner with the Doziers

Henry showered and changed into the fresh clothes he had gotten in town that day, acquired in a trade for some deer meat.

His father had been watching his progress. "Must be headed to some place special for you to get dressed up like this."

"No. Just meeting some friends in town."

"Yeah, friends. Well, you just need to remember that sheriff is no dummy."

When Henry arrived for dinner at the Dozier house, he ran into the sheriff and one of his deputies talking in the living room. The sheriff told Henry to have a seat in the kitchen while he finished up with the deputy.

Henry handed Iris a package containing the deer meat he had brought from the swamp for her to cook with some vegetables she had gathered that afternoon from the Doziers' large garden. She declined his invitation to help with the cooking, so he sat in a chair by the door visiting with her and petting Midnight, who was excited by the deer smell on Henry's hands.

Then she decided he could help. "Here, set the table. I don't know why you still haven't brought your father over for dinner." She gave him a puzzled look as she handed him the silverware and dishes.

Henry didn't answer her question, but instead went into the adjacent dining room and tried to figure out exactly how all the stuff he was holding was supposed to lay out. He remembered that the knife and fork were on opposite sides of the plate, but was not sure which. As he was debating what to do, Iris kept a banter from the kitchen.

"It that a new shirt? It looks like a dress shirt."

Henry looked down at his chest absentmindedly. "Well, yeah, different anyway."

He put the plates in front of the chairs, laid the silverware all together in the center of each dish and moved quickly back to the kitchen. He reached down to continue petting Midnight, who immediately put his big head in Henry's hands. "I was thinking I might give you and your father a hand by fixing that fence out by the road before your cows push on through it."

"That would be nice of you, but you don't really need to do chores around here. We don't have any extra money."

"No problem. I don't have a regular job and paying work is hard to come by."

She gave him another overall appraisal. "Anyway, the shirt looks good on you, and by the way, there is a tag still sticking out of the collar." She returned her attention to chopping up the vegetables by the stove.

Henry tried as deftly as he could to reach around and remove the tag. Sitting there about ten feet away from the living room where the sheriff and the deputy were talking, he could not help but overhear their discussion.

"There's been another killing on a farm just outside of town."

"Shhh."

The deputy dropped his voice. "Down the road toward Sylvester. Stole everything and shot the man and woman. Kind of like what's been happening in isolated places elsewhere. Left a little girl and boy there alive. They had to have been there when it happened to their parents. They told us about it as best they could, but were too young to give much of a description of who did it. I left one of our guys out there to look for any clues and tape it off from more looting. Sent the kids over to their church."

Dozier nervously glanced over toward the kitchen. "Okay. We'll talk about it tomorrow. If anything comes up that looks like we might find the perps, come to get me." Dozier started to turn as though he was ending the discussion.

The deputy cleared his throat. "Sheriff, another thing. We got to do something. People are out there are trading food for things that are not legal, like sex. Some folks are hoarding food and others will do anything to get it. Same with guns and other stuff. There's bad feelings building up, and I'm afraid there may be bloodshed between neighbors. I just don't think we can handle something like a riot."

Jerico nodded. "I agree times are hard. We're into a place none of us have been before, and we've all got to think clearly and have some patience. There's always been illegal trading, some of it for sex. You and the other officers just need to do what you have in the past and talk down the problems y'all run into. Everyone is running out of food or whatever. In a few weeks, any barter that's going on now, even trading for… that kind of stuff, will mostly have run out.

"Our job is to keep the lid on things. We've got to prevent people from killing each other until we get some sort of plan in place to cover power, food, medicine, and other things that are fast disappearing. We can't sweat the small stuff right now." He thought for a moment and slapped his leg. "Tell you what, call a meeting tomorrow sort of midday with all the city and county law officers and I'll talk to all the shift commanders. We can discuss these kinds of problems with everybody. We all need to be on the same page. Get me an update on the latest killing. Ask everyone to bring a list of things they are worried about. We need to talk about what else we can do with the militia to help support you guys. I don't have all the answers, but together, we can solve at least some of them."

"Thanks, Jerico. I knew you'd find a way to help us out. I'll get everyone together. You have a good night, now."

As the sheriff was meeting in the living room, Henry continued talking with Iris. "You look worried. More trouble a work?"

She sat down a platter with a clank. "It's endless. We going to have to bury our dead without embalming, and burying them quickly in graves that are often not in graveyards... but in spaces close to where the person has died. Since we are not getting caskets delivered anymore, the bodies will deteriorate quickly and become part of the soil. The decay could leach into the aquafer.

"Also, the people who are drug or alcohol-addicted are in bad shape. The sources of their addictions have dried up, and they're having to kick their habits or suffer the consequences. Same with smokers. It's not pretty."

She picked the platter back up and continued. "The good news is that our labs are working to develop medicine to take care of diarrhea, as well as constipation, and we're getting more coagulants and something for basic headaches. Oh, here comes Pop."

As he entered the kitchen, Jerico Dozier said to Henry, "Good to see you again." He stopped and smelled the bundle and put it back down. He glanced at Henry, "Thanks for bringing us the meat." Then he looked over at Iris. "Remember how much your mom liked deer?"

Then quickly back to Henry, "You should have brought your father with you. Iris tells me you live together."

"Well... He's not feeling too good and likes to stay close to home."

"Just the same, he's welcome. I met him years ago when he got out of the military. He had quite a record. Was well respected from what I remember."

After they finished their meal, Henry helped to clear the dishes and watched Midnight sleep on the floor making snoring noises. In the past few weeks, he had overcome feeling intimidated by Sheriff Dozier, and the sheriff had begun to tell Henry more about his theory of plastic becoming a valuable commodity. Henry came back in the den and sat down next to Jerico, bringing him what Iris said was the last of the coffee they had. "Sheriff, I wonder what we all might do if we were attacked by a large force."

"What? Well, Henry, why would you think that might happen?"

"We're the largest town in Southwest Georgia and we've got the Marine Base."

"Marine Base?" Dozier did not want to let on that the Marine Base was a key ingredient to the security of Albany. He was impressed with the intuition of this handsome young man who was becoming closer friends with his daughter. "Why?"

Henry smiled. "I've got this friend I've known for a long time and he has a military surplus store out by the base. He told me they are the largest Marine Supply Depot in the Eastern United Sates." Iris came back into the den and joined her father to listen to Henry. "You know when a Marine unit deploys, it has everything they need to survive for a long time. They've got generators and gasoline for power and running vehicles. They've got trucks, tanks, jeeps. They've got tents and all kinds of clothes for all kinds of weather." Henry put down his cup to use his hands when he spoke. He glanced over at Iris and noticed she was listening carefully.

"They've got food. And the food they have is the kind that lasts a long time on the shelf... canned or packaged food like when you add water. My dad told me that a U.S. military company at full strength is about a hundred fifty or more soldiers. There are four companies to a battalion and four battalions to a regiment. A regiment is the kind of go-to war unit for Marines. So that would be, theoretically, about three thousand or more soldiers. Three meals a day for a month is, say, ninety meals per person. And these are strong people, so the meals are full of protein and vitamins for active, full-size soldiers. So, if we round that up, a regiment would eat almost three hundred thousand of these meals in a month. And the Marine Base has food to support a lot of these kinds of units. So, say in this situation when we are rationing food... My guess is that if you were careful, and supplemented the Marine meals with other food, you could feed three townspeople pretty well for what you could feed one of the Marines. That's like a million meals a month for the food allocated for each regiment. They likely have food at the Marine Base for many millions of meals stretched out over many months.

"And because they are Marines, they have warehouses full of lots of weapons and ammunition. I'm saying that any large group of hungry and desperate people who wanted to survive for any length of time would see the Albany Marine Supply Depot as a target. It's not exactly a secret that it's here."

Dozier nodded and pushed back his chair, which squeaked. Midnight raised his head and then let it slowly drop back to the floor.

Henry continued. "The other thing is that Albany is a supply dump, not a regular base. They don't have platoons of combat Marines marching around there. They have clerks, equipment maintenance, and warehouse people. They've got guards and stuff for sure, but lots of what they do is done by civilians. With all that has been happening with the economy, my friend who has the surplus store said they've cut way back on the civilians, and there are not as many Marines as before. The general slowdown everywhere has affected them as well. Yeah, they are Marines and tough folks and all, but they've been stacking boxes and taking inventory… And there are not too many of them on site anymore. I've been by the property, and there is a six-foot wire fence with three strands of barbed wire on top surrounding the place. That's not much of a deterrent for like… three thousand acres. It would take thousands of Marines just to protect the boundary. They don't have thousands of Marines to do that.

"So, I'm thinking maybe if they would throw in with you and the mayor, Albany could hold out better than most places for as long as it takes to get the United States and wherever else back like they should be. I'm also thinking we have the manpower in town to help cover the base perimeter."

Sheriff Dozier looked at Henry thoughtfully. "That's an interesting idea. Well thought out too." He turned to Iris. "This guy is not the dumb hick you told me he was. He's smarter than he seems."

"Papa!" She gave him a playful swat. "You know I didn't say that."

Island in the Storm

Jerico laughed. "I do. Just kidding... both of you. Henry, I'd like you to join me in thinking about the defense of Albany." He tried to keep a poker face to hide the depth of his real concern. "We could use some of the knowledge that you said your father taught you, particularly if you can translate it into some of our new militia soldiers. Probably start with my deputies and other local police.

"I've actually been thinking the same thing about the Marine Base. I'll talk to Mayor Ballard and we'll see what the Marines have to say. It's been a while since I've visited out there, and you're right to be thinking about all the resources they have... and how much we may need them in the mess we are in now."

"Sir, I'd be glad to help in any way I can. I've got some friends who have been through the same kind of training my father gave me. We may not be much for marching around, but we know how to hide and shoot."

"Good. That's likely going to be in greater demand that parade ground theatrics. Come see me tomorrow and we'll set up a plan."

Henry frowned and made a puzzled face. "Let me ask... I kind of understand where we are now in this mess, but I'm a little fuzzy on how we got here. I thought as sheriff, you might have a better idea."

Sheriff Dozier took a final swallow and, realizing he may not have any more real coffee for a long time, looked lovingly at the empty cup and leaned back. "Well, as best as I can figure... Back after the experiences of the Great Depression in the 1930s and World War II, government and business got the idea that centralization and mass marketed products through big national industries was the way to go.

"Over time, the mom and pop world of America couldn't compete. Folks moved from small towns into cities, and the collection of people into big cities reduced civility. The dependence that small town people had, trusting each other and sharing what they had, simply disappeared. It didn't happen overnight, but built up over several decades of the U.S. economy going up and down like a yo-yo til, at last, the string lost its bounce.

"Another thing… We all seemed, in recent years, to live to do nothing. It got to where sitting around and watching television and tapping on computers was the ultimate goal in life. Got to where the biggest businesses were about developing mindless escape entertainment to give people something to do in their leisure time. Like a big narcotic. Nothing to teach them to be better people, just to babysit them.

"Our brains got soggy and we no longer appreciated hard work or going the extra effort of providing initiative and creativity where they were needed. People tried to figure how to get out of work, rather than how to do their job better. We didn't appreciate our friends and family enough. There seems to have been an increase in our desire to escape our daily lives… drugs, booze, technology, whatever. People just were not satisfied with what they had, and yet, couldn't get up the energy to make it better on their own.

"We got more depersonalized and got used to living in tubes of elevators, depositing workers into tall buildings crammed with cubicles of paper shuffling. Greed got us into economic stress and the economy got wobbly. Business became more interwoven and interdependent. The world was in effect, one nation economically, but we still fought among each other and spied and cheated each other.

"Distribution systems for what we did create and share started to fail because of the lack of available gas, compounded by computer glitches and power outages. Hell, it got where nobody wanted to drive those big semi-trucks all over the country. It was hard, lonely work. Our food has been mass produced in large industrial factories and then shipped out to consumers. With a transportation crisis, how could that work? It got where it didn't pay to send the necessary products and materials out to dwindling communities. Without merchandise, shopping diminished and the economy began to tank even more.

"As we got into a recession that led to the depression, the larger industries failed because the business model of mass-produced items depended on a mass of consumers able to purchase the goods. So, fewer items were made and repurposing them became more important. Nobody figured out how to create all the jobs lost through automation and robots and stuff. We never fully recovered from the effects of coronavirus. The economy kept getting worse and people got more frustrated with each other. Got madder.

"It got to where nobody cared anymore who was elected to office up in Washington. Those people we had up there did nothing but complain about each other anyway. Here lately, government became unimportant to most Americans, who were more interested in survival than fixing the political corruption and incompetence. Nobody trusted anybody anymore. What anger there was went into battles between the masses of the have-nots, and the haves who could hire the have-nots to protect them. People just didn't believe in the government or industry anymore, so they chose not to believe in anything outside themselves."

Iris interrupted, "Oh Pop, it is not as bad as all that."

Jerico looked over at her with sad eyes. "It's close though, and close is bad enough." Then he turned back to Henry. "Here recently, computers and electronic gadgets became less useful because of unreliable power grids. I know you remember the blackouts here and around the world in the past couple of years.

"Cell phones started failing more often. A kind of cyber war started between nations and businesses. We had gotten to be a society of secrets and security, and all that was hacked. Because all the computers were in some way linked together, like the cloud, apps, cell phones, wi-fi, a thousand TV channels, all this stuff, and no one really knew the whole of what it was. Technology got too crowded. When someone pulled the plug, no one knew where it went. No one knows how to fix stuff that is in the ether. When that crashed recently, it destroyed all communications, and everything crashed. Like a water choked hillside, it began to slide down, following subtle cracks, slowly at first, then all at once in a rush.

"Henry, everything is run by computers, and computers are run by electricity. All the computers are interrelated and tied together one way or the other. Computers even make the electricity work. Kill electricity and you kill everything that makes the world function.

"Pulling that plug has created broiling masses of people struggling to find food and power. We have a wasteland of deconstructed and decaying small towns. Although, to tell the truth, I hear it is worse in the bigger cities. People who had been eating in restaurants or taught to open cans and microwave food for all their meals now lack the survival skills for any other way of living.

"Now, because we don't have enough resources, we're gonna have to button up and build a ring around ourselves. We've got to save who we can here, and turn everyone away who can't directly help us survive. That goes against my core faith and everything the United States has always stood for, but I don't see any other way.

"I think it's likely that tribal bands are forming and becoming nomads or building small forts to survive in increasingly hostile environments. I assume there are smart people still out there in government and business trying to figure out how to fix this mess, but we are stuck here on our own until they do."

Training

In an empty lot near the county landfill, Sheriff Dozier met with several of his deputies and a number of other handpicked people he knew from around town. "EVERBODY! We got ourselves in a mess here that looks like it may be the same problem that's happening everywhere else. We've got to maintain law and order, and need to do something about the raids on our outlying farms. The sheriff's department and police agencies don't have enough officers to take on large bands of armed thieves. We've got a very big perimeter to defend, and need to get organized into military style units.

"We're gonna form three teams. The first will be neighborhood militias made up of anyone armed in the neighborhoods. I can see from the kinds of weapons you brought today, we have a hodgepodge of firearms... and that's gonna make supplying cartridges more difficult. We're going to have to organize you into squads using similar weapons. Most of you will eventually be asked to go and help train, and maybe lead, the neighborhood teams. Then we're gonna have all of you as our main force, and we hope more folks like you join us. You'll be trained to act as a cohesive military unit. You'll be our big ass S.W.A.T. team. The third and smaller group is going to be trained as sniper-scouts.

"We got to get organized here and fast, 'cause without a real serious plan, this town is as open as a Ford dealer on a Labor Day sale. I'm asking for you to help me find people, men and women, who are fit and good shots and have had military or police experience, to join us. Now, you all will be taught how to negotiate with anyone you meet to calm down a bad situation and try to get folks to cooperate. We're not looking for trouble.

"We're all gonna do our best to reach out to others in towns living near us and form a kind of alliance to keep the peace and keep down any looting or other criminal activities. Anybody who has close friends or relatives in the surrounding towns needs get them to join with us and not be against us. We're hoping they will be a kind of buffer for us, but we're not sure how that's gonna play out as yet.

"Now, if you see anyone sneaking around or stealing or threatening one of your neighbors, you need to let us know. When we get the militia set up, hopefully in the next few days, we plan to have representatives in every neighborhood working with the Neighborhood Managers, and that is the person to tell what you saw.

"Don't anyone just start shooting because you think something bad is going on. You're likely to shoot your neighbor or one of us. Hunker down if you have too, but don't try to take on things by yourself or be some kind of hero. Any questions?"

One man asked, "What about the Marine Depot? They got trained soldiers and guns and stuff?"

Dozier scratched his head. "Not sure. I'm gonna assume no one will try to attack them. We've finally got a meeting with the commanding officer coming up soon. I hope they will join us, and we can all help each other. Many of them live off base, and their families will need protecting just like ours will. We just need to wait and see if they can throw in with us, or if there is some bigger plan coming from Washington or the Marine headquarters." He took a deep breath.

"You're gonna have to help us keep the peace. You'll likely run across unusual stuff like… Well, I guess you all know we're saving the fertile seeds from any produce that has seeds. The college professors are finding which ones will grow, and then they are turning them into seedlings for growing trees, plants, vegetables, whatever. We've got to look down the road at how we are going to stay alive.

"Recently, we caught some people trying to get into where we're growing those seedlings and eat them. That kind of selfish behavior could kill us all. We had to shoot one of them. It turned out it was somebody who used to be rich. I guess we are not a society that is used to being deprived. Let me tell you, we are serious about doing every damn thing we can to save everyone we can for the long haul. If anyone does anything to jeopardize that, I don't care what you were before all this started, your ass is mine. That may be hard and unfair, but that is how it is.

"So, while we're getting better organized, we're gonna rely on the neighborhoods, and local militia in each neighborhood, to hold down the fort as much as all of you can in your own local areas. Without cars, we may be reduced to battery operated golf carts, horses, or walking to move around. So, we're not going to be able to rush with a large group of reinforcements anywhere. I can say one thing. We will not have any tolerance for anyone stealing, robbing, picking fights, and any other horseshit.

"Now, look at that small group over yonder by the fence. I've asked Henry Graham there to train some of my deputies and others in town how do to the stealth activities Henry's father, showed him. There gonna be the sniper-scouts I mentioned."

With limited time and equipment, Henry began with a core group of the most likely candidates in terms of physical ability and marksmanship skills. He showed them the basics of disguising themselves through the use of camouflage and how to enter and leave a place without being seen or heard.

He also showed them how to build a series of disguised nests in the woods he called "hides," how to walk without leaving a trail, how to be still and not speak, to listen, and even how to elude in an urban environment. He explained that the hide is best if it is not obvious. No one should be able to spot it, even if they are looking for it. So, behind a pile of rocks is not a good place.

They played memory games so they would be able to report what they heard accurately. There was not enough spare ammunition to do much target shooting, but he did take them on the range to determine if they were proficient. He assumed most of the actual shooting would be within two to three hundred yards, so really long range accuracy was not as important. His students lacked the experience to be excellent as sniper-scouts, but they gained skills to make them more of a threat to whatever enemies were headed to Albany. Those who were not cut out for scouts were put into the main force group, and both of those teams trained diligently. Henry soon realized he needed help from his friends.

Fatherly Advice

Henry had been staying away from his father more than usual. He would bring in water and food when he thought he was asleep, rather than eating with him as had been their custom. Instead, he spent much of his swamp time talking to people his own age about the need to join the new militia and help train others. He was preparing to shove off in a jon boat for another organizing meeting in town when Willis Graham found him by the water. "I've been hearing you out there talking to the others. You're getting into something complicated with those towns-people."

Henry felt nervous having to explain himself to his father and looked out at the swamp, then at his gear in the boat, to steady himself before answering. "I'm just trying to help other folks who live in Albany. They've got all these problems and there are some people who are likely coming here to take everything we have. They will be killing us, our friends, neighbors, and everybody's family. What are we supposed to do? We've got to defend ourselves. We have to protect each other."

"Yeah. I understand that and the nurse lady is very pretty, but you got to try to see things down the road. All the getting ready and training and such makes sense when it is right in front of you, but Henry, you got to wake up! You got to think where all this is going. When people train with guns and start playing war, war has a way of finding them. I've seen it. I've been in it. Those ideas of hero stuff go away fast when the bullets start."

Henry looked at his father. "Daddy, we're just doing what's

for our own good to protect everybody. Right now, our job is to stay alive. We've got to get ready so we can protect others. I don't want to shoot anyone. I damn sure don't want to kill anyone, but if that is what it takes to protect and keep you safe, and our friends here and the people in town... and yeah, to keep Iris safe. I'm ready to make a choice to help everyone from being overrun and killed."

"You're talking like an honorable man, the kind of man I wanted to raise, with those ideals." Willis hesitated, "You also need to realize some of that honorable man stuff is bullshit. That's the kind of talk people have before they get shot at. Take all that idealistic nobility and set it aside for a minute. Try to move time forward in your head. Things may feel safe now, but when people with guns come, all the playacting will get real and get nasty and get bloody and get stinky and get sticky. Your friends can die. You can die or get hurt. Think about that when you and your friends are marching around all puffed up. It never ends up like it feels in the parade. Think about Trey with his guts laying on the ground."

"Okay. I get the picture."

"No, you don't." His father staggered slightly and steadied himself by holding onto a tree. A look of discomfort passed over his face. "I'm talking shooting and killing people. This situation you all are in is not some video game. Think what happens when someone gets shot." Willis stroked the seashell tied around on his neck. "A bullet rips apart everything it hits. When a bullet enters, it tears everything up and shatters bones, which also become a bunch of sharp objects penetrating, cutting, and tearing. Bullets bring in other foreign objects like cloth or bits of button or zippers into the body, and all that crap causes more damage that has to be cleaned out. When the doctors clear out things that are not part of your body, it causes more harm... but it has to be done.

"Because the body is so torn up, it can take several operations to fix problems. It takes a long time to heal, and when it does, it usually heals as scar tissue. Nothing works as well as it did before. Some things never work again. Ask your friend Iris what a bullet wound is like."

"Yeah. She told me some stuff."

"Henry, everybody's gonna wet their pants and cry for their mama when the shit comes. Do everyone a favor and make the training real for everybody. You're still likely to do the same thing going into it, but it might help some of you find your way back out of it later."

"Dad, you still haven't answered the question about what we are supposed to do to stop people who might be coming here to take over and kill us. Right now, we just have to survive."

His father let out a long breath. "I just want to make sure you're aware of what may be coming along with those bad people. Are you comfortable with killing people who live the next town over, people you might have known?"

Henry bowed his head. "I'm not comfortable in killing or shooting at anybody, no matter where they live. When I started to hunt, I was just proud of myself for being able to bring something back to show you, and to share something that everyone needed to eat. At first, I did it for fun, or just because I needed too... But later, after killing so much, I got to where didn't like killing anything that was alive, like a deer or a hog. I can't imagine what it would feel like to take a human life. It bothers me, but I realize I may have to do it. I know it sounds weird."

Willis nodded. "Not to me. What you said is a good first step. Killing anything should bother you. That makes us human. You need to know that, so when the fear hits you, and it will, you'll know better how to handle it. Being brave is not just overcoming coming fear, but doing it with caution. Understanding that gives a warrior the edge to avoid mistakes."

"You know, Daddy, we're training everyone to talk anyone out of fighting and asking them to join with us. I don't know if it will work, but we're all supposed to try that first." Henry was fidgeting and rubbing his hands on his pantlegs, which he often did when he was nervous.

Willis sighed. "My point in this conversation is that you need to man up when you get ready to kill. Use what I taught you and teach it to the others. It may help to keep some of your friends alive, but it takes some work to come back from killing. But son, if you do have to get into it, don't hesitate. Shoot to kill and keep on firing til you're sure they're dead."

"Yes sir."

"Also, tell whoever is building those sorry ass barriers to clean out all the brush, buildings, trees, and such to maybe out to three or four hundred yards. If you are going to be attacked, don't leave them any cover up close."

"Yes sir. Good idea."

"One other thing, and I'll only say this once. If that young lady is worth her salt, and I think she is, she'll not like you any better if you go strutting around all macho-like up and down the street. Don't let your pride write a check your abilities can't cash."

Near Griffin

Rowdy Burdett checked the rearview mirror and patted the .357 pistol by his side, "I think we lost those hick cops."

The man riding shotgun looked back. "Yea. They kinda didn't know it was us. We got out of there just at the right time."

As they pulled onto the interstate, just north of Griffin, Rowdy frowned. "Damn. Looks like everybody is headed home. Crowded. See over there where there are cars pulling off to the side? They must be running out of gas. Let's sell this gas at these exit stations. Save enough to get us to central Florida."

"Yeah. Let's do just a little each stop. We should trade the gas for food and other stuff. Don't want to raise too much attention."

"We should do all right, 'cause if people are pulling over like that on the side of the highway, it means everybody's about hit the bottom of the gas tank everywhere."

"Gonna be a lot of 'em out there walking soon."

Neighborhood Managers

Henry met the sheriff outside the mayor's office to go to the next leadership meeting. In the anteroom, Henry could hear loud voices as three of the Managers were arguing about a recent food distribution. He could hear the mayor saying, "There are no confirmed reports of cannibalism, but we've given orders that anyone who does not live here is not welcome. Those who want to throw in with us need to have something to contribute to our survival."

He recognized the voice of Larry Goldwin. "We've gotten into this mess because our leaders failed us, and that includes you."

He couldn't hear all the words, but could just barely understand the mayor's calm voice saying, "Thank you Larry for your usual constructive suggestion." Then the volume of the voices dropped back to where he could no longer distinguish the words.

Henry looked over at the sheriff. "I never realized the mayor had so much to handle."

Dozier snorted, "Politics! Bunch of babies whining over who gets the bigger piece of candy."

"But, the mayor... He's..."

"We're damn lucky to have Lamar Ballard as our mayor, is all I've got to say." Henry was surprised at the sound of anger in the sheriff's voice. The noise in the mayor's office rose in volume again, with several voices talking over each other. The sheriff, not listening to Henry, looked down at his watch. "Those blowhards are making us late to the meeting." The door opened and three red faced men, one of them Larry Godwin, left hurriedly, each keeping their distance from one another as they headed for the century-old municipal auditorium.

Dozier nodded where the men had gone. "You've heard the saying, 'An idle mind is the devil's workshop?'"

"Yeah. My father uses it."

"Well, Godwin's mind is not only idle, but other than schemes of ways to promote himself, it's mostly empty."

Someone had rigged up a battery-operated speaker system so that with quiet, the voices from the podium could be heard in the back of the room. The emergency lighting was supplemented with other battery illumination that was adequate enough to see around the room and not stumble over the rows of chairs. They had opened all available windows and doors. Everyone was casually dressed, and the openings helped with the stale sweat and sour onion body odor in the packed space. Many had improvised, handheld fans flapping back and forth.

On the stage, Mayor Ballard repeated the mantra to himself he had frequently used since the crisis started. "Hold it together. You can't afford to piss people off. Got to unite them. Hold it together." Now calmer and focused, he stood, waved his hands, then cleared his throat through the microphone. "Quiet please. The rest of you take your seats." He waited for the noise to die down. "We're meeting here with our neighborhood leaders, and to welcome all of you that have recently joined the team. We're relying on you as an extension of our local government. Your job is to communicate to the citizens strung together over many blocks in your neighborhoods.

"We've asked you to take on this particular job because

we need leadership down into the neighborhood block level. Your first job will be to assemble a meeting similar to this one and relay to everyone what we will discuss today. Without a real communications network, you'll need to do that after every group meeting we have. Go door to door if you have to. Most people will cooperate. Some will not. Do your best. In time, we will try to get you more support. We're going to have to open up some of the empty commercial property closer into town for housing, so there will be more people packed in together. Keep up with everyone who is in transit.

"To start, let's look at where we are. Money does not matter anymore. A very wealthy person with lots of money in the bank and a poor person with no money at all are both the same if they have nothing to eat. There is not any good news here. We're are going to have to make some very difficult choices. This is a time when we need to concentrate on how to survive."

He raised his voice. "We are working on setting up water wagons to go to the neighborhoods and distribute water, but everyone must boil any water they drink. You are going to have to set up a rationing system for people, with a goal of a gallon of water per day for all uses. Setup a cistern, kids inflatable splash pool, or buckets or barrels to catch rainwater in drain spouts. Just dab yourselves with water to get clean. Reuse that water for crops in the garden. Save water to drink. We've go to balance that against what we take from the streams so we can still use the waterwheels to make electricity."

"Another thing, with all the wood used in cooking today, we're gonna have house fires. You need to set up fire brigades in your neighborhoods and throw dirt or sand on it... NOT clean water. Practice getting the fire brigades together on short notice."

There were murmurs.

City Counselman Larry Godwin shouted. "You're trying to tell everybody how to live. That's playing God! You can't do that."

Ballard nodded. "It's as close as it can be. Nobody likes it, but we don't have the resources to survive if we don't make choices." Ballard raised his voice. "Listen everybody! We don't want to declare martial law. We want people to do what is needed because it is the right thing. But let me tell you… What we are going to do will feel a lot like martial law. This new system is gonna require leadership. Educate your folks and be straight with them. Think of yourself like you are in a small town where you're the mayor. If you can't do the job, let me know and we will find someone else. The sheriff and I are going to make a lot of judgment calls and we're not going to have the time to litigate everything." He paused.

"We've got to hang onto everything we have. We can't make anything here that requires large or sophisticated factories to manufacture. We can't get any more supplies delivered. Don't waste anything."

A man standing on the side wall near the front spoke. "Look, we all live in town. We can't grow enough stuff in our back yard to feed our families, much less everybody else. How are we all goanna get enough to eat?"

"Okay, as to food. Here is a short list of what we've thought of for now." He raised his voice. "We're all gonna have to ration what we eat. Our plan is to work with other towns nearby that have more land and big farms that can grow more food than they can eat. There is enough food for everybody who lives in

Southwest Georgia to share for a short time, and if we can figure how to grow, preserve, and process food, we'll have something to trade or sell to other places.

"We are digging outhouses as fast as we can and putting our fecal matter into the yards to be use as compost to help us grow crops. After a few months of shifting, the outhouse around the yard should have a row of... ah, well, fertilized dirt ready for planting food crops next spring.

"Everyone needs to dig up their yard, front and back, to plant food. We've got seeds and seedlings from the farm stores to share and will be passing them out. You are going to be issued tools to share. Make sure you get them back for the next person. Also, because the water pressure is so low, you will likely have to water with a bucket. We're working on a system of hand pumps to get water, but we're not there yet.

"We are creating massive compost piles, which we will use as fertilizer for the next planting season in the fields outside of town. I know that sounds nasty, but it is what people did for thousands of years. We can't go to the grocery or garden stores anymore. We have to learn to grow our own food. That means making our own fertilizer.

"People need to urinate in containers that can be used to irrigate their garden crops. Mix the urine with about a tenth to a quarter of the liquid being dirty water, like from bathing or runoff from cooking."

There was new murmuring in the audience.

The mayor used his hands to shush them again. "Okay, I see your faces out there. Here's why you need to do this. It takes electricity that we don't have to bring up water from the ground reservoir to flush toilets. We must grow crops to feed ourselves everywhere we can. It may only be a supplement, but it is a vital supplement. Urine is a natural fertilizer containing nitrogen, potassium, and phosphorus, which crops need, and we don't have those nutrients readily available. It's fairly sterile and there is not much risk of contamination from it, even though it's kind of gross.

"Okay. Folks are hungry and they're foraging in the woods after something to eat. We've made handouts on what food may be safe to eat and what you should avoid. There are some suggestions on how to prepare food you may not be used to eating like squirrels, possums, rabbits, leaves, and roots. That kind of makeshift food will extend things somewhat, and can be mixed with other food to make it go further."

Someone shouted, "People will actually eat that?"

"They're doing it. From now on, wherever we can, we must plant trees that can bear fruit or nuts. We should only plant bushes that can grow berries, peanuts, soybeans, whatever will feed people. Everything we do must support something to eat."

There was more murmuring.

A large man stood and crossed his arms across his chest. "I hear what you are saying, but what if we've got people who just want to take care of their families and don't want to be involved in all this stuff?"

Mayor Ballard leaned into the microphone. "Anybody wants to go off on their own will have to stay that way. They can't come back begging to get help later, after they run out of everything, if they're not willing to pitch in and share it now. And let me say, those folks won't have medicine, security, energy, or the advantages of collective food and shelter. Together, we have a chance to make it. By yourself, when those bad men come to your door with their guns in the dark of the night after you and your family… Good luck."

Larry Godwin stood and shouted. "All this talk sounds like a power grab by you."

Ballard spoke quietly so people would have to listen carefully to hear. "Larry, we're trying to survive here. If you have a better suggestion on how to do it, please let us know… Right now." He waited. "Okay then, let's move on."

"Now listen, there's more! We can't just eat everything now and cause everyone to starve later on. We will have to save enough animals to breed for next year. Same with vegetables, seeds, and such. We've got people working to determine how much food we can eat and how to save seeds to plant for the next year. You've got to get everyone under your area of responsibility to follow the rules we set down, or we will all starve."

A woman in the back who was unwinding thread from a piece of cloth onto a stick to use for sewing stopped and shouted out, "What if you live in an apartment or condo?"

The mayor pointed to the back where the voice originated. "Good question! Then you will be given a job to plant crops by hand and harvest by hand. Everyone's gonna have to pitch in to help each other with food in the fields, you know, harvesting, handling chickens, cows, pigs, and other thigs. We can't afford to pay people to sit on their ass anymore. We need people who can water and debug the crops. So, there is plenty to do to earn your keep."

Someone shouted. "What do you mean… debug?"

"We don't have equipment to fertilize or spray insecticides. We're going to have to do that by hand, just like they did a hundred or a thousand years ago."

Another voice shouted. "What other good news you got

for us?"

Mayor Ballard looked down at his list. "One thing we will need for sure is to gather anything on wheels that will roll. We're gonna run out of gas before long. We won't have heavy equipment to move things, so we're setting up a system to convert our lightweight vehicles by stripping them down to the wheels, steering, and brakes. We can install large basket frames on the wheelbase to carry produce or other goods. They can be pushed by people and horses, or winched up hills.

"I suggest you consider that for each of your neighborhoods, and those vehicles can get loaned out for moving big piles of materials. Save any grease or other lubricants. That'll be important to keep wheels, ball bearings, and other things turning. There are lots of changes, but we're adapting.

"Keep track of whatever folks provide for the common good, and we'll figure how to repay them with food, electricity, or whatever we can when we split that stuff up. You can choose not to help everyone out. We're still America, but if we don't work together, I'm not sure if we will make it."

Another man in a red shirt, sitting near the front next to Larry Godwin, stood and waved his arm. "I've heard you want to take over food factories around here. You can't just go out and take something that belongs to somebody else."

Ballard looked at him. "You are right, but most of those plants are owned by big corporations somewhere else that have now gone bust. Plus, if we don't protect those places near us, someone else will likely come in and take them over by force. It will be better for us if we cut deals now to share what we can and barter the rest until the economy returns. All of you need to tell us who you know in nearby communities that work for those companies, particularly food processing companies, and to try to come to some agreement."

The same man in the front spoke again with some anger. "You can't just tell everyone what to do. We have rules... laws." The man crossed his arms over his chest.

Ballard shook his head. "Mister, a few weeks ago you would have been absolutely right, but we are in a new world now. Money is no good. The only thing that has value right now is what you personally can bring to the table. Anybody's fancy silver and china are only valuable as spoons and plates. The four gas guzzling cars someone may have in their garage are just big paperweights. Computer programmers and stockbrokers and television advertising people just took a step back in line to a mechanic, farmer, or person that can build a waterwheel."

He waved his hand in an arc over the audience. "Ask yourself... What can you do?" He paused to let that soak in.

"Can you make the equipment to make power? Do you know how to wire a windmill or a water wheel? Do you know how to plant and grow crops? Can you tend the sick and make them well? Can you make things we need with your hands like sewing, weaving, construction? Can you form an alliance with other towns and people so we can support each other? Can you fix an engine or a machine to run on something other than electricity? Can you organize others to do all this stuff? Can you entertain the rest of us with songs and skits or something that will give us pleasure and renew our energy to keep is plowing ahead to do what we need to get done?

"Everyone here... Your skills are your value. What you can actually do will define the new rules this gentleman has referred to." He pointed to the man in the red shirt, who dropped his crossed arms and sat back down. "Nobody has all the answers, but one thing is clear. If we are going to make it, we all will have to work together and support one another. And... In this new game, nobody is going to get a trophy for just showing up. Everyone will have to find the thing they are good at and work like hell to make everyone else appreciate their efforts. There is a tough road ahead, and there will be no free rides."

Another person stood in the middle of the room. "All these things you are proposing to do sound like socialism or communism."

Ballard recognized the man. "You're right, Bob. It is sort of like that because our money is worth nothing now. I've been talking to economics professors at the colleges about working on a financial plan of chits or vouchers for work or exchange of products that incentivizes people to work harder and create things. We need to use the motivation of free enterprise, but without the money. We need to evolve back to where we were in terms of real free enterprise and capitalism, like it was years ago, before Wall Street got involved, but we've got to survive first. Our immediate survival may involve some socialism or even dictatorship properties, but whatever gets us to stay alive, I'm for."

There was murmuring both pro and con in the audience.

"Lastly, the sheriff is creating militias to protect each neighborhood. Okay, for now, let me see your hands... Are you willing to organize and practice military tactics in your neighborhood groups?" A show of hands indicated almost everyone was in general agreement.

Ballard raised his voice again. "I'm asking you to be patient with us now, and to have faith that we can find something more equitable, like what we were all used to before the crash.

Go back to your neighborhoods and share what we've been discussing. Get those good new ideas and bring them back to me."

After the meeting, Sheriff Dozier and Mayor Ballard were sitting together in the now empty hall reviewing the discussion and the reaction of the crowd. Dozier looked over at Ballard with a skeptical smile on his face. "You think all those people are going to do what you ask? Take baths in dirty water? Use their backyard as a toilet? Think they'll plant potatoes in that dirt where they have been to doody? Pee in jars? Man, you'd be lucky if anyone did that. Lot of them are going to think like your good buddy Larry."

Ballard smiled to himself and replied, "Not all of them will at first, but we got to start somewhere, and I'd rather start strong if some of them are going to back off anyway. Jerico, you know Larry Godwin will never agree with me on anything. He wants my job, and one of the first things he will do is go after yours."

The sheriff nodded. "I 'spec so."

He shook his head. "You know, Jerico, I don't want to be heavy handed. We've had it so easy. People have been used to having their own way for so long, we need to be gradual about turning up the pressure to conform."

Dozier patted Lamar Ballard on the shoulder and turned to start back to his office. "Well, that's good, 'cause we sure don't have the manpower to throw people in jail just for being selfish. You know we're going to have to build us a small army in case things get out of hand and people start rioting." In another part of the room, as the cleaning crew was working, the clinking glass sound of a bottle falling over stopped the conversation. He nodded in that direction, "Well, at least someone was enjoying the meeting."

Ballard rose also and stretched. "You are probably right. We've got to rely on the neighborhood groups and better equipped militia like you've started. We're going to need more people to guard and protect the supplies we've confiscated."

A deputy came up to the sheriff. "What is it?"

"Sorry to bother you, but Shep just got back from that trip over to the interstate highway."

"And?"

"He said traffic was down to a trickle. He talked to some of the people in stores by the highway, and they said folks were frustrated and looking for someone to blame. He said the sides of the road were littered with cars and trucks that ran out of gas."

"Thanks. Tell Shep to get some rest and write up a report on everything he saw. I'll see him tomorrow after he's had some sleep."

As they waked out of the auditorium, Ballard and Dozier overheard two people from the cleaning crew talking just outside.

"Sounds like they think we're gonna have an apocalypse."

"Oh my God. I saw that on TV."

"No. That was the zombie apocalypse. This here is the regular kind."

Swamp People to the Rescue

With his growing attachment to Iris and her father, and after listening to the earlier meetings, Henry felt strongly that he and some of his swamp friends needed to get more involved to teach skills that would be useful to the newly formed Neighborhood Managers. He weighed his father's cautionary advice, but reasoned that his father did not have all the information he had gained from talking to the sheriff and others. He felt there was no other choice but to work with the townspeople.

Henry wanted Trey and Bubba to be as motivated as he was to help the townspeople, so he had taken them with him as self-appointed Neighborhood Managers at large to the next meeting held at the municipal auditorium. Afterwards, they stood outside on the street after listening to seemingly endless gathering, as the mayor deftly weaved through the many unusable ideas and gave praise to those that would be beneficial.

Trey let out a breath. "Damn. That man can talk!"

Bubba nodded and said, "Yeah, but we've already been living like most of what he talked about."

Henry patted Bubba on the back and said, "That's kind of the point. We have some skills we can share to help these folks. You two help me get some others from where we live, and let's teach some of these people the things we know that could help them."

Bubba made a face, "Yeah, but our folks may not want us to do that."

Henry smiled. "I've been talking to them. We're in a new

world now. I don't think we need to worry about hiding where we are and who we are as much as we have in the past. Let's just remember not to talk about the banks."

Henry leaned in. "I think we need to train other people, like we were trained, to sneak around and listen to what people are saying. Albany needs the intel, and we can show these townspeople how to get it."

Bubba frowned again. "I still don't think lots of our folks will want to put out that effort. They're used to laying back."

Trey looked at Bubba. "Hell, Henry leave him. If he doesn't want to come, he can just sit out there and listen to the frogs with Linda and her daddy."

Henry smiled at Bubba. "Well he could, but Bubba is a better shot than either of us. He may be slower in the running and stuff, but he's a bullseye with a gun."

Bubba pointed at Trey. "Yeah. And don't you damn forget it."

Henry slapped Bubba's shoulder. "You may be right about some of our folks in the swamp. Some of them will just sit tight. Others will get that we're in this together. I'll go around back home and explain things from family to family. You guys back me up if you are asked. We can't get what we need to live anymore just by relying on people in the swamp to provide for us. We've got to join with these other people out here to survive.

"We can show these folks what we've been doing. They're not used to it. You know, using clotheslines to dry wet clothes and letting the sun help warm the house. In the summer, without air conditioning, they need to learn to shade their houses, and if it gets too hot, open the doors and windows and air it out, don't let the heat buildup. They should be sleeping out on any screened in porch to get a breeze. All that's stuff we've been do-ing for years. When they see how we've been accepted by the town, our folks will come around."

Bubba Shrugged. "Hell. Most people can figure that stuff out on their own. "

Henry smiled and leaned into Bubba. "They can't figure it out if they've never done it and no one ever told them. You know, Bubba, we'll able to give them something they could not have gotten on their own. You could show them how to improve their hunting skills and teach them how to hide and such." He leaned closer and smiled conspiratorially. "Bubba, after we help them like that, you'll be a hero and all the young women in town will be after you. You've seen them walking around inside there at the mall. Not so bad, huh?"

"Well, okay. That does it then. I'm in."

Mental Health

Iris sat in the mayor's office with her father and Mayor Ballard. "I wanted to give you an update on something we discussed a couple of weeks ago. I've been working on this idea with the hospital staff. I think this information needs to be distributed to the neighborhoods, but because it's sensitive, it's your call."

"Go ahead."

"Well, first, the fact is that many people have died and that has a side effect of allowing us to have more of the existing the food supply, but it is a horrific trade off." She stopped and took in a breath.

"But the main point I want to make today is that the gradual decline in food and the deaths have everyone depressed. Lethargy has increased. Suicides are climbing dramatically. There are now people being buried everywhere. We can't cremate bodies because we need the wood for cooking, and we're using human excrement for fertilizer, so everything smells really bad. This is not an environment that engenders feelings of joy.

"Also, almost all mental health patients have run out of their meds and some patients have become dangerous. When they get hostile or suicidal, they could injure others along with themselves in a violent act. Everyone should watch for excessive erratic behavior. We just can't take chances on being polite and inoffensive like we could in the past, when we had the meds to treat some of these kinds of illnesses."

Ballard frowned. "We're in a situation where everyone is erratic. You're recommending that if we see someone that will not cooperate, your dad here might just send someone to arrest or shoot them?"

Iris grimaced. "None of us would want that to happen, but it's happened before this crisis. I'm saying we need to identify problems and handle them before they get larger. We'd prefer to isolate them, examine them, and hopefully calm them down. We should continue to be caring and humane with every patient. However, we can't afford to be accommodating to people who have the potential to kill us with an infectious disease or mental condition that makes them captive to a violent and aggressive behavior and threatens everyone around them. Hopefully their families will step up and take care of them, but we have to be ready if they don't. We don't have the facilities to handle a surge of the mentally ill." She continued to stare at the mayor.

"Oh... I guess not. It still sucks."

She nodded in agreement. "Yes, it does. Enough on mental illness.

"I've been talking with some of the social workers and psychologists, and we've organized a civic committee to set up more group entertainment. We're working with the neighborhood groups through the Managers. They are getting musicians to start concerts all over, starting plays that can go from one place to the other. Having poetry or other readings. Setting up card game days at the old bank branch buildings. All positive stuff. We're getting kids involved. We need to find anything to do that's entertaining and gets people out of their funk. I'm asking you to support this effort and encourage the neighborhoods to help entertain each other. Some of them are not taking this seriously, and others, following the attitudes of some of the leaders, have a kind of negative mindset and don't participate. That hurts our efforts."

The mayor waved his hand. "Iris, of course we will. I'll get a word out to the Managers. I've heard about some of that, and we can help by sending out small groups to play in neighborhoods from what's left of the Albany Symphony Orchestra and high school bands."

Iris gave a wan smile. "I realize entertainment may be a band-aid over a large wound, but we have to try to do something to help." Iris swallowed and looked from the mayor over to her father.

Mayor Ballard shook his head. He looked at the young woman he had known as long as he had known her father. "Iris I'm sure glad you're doing this. You've really grown into that hard job you've got over at the hospital. Keep me up to date on what I can do to help."

Crossing the Georgia Border

Walter was worried about his family as he marched along to the east with a renewed determination. The group from near the Fort Rucker base had grown to almost three hundred people by picking up disgruntled troops from the National Guard and reserve bases who were intimidated by their ferocity and military precision.

On the southwest side of Dothan, another armed group had formed. The two companies had clashed in several skirmishes. The west side gang then created barricades that looked too formidable to attack. Leading up to that stalemate, there had been run-ins with the law and other citizen groups. People were shot and killed on both sides, including Walter's cousin, who was left with several other wounded by the side of the road. Now denied access to the west, they ransacked the eastern side of Dothan.

Walter worried that any hope of moderate behavior or quickly obtaining supplies to take back to his family were long gone. Anyone who tried to leave the pack of Fort Rucker marauders had been shot as deserters after they were tortured, and everyone was made to watch. The leaders of the group were assuming more grandiose ideas along with their new power. Walter thought the rapes of both men and women were the worst of it. When that was going on, he would find something else to do and become as invisible as he could, away from all that activity.

Now instead of scavenging for more food, they were moving to cross the Chattahoochee River into Georgia. They had with them a ham radio operator with battery powered equipment who was in contact with others that let them know of large farms and supplies ahead in the southwest part of Georgia. Earlier they were pulling two 105mm howitzers and a significant supply of thirty-seven-pound shells with two large trucks. However, after maneuvering through two brief battles and several days of travel, they recalculated and found there was not enough gas for everything they wished to take. The big guns and shells ended up in ditches near the river.

They were going to scavenge their way to Albany slowly, picking up more troops when they could. The small army had enough gas to make it to that hub of Southwest Georgia, but hoped to find more on the road. It was the biggest town in the area, and had what some people said was the largest supply depot in the Marine Corps on its outskirts. There, the bunch hoped to find all the food and weapons they would need to survive whatever was coming. Fortified with the resources from the Marine Base, anyone who tried to stop them in the future was as good as dead.

Energy

Earlier in the day, there had been pounding rainstorm. Almost everyone in Albany had run out of their homes or workplaces carrying pots, pans, buckets, plastic bags, children's wading pools, or whatever they could find to catch as much water as they could. Some ran out with bars of soap to take an impromptu shower. Some with modesty, others not so much. The rain lasted for over two hours, and people continued gathering water until it slowed to a trickle and ran off into the gutters and culverts, where several of the more diligent citizens still tried to capture more.

Sheriff Dozier and Mayor Ballard left city hall as the storm was subsiding. The sun emerged and shone brightly through still sprinkling rain on the street. Jerico turned to the mayor and said, "Look, the devil is beating his wife."

Mayor Ballard looked up. "My grandma used to say that to me. You remind me of her sometimes."

Jerico Dozier gave the mayor a surprised look and shook his head. "Lord, help my time!   Lamar, sometimes I just don't know where you get these things. Your grandmother had to have been a more sensible woman than to give you secrets like that to blab about. I can't imagine her having to put up with you as a little boy." As the rain finally subsided, a rainbow appeared momentarily over downtown Albany. He pointed. "Did your grandmother have an old timey a saying for that?"

The mayor looked back at the sky and the fading rainbow before giving Dozier a serious look. "Yeah, she did, but if we don't get our act together and get all these people at least a little power, the devil is going to be beating on all of us and we're not going to find a pot of gold anywhere."

They were going to the parking lot of the James Gray Civic Center to observe one of several dozen exhibitions on making energy that were organized simultaneously all over town. The trade school had precut large quantities of the materials to make windmills and waterwheels, and these materials had been distributed to several locations where the demonstrations were taking place all around the county.

They spotted Julian Cordell from the Albany Utilities Company standing to the side and joined him. Ballard greeted Cordell with, "What good news do you have for us?"

Cordell perked up and pointed to the crowds gathered in the large space and dividing onto smaller groups. "Good news is, with electrical power from the wind and waterwheels, we can use our old laptops to keep records and access information from hard drives to give us tutorials on how to do stuff. We have the basic files, schematics, and instructions. Of course, there is no internet, but over time, I think we will be able to rebuild what we need, not just for energy, but for most everything. Today is going to help us turn the corner on getting more energy. We're gonna build more windmills and start to set up windmill farms, maybe put them on the tops of buildings or anywhere we can get a good breeze. We've still got a good bit of gasoline for emergencies left, all locked up securely thanks to the sheriff here." He nodded at Dozier.

Ballard smirked. "You know, all those billionaires that went off to live on their own islands... Well once their wine cellars run out, they'll be in as bad a shape as the rest of us. So, it's about time we start being equal to each other."

Dozier patted him on the back. "Now Lamar, we're all in this together. Rich folks didn't start this mess. You need to stop blaming them. Julian, tell us about the energy. How bad is it and what do we need to do?"

The clean cut and bespectacled manager of the Albany Electric Company adjusted his glasses. "We can't store large quantities of power with the equipment we have. We're gonna use the streams of running water and wind to generate some energy, as well as our own muscles. In fact, water is our largest continually renewable energy resource. Making these windmills and waterwheels will let us claw our way back over time and survive as best we can. We're gonna do all right.

"The students and teachers from Albany Technical College have been particularly helpful at these projects, since they have been studying these subjects in the school. They've become far more important than the computer geeks and marketers. They're making equipment that will transfer that power with dynamos or other electromagnetic widgets that are used with generators to create some amount of electricity. We're gonna store it in batteries, which can be recharged. I need your help to get the word out to Neighborhood Managers to take an inventory of batteries and get that information back to me.

"We also need to find windmill parts and working windmills outside of town. Everyone needs to try to remember places where there are old windmills or old hand pumps, with the pipes bored in the ground, that we can rig up to generate power as well as bring up water. We need to know where the wind blows most often and in what direction. We'll mostly be using those and waterwheels. We need to identify every creek or stream that has a current. Neighborhood Managers need to map those out in their areas."

Dozier said, "What about solar power?"

Julian Cordell shook his head side to side. "Buildings that have solar power need batteries to store it. Not many homes or commercial properties have got significant battery backup. Unfortunately, solar configurations are too complicated for us to simply dismantle sections of systems and repackage them into smaller configurations. We don't have the equipment for that."

Ballard said, "We did what you suggested and identified several large patches of empty land that were hard hit by the tornadoes and high winds of the past few years. There are likely lots of downed trees there that should be easier to cut up. We sent carts to those places that people can push to haul the wood for cooking or heating. We've also let people get available bricks, cement blocks, or old iron tubs or sinks to use for outdoor cooking."

As they walked closer to the demonstration, Ballard pointed. "Isn't that one of the kids from the swamp?"

Cordell answered, "Yes. They've been making these waterwheels out there for years. Several of them are helping us teach others."

Trey, with the help of some county workers, had set up a temporary sluice sending water down a small stream. He was demonstrating to the city people how the swamp people set up channels in running water so it would flow faster than normal and rotate flat spoked waterwheels to produce energy that would charge magnetic alternators or generators.

From the other side of the parking lot, Henry watched Trey's class, where thirty people divided into groups of five or six were learning to make similar waterwheels. In the nearby sluice trough, they practiced with their creations and learned how far they could space out the wheels so the continuing rush of water would spin several wheels sequenced along the stream. They all could use the same water over and over to generate more electricity. One of the teachers explained that these classes were scattered all over the county to encourage the use of the local streams, and that the results would be enjoyed in the nearby neighborhoods.

A woman was speaking to a group of about fifteen Neighborhood Managers. She explained, "I work over at one of the doc-in-a-box former bank branches. We've got lots of neighborhood trading going on in the parking lot, and we lend out tools to dig holes and stuff. We've also got the health clubs nearby to bring us stationary bicycles and other exercise equipment so people can use their muscle power at the neighborhood center to charge batteries through dynamos. You guys ought to try it."

Henry walked down toward the river and saw a group of younger teenagers were having trouble trying to assemble a water wheel. He smiled as he thought that a few months ago, they would have been lost in their cellphones. He remembered the independence he felt at that age, when he assumed he did not need any adult to tell him what to do. He spoke as he sat down by them. "You guys know I grew up in the swamp outside of town. I can show you how I learned to make one of those when I was your age."

They smiled and leaned back from the pile of boards, wires, and rubber bands. Evidently, growing up in a swamp still brought him credibility with kids. He sat and began to assemble the wood slats as spokes to make a wheel spin and showed them how to attach that to the belt that would make electricity for a nearby generator. He slowly explained what Trey would have shown them in the larger group of adults near the Civic Center.

"Now, you all and other folks will be using a lot of smaller waterwheels. You can see a demonstration right over there." He pointed back to where Trey was going from one group of adults to another, doing much the same as he was here. "We're going to make waterwheels of different sizes to use wherever it's practical. Every system we use will convert that spinning wheel into energy through the wires into generators and batteries to run the machines we need to reestablish society. After today's rain, the waterwheels we have will be spinning faster to create even more energy. They can make electricity twenty-four hours a day, but windmills and even human powered bikes can also make electricity with this simple system.

"We have figured a formula for everyone to use that tells them how to set up a windmill or waterwheel to supply battery power to their house. The county is gonna supply the equipment, but that will take some time. Because of the lack of electricity, we didn't have a copy machine running to make everyone copies. If you want, you can get the plans back over there and paper to copy them down. Then you can make more for your friends or other people near where you live. You can show them how. The city is going to need help to dig channels for flowing water to be more efficient in spinning wheels to make electricity. They'll get instructions to the leaders for that."

He held up the finished wheel, passed it around for all of them to look at, and then showed how it attached to a pully leading to a generator. "Here, you guys can finish this up. Go check it out with that short guy over there. He can set it in that flow of water, and you can make some electricity." He pointed to Trey.

As Henry walked down toward the river, he looked into the nearby neighborhood and across the river, he saw flags of clothes drying on lines strung up in the back yards on cords of rope, or along fences or tree limbs thick with string. He knew that inside those houses, there were stacks of dishes drip drying. He could hear the distant noises of people chopping wood that would be gathered and used for cooking food. People not just in the swamp, but here also were sweeping with brooms and manually taking care of daily activities as they discovered that there was not as much time just to sit around and relax. He was seeing what Mister Cordell and the mayor had discussed in action. It was happening. People were using the little electricity in their homes mostly to recharge batteries so they could have one or two lights at night, or some refrigeration and fans in the most severe heat, just like they had always done in the swamp.

He smiled as he approached his bicycle in a rack. People all around him were learning to make do with what they had. Now for the first time, he felt a part of it. He was helping where he could, and he had brought others from the swamp who were good at many of the things that were now needed. Hand saws were used in construction. Plumbing was patched. Equipment was repaired and made to last longer. He could see the entire town was changing and he was involved. It felt good.

As he unlocked the bike, he noticed another group of young teenagers playing music together as they were hanging out. There were several different instruments in addition to the mandatory guitar. They were talking about attending a concert at a public park with a bunch of their school and neighborhood friends. That reminded him of the play he had seen at the little theater with Iris two nights before.

He felt himself caught up in the stream of social activities that had begun to take place day and night that served to entertain everyone. He was discovering more about the town he had always lived near, and in doing so, was discovering more about himself. He liked going to plays and concerts with Iris, and with others as well. He liked talking about the events afterwards, sitting around and listing to others critique what had happened and the quality of the performance. He realized this interaction was something he had missed in his life until now. He was also beginning to participate in these conversations, and realized that all the reading he had done in the swamp gave him the background and confidence to share his opinions.

Then he realized that everyone else had missed these discussions as much as he had. Until now, many of them had been coasting through their lives watching television or playing electronic games. All the people he was around had come from different paths to the same place. He belonged.

Interstate 75

The truckers and other stranded travelers were getting short on food and the whiskey had almost run out. They had started to collect at the exits to Interstate 75 near Cordele where one by one, the trucks, cars, and vans had pulled off the interstate for gas and food only to find out there was little left of either.

A batch of them had gathered for the first several days near exit 99, and after exhausting the food and drinks there, moved up to exit 101 by U.S. Highway 280 where there were more fast food restaurants, motels, and liquor stores. By this time, they had formed a pack of over thirty men and six women who decided to band together. Almost all of them had at least one gun they were carrying for protection. The ringleader - there was always a ringleader - was a burly man well over six-foot-five and two hundred eighty pounds, who called himself Rowdy Burdette, and he loved the power of command. For the short run up the interstate to the next exit, they joined together in pickup trucks and vans they had taken from fellow travelers. Once they made their minds up, rather, once he had made their minds up to move in a large group, no one they met after that tried to resist them.

When they reached the U.S. 280 intersection, they found more stranded travelers milling around the motels and restaurants, all angry that they could not get any gas and that the food was running out. The shortages of everything fueled the gang's temper for the next week, along with the liquor. The group expanded, adding others they found equally pissed off and half-drunk, until they became a ruling force covering the entire area of the interstate's enormous intersection of motels, restaurants, and gas stations. By now, the growing mob smelled of piss and beer and there was an edge of impending danger in the air.

The big man gave orders and a wad of hungry people swilling warm beer moved to obey. There were some locals of like mind that also joined them – milling about, drinking, talking trash, and getting more pissed off. One or two local police watched from the edge of the road, but did not interfere. Now there were over two hundred fifty people sticking together like Velcro, growing all the time, intent on some action to vent their frustrations and find something they could latch onto and control, something to give purpose to all the madness.

No one had any good ideas, but there was a common assumption that the people who owned the motels and restaurants and the people in town were holding out on them. That hypothesis was enough to give them a target, and spurned on by the opinions of Rowdy Burdette, they decided to head into town to see what they could find.

First, they took care of the police watching in the squad cars. After casually walking up to the cars, they pulled guns, pointed them at the surprised officers, and easily overpowered them. Then they took their guns, gear, and cars.

The big man called the mob together and spoke to them as he stood on the back of a flatbed trailer. "Okay you folks," he said, pointing, "take these police cars and go to the police and sheriff's offices and take them out. Get all the guns and ammo they have. Look in storage areas and places where they likely got automatic weapons. See if they got an armored car or military stuff like an armored SUV.

"Break into the National Guard and Army Reserve office and storage area. It's on the local map. I saw a sign for the Defense Department over on Eighth Street. See what they got. And find out where they got some gun ranges in this town. They're bound to have guns of all kinds, automatics, AKs, M-15s and M-16s and lots of ammo. We need to get all the guns we can find. Hit every store in town… Hardware, whatever. Get it all. Be back here with all that stuff by sundown." The crowd scattered, happy to have direction and finally a purpose.

He turned to another group, still pointing. "You all! We need to siphon every drop of gas we can find in all these cars and trucks around here. Go up and down that interstate and get us several buses or flatbed trucks that can carry a lot of people. Need some good pickup trucks too. Go to town and siphon all the gas there. Get all the food. Ask first if anyone wants to join us, but don't get any wimps. We need some hard-tail boy dogs ready to hunt."

He looked down at one man standing near the front. "Didn't you tell me you are hauling supplies for the Marine Base over in Aw-bany?"

"That's right. Got a semi full."

"Take some of these people, open it, and get what's inside." He turned to the group standing nearby and pointed again. "Go with him and get what that guy has on the Marine Base truck."

Over the next week, there was widespread looting. It roamed into the residential neighborhoods house to house. People who resisted were beaten or killed. Some, fearful of what might happen to them, joined the growing band.

Rowdy Burdette organized and directed squads within the

growing mob. He told a smaller group of people he had started to call his lieutenants, "You all break up into groups of the people who you've been working with. Each of you need to take your team, make some visits to the little towns nearby, and see what they got that we can use. Get people who are fit, pissed off, and rangy to join us. Tell 'em we are going to a place to get all the food we can eat. Get everything that will shoot and all the ammo. While you're at it, find some young women you can bring back here. I need me a harem. I got a plan that's going to get all of us through this mess, and I need to be kept happy to make it happen."

Mayor Ballard came to see Sheriff Dozier with a big smile on his face. "I think I've got something out here in the parking lot you will like." He took the sheriff to his truck where there was a sizeable drone in the pickup's bed. "This belongs to my son, but I've commandeered it for our cause."

Dozier looked and blinked.

"He was going to use it to make home movies. See, it's got a little camera here." The mayor pointed. "The battery's here and you control it with this gadget. It's like a video game thing."

Dozier frowned and shrugged his shoulders. "I don't know..."

"Look, Jerico. Neither you or I can run this thing. We need a fifteen-year-old or something like that. It can be controlled from three of four miles away and can stay up for about thirty minutes. You can watch it on a laptop like a movie"

"But..."

"So, if there I something we need to see, but is dangerous, like the potential of bad people coming into town or something toxic, whatever... You can use this to fly over and send back pictures to a laptop or iPad screen to see what's happening. We never did get any replacements for all those parts and gas that guy stole months ago to fly regular airplanes, so this is all we've got for aerial surveillance."

"Oh... Yeah, that's kind of cool. I've seen stuff like that on videos."

"Thought you'd see the value of it. Anyway, it's yours to use. When all this craziness is over, get it back to me in one piece if you can so my son won't disown me."

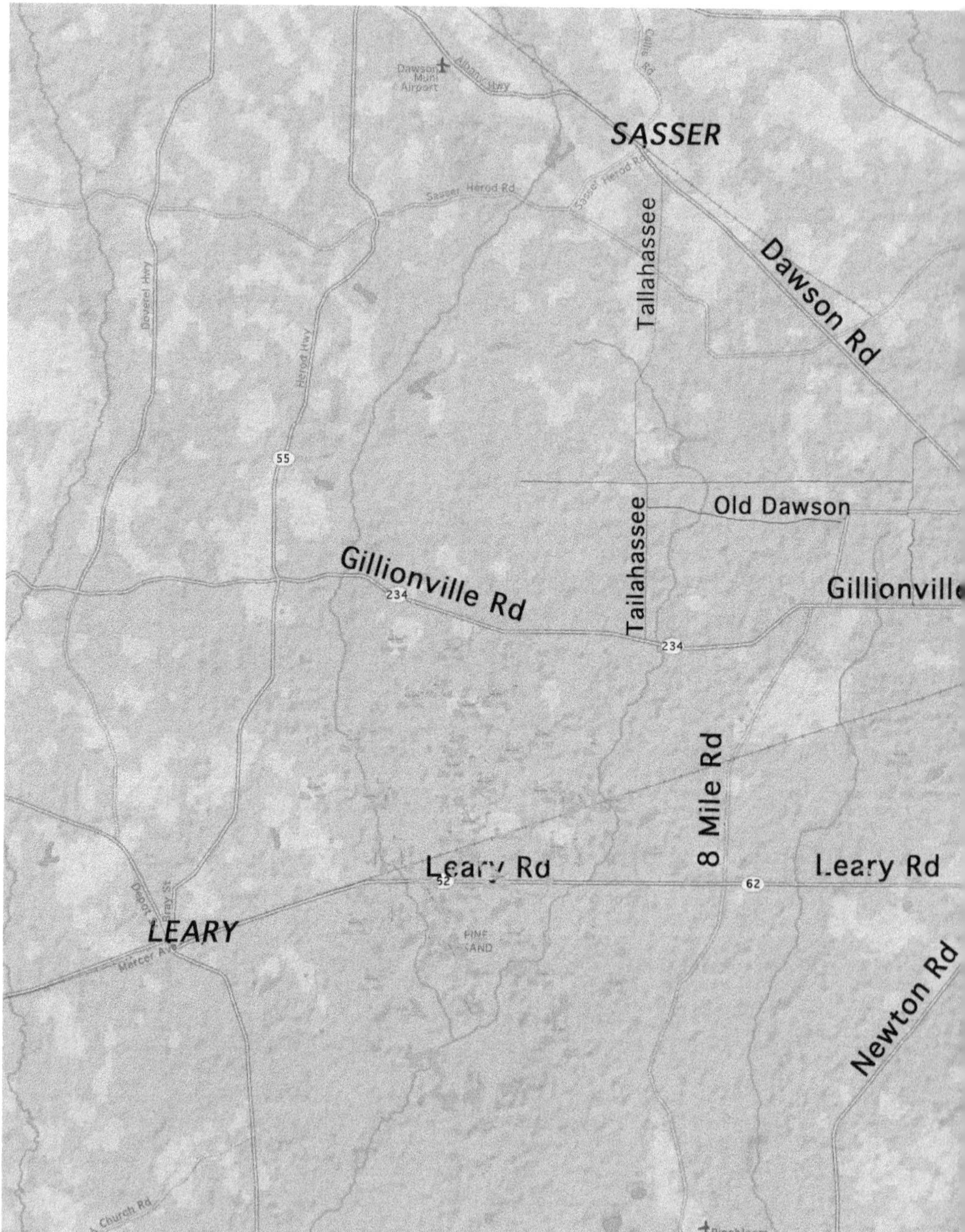

SASSER
Dawson Muni Airport
Albany Hwy
Sasser Herod Rd
Sasser Herod Rd
Tallahassee
Dawson Rd
Doverel Hwy
Herod Hwy
55
Old Dawson
Tallahassee
Gillionville Rd
234
Gillionville
234
8 Mile Rd
Leary Rd
62
Leary Rd
62
LEARY
Depot
Gray St
Mercer Ave
Newton Rd
Milford Church Rd
Pinebloom Plantation Airport

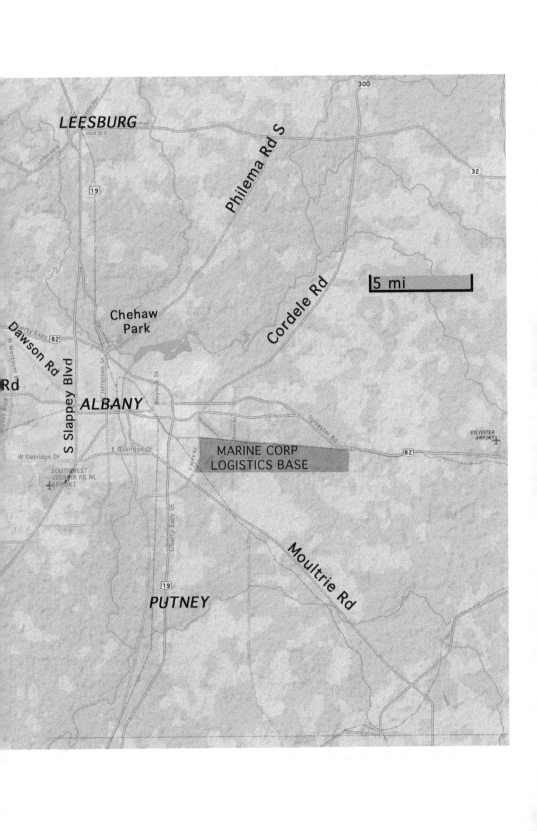

Challenge from Leesburg

Since the crash, candles and battery powered lanterns were largely used for lighting, and horses had become one of the favored modes of transportation.

One day, a gang of twenty determined men rode south on U.S. Highway 19 into the outskirts of Albany past shuttered stores, overflowing dumpsters, places with broken windows, and strip centers with weeds beginning to grow in the parking lot. They continued until they were stopped by a barricade stretched across the south end of the Slappey Drive bridge over the Kinchafoonee Creek.

The riders were strapped with rifles, pistols, shotguns, and aggressive attitudes, spreading out across the highway as the approached the bridge. They stopped only when they reached the railings on either side of the bridge and saw six people behind a barrier of two cars wedged together pointing rifles and shotguns at them. In the distance, there were more people running in the direction of the bridge carrying guns.

One of the riders leaned to the side of his horse, squinted, and suspiciously asked the Albany defenders on the other side of the bridge, "How come you blocking the road? We're just coming to visit."

One of the men behind the barricade gave his answer, "No more free visits in and out. I'd think about stopping right where you are if I's you."

One of the younger men in the bunch of horseback riders impatiently started to move his horse forward. "Screw him, he ain't gonna shoot and they couldn't hit all of us anyway."

The man who had spoken first, and who seemed like the leader, looked back at the younger horseman and said in a louder voice, "Hold up there, hot shot. We didn't come all the way down here on this warm day just to get in a gunfight. I don't need to be the one to tell your mama I got you killed by coming with me."

He turned back to the Albany sentries behind the barricade. "Folks, we just come to ask you to share some of that electricity you got. We can see you lit up at night from out there. We want some."

The man standing behind the car replied. "Mister, I can't answer that directly. Now, I don't mean to be unfriendly, but you need to get those other guys out of here and on back down the road a ways. You stay back where you are on the other side of the bridge. I'll get someone who can answer you, but it'll take a little while for them to get out here on a bicycle or a golf cart. We can talk about what you want. Just chill out and get those other folks to go on back toward Leesburg where I can't see them. Tell them not to even think about sneaking across the creek and trying to get behind us 'cause we got folks watching. We'll shoot them and I'll light you up at the same time." More people arrived out of breath and took up places defending the bridge.

The horseback leader nodded and spoke to the others, who turned and walked their horses slowly back north on U.S. Highway 19. He dismounted on the other side of the bridge and let his horse graze on the tall grass and weeds that had not seen a mower in well over a year. He loosened the saddle, took it off, and laid it on the bridge abutment to give the horse a breather. He patted the horse down and got some water from his canteen for himself. The horse stomped one foot because of the tickling grass and swished his tail at the gathering flies.

After about fifteen minutes, a man rode up on a bicycle followed by the man who had gone to get him. Three others, including two women, also pulled up heavily armed in an electric golf cart. They took positions to the left and right. The man who had recently arrived gave directions, pointing to the others on where to take up positions. He then moved toward the center of the cars and nodded at the dismounted rider forty yards away.

The man across the expanse of the bridge pushed up from where he was leaning on the support and started to walk across the space toward the barricade and the guns, which continued to point directly at him. He walked carefully about halfway across and rested against the edge, looked at the barricade, then leaned over and tossed a pebble into the Kinchafoonee creek. He watched it plop before turning to stare at the Albany defenders, particularly at the newcomer. "You know, friend, we don't want to fight you. We just trying to stay alive. We've seen some kind of marauders out in the woods and on backroads robbing people. That's why we are carrying guns. We saw you folks got light at night and thought maybe you could share some of it with us. We've run out of gas for our generators." He looked down and swept his foot side to side in the dust on the bridge road.

The newcomer behind the car barricade, wearing a deputy sheriffs' uniform, said, "Mister, I don't know if you have bad intentions or not. We're doing all right here and intend to stay that way. We've figured out how to do some things and get back some of the comforts we lost when they pulled the plug. If you want to know how to get some of this stuff for yourself, we'd be glad to teach a small number of you how to do it, and then you can go back and show the others wherever it is you came from. We're not trying to hide how we got our electricity and other stuff.

"Now, another thing. You can see we're ready and fairly well able to defend ourselves from anyone who wants to come in here thinking they can try to hurt us. We don't have any bad intentions, but we're not gonna let anyone just invade us and take what we got.

"So, if you want to fight us, we're ready for that, but we aren't looking for trouble either. However, if you have resources or skills to offer and want to throw in with us, we'd be interested in talking some more about that. I'm guessing there are a lot of small groups around here in South Georgia, like both of us, and if we can stick together, we all got a better chance of surviving and figuring how to get back to some level of where we once were.

"Now, we're not gonna give you stuff without getting something back. You need to figure what you got to trade us for some of the things we got, like electricity. If it makes sense, maybe we can deal together, and then we can drop this barricade and work directly with each other. But let's take it one step at a time. Come back to me on what you got to offer, and what you want for it, but don't come back here showing off your guns and demanding anything."

The horseman put his hand on the bridge side and nodded. He waved at the gnats and other bugs, attracted by the smell and sweat of the horse, which had gathered in larger numbers to bother people on both sides of the barricade. "Okay. We'll think on that and get back with you. Off the top of my head, we mostly got crops, farm stuff, livestock, and such. Got a bunch of chickens from those growers near Smithville. There's a dairy farm just north of Leesburg and some chickens there as well. I spec we got some things more than we can use. Here lately, they can't get the feed to keep them all alive and they're gonna die soon if we don't dispose of them. I'm thinking most houses or neighborhoods you got here could do with a few chickens in the backyard for the eggs and meat. That ought to be worth something for us."

The deputy smiled. "Well you may have something there. Seems like we've got the makings of a trade. We can show you how to make electricity and maybe give you a generator that's set up so it can run off a waterwheel and some other stuff for the chickens. Then let's us start to talk about supporting each other in case someone else wants to attack us. I think we can help each other."

"Well, now that you mention it, I got a cousin that came to my house from over near Cordele. She was kinda like a refugee and said there was a bad group getting together over there. Kind of took over the town. Some of them came up from the interstate and others were locals that threw in with them. Anyway, there's a whole bunch of them, and they got all the guns over in that area. We'd actually feel lots better if we could throw in with somebody like you guys, rather than trying to face a badass gang like that alone."

The man saddled his horse. "I'll be back in about three or four hours with some chickens. It'll just be something to get us started. They'll be on three carts. If you can get us up some stuff for me to take back, maybe some charged batteries or something that can make electricity like that spare generator, we'll be off to a good start. I need to show my folks that I got something for the chickens. That sound fair?"

"It does. We can also give you some directions on how to make your own wind or waterwheels that can make the electricity from the generators you already have to recharge batteries. That'll work, even though it takes a while and only gives a little bit of a charge at the time, but that's what most of us are using. If you have questions, next time we can send someone back with you to show you how to make some more."

"Sounds like a deal. See you in a few hours."

One of the women holding a shotgun turned to the deputy who had done all the talking. "That seemed too easy."

The deputy smiled. "It's like the sheriff was saying in one of our meetings, people let things build up in them til it starts to boil over, and then they rush toward a confrontation. We offered him an out and gave him something of what he wanted. Everybody got something out of the deal, and nobody got hurt. It should have been easy except for those boys letting things build up in them and getting all hot back up that road there."

A half mile up the road toward Leesburg, an Albany sniper team watched from the woods as the man rode his horse back toward the bunch resting their horses and themselves in the shade of the trees behind a shuttered fast food restaurant. They would stay there until the intentions of the men who had ridden to the bridge we fully known. They'd practiced waiting in hiding, and they were far enough away so to move around slowly and keep their muscles from cramping. They also could take turns watching so their eyes didn't get too tired, and they could stay alert and sharp. Henry's training was starting to pay off.

Barricades

Soon after the Leesburg incident was settled, Sheriff Dozier called the key defense team and the mayor together. "I realized, after what happened out on North Slappey Drive with the people from Leesburg, that we need stouter barriers. We don't have any way of knowing if folks outside of Albany are with us or against us, and we can't afford to feed any more people anyway. Here is what we will do until we can sort this out and get a military system in place…

"We're going to set up blockades around town to cover all the main roads coming into Albany. We'll need to figure a schedule for people to be on guard at those barriers, look for trouble, and alert the rest of us if we are threatened. To start with, the neighborhood militias will handle protecting any roads coming into town in areas close to them. We'll come up with a better system, but it will take a little time.

"I've been stockpiling bales of plastic for many years as a business venture. Well, that's likely not going to happen now, so we are going to use those bales of thick plastic to construct the barriers. Each of the bales is three or four feet thick with hard pressed plastic sheets banded together. They would stop any bullet I can think of. It's not the same as Kevlar, but those bullet proof vests are not four feet thick either. Processed and pressed plastic has been used for bulletproof protection for many years, and it will protect us here.

"We need to send those rolling truck bodies to my storage houses to get the bales. Put them on rollers or carts as much

Island in the Storm

as possible so they will be easier to move around. That way, we can be more flexible in how we configure the barricades. I'm gonna work on a plan for this, and will be calling on the Neighborhood Managers to help build the barricades in their areas."

A voice from the back of the group said, "Everybody is tired as it is. How you gonna encourage people to go stand around and be on guard?"

Dozier responded, "I'm gonna get anybody manning the barricades an extra ration of food for every shift they take."

The voice said, "Sounds good to me."

As they left the meeting, Ballard commented to Dozier, "Lord what a mess. What's it gonna take to get these people into shape?"

The sheriff scratched his head. "We'll have to keep working through the Neighborhood Managers to recruit more of our main militia. I'm gonna get my young friend over there," he pointed to Henry and his friends by the back door, "to set up some demonstrations on how to walk stealthy in the woods. That might attract some more folks who want to learn that kind of stuff. He's already teaching some people the kinds of things his daddy taught him. He said those other two," he pointed again, "know how to be snipers also."

As the teams of people moved the bales of plastic into the intersections of key roads leading to Albany, more than one person remarked how they felt like they were building the pyramids. They left some of the bales on rollers at each intersection so they could be pulled aside to allow any traffic through the barricades.

Once the bales were in place, other teams of workers directed by the Managers began to cut down trees near the main highways entering Albany so the tops of the trees were pointing toward the road. These were placed in rows on each side of the bales to extend the line of defense, and sometimes curved so the shape of the defensive roadblocks looked more like a bow bending one way or the other to follow the landscape.

They either left a portion of the tree attached to the stump to make them relatively stationary or dragged them to a desired position and staked down the stump end or roots to keep them immobile. Where practical, firing positions with shields to protect the defenders from bullets were nailed into the trunks or thicker branches facing the road. Then the central and top branches of the trees were interlocked, and the all the limbs facing the road were shaved to sharp points.

Some trees were bunched together to make the branches thicker. Smaller trees were wedged inside lager ones. In places that only had a few limbs, they drilled holes in the trunks or the larger limbs and inserted sharpened stakes or pieces of rebar with sharp, pointed ends. This configuration, called an abatis or cheval de frise, formed an almost impenetrable set of wooden spears, menacing anyone trying to get at the defenders. One of the history professors at Albany State University suggested this ancient method of defense that had been used for many centuries.

Soon there were abatis structures reaching out from the sides of all the bales of plastic, extending the barriers and guarding the flanks of those borders. They were also used on other roads deemed too small or less of a threat than the main highways to receive the heavy plastic bales.

Everyone realized that sooner or later, all the abatis material would become firewood for cooking or heat for the coming winter, so the recruitment of workers with axes was not as difficult as it might have been for a less practical military project. In the scattered neighborhoods where the wood was used, it was eyed by those living close by as the beginning of the winter stockpile. However, the sharp spikes were to be avoided. Kids and running dogs soon learned to keep their distance from the front ends of the breastworks.

Radium Springs

A week later, Henry followed Sheriff Dozier and Mayor Ballard over the bridge across the Flint River to East Albany, then out Radium Springs Road to the fabled springs caused by a fissure from the underground aquifer running below much of the south through porous limestone, all the way down into Florida.

Though greatly diminished from its heyday, the recently cleaned surface shimmered with blue-green waters, emerging from a deep, cylindrical hole and forming the largest natural spring in the state. The fissure pumped clear, bubbling water containing traces of radium and other minerals through an extensive underwater cavern system into a large, opening spring the locals called "the boil."

The mass of water collected in a meandering eddy and then flowed down a broad, chilled stream to join the Flint River and continue south. Here in the boil, however, fresh from its journey from deep in the earth, the water was filtered naturally through limestone so that its content was almost pure. From the underground aquifer, this water rushed at seventy thousand gallons a minute and at a cool sixty-eight degrees in temperature, and the contrast for swimmers in the ninety-degree heat of a South Georgia summer made it feel like ice water.

Henry was going to stay on the site to plan and organize a system to collect the Radium Springs water, filter it through a fine-meshed cloth, and then take it to be boiled or otherwise processed safely for mass consumption at a microbrewery in downtown Albany and the Miller-Coors beer bottling plant. The sheriff and the mayor were going to continue to the Marine Base once they felt comfortable that Henry could manage the plans for the water collection.

As they walked around inspecting the stone and concrete sides that framed the walls surrounding the bubbling water, Jerico Dozier became excited and began telling Henry stories about the history of the place. "Man, this is great. My parents used to bring me here when I was a little kid. Everyone came. We'd jump into the freezing cold water and then lay on the hot sand to warm up. It was the best place to spend the summers before it closed. Over there was an enormous casino and restaurant.

"Before the big flood wiped it out, the casino and adjoining hotel were the most beautiful architectural things in Albany with maybe, I don't know, five or six floors that terraced down to the water. All of that building on the water side had these windows that looked alike, and you could eat inside and see everything out here. Man, there were kids swinging from a rope, or jumping from high and low diving boards into the boil, where they would sink into the pit only to be pushed up to the surface screaming in shock! Not from the leap, but from the chill of the water. Everyone who jumped into Radium dog paddled like hell to get to the nearest side, rush out into the sun, and run for a towel." He walked back and forth smiling and remembering as the years melted from him.

"But, Henry, the thing that defined Radium was its smell. As soon as you got close, you were hit in the nose by the limestone in the water. No sleazy YMCA or high school locker room shower after a big game could have equaled the smell of lime. It was in the rocks, in the puddles of water in the leaky faucets and water fountains. The smell pulled you in from the road out there, through the lobby toward the light and the water. You went down some steps that opened onto a big concrete slab with railings surrounding the water. Behind that were all the people. There was a whole world at Radium Springs.

"We came here almost every week of every summer of my youth. It was the thing to do with visitors, with family reunions and cold fried chicken, potato salad, and gallons of iced tea. And there were the people we knew, saw in school, in church, at the downtown stores. We saw each other grow up on this common ground. This was our equalizer.

"And over there," he pointed in the opposite direction, "was a pavilion on stilts with open sides and a tin roof. A jukebox contained the only lighted area in the space. A wooden dance floor was littered with sand.

"After dark, teens met there to dance and stare and learn to talk to each other. I met Iris's mother here when we were just kids." He looked over at an empty place where sand came down to the water. "Back then, she looked like magic." Jerico's voice caught, and suddenly he stopped talking. Henry saw the emotion of the memories and stayed still.

Mayor Ballard listened to the sheriff and the young man who he knew had taken an interest in Jerico's daughter, and smiled to himself as he looked down and walked the perimeter along the water.

Dozier, coming out of his reverie, noticed the unusual expression on the mayor's face. "What is it, Lamar?"

The mayor shook his head. "I'm just not used to hearing you go on along like that." He smiled again. "You know... Hearing you talk so personal about your recollections of Radium Springs just now. I'm glad for you to have those good mem-

Island in the Storm

oires." He continued to walk forcing a smile.

Dozier cocked his head at his friend. "But, Lamar, I know you. There is something else."

The mayor shrugged and stopped his pacing. "It reminded me of hearing from my parents that they could not go to Radium Springs when they were kids... When it was still segregated. That's ancient history now, but some of us have different memories that also need to be respected."

These comments drew Dozier up. "Sorry, I didn't think... Was not thinking of it that way."

Ballard waved his hands. "Don't worry. Times have changed and anyway. We've got to get someone scheduled to bring containers to collect the loads of water. We need to fix a ramp to take it out over there." He pointed. "I'll get the people over at the water department to figure out how to test this water to see how much more we need to do so we all can drink it safely... or whatever. For now, we can boil it here or take it over to the microbrewery or the beer plant and have them process it. They've rigged up a generator to run some of the equipment, and are also going to be processing river water.

"We can't get it by turning on the faucet anymore, so we're gonna have to use every well we can find to pump water manually to the surface, collect it, boil it to be safe, and then put it in tanks or barrels. We'll get folks to distribute it through the neighborhoods and to the homes. We need to work with the county agent to find where we have high water tables and try to dig new wells where we can pump more water." He looked down at his watch. "Come on Jerico, we've got to get to Marine Base or we'll be late for our meeting."

Two women and two men who had just arrived came

down the steps to the water's edge carrying large containers. They decided to start a clean water factory on site by filtering some of the water and bringing it to a boil over a wood fire. They would distribute some water in the neighborhoods near the springs and take other water to the Miller plant and microbrewery to use their generators for processing. This way, they would have several systems going at once to obtain clean water. They realized they would need more help, so Henry rode back to city hall on his bicycle to get more workers.

Island in the Storm

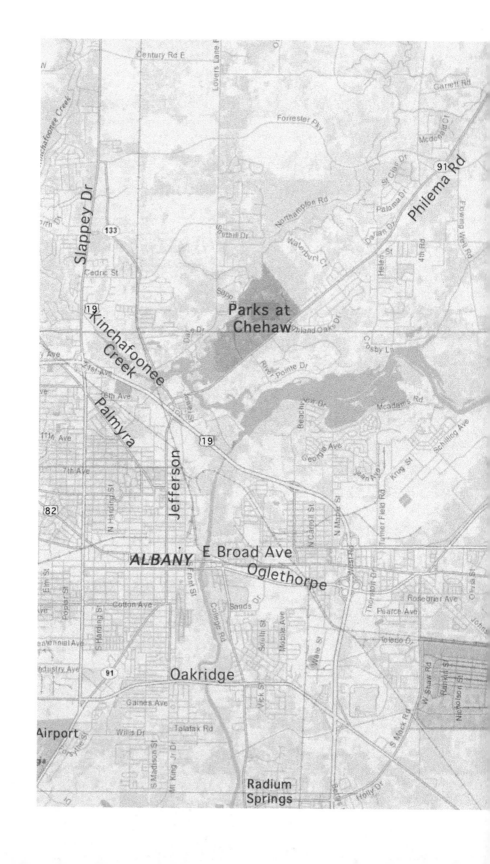

Marine Base

After a short drive from Radium Springs, Sheriff Dozier and Mayor Ballard arrived at the massive U.S. Marine Base to see the commanding officer, Colonel Spencer. Sheriff Dozier's recent conversation with Henry had him looking at the base defenses for the first time in the new light of civil unrest, and he was surprised that Henry had been correct about the flimsy fence. He wondered if any electric security monitors, used with commercial power from the outside by the base, were cut off with the power failures. The expansive border around the facility would have taken literally thousands of armed soldiers to defend.

As the base was located on the southeast edge of town, it was also vulnerable to attack from that general direction, which would not be buffered by any nearby Albany militia defenders. The facilities on the base were set back at least a hundred yards or more, but there were no hard barriers to prevent anyone who breached the fence from penetrating well into the base before facing any opposition.

The current crisis had whittled down the cars of civilian workers from several hundred a day to only a handful. That lack of normal automotive clutter made the open space in the parking lots seem abandoned.

They were escorted in a Humvee painted in desert camo past row after row of enormous warehouses, each one over a thousand feet long. Perhaps in anticipation of difficulties, like a squirrel preparing for the winter, the base was packed with a massive amount of food, clothing, handheld weapons, mu-

Island in the Storm

nitions, and other materials better not left to the elements, all jammed into the warehouses.

In the distance, there were lines of heavy vehicles mounted with an array of weapons, including what looked like rockets, long barreled tank guns, and howitzers, as well as crates and boxes of every imaginable kind of support equipment and weapon. Parked in large lots were over two hundred Humvees, dozens of tanks, supply trucks, and semis, and thousands of crates of parts and supplies. They drove past the base's field of solar power, and Dozier wondered how much actual energy it could generate and where that power was directed. In the distance, there were also several large municipal-sized storage tanks of petrol. If ever there was a place that could survive a food and energy crisis, with massive amounts of weaponry to defend itself, this was it.

Even though there was little activity in the massive compound, once they reached the main administrative building with the VIP offices, they had to wait almost thirty minutes before being shown in to see the bird colonel. Although they felt slighted by the wait, it gave both men an appreciation for the air conditioning and electric lights the base still maintained.

Just before he had them enter, the base commander sat at his desk, looked once more at the troublesome letter he had received two days before, and put it into his desk drawer as he prepared to greet the visitors.

As they entered, they noticed everything in the colonel's office was absolutely neat and in place. Mayor Ballard felt the room had been organized to present visitors an impression of power, but instead it felt flat, stale, and still. The colonel rose to great them at a desk free from any papers or folders, and with a hand gesture, offered them a place to sit in a nearby group of chairs around a low table. He was a big man, impeccably groomed and filled with self-confidence. His hairline was receding prematurely, which made his proud, dark face seem older. A plaque from Howard University, along with several trophies, referenced his former athletic achievements and were displayed in a large glass case next to military memorabilia.

He started as though nothing was going on to cause any alarm, and spoke in a deep, soothing voice. "How can I help you gentlemen?"

Taken aback, they both looked at each other. Lamar Ballard started, "Colonel Spencer, I'm sure you are aware of the stress everyone is under with the bad economy, energy crash, and failing infrastructure. We are here because we are concerned about civic unrest in this part of Georgia, and that it might actually affect you and the base here."

The colonel smiled and crossed his legs. He flicked at a piece of lint. "I'm not too much concerned about that. We have things locked down pretty tight here. Our external communication is spotty, as I'm sure yours is in town with the problems everyone has with electricity and the internet." He absentmindedly looked out the window, then back at his guests. "However, our internal coms and our perimeter are still secure, and I'm hoping the problems you are having in civilian life will soon be settled."

Ballard continued, "I hope you are right, but Colonel, we are concerned that these problems could very easily get worse. We have serious shortages of food, fuel, and medicine. There have been incidences of theft and some violence. Your base is located right here with us and..."

The colonel held up his hand. "Mister Mayor, sorry, but before you go on, I have orders to protect this base. If any of those rowdy people were foolish enough to try to break in here, I can assure you that they would find themselves in a very unwelcome situation. We are safe and intend to stay that way."

Ballard continued, "Actually, we could use your help. We've been organizing militias and have increased our police and security presence, but we are stretched thin and..."

Hand in the air again. "Let me stop you there. We do feel a strong affinity for the civilian life in Albany, and the Marine Corps has had this base here for many years. However, we are the U.S. Government. We have orders on what we can and cannot do. My orders have been given to me very specifically by people up the chain of command, who I'm sure are quite aware of the civilian situation and prob... your issues. What I can do and must do is defend this base. What I cannot do is to get involved in civilian affairs and disputes, especially violent civilian acts. I have orders to stay on the base and look after it. As much as I might feel sympathy for your position, and the citizens of Albany, I cannot do anything to help you or your issues, as I have my orders to the contrary."

Sheriff Dozier spoke. "I understand orders. I was in the military many years ago. However, perhaps you can loan us some equipment that we can use as a deterrent for any harmful actions such as..."

The colonel interrupted, "Sheriff Dozier, I appreciate your situation, but my instructions have been made clear to me. We're on an island here. Whatever takes place outside of our perimeter, we cannot be a part of. If my orders were to change, I'd love to help. We understand the problems of civil unrest and we don't condone violence directed at any state or local governments."

Mayor Ballard leaned forward. "Colonel, perhaps you

could stage a military parade that showed off your equipment, you know, tanks and jeeps and stuff. That would reassure our people, and the word would get out to surrounding areas and imply that you were helping us even if…"

The colonel interrupted, "I'm sorry, Mayor Ballard, but that would just be the first step of pulling us into your conflict. There is a line I cannot cross without a different direction from my superiors."

Dozier looked disgusted and reentered the conversation. "The same superiors who cannot communicate with anyone now that all the electricity is off?"

"That may be a temporary setback."

Dozier leaned forward. "So, if you are attacked, you don't want us to help you?"

"I think we can take care of ourselves."

Ballard tried another tack. "Maybe you can tell us a little more about what happened. We know the finances were stressed with all kinds of debt. Kind of like with the economy back in 2008 and with the virus in 2020, but worse. I thought they were going to fix that up in Washington."

The colonel sighed. "Mister Mayor, and let's keep what we are saying in this room, I think you know it wasn't just us, but the whole world that was in debt up to its eyeballs… And affected by the virus. From what I understand, no politician wanted to make the hard choices and kept on printing money.

"Everybody got suspicious of each other, including all the countries around the world. They started screwing with the internet and computer systems and things started crashing after being infected with all the bugs and worms. We've all just got to hunker down until they figure out how to fix it and get the power back on. We've all taken a good hit, but we've got to trust our leaders to be able to fix things."

Dozier said sarcastically, "The same leaders who could not make a hard decision when we were functioning, and could have actually done something months and years ago."

The colonel nodded and smiled wanly. One hand waved to the side. "That's above my pay grade. I'm here and I've got my orders. I'm going to follow them until someone above tells me differently."

Dozer continued with his temperature up, "And there is no equipment or supplies you can share with us to prevent riots or bloodshed? You can't help, even if we are attacked by a mob from elsewhere?"

"I'm afraid that with the orders I have, I cannot do anything to help."

Ballard now decided to try yet another approach. "Colonel, I understand your people have not been paid for a few weeks. We could help with that, you know, giving credit in town... And for those living off base, forgiving rent and such. We're looking for a way to work with you here."

Colonel Spencer shook his head. "My men and women are Marines and we can take care of them without your help. Thank you." He gave Ballard a hard look. "I'd appreciate it if you would keep any suggestions of deals like that to yourself."

Ballard slapped his knees and rose. "Well Colonel, you have given us a very clear idea of where we stand. It is a good thing you weren't at Lexington or Concord. Back when we started this country, we all worked together. People stood up to help each other and didn't hide behind bullshit orders."

The colonel now also stood quickly. The two African American men faced off, one standing a foot taller than the other. "I don't need any lectures from you. I'm wearing the uniform of my country and I am likely going to be needed, maybe very soon, to step into a fight. One thing I do know is how to follow orders from my superiors. That is what a soldier does. We may not always like it, but if we lose that discipline, we are no longer an army. Good day, gentlemen."

As they were turning to leave the office, Sheriff Dozier said, "Colonel, I understand you are military and not only that, you are the U.S. Marines, but this is a supply depot not a front line combat unit. I'm sure you can handle most small gangs of rioters or hungry American citizens coming to you for help. But it's one thing to talk confidently and another to shoot down your fellow Americans. Those young men and women driving forklifts and taking inventory may not be the soldiers they once were just out of basic training or back from combat experience, and you don't have thousands of them war ready. I hope you will eventually understand that, orders or no orders, we're in this mess together here in South Georgia, and that is the way we will have to be to get out of it."

As they were driving back to the office, Dozier looked over at Mayor Ballard. "I thought, for a minute there, you were going to punch him." "Jerico, I was angry, not crazy. The guy's big as a moose."

The sheriff blew out a breath of disgust. "That smug, stick up the ass son of a bitch. I was so tempted to shout to him that I bet his own precious Marines are selling stuff out of the back gate right out from under his spit shined nose. He has no idea what not getting paid has done to their morale. Makes me appreciate young people like Henry Graham all the more."

Alone in his office, Colonel Spencer sat back at this desk, opened the middle drawer, and pulled out a letter that was on the stationary of the president of the Albany City Council, Larry Godwin. He scanned down the first two paragraphs of flattering comments to the meat of the message.

"...And most of us on the city council think the Mayor is being unduly rash and irrationally concerned with the security of Albany. We believe in and trust that our elected officials in Washington will take care of our needs, and do not think it necessary to form a militia. We hope you will not be unnecessarily bothered by the fearmongering of our somewhat unbalanced mayor. Rest assured, we intend to rectify his bothersome actions in the next election."

He steepled his hands and rocked back and forth while contemplating the two widely different views on the future of Albany.

He folded the letter and put it back in the drawer. Next, he reviewed once again the medical report marked "personal and confidential" lying next to the letter from the city council president.

Tift Park

After setting up the system to gather water from Radium Springs, Henry stopped by the hospital to see Iris. They walked down to Tift Park, where they could have a private conversation and Iris could speak more freely. As they were negotiating a path through the water oak trees, their conversation was interrupted by the noise of carts rolling by, each carrying a large bale of bound plastic down Jefferson Street toward the perimeter road. Henry commented. "Your father is shoring up the northeast defenses." Iris was unusually quiet and walking with her head down. "What is it?"

Iris stopped and took in a deep breath. "Recently, we've lost everyone who was on dialysis, all the preemie kids, and most people who needed heart, cancer, or diabetes medicine to survive. We could not perform needed operations. Even simple things like appendectomies proved disastrous. Infections are killers and sixty percent of everyone who had surgery recently has died. I believe the population of Albany has dropped by almost twenty percent in the past six months."

She looked back at the hospital and continued to walk. "I just hope, with the energy we expect soon from that power plant out toward Chehaw, and the waterwheels down by the river, we will have a steady supply of electricity that will let us provide life support. There are also simple problems... Like we no longer have pasteurized milk, and we mostly don't have refrigeration for milk, so our children and adults are at more risk from all kinds of things. What do I do about that?

"Because much of our food is being grown using human excrement for fertilizer, we've got to make sure people clean the food well and then cook thoroughly. We need people who have teaching experience to put together hygienic cooking classes. I'm worried that these neighborhood groups are not doing that.

"To top it all, my boss told me that without his medicine, his diabetes is starting to cause other medical complications with his kidneys and eyesight. He also has diabetic neuropathy. I'm going to have to take over administrative management."

Henry rubbed her shoulder. "I had no idea it was that bad."

Iris, hardly hearing him, continued, "Our job as medical professionals is to protect and nurture the living. The hospital is relying on me to reach everyone with messages of nutrition and cleanliness, and to caution them about our limited medicine. We are in danger of a cholera epidemic, not to mention other communicable diseases, because of bad sanitation... And we can only reach people by word of mouth.

"How do I alert everyone that diarrhea and vomiting could be signs of transmitted diseases like cholera, hepatitis, and typhoid? There aren't any bananas left, so we try some white rice, peanut butter, mashed potatoes, or chicken broth to treat diarrhea and clog the stomach. Henry, if we get a contagious epidemic, it will have the potential to devastate us all. Everyone is all packed in closer together because of the lack of transportation. We don't have enough sophisticated medicines. We are on our own to do what we can."

Henry said to her, "I'll get the word the people at the barriers to be on the lookout for sick people who want to come in here. Let us know how to spot a dangerous illness. We can stop people coming in to protect the rest of us."

She stopped and sat down hard on a bench. "This is getting to be more than I can handle. It's so frustrating. I have to be the strong one in all this." She looked over at him, her eyes brimming with tears. "Everybody just sees me in such unrealistic ways. They can't get past how I look. I'm such a fraud. People think I have all these abilities and that I'm smarter than I am. I'm not trained for this."

"But you are great."

"Henry, I never went to medical school." She shook her head. "Most of what I know about medicine I got from just taking courses here and working at the hospital... Being observant. I'm not qualified to be giving orders to doctors and people who really know what they are doing." She dropped her head and shook it again. "I'm going to get people killed. I'm just half guessing at what needs to be done. It's like when I was taking care of my sick mother, and there was nothing that would make her better." She picked up a rock and threw it. "I don't know what to do and I'm scared."

He reached over and rubbed the back of her neck. "Okay, I get what you are saying. But Iris, none of us have been in a crisis like this before. We're all just doing our best here. You understand the hospital because you've worked it from the ground up. You're not making medical diagnosis or conducting operations. You're really good at communicating with people."

She took a deep breath and closed her eyes. "But I feel like I'm trying to play a game with people's lives because I don't know if what I'm telling them is right or not."

He turned her shoulders so he could look into her eyes. "Look, I'm teaching people I only just met how to go out in the woods and spy on others and maybe shoot them. There is no way they can know everything that has taken me a lifetime to learn. I'm playing God. I have to tell them that they are okay to do a dangerous job... When it's likely they'll not be very good at it and get killed.

"Iris, our main job is to stay alive. Everybody has problems. You are trying to help people have better health, and I'm trying to help your father protect us. Look, I'm worried that I may be forced to kill someone, but if that is what it takes to keep you safe, and keep my family and what we have from being overrun, I'm ready to make that choice. This stuff is hard on us all."

Henry leaned back on one elbow. "You told me once that lots of medicine boiled down to making a hard choice... Picking one among several bad options. Nobody has a lock on knowing what to do, particularly in this situation. One thing that you do have is people's trust. They do what you suggest because you have picked that option for them. They rely on you to take that burden off them. When you look like you are certain about what you do, it gives them hope and makes them stronger. Maybe it puts you in a position that seems unfair, but that's where you are. It's what you have worked toward all your life, and you're good at it. Things stabilize when there is a leader.

"Let the doctors do the medicine. Let the others do what they do best. Everyone will make mistakes. They are counting on you to do your part. You are smart and you've got to suck it up to help. We're all fragile here. Be strong, like you can, for all the others. Doesn't matter if it makes you uncertain inside. We're all uncertain. We're all putting on a face of sorts. You're the rock over there at the hospital. It's okay to have some cracks, but you can't break."

Iris wiped the tears from her eyes and sniffed. "I've always known there was a reason Midnight liked you."

Lake Blackshear

The big man, Rowdy Burdette, who was firmly in charge of what was now well over four hundred armed people occupying Cordele, smiled as he looked at the map. He turned to a small group of his assistants, "We're just about got this place skinned. Get everyone ready to move about ten miles over to Lake Blackshear." He pointed to one of the eager locals who was delighted to help. "My new best friend here tells me that rich folks got cabins and vacation houses all around that lake. We're gonna go visit with them for a few days." He pointed around the room. "Get your teams ready. One of the groups will ride over by the north road and start down to the lake from there. I'll bring the other group in from the south. We'll take care of that place they call Warwick."

On the map, Lake Blackshear looked like a partially blocked and swollen artery on the Flint River as it meandered south from central Georgia. The dam near Warwick, Georgia backed the water into a fat finger, stretching more than dozen miles north to south. The swelling of the river into a lake allowed the additional waters from Swift Creek to join together until they formed a narrow lake filled with game fish and water skiers, surrounded by cabins and expensive vacation homes.

Rowdy pointed to the map. "By the time we've met up, I want that place picked clean, just like we did here in Cordele." He turned to the local man. "Now, you say your friend got a short-wave radio that works?"

The man smiled. "He sure does. He lives on the lake, so I

need to go over there and get him to help us. Don't be tearing up his place. He told me that he is what they call a 'ham operator,' and can talk to other people that have a radio set like his."

One of the other men covered in tattoos said, "What the hell is that?"

Burdette nodded at the local, "'Splain it to him."

"It's this radio that uses what they call shortwave signals. You can speak to someone else that has one when they dial into a signal, like a telephone, but it's just for you two. It'll run off a battery or a generator. He's got both. It's kinda like what they use in ship to shore talking, or on the old highway truck rigs years ago. They made a song and a movie out of it called 'Convoy.'"

The other man impatiently interrupted. "So what? I never heard of it. What do I care?"

Burdette said, "Just shut up and listen."

Grateful for this show of support for what he had to say, the local man smiled, "Anyway, he's got this buddy with one of these things over near Dothan, Alabama. And they've been talking back and forth. Seems like there is another big group over there, kinda like yours, Rowdy." He nodded over at Burdette. "Some of them are people from the military base and others are locals. They got organized to do something like what you are doing. Anyway, they decided to head to Albany to take over the Marine Base."

The man who had interrupted burst out, "Hell, that's what we're gonna do. We can't let those sons of..."

Burdette held up his hand. "That shortwave thing is one reason we're gonna stop at Lake Blackshear. I'm gonna get that fella to hook me up with whoever they got in charge over in the Dothan area. No point in us fighting each other over the base.

If we work together, we can hit Albany at the same time from two different directions, with maybe close to a thousand hard ass people coming from both ways. Here, look at this map." He pointed out how the access road to Albany coming from Dothan from the southwest was exactly opposite from the road they would use from the northeast. "If we both get there on the same day and hit the town at the same time, there is no way the people in Albany can stop us."

"Damn. You're right."

"Let's get over there. I want to talk to whoever is in charge in Dothan. We're gonna kick some ass."

A few days later, the moving storm of outlaws had occupied all the homes, stores, hotels, and barns around the man-made lake. The former local paradise was now the temporary home to new arrivals intent on sucking it dry.

Gathered in the home of the shortwave enthusiast, the big man met again with several of his lieutenants. "Okay guys. We're gonna use this radio rig here to get in touch with that other group over in Dothan."

The man with a ruddy face and tattoos all up and down on his arms spoke. "I still don't see way we need to fool with those guys. They may take over when we get there and get ahold of what should be ours."

The big man looked over at him, turning his head slowly in increasing disgust. The continued questioning of his authority had been happening for the past few days. "Buddy. I'm going to explain this to you one more time..." He looked around the room and nodded. "And to any of these other folks who either don't know or haven't been listening." He pointed to a map of the southeastern United States on the wall with numbers marking places where the shortwave operator had contacts he used frequently.

"We don't know how many men they got, and that is one reason we need to talk to them. We don't know how many men the Marine Base has, and that is one reason we need Dothan's help to make sure we can take it. Us, along with those Dothan people, make a larger army. If we get control of the base, there is likely enough stuff for all of us. I'll bet any soldiers we don't have to kill on the base will be glad to join us. Once we have the military base, we can go and take over other places around here, or maybe even go down into Florida using all the stuff the military has on the base. If those Dothan people are not agreeable, then we will take care of them quietly at night."

The man said, "But..."

"Listen asshole! The only people that are gonna survive this shit are the strong. We gotta be strong to survive. We also got to STAY strong to survive, and we gotta keep our troops happy by winning all the time. To me, that means being the biggest and baddest we can be. So, we need those people from over in Dothan."

"Were you in the military or something?"

"Yeah. Or something! More importantly, I got good common sense and I understand people. One thing you need to understand is that I don't need you. I've been around tough sons of bitches and I've squashed them for breakfast. Mister, I'm tired of your interrupting and I'm tired of you questioning me. You want to stay alive and be part of this outfit, button up and do what you are told. You pass on what orders I give, and you carry them out. Remember, only the strong survive... And I'm stronger than you." He looked around the room again. "Any of you other sons of bitches got anything to say?"

The room was quiet. "Okay. Now go out and finish getting all the food, guns, ammo, and any other thing we can use from every house on this lake. Go out to nearby places like that town, Leslie," he pointed to the map, "and bust their ass well. Recruit any people who can shoot and want to join us. I'm gonna coordinate with these Dothan people, and then it's on to Albany."

This time, the tattooed man raised his hand like he was asking for permission to speak. "But I thought we were going to the Marine Supply Depot."

The big man wiped his face from the top down like it was covered in something unpleasant. "Yeah, but it's in Albany. We gotta take the town to take the base, and the town will be easier. Once the people on the base see we've got them surrounded and own the town, they'll be easier to handle. If we don't take the town first, we'll have a bunch a people attacking our asses from behind. We get the town, then we can attack the base from all sides and there is no way that they can stop us."

The tattooed man nodded. "That's slick."

Burdette rolled his eyes. "So, while you all are finishing up Lake Blackshear, I'm gonna send a team over to just outside Albany at this here park to camp out." He pointed to Chehaw Park on the map stuck to the wall. "They can clear out the road from here to there for the rest of us, scout out things over near Albany to see what's the best way to attack, and let me know what we may be up against when we go into the town."

Tattoo said, "Damn, you're not just a pretty face."

"Yeah. And when I get all that worked out, I can let those folks over in Dothan know. That will set a timetable for them to come over to Albany and hit 'em hard from that direction."

As the men were filing out, the big man stopped his most trusted assistant and whispered, "Get all these people back to where they need to be to pick the lake clean." He nodded to the door where the others had just left. "That tattoo man has torn his ass with me. When you get the chance, shoot him in the head and toss him in the lake."

The man nodded eagerly. "Got ya covered."

Bad News

Julian Cordell raced down Jefferson Street in the golf cart that the power company was using to refit the dam at Lake Chehaw. He was traveling just under twenty miles an hour on the empty street and he felt a desperate need to go faster. With the adrenaline churning in his gut, his body was rocking back and forth against the steering wheel in the hopes of gaining more speed. A casual observer might have mistaken Cordell's hunching motions as a somewhat deviant public expression, had not everyone known him as the ultimate straight arrow.

As he turned toward the courthouse and major civic offices, he shouted at a policeman standing on the corner, "Where is the sheriff?"

The man turned and pointed as the cart hummed by, "Over at the court chambers in a meeting."

He banged on the steering wheel, impatient to get there. Finally, he pulled up to the curb and took his foot off the power, which stopped the card dead still. He ran up the steps two at the time, down the hall, and burst into the big courtroom. Everyone looked up, shocked to see him slamming open the door.

He had to catch his breath before shouting, "They're coming. Coming down the river on boats. Bunches of them. Call out the militia. Hurry, they'll be here any minute." He leaned over, holding to the door and breathing harder.

Sheriff Dozer quickly moved over to Julian and asked, "Tell me what you saw. What happened?"

"I was crossing the road, going out to the dam, and saw

a flotilla of maybe ten or twelve boats full of people. Some of them had guns. They had cut around just above the dam and went down the Muckafoonee Creek bypass to catch the river and head south toward town."

By this time, there were two deputies and several members of the militia crowding the doorway.

Everyone in the courthouse grabbed whatever guns they could find, rushed over to Broad Avenue, and then sprinted down to the River Front Park not knowing what to expect. As they fanned out, pointing the guns as they approached the riverbanks, about a dozen boats had already docked near the area where a series of waterwheels charged golf cart batteries and ran generators for the city. Both ski boats and fishing boats were tied together on the bank as people were helping each other off onto the dry land. Several were holding weapons, which were dropped when they were challenged by the Albany law. Their presence showed a glaring flaw in Albany's defense system, although it was soon apparent that these were refugees not invaders.

Sheriff Dozier began to question them at the same time Mayor Ballard arrived to listen, and the man who seemed to be in charge began to explain why they were there. As the sheriff was talking to the newly arrived people standing on the shoreline, Larry Godwin arrived with a colleague from the city council and watched from halfway up the riverbank.

The man from the boat directed his comments to the sheriff. "These people came out of nowhere. Gangs of them. They swept into the neighborhoods and subdivisions of Cordele and just grabbed everything. People who resisted were beaten or shot."

A woman next to him said, "God knows what they did to the women."

"We got together and made a run for it over to Lake Blackshear, where we have a lake house. We got our boat and all the supplies we could carry and told other neighbors. Some folks wouldn't listen. Anyhow, we got this group of boats together and came downriver to here. Took us two days 'cause we floated some to save on gas, and because we had to tow some of the boats. Now we're all just about out of gas. You got to help us."

Mayor Ballard, who been listening, stepped forward. "I'll tell you want we can do. First, there are not enough food and supplies for us to take in refugees."

"What? Mister we've come through hell..."

Ballard waved his hands. "Hold up." He turned to one of the deputies. "Go and get these people some food and some good water from the microbrewery." He looked around and counted the boats. "Get about ten gallons of gas from the reserves." He looked at Dozier, who nodded his approval to the deputy.

Godwin stepped carefully down the bank and moved closer to the front of the group of people. He crossed his arms and looked back and forth from the mayor to the refugees.

Ballard, ignoring him, turned back to the collection of people from Cordele and Blackshear. "You can earn your way to staying with us by pitching in to help where we have needs. Those of you who look to be fairly well armed and have gas left need to go back up the river to the power dam a couple miles back upstream. Dock there and support the people who are repairing the electrical systems. You had to scoot around it to get here. Do that, and you can stay there near the dam and power station. You'll get regular rations of food like everyone else, but you will have to defend it if it is attacked. If it gets overrun, bring all the people back down here in your boats, even if you have to float or row."

Ballard looked at the sheriff. "You need to get some people up there to block off that passage and check out any other people coming downriver. We need to stop them upriver before they pass the dam." He looked at the people with the boats. "We might need to give these folks some extra gas, and they can help you with that."

He turned to look downstream. "The rest of you can go downstream to where we are building a big vegetable farm. There will be a place to live out near a bend in the river, but you will have to work the crops and help bring up water from the river for irrigation. They're making a system to pull the water up by manual labor. I'd suggest all the kids go there. Or... You can keep on going downstream and take your chances with the next towns that way." He pointed to the south.

The people talked among themselves and divided as Mayor Ballard suggested. With the kids going to a safer place, only workers and potential fighters would be left.

Larry Godwin stepped up to closer to the group of new arrivals and waved his arms. "Hold it! I've had just about enough of this bullying. You can't be playing God with these people. I've got a good mind to..."

Sheriff Dozier stepped past Ballard and up close to Godwin. "Larry, take your good mind and shove it up your ass. All I've heard from you for the past several months is criticism. No good ideas, just whining. Now the mayor may have to listen to your bullshit, but I don't. You either make constructive suggestions or get the hell out of my way... And keep out of meetings."

Godwin sputtered, "You can't just... You have to..."

Dozier stepped even closer, now inches from Godwin and overshadowing him in height. "What I have to do is to try to protect this town. What I no longer will do is listen to your complaining. The next time, I'm going to put you in my jail for disturbing the peace. Either grow up or keep away from me. Go back to your real estate office."

Godwin started to speak. "I..."

Dozier have him a hard look. "Don't do it, Larry. Don't test me."

The group of refugees momentarily looked from one to the other, seemingly unsure if they would be forced to take sides in this local dispute, or if this was actually the spot where they the wished to disembark. However, as Larry Godwin made his way back up the riverbank, they relaxed.

Sheriff Dozier turned to one of his deputies. "Get a team over to the dam and set up a watch there. Figure how to stop hostile boats coming down and find a way to help any others escaping from Lake Blackshear."

As they were walking back to the courthouse, the mayor snapped his fingers. "With the river emergency, I almost forgot some good news. Someone found a pile of old crank phones used for telephone repair and can rig them up to some land lines. When you crank them, it generates electricity to communicate over the line. That will give us the chance to have a point to point conversation over some distance on that one line. We can set one up at the power station at the dam and others at every barricade.

"If we are lucky, we'll find one of those old phone jack

boards you may have seen in the old movies, then the outposts can be plugged together to communicate on one central switchboard. Maybe if we can find more of them, we can connect the neighborhoods through the branch offices."

One of the deputies said, "There is a museum over in Leslie that has the largest collection of antique telephones, like maybe in the world. I bet they have some of that stuff."

The mayor pointed in the direction of the voice. "You're right! I forgot about that. We need to organize a group to go over there and bargain with them to let us have some of that equipment. We can trade some food or bring them into our protective defense."

Sheriff Dozier leaned in and spoke. "Well, Leslie is almost thirty miles away, so the defense thing is not practical right now. In any case, I'll send some people over there. They'll have to be super careful to avoid that Cordele bunch we just heard about."

The mayor nodded. "Okay. At least it will give us some method to communicate, however primitive." He slapped Jerico Dozier on the back. "I believe we are getting to the point where we've almost got what we need to sustain us. The key thing will be to work together and to stay safe."

Sheriff Dozier frowned, "Well, that's going to be much harder if there is a marauding bunch of militants over near Cordele. We need to keep our eyes on them. Henry, I need a couple of your sniper-scout people to go with my deputies over to Leslie. We've got to have better communications if we hope to become a more sophisticated, military-type organization. Okay everyone, let's get going. I need to see how that river watch patrol is getting set up."

As they were reaching the courthouse, Sheriff Doz-

Island in the Storm

er pulled Henry aside. "Are you ready to go on that little shopping trip we talked about?"

"Yes sir. I got the list of things you thought the city might need, and I'm gonna get some things for the neighbors where I live."

Sheriff Dozier rolled his eyes. "I can't believe I'm condoning this. You did say you were going to pay for the stuff."

"Yes sir."

"How?"

"We took up a collection among our neighbors. I think it will be enough. We're not paying full retail, you know. I'll let you know if we come up short. We need to do it now while the PX is still taking cash."

"Well, it's generous of you all, and we'll not forget it." Jerico Dozier had a suspicious feeling about the money, but given the critical need at hand, he was not going to get into that detail just now. "Just don't get caught or shot."

"That sounds like something my dad would say."

"He'd be right. Now, we'll be waiting about a mile away. When it happens, get out quickly and we'll meet you, escort you, and help move the stuff, but we've got to stay in good graces with the base commander and can't be seen as working with you on this… Thing."

"Not a problem. In and out."

"Maybe we should not discuss this with Iris. I don't feel good about what we are doing, and she might get upset with both of us if she knew what we were up to."

Henry frowned, "I don't like it either."

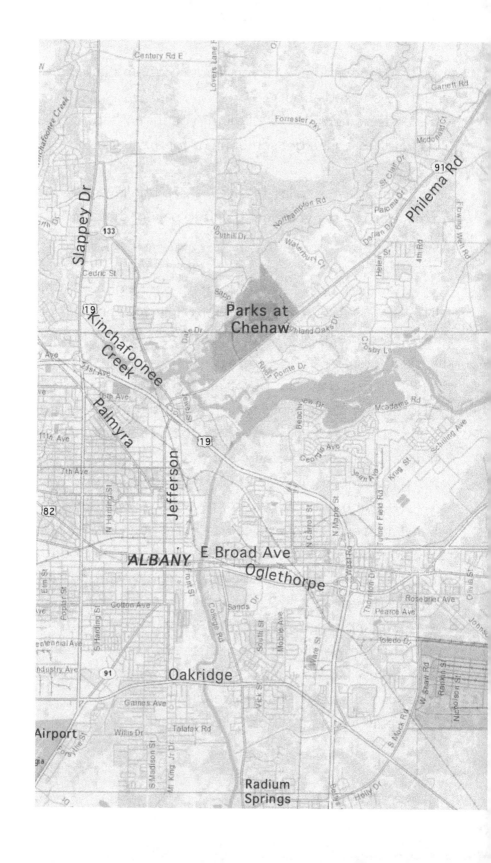

Part III – The Crunch

Henry Graham Emerges

Henry nudged Trey in the ribs. "You ready to go help me? We got work to do."

"What you mean?"

"The world's going to hell and we need better provisions for the trip. Up til now, I thought some of this stuff that's been going on out there would sort itself out, but from what the mayor and sheriff have said at the meetings, that's not going to happen. I've got that friend who has the surplus store over by the Marine Base. We need to get over there and see what we can do about getting more supplies and better weapons."

"Who's that?"

"Back before we moved to the swamp, when I was just kid, I had a playmate in the neighborhood named Bobo, a best friend actually, who later on went to work at the Marine Base. It is near about the biggest supply depot in the Marine Corps according to this brochure I've got here. It says, 'to serve as a designated safe haven for the Marine Corps and other Department of Defense agencies during times of threat and recovery from emergency situations.' That's a mouthful saying they have a lot of what we need.

"In addition, the brochure says, let me see here… The base will, and Trey, listen to this part… 'The base will reach out to the surrounding community to find ways to share common goals and values, and will build relationships that are good for the Corps and the community, which will last far into the future.' Well, according to what the mayor and the sheriff were told a couple of days ago, the Marine Base is going to ignore the cooperative part with the surrounding community. So, that's why we need to act. Let's take an inventory of what we need. We've gotta make a visit to my friend's surplus store."

Willis Graham was lying on his cot across the room listening to Henry and Trey with both excitement and fear in their voices. He felt the same increasing dread he had felt before a battle, when he had been sent into the field to track and kill. They did not know what would be coming at them or how violence would affect them. He knew. He leaned up on one elbow, "What you really got on your mind, Henry?"

Henry said, "You know, the Marine Base is a supply base. They've got everything anyone would need to survive for damn near forever. The surplus store where my friend works will have some things, and we may need to get other stuff from the base itself. Bobo told me that over the past few years, he has been able to give a list of what he needs and one or two of the Marines will bring it to him. They make money on the side that way, and there is so much stuff on the base, no one will miss it."

Henry and Trey continued to make their list, and when Henry got into more of the details about what he and Trey planned to do, it got more of his father's attention. Willis continued, "I kinda figured you have been getting closer to that sheriff 'cause you been seeing his daughter. He doesn't know how we've been getting our money?"

"No sir."

"Well, what you are describing sounds risky. Don't do this

thing alone." He turned to Trey. "Trey, go get someone from each of the other families to come over here. Lemme…" Willis stood and staggered, caught himself, and nodded that he was okay to Henry, who was making a move to help him.

"Dad? I…"

Willis held onto Henry's arm to steady himself, then stood tall. "Let me help you. You need to dip into our money, and we need to get everyone to agree on that."

Trey returned with representatives from the other families. Willis waved his hands to get their attention. Even in his weakened condition, Willis Graham had everyone's respect. "I'm gonna let my son explain something to you, and you need to listen."

Henry let everyone know what he was planning and brought everyone up to speed on his discussions with the sheriff and their training of the militia groups in Albany. Several of them who rarely left the swamp were not fully aware of the severity of the crisis or the threat of an armed invasion from outside Albany. A heated discussion began, as this was the first time the swamp families had collectively considered what was happening to the rest of the world after the total failure of electricity.

After Henry finished explaining the situation, John, one of the older, founding members of the group, commented, "Damn. Where can we go to get away from this?"

Another said, "It's likely you're in as good a place as any. We just got to hunker down til things get better."

"We can just stay here. We don't have to get involved in someone else's fight. We can survive on what we have here, and those people ain't gonna come in here looking for us. If they do, we can take care of them. Nobody knows this place 'cept us."

"Aw, hell. Lots of people know we're out here, just not

exactly where."

John punctuated the conversation. "Well, we don't need them."

Henry nodded. "What y'all are talking about might work for a while, but at some point, we are gonna need the others or need something they have. We can't just pretend we're not part of a bigger world out there."

John's wife pointed. "But we can't let them find out what we've been doing for all these years to get our money. They'd arrest all of us."

"She's right! We gotta hide that, for sure."

Henry continued. "We can pick our shots at what we do and how we work with them, but we're gonna need them for the stuff they've always provided like food, ammo, parts for our equipment, medicine, gas."

John was now taking the lead in confronting Henry. "But I ain't gonna fight and maybe get killed for a bunch of people I don't hardly even know."

"You get to make that choice. But if they are risking their lives to protect everything around us, and we are not willing to help, that makes us cowards."

"Makes us smart."

The discussion went on for some time and finally Henry, Trey, Bubba, and some of the younger men and women said they were going to the help defend Albany no matter what the older adults decided.

Finally, John said, "How you gonna pay for all that? You are gonna pay the soldiers for getting the stuff, aren't you?"

Henry got a look on his face like he had been caught taking too much dessert. "I'm gonna use some of the money I got from the banks."

"That's our money. Our money together."

"Well, it's just sitting there and the only people using real money are those Marines on the base."

John took a step toward Henry. "Still our money."

Willis, who had been letting everyone else talk, said, "Well now, John, you know I think Henry's right. From what I hear, money is not being used anymore. Everybody's bartering. So, it's worthless. We've got a bag full of it from the bank robberies, and Henry's right that we need to buy the supplies. We need to stockpile more equipment and get power for our generators, as well as a fresh supply of ammunition, just as a precaution. It sounds to me like a visit to Henry's surplus store friend is a good place to start."

Willis spit to the side. "Johnnie, you and you other folks also need to remember, it was Henry and Trey who went out and got the money and risked getting shot the past few times. They did that while you all were sitting on your asses. So, I say let them do what they're gonna do anyway."

The swamp families provided a long list that was added to the one prepared by Henry and Sheriff Dozier. After the discussion ended, Henry and Trey left the swamp with a box full of cash to get what they needed. Willis Graham had settled the discussion, and everyone agreed that those who wanted to fight with the town could do so, and others who wanted to hide out in the swamp could do that too.

Shopping at the Marine Depot

Henry and Trey met with Sheriff Dozier in a seldom-used back office at the Thronateeska History Museum housed in an old, abandoned railroad building. He gave them a fully charged walkie-talkie and offered some concerned advice. "Look, I'm very nervous about you getting everything directly from the base. Get as much stuff as you can from that surplus store. That will let you get on and off the base quicker, and reduce the chances of getting caught. Just be careful." As Henry was packing the walkie-talkie, the sheriff noticed a strange look on Henry's face. "What is it?"

Henry had been thinking to himself, and was surprised that the sheriff had gotten to know him well enough to tell when he had something on his mind. That realization made Henry feel more accepted, but also a little afraid because of his past activities with the banks. He smiled and said, "I was thinking that it's ironic to be meeting here because Thronateeska was a Creek Indian word for the Flint River. Trey and I have been living in the swamp from the river's watershed, near where the same Indians that are honored in this place fought their last battle in the 1830s. And here we are, going to sneak things away from the modern version of the same army that fought the Creek Indians."

Dozier looked around the museum room at the relics on display. "Well, make sure you come out of it better than those Indians back in the 1830s."

Later that day, Henry sat with his childhood friend Bobo in the surplus store located near the Marine Base going through the list of items he thought they needed. Bobo had sent a note to his main contact at the base, who still had not joined them a couple of hours later. While waiting for the Marine sergeant, Henry looked around the store and gathered merchandise he thought they could use including weather gear, tents, boots, tactical vests, clothes in the new camouflage material that was almost invisible, powerful flashlights, and other items.

Bobo followed Henry around the store. "Hard to believe you are still out there in those woods. My grandad told me that when he was young, all the land within a forty by forty-mile square patch was that swamp. Folks over there cut into some of the old swamp land, down to about… maybe half of what it once was, but what they left is still near about as big as the Okefenokee Swamp over in East Georgia. He told me that when he was a boy, he worked at Cordrays Mill over on the edge of the swamp for fifty cents a day, grinding grain on the stone discs that were turned by the waterwheel below the dam."

Henry smiled. "Yeah. I'm guessing everything was a lot thicker back then 'cause they've been cruising timber on the high land in recent years, and they thinned out the original growth." Henry stretched. "Hard to believe the Flint River started from under some damp spot near Atlanta and wanders down to join the Chattahoochee to form the Apalachicola. With the farming that's been going on, you'd think all that water would have been pulled out before it got to the Gulf of Mexico."

Bobo nodded. "Yeah, there are places back there that have only been seen by the nasty-ass critters living there. When you gonna move out?"

"Maybe after all this crazy stuff gets settled." Henry pointed. "Look, I think your buddy just came in over there."

After listening to the idea and reviewing the list of what they needed, the young Marine staff sergeant named Sidney said to Bobo, "This is a lot more complicated than me bringing you some boots and bayonets. In the last few months, things have changed. The fact that many of us are not getting paid regularly is only part of it. They have laid off most of the civilian workers, tightened up lots of what we do, and more of the military staff has been moved back to D.C., out to Camp Pendleton near San Diego, or somewhere else. We shipped out lots of the helicopter parts, the bigger rockets, and most of our big ass M1A2 Abrams tanks just before the big crash."

Henry leaned in, "What you're telling us is that everything is falling apart. The military brass are hunkering down on bigger bases and starting to strip this depot of the big hardware and most of the people."

Sidney nodded. "Correctamundo." He looked into the cup he was holding and made a sour face. "Damn, Bobo, what is this crap you are putting in your coffee instead of coffee?"

Bobo said, "Well it kinda looks like coffee, but we ran out of that stuff several weeks ago. Next time you come, bring me some from that big sack of it you got over in one of those warehouses."

Bobo then looked over at Henry, who picked up the conversation on the crisis, calling him by the name from their childhood, "Yeah, Henny. They began to strip out the big stuff just before the crash. These guys they left on guard, like the sergeant here, haven't been paid in three or four weeks and are just holding out. Staying on the base for food and a place to sleep. Some of them even traded us stuff that is not exactly surplus for some extra food and other stuff." He thought for a moment. "Hen, maybe you should add some coffee to that list of yours. I think they got the last of it in the whole state of Georgia."

Henry asked, "What's it like on the base?"

Sergeant Sidney set down his cup and looked round at the dim, makeshift battery-powered lighting in the store. "Being out here feels kind of creepy. On the base, because we have solar power and lots of generators and gas, we've still got regular lights and electricity. Things are running pretty much like they did before. You can still go into the PX and buy stuff using cash. Watch videos and go to movies. We haven't been paid for several weeks, but if you have money, you can get whatever you want. Everybody is still driving around in jeeps. We're all buying booze and food and music and all kinds of stuff. Not like it is with you guys out here."

The Marine sergeant nodded at Henry and explained further. "Looks like not too long after the big recession or depression, whatever you call it hit, the cyber war began. Folks all over the world started zapping each other and killed off the electrical systems and the big computer storage places. The cloud. The internet. So, then nothing worked anywhere. Last thing we heard was an order to secure the base, and hey, get this, 'repel boarders.' Like it was some old frigate with cloth sails."

Trey, who had been observing from nearby, laughed and said, "Those military guys are full of shit."

The sergeant gave him a look that shut him up. He then took a hard look at Henry. "Dude, don't you think for one minute because I can kid about all this, we are not lockdown patriots. A good many of us live off base, and our families are worried about what is happening. We want to protect them, as well as this base. If the generals and the politicians have their heads up their asses, we can't just sit by and let a bunch of crazy people come in here and take over. But let me tell you," he pointed in Henry's face, "you try to use any of the stuff on this list in a way that threatens this base or this country, then we'll come out of there and have your ass."

Henry nodded. "Got it. Our hope was to be working this together, and we still hope to be with you to face whatever comes at us in the near future. Like you just said, some of the leaders have their heads up their asses."

The Marine nodded and said, "Okay, what do we do?"

Henry nodded back and thought for a moment, looking at the ground then back up at the sergeant. "If the shit's coming down, then we're gonna need all of the stuff on the list that's still on your base. I've got money for you and those guards, you know, to let us on the base tonight to fill up that deuce and a half truck."

He pointed to a large military surplus truck with six wheels, one in the front and two paired in the rear of each side, parked nearby. "Get word to your buddies to be on guard duty at that gate near us. We'll come in at midnight and load up. We'll take care of whatever other guards who are in on this also. We don't want to get shot over doing what we need to do to protect our-selves." He pulled out a wad of money and gave it to Sidney. "Here, use some of this here ten thousand dollars to seal the deal and tell them there'll be more after, and lots more for you."

He looked over at his friend Bobo and then back at the enormous truck. "No. Wait. I can use both those big ass trucks." He pointed to a second six-by truck parked nearby. "Bobo, get both of 'em cleaned up and running, with enough gas to get them back to the other side of Albany."

Bobo started to speak.

"I'll double what we talked about."

The sergeant frowned as he put the money into a pocket on the right leg of his fatigues, just above his knee. "We may have a little problem. You see, opening and shutting the big vehicle gate after base lockdown is hard to fix. There are some redundant alarms on them. Stuff I can't control. Once you are inside the perimeter, it is easy enough to move around. Our security is mainly designed to repel boarders." He looked at Trey with a frown. "Mmmm. We're gonna have to get the trucks on base during regular daytime hours when the gates are open, fill them up overnight, and have them drive out the next day."

He pointed to the map of the base. "The night we do this, I'm gonna have to let you all walk on the base through the personnel gate at curfew, and that will involve taking care of," he counted on his fingers, "the guys on the gate, sentries walking around, the person watching the security cameras, and some people in the warehouses." He looked again at the list. "All this stuff is going to be in several warehouses. I don't have a hard count right now, but that's something like at least twelve or maybe fifteen people on our side of the fence to consider. Once we get the stuff you need out of one warehouse, we'll seal it again and move on. We'll split up the trucks to get different loads and cut down on our time on task. Based on what you need, I'll figure out how to stack and load the materials in each truck, and what sequence of warehouses to go to. If I have enough time, I'll get the people helping us to pull the stuff down off the stacks and get it near the door so it will be ready to load. We'll need to move quickly to get all these things you have on the list."

Henry frowned. "That's a lot. Can trust that many people to go through with this and not tell on us?"

"Man, I don't know. This is hairy shit, but I don't see how we can do what you want otherwise. I'm going to make sure I can trust the people I approach before telling them what it's about, but I can't tell you for certain who might decide to help us and later chicken out or decide to blow the whistle. I can't say who might get drunk and talk about it.

"You're gonna need at least..." He counted. "Maybe fifty thousand. This is a lot of risk and we could all end up in the brig if we get caught."

Trey sputtered. "Damn. That much!"

Sidney looked over at him then back to Henry. "Yeah. We're risking our asses and our careers. I'm not sure if money is ever going to come back in use or if it's going away for good, but right now, it's still something we can use on base. Next week or the one after, maybe not. If you don't want to do this..."

Henry held up his hand and nodded. "Yes, we're doing it."

Sidney mused, "I'm going to need a couple of days to round up the right people and set this up. See who's on what shift and what I've got to change around. What I can do is get those two trucks onto the base tomorrow. They are already painted to look like our other vehicles, so you can park them in a row of other trucks and they won't stand out. I'll show whoever drives them in where to park, and then they'll leave through the personnel gate. That will be the same gate you use on the night you load up. I'll get passes to Bobo here later today that authorize the return of two trucks that have been sent off base for civilian maintenance."

Henry asked Trey to stay with Bobo for the next few days and be his person on site in case things changed radically. As he left the surplus store, he leaned into Trey, "Try not to piss off any more of the Marine sergeants we need to get this job done." Trey shrugged, pulled out his Game Boy, and took a seat in the back of the store. Henry used the walkie-talkie to contact the sheriff and explained the logistical and financial problems on the base, as well as the delay.

Later, Henry and the sheriff went to see the mayor together. They settled in the mayor's office and Henry explained. "Because so many low-level soldiers are getting involved, I'm gonna need more cash money than what I've been able to collect."

"How much?"

"I'm guessing, counting what I'm going to have to pay the surplus store for the trucks and supplies, and then a bunch of Marines on the base, about forty thousand dollars more."

"What?"

"I've got a long list of things to get, and we've got lots of people to pay off on the base, as well as outside."

The mayor asked, "What are those young soldiers making that they have to stiff us for such a big payoff?"

Sheriff Dozier interjected, "Well, they haven't been paid for several weeks, and if the colonel caught them doing this, he'd fry them and have them for supper. It's a big risk for them. It's not like we have a bunch of other places we can go to get this gear, and it's stuff we need."

Mayor Ballard threw up his hands. "Damn! This is getting more out of hand. There is no way we can keep this a secret. We're going to get in a hell of a lot of trouble. Jerico, are you sure we need to do this?"

"Lamar, we need those guns and all the other supplies they have. Like I said, we don't have another choice. If we don't get it, we're going to be a pushover for the first well-armed band of marauders that comes our way."

Mayor Ballard shook his head. "That damn colonel. He could have made this so much easier."

"But he didn't."

"Okay. I'm going over to the bank to get the money. Cash?"

Both Henry and the sheriff nodded.

"This is going to make me tell some world class lies to the bank people."

Dozier smiled. "You're in politics. You're good at it."

Ballard gave him a sour look and tapped the desk. "Oh well. Good thing money is not worth much anymore. Be back here at five o'clock."

As they left City Hall together, they passed Iris entering the building on a hospital errand. She looked surprised. "What are you two doing together?"

Jerico stammered, "You remember I asked Henry to help me with some maneuvers? We had to get together to go over it."

She cocked her head to one side suspiciously. "Maybe, but you guys look like you got caught with your hands in the cookie jar. I don't know about you boys." She waved a finger at both of them.

Henry mumbled, "It's just we didn't expect to see you here. Caught us by surprise."

She continued to look at them skeptically as she started to

walk on to her meeting and said laughingly, "Okay, but I'm going to keep an eye on you two."

As she left, Jerico looked at Henry sternly. "You know, someday we need to have a serious discussion about where you are getting all of your cash dollars."

Henry nodded. "Someday, yeah. Maybe. But someday is not now."

On the Base

As promised, Sergeant Sidney got the passes, and when the trucks rumbled onto the base, he met them and showed them where to park. Trey drove one of the monsters to get a better feel for the layout of the base and the proximity of the trucks to the warehouses, and Bobo drove the other. Later, Bobo got word from Sidney that everything was a go for the next night. Trey and Henry were issued passes to mix into the group of off duty Marines who would be in civilian clothes, and who usually timed their return from the nearby bars right up to midnight, before they missed curfew.

It was a dark night and heavily overcast, which everyone thought was a good sign. By the time Sergeant Sidney met Henry and Trey at the gate and took them to the trucks, a light rain had begun to fall. Sidney spoke into his walkie-talkie to start the process with his team, then jumped on the running board of Henry's truck and hung onto the side as both of the large trucks lumbered over to the rows of long warehouses. There were two men standing by a door on the side of one, and the sergeant pointed for Trey's truck to stop there. He continued riding and directing Henry to another warehouse off in another row. They passed a man on guard duty wearing a plastic poncho. He was walking and carrying a rifle turned upside down to protect the barrel from the rain. The man looked at them with caution at first, but then waved at Sergeant Sidney. Henry wondered how fast that guard would flip the weapon around and point it at him if they were caught by the base authorities.

There were two more soldiers standing by another door, who opened it as the truck approached and motioned for them to enter. Henry drove into the cavernous space and the heavy door rattled closed behind him. He worried about the wet tire tracks leaving a trace on the clean floor. Somewhere in the distance a dog barked. A man and woman moved with smooth efficiency and already had several crates of materials ready to be loaded onto the truck. They dropped the back hatch, which made a loud clank in the dark, quiet warehouse cavern, and used a forklift to shovel in several pallets of material. Henry and the man muscled the pallets using used lever bars on wheels to move them to the front of the truck bed and get ready for the next stack of items. Once they had gathered what was needed from that warehouse and tied it down, Sergeant Sidney, who had returned from seeing how Trey was doing, looked at his list, checked it off, and directed Henry to drive over to the next one. The two Marines cleaned the floor and clipped metal binders to seal the door of the warehouse as they left, then went with Sidney, all three riding on the truck's running boards to repeat the procedure to gather and load whatever material was next on the shopping list.

As they were almost through collecting the materials from the next warehouse, Sergeant Sidney got call on his walkie-talkie. Henry, standing nearby, overheard the whispered voice. "Get out of sight and close the doors. Major Wheeler is on OD duty and is taking an unscheduled drive around the base. He'll be on top of you in three minutes."

The three Marines rushed to the doors and made sure they were locked in case anyone came by to rattle them. The doors, however, did not have the seal on the outside indicating they had been secured. Sergeant Sidney turned down the external speaker on his radio and put in an earplug to hear any more messages. They killed any lights and sat still in the dark. The clicking of the forklift motor as it cooled in the dark sounded to Henry like someone beating on a brass bucket with a hammer. He felt he could hear its echoes in the enormous, dark repository. Henry wondered if the rain had washed away the tracks of the big truck driving on the tarmac outside the warehouse and entering this space. In his nervousness, he felt a strong urge to pee. One of the Marines was looking out of a small window in the door that telescoped the action on the other side, like a hotel door security device. Waiting in the dark, Henry felt like it had been forever since Sergeant Sidney had gotten the alarm.

Finally, the corporal watching the door raised her hand head high and pressed it down for additional quiet, as though that were possible. They hoped the rain on the warehouse roof made enough noise to muffle extraneous sounds. In the distance, the motor of a Humvee jeep passed by outside.

She turned back to them, and they could see her in the dim security lights as she rolled her eyes. They decided to wait longer, and a few minutes later, Sergeant Sidney heard an "all clear" in his earpiece. They continued going through the list and traveled to several other warehouses.

By the time they had finished, it was close to five a.m. and the rain had stopped. They rejoined Trey and parked both trucks back in the same spot, next to rows of many other similar looking trucks. One of the Marines dragged a small tarpaulin back and forth over the tire tracks on the still damp concrete, moving backward to the main lane leading to the warehouses to muddle the trail of the tires.

In the rear of one truck, there were stacked boxes of alternators, generators, powerful magnets, two large industrial sized generators, and extra coupling cables. They also had several thick rolls of various grades of heavy-duty copper wire. With the help of the Marines, they found some fittings that would work with alternative power sources such as solar and wind, and also grabbed several portable solar powered devices with the solar panels rolled up like a small rug. After all, the Marines could not always count on gasoline where they deployed. They also obtained several large crates of generic medical supplies and field medical supply kits. They were not sure if these were the meds the hospital really needed, but felt they would expand the inventory available at Phoebe Putney. They also packed a large crate of coffee.

In the other truck, they had piled crates of large batteries, MREs, and crates of freeze-dried food. Then they added weapons and ammunition, including several crates of M-16s with sound suppressors, MP5 submachine guns with sound suppressors, M18 9mm pistols, Claymore mines, hand grenades, grenade launchers, and ammunition. Henry got several crates of .223 cartridges and extra magazines. He knew that the M-15 or AR-15 was a popular weapon with homeowners and they needed the ammunition. They also got several sniper rifles with suppressors and ammunition, plus communications gear so the shooters could talk to each other from a distance. To this, they added shaggy ghillie suits for camouflage, night vision equipment, additional communication equipment, and sophisticated, battery-powered walkie-talkies.

As part of the arrangement, Sergeant Sidney was going to drive a fuel hauler with a large capacity container full of gas over to Bobo's surplus store the next day. The fuel would be transferred to smaller containers in the back room of the store, picked up by the sheriff's people a day later, and taken to the hospital to run the big generators there.

The machine guns they "procured" were the 7.62mm M240, which was the US military designation for a .30 cal. machine gun. It was a proven weapon that weighed almost thirty pounds and was fed with belts of ammunition that weighed seven more pounds per hundred rounds, which meant it needed to be used with a tripod. However, as a utility light machine gun, it provided a welcome sense of security.

Later that morning, after the sun came out to dry the concrete, Sidney walked past the trucks and knocked on the doors, giving the signal to Henry and Trey that it was safe to get up off the truck floor. They drove the heavily loaded vehicles slowly off the base with written orders from Sergeant Sidney that the trucks were to be taken away for civilian maintenance. They first stopped briefly at the surplus store for appearances before driving to a warehouse in town where Sheriff Dozer and others waited to unload.

Bobo and the other employees at the surplus store now had more money than they had ever seen at one time. The Marines on the base who helped now had wads of cash to use however they could find a way and place to spend it. More importantly, after talking with the Marines all night, Henry now had a confirmation from the government, however indirectly, that there was a catastrophic shift in the world going on, and that even the government and the military were frightened of the consequences.

Two large military cargo trucks are not inconspicuous, even though it was almost noon when they got the trucks off the base and headed back to the militia staging area. The trucks, painted with military colors and signage, attracted the attention of many people on the street, and watch committees from several neighborhoods sent in word of the trucks passing through their area to the central office over the hand cranked phones.

A county police car picked them up and gave them an escort for the last few blocks to a series of maintenance shelters that had been converted into the militia compound, once used for the city and county trucks and other equipment. There, Sheriff Jerico Dozier congratulated them and began to supervise the distribution of materials.

Henry set aside some of the energy producing equipment, medical supplies, and military hardware for the swamp as he had promised. He would borrow a truck and use some of the city's precious gas supply to deliver them as soon as they were packed.

Jerico called the mayor to come to see what they had gotten, and after a thorough review of the inventory, Lamar Ballard declared that he was impressed.

Julian Cordell and the energy committee took most of the energy equipment, including the alternators, generators, cables, couplers, magnets, and wire. Some of it was designated for the hospital and a couple of the higher priority places, and the rest was to be used to make new parts and equipment to generate more energy to be evenly distributed in the neighborhoods. Jerico got one of his deputies to take the medical supplies over to the hospital, and to tell the crew at the loading dock to get to them to his daughter, Iris, for distribution.

Mayor Ballard walked over to Henry, who was at the truck packing the supplies for the swamp. "That's quite a haul you're putting in that truck. What you planning on using it for?"

"Out where I live, folks are gonna be on their own. Those supplies will get them better armed and situated to last through whatever is coming."

Ballard licked his lips and took another swallow of coffee from the fresh supply obtained at the base, then smiled. "What you have on that truck is exactly what we all need to survive. Everything we have is falling apart." He looked around. "You know under normal circumstances, I'd have you and your buddy in the slammer and would be pressing local and federal charges for what you did last night, but these are not normal circumstances." He took a deep breath and looked fondly at the coffee cup.

"Sir, I know all that but..." Henry pointed to the truck loaded with material for the swamp. "I made a deal, and the stuff in that truck is part of that deal. You know that."

The mayor put the coffee cup down and leaned in toward Henry. "That's kind of my point. You are turning out to be a big help to us here in town. We need people with your skills working with us," he waved his hand, "not hunkering down in a hole way out there by yourself. I'll gladly let you take that stuff you say you... purchased... and drop it off. Then I want you back here. We need you to keep on coaching others that will be needed to defend Albany. Also... We could use some more of the people with your skills here."

"That's kind of what I've been talking about with the sheriff." Henry looked over at Dozier, who had been standing about six feet away. Through the visits with Iris, he had come to think of the sheriff as a second father.

Dozier nodded. "Well, you know Henry's already started training our law enforcement folks in some of that sneaky stuff, and he and some of his buddies have started to do it for others."

Mayor Ballard raised his eyebrows. "I didn't know you had already started with more people on that. Good."

"Well, you got a lot on your plate. Now you know."

Henry interrupted, "I'll be back here later today, and I'll bring others if I can convince them to come to help your folks. There are already a couple of our people working with the militia." He pointed, "My friend Trey over there and a guy named Bubba you haven't met. I've already started to discuss this with more of my friends who live out of town. You need to think of the snipers as your first line of defense, and a way to gather intel.

"We'll need to continue to look out for fit young people who already are good shots. They will prove our greatest asset. Some things you don't have time to train. My daddy has told me for years that people who can fight invisibly and from a distance are worth many times their actual number, so if I have the time, I'd like to train several more teams of snipers or scouts. They will not only be valuable in a fight, but they can go out in all directions and bring you information from the field and spy on invaders or whoever are your enemies. You will need that if we get into a real fight. We can show others the general military stuff, but to be sneaky in the woods, it takes time to train a special person."

Henry walked away to give directions on distributing the military hardware from the trucks, and then drove the pickup truck load to the swamp. Mayor Ballard stood talking with Sheriff Dozier. Ballard nodded, "That boys got some skills."

"He does. You know, it was his idea to get all this stuff from the Marine Base, and he came up with almost half the money."

Ballard's forehead wrinkled. "I'm conflicted about what we are doing. We're on a path that will take us out of normal legal niceties and getting into a might-makes-right situation."

Dozier kicked the dirt. "That we are. Don't know what the alternative is though. We've got to secure what we have first, and then bring back what we had before our leaders failed us."

The mayor exploded a loud breath. "Goes against my grain. Anyway, that boy Henry's been a big help. I hear he's been over at the hospital… Visiting."

"Yeah. He's been over to the house for dinner several times. Don't know much about his background, but he seems solid."

"I thought I remembered one or two others who had their eye on her."

"Well, she's had lots of attention and she's exceptional in many ways. I'm guessing the days of any father hoping his daughter would marry a Wall Street Harvard graduate or a Silicon Valley computer nerd are over. Women may be better off today marrying somebody who can repair a generator, raise chickens, or who knows how to dig a well. Whatever she decides to do, I know she'll make a good decision."

"Yep. Despite all you have been through over the past few years, you are a lucky man, Jerico. Oh look, speak of the devil."

Iris brought her father a sandwich, as these days he was often so busy he forgot to eat. Earlier, she had inventoried the new supplies at the hospital and was curious to see what else they had. She talked to Jerico and Mayor Ballard for a few moments, then walked over to see what additional medical supplies were near one of the trucks. As she was going over the items and looking at the materials, Trey and two of the other men who were unloading the trucks stopped to talk to her. They had started a celebratory drinking contest two hours before with one of the rare bottles of liquor one of them had stashed for an occasion like this. Iris had met Trey before when she had seen him with Henry. As Iris and Trey talked, the other men took a load of MREs to the central food warehouse.

"Trey, tell me about it."

Trey was elated at the success and stimulated by the booze, lack of sleep for the past two days, and the excitement of getting off the base undiscovered. "We had quite a night. Sent you some supplies over to the hospital."

"Thank you. I heard you might have some more here so I came to look. How was Henry?"

"Iris, you should have seen your boy. He was just great."

"Well, I didn't know much about what you were going to do beforehand. I think he and my father were the ones talking about it. I heard something about Henry getting some money to buy some stuff." She looked around. "I guess it was for this."

"Yeah. He is so good at figuring out how to do these things. Man, the Marine Base thing was lots more complicated than hitting the banks."

Iris shook her head. "I... I don't know what you are talking about?"

Trey drew himself up with wide eyes, suddenly sober, and realized what he had said. "It's just an expression. Don't mean nothin." He started to move away toward the other truck. "You'd have been real proud of him. Anyway, I've got to get this next load ready 'fore those guys get back. You take care now." Trey climbed into the back of other truck and moved toward the front of the interior to be hidden by the baggage, out of the way where Iris could no longer see him.

Bobo

Bobo came to visit the supply depot a few days later, where Henry was instructing a group of snipers. Henry stopped the trainees for a rest from running around the container boxes placed as obstacles in an urban warfare environment. "Bobo, what's going on?"

"Did you hear what happened at the Marine Base?"

"I've been stuck here organizing this stuff and training scouts. Don't know how I'd hear anything about the Marines."

"Well, those trucks rolling through town got some city official's attention named... Goodwin or Godwin, who got in touch with the colonel. He made the colonel think somebody had gone around behind his back and got the Marine Base to help Albany. It embarrassed him, so he sent some motor pool major named Wheeler over to ask me what I knew about it. I told him that I'd sold you those trucks for the city to use, and he said before I do that, I should ask them for permission first.

"Well, I told him that anything that happened on my side of that fence was none of his business. He didn't like that very much, and took a hard look at my inventory. Anyway, they've tightened down everything at the base. Stepped up perimeter security. I've afraid what you got on that midnight trip is likely to be the last haul you're gonna get."

"Did Sergeant Sidney or any of the others get in trouble?"

"Nah. The colonel and them on the base don't know what happened, but they are starting to get suspicious something like that could happen, so that's why they tightened the screws."

The Militia Matures

Using some of the additional weapons Henry brought out of the Marine Base to supplement personal rifles, Sheriff Dozier and others began to organize the younger and fitter citizens into a company of military squads and units. They divided the town up into sectors to patrol, then continued to construct the barricades at choke points on roadways using Jerico Dozier's remaining bales of plastic. With the hand cranked phones creating their own electricity and extra wire from the Marine Base, they also developed a system of communications to alert each other when anyone needed help from a serious threat. Dozier hoped that when the people they sent to Leslie's telephone museum returned, they would have more equipment to use to improve the hastily rigged communications network for the barricades they had started earlier.

They continued to implement the plan to co-opt people in the surrounding towns to mutually support and trade with each other, and to expand that perimeter for additional protection. Every person in the militia was given instructions on how to defuse tension and tone down heated rhetoric. They began to roleplay at the choke points, teaching the defenders how to talk down hostile invaders. At the same time, they practiced small unit combat and sniper tactics to be ready for whatever came down the road that might be averse to polite conversation.

Henry and his colleagues from the swamp also started intensive drills to teach stealth and sniper tactics to a band of excited students. After weeding out those who were not fit emotionally or physically, Henry began a new class of snipers with a group of the ten most promising applicants.

They selected people who were already good shots, but they did not actually fire the weapons often to save ammunition. He taught them about camouflage, being quiet, staying hidden, and anticipating their opponent. They practiced until they were all good at hiding and being aware of moving in the woods. Henry also infused in them the importance of being sneaky. They often came in from the intense workouts soaking wet, sweating from the tension of hiding and the humid heat of the summer. When he thought they were ready, Henry turned them over to his two associates for group exercises and took on another group of rookies.

The other two teachers, Trey and Bubba, had learned the basics about stealth years earlier, and took the graduates from Henry's course into the second phase of working as a team to employ the basic sniper tactics Henry had taught them.

As those students graduated from sniper school, they began to teach the lessons they had learned to other militia members in the neighborhoods and took turns guarding the barricades. They particularly focused on being quiet, accurately reporting what they saw, maintaining discipline, and street-to-street fighting. It took some time to upgrade the defenses, and during that time, they realized how vulnerable they all were from the real danger of hungry, scared people coming to take the little they had.

At first, the attacks came to the furthest outlying places - small farms or suburban houses with big lots on the edge of town. There, a small group of people would rush in and take whatever the people had, sometimes kidnapping kids for later ransom or threatening women, then rush back to where they came from. These attacks had been ongoing, and before there was not much that could be done to prevent them. As Henry trained the snipers, however, they learned to follow the trails and take back what had been stolen. When they found the thieves, a fight often ensued, which sometimes involved killing the outlaws. On one occasion, an Albany sniper-scout was wounded and another was killed. After an attack far to the west, militia members tracked the culprits for two days. The band of pillagers were routed, and one of the sheriff's deputies found some supplies in the camp from an earlier attack on a hunting plantation lodge on Gillionville Road, where the overseer and his wife had been killed.

The snipers intensified their practice, and rumors of their abilities began to spread to the outlying communities. Afterwards, the threats ceased from almost every small band of criminals intent on harming the people of Albany. They extended the boundaries of the protective perimeter slowly by one farm or small crossroads community at the time. Gradually, they either found out who wanted to be left alone, or who wanted to join them in a cooperative environment of self-preservation.

Henry and Iris were having one of their lunches, sitting on a bench in Tift Park, when she changed the conversation from her concerns about hospital shortages. She looked up at him from her head tilted to the side and said, "I saw your friend Trey when you brought back all that stuff from the Marine Base.

Thanks again for the medicine, by the way."

Henry scuffed a pinecone out of the way. "I'm just glad we could help, and that they had those supplies where we could get at them."

"Me too. My father mentioned that you helped to purchase the supplies with some money. It made me wonder how you got your hands on a that much money to help everybody here."

Henry rubbed his foot in the dirt where the cone had been. "Where I live, we had some money saved, and money is not worth much these days."

Iris put down her water bottle and looked at Henry. "Well, thinking back to the day you brought all that back from the base... Like I said, I was talking to Trey."

"Yeah."

"He said something about how skilled you are at organizing and 'hitting the banks.' So, what was that about?"

Henry's shoulders slumped as he stared at the ground. He tried to breathe normally and waited a few moments to gather his thoughts. "I have not been completely honest with you and your father about everything in my background." He looked around at the trees, with the leaves blowing in the soft breeze and the light shining through, then turned to her.

"You've never been back there where I grew up. I have lived with a group of people who didn't like the government and have lived off the grid, and sometimes outside the lines of the law. Now, we've never done anything to hurt anyone directly or anything like that. However, starting when I was still very young, some of the people, including my father, would take money illegally from places where the insurance would repay them."

"Like robbing banks?"

"Well, yeah. They'd take just enough to get them by for a several months or a year. They were always careful not to hurt anyone, and they were sure that the money they got was from a place where the government would pay it back."

"Henry, that's still stealing. It's a federal crime. It's criminal!"

"Yes, it is... or was." Henry looked back down.

"You said 'they.' What about you?"

"When my dad got sick… Too sick to go and get the money, I was asked, or I guess I was expected to take his place. So, I did."

"Henry, your father had a hard time in the military and couldn't get along in regular society. He moved into a swamp and trained himself into becoming a bank robber. I don't see anything particularly noble in all that. However, that was his choice. Just because he did, it is no reason for you to make the same decision."

Henry flushed. "Look, at first it gave me respect from those folks out where I lived. Made me feel responsible. Then there was a kind of bad boy cool to it. That was before I realized how stupid and naive I was being, and how I could get shot or put in jail. After that, I never liked it and did not want to do it, but everybody depended on me. It's not who I am. It is what I had to do."

"That's no excuse, and don't blame this on your father or other people. He had his life to live and you have yours. I don't think he's the kind of man who would hide behind you for something he did wrong, like you're suggesting.

"God! Here I thought I had found a man I could admire

and trust. You are not some over-confident blowhard. I have spent so many years taking care of my parents and working to help people at the hospital. I've turned down the advances of so many men who didn't have the combination of qualities you seemed to have. Now…" She broke off.

Henry nodded. "You're right to be thinking like that. I was not up front with you, but my worry about going to jail seemed like a good reason not to talk about it. That… and we stopped robbing the banks when the economy started to crash. I don't want to seem like I'm a bad person to you, but I'm telling you the truth. That's where the money we used to buy the supplies from the Marine Base came from. Doesn't excuse what I did."

"My God." Iris exhaled a long breath. "This is a lot to digest. You realize that if we were not in this current situation, I'd march you down and turn you into my father myself." She thought with her head down for a few moments then looked back at him. "You don't seem like a criminal, and I just don't know how to process what you have done in the past." She looked away from him.

Henry nodded. "Whatever you decide to do is okay with me. Well, not really…"

"Why don't you stay here, and I'll walk on back to the hospital on my own? I'll need a few days to think about all this."

Mayor Ballard walked up to Sheriff Dozier watching the team exercises for a platoon of the main militia as about forty young men and women were running around a track. "Jerico, those folks look worn out. You may be pushing them too hard."

"Naw, they're just malnourished. Even with extra rations, they can't hold up to exercise like people used to do. They're stymied by the lack of calories and protein. Still, they got to train. It's not easy taking a group of average citizens with limited military backgrounds and organizing them into a functioning fighting force."

As a group trudged by, the sheriff shouted, "You folks look smart out there, the mayor came to see how you were doing." A few of them gave a feeble wave.

Jerico leaned closer to the mayor. "Got to keep them encouraged to make up for being so out of shape. Some of them alternate from being afraid of a real threat from the outside one minute to thinking that these maneuvers are an exhausting waste of time in the next." He waved his hand at the mayor. "Just a sec." Then he shouted across the track at a laggard. "Pick it up, Jessie!"

He shook his head back at the mayor. "Most of these folks are used to watching television and drinking a six pack of beer as their main form of entertainment. Now they're walking several miles a day and moving heavy objects to build barricades and crawling under obstacles and rushing around in a group formation while carrying weapons."

"Why couldn't you get people who were more fit to start with?"

"For this military team, we need people who will follow orders, be disciplined, and can already shoot fairly well. Aerobics instructors may not fit that criteria. Besides, we don't have the ammunition to teach people how to shoot from scratch."

"I thought you were making bullets."

"We can make the projectile, reuse spent cartridge cylinders again, and we're making something like gunpowder. The problem is in the primer. It's small and precise, and you really need special equipment to make a bunch of explosive devices charge the bullet when it's hit by the firing pin. We're working to make them by hand with the college engineers and an old watch repair guy. They're trying to make equipment to press and crimp small bits of metal, but they need to be safe and not blow up in someone's face when they go to use them, so that's a work in progress." As they were talking, another group jogged past.

Mayor Ballard made a sad face, remembering his days running track in college, "Well, gotta keep it up. We're hounding the neighborhood militias to get fit also. Got to keep pushing them on practicing the military maneuvers. Managing all the food we need to get in here is linked with our security." He waved and smiled at another batch running by and spoke to them for the first time. "Keep up the good work, folks. We're all counting on you."

Jerico leaned back toward the mayor. "That ought to do it. I'm sure with your encouragement, they'll all want to run another five miles."

Ballard made a half smile, still looking at the exhausted runners. "You know where you can put that sarcasm. Now, get me up to date about those rumors of big attacks on other towns and stories about the raids on our perimeter farms and neighboring homesteads. The worst rumors we've heard filtering in were of cannibalism. That has frightened everyone, but no one's got any proof that those whispers are real."

The sheriff got a serious look on his face. "So far, outside of Cordele, most of that stuff about big raids are just rumors, and we're sending people out there to check them out. We've had some conflicts and poaching between neighborhoods, so our people put strict rules in place for the theft of food. That mostly stopped when we tracked down the perpetrators of those raids and three people were executed."

Ballard forced out a breath. "Tough stuff."

"Yeah, but some of the neighboring small towns, like Leesburg and Smithville, have now joined us and shared resources in exchange for protection. It's an ad hoc expansion of our defensive perimeter, and some of it does not fit into a logical military defensive formation. Still, working together has created stronger bonds and some people from those communities came into the militia program. See those four over there?" He pointed. "They're from Leesburg. Now, give me an update on what you've been doing on the food."

"The feed stocks for the chicken, cattle, and pig producing farms near us ran low, so we're keeping the breeding stock on those farms to continue to produce food animals and now we're using any of the remaining nourishment to feed those animals. We're using some of the excess animals as barter with other towns to get other things we need instead of letting them starve. That sort of trade has become the new way of commerce.

"Henry's scouts can watch and listen, and if they detect signs of potential cooperation that seems promising, then we start a second phase of outreach. For that, we're using anyone who knew people or had close relatives in the potential expansion area. Often, we'll pair them with lawyers to help negotiate. Together, they walk into those communities, propose cooperation, and try to close a trade deal. They set up a barter exchange with guidelines and rules that are acceptable to everyone involved."

The sheriff wiped his face. "I've been busy with the military exercises, but that all sounds good to me."

Mayor Ballard continued, "We also decided to divide the rest of the excess livestock among the neighborhood groups so each could share their own food and feed those animals from their own gardens, shrubs, lawns, hedges, or whatever they could find to prolong their lives and stretch out the food sources. The agricultural extension staff told everyone what was safe to feed the animals and what was not. The neighborhoods can decide when to slaughter the animals and divide the food. That gives some autonomy to the neighborhoods, which they seem to like."

"I bet your friend Larry Godwin enjoys having control over that in his sector."

"If it'll keep him off my back, he can be lord of the chickens for all I care."

Sheriff Dozier leaned and stretched. "Look, I think we're doing what we can with food and security. If we can get this band of militia up to speed and trained over the next few months, maybe up to a thousand part-time soldiers, and if the food can get stabilized, we may make it. Once we've got a significant perimeter established, I don't think we will have to worry so much about armed forces traveling more than eighty or a hundred miles to try to take over Albany. They wouldn't have the supply lines to support a big enough force for such an attack."

Ballard nodded. "Yeah. A large military force trying to live off the land would starve because that food is already being eaten by everybody who lives there. I still feel sorry for those people when I hear the rumors of tragedy out there. While our food supplies continue to dwindle, we can't afford to help people like we used to. Everybody's getting depressed. Lots of people are eating their family pets. Doesn't matter that most of the pets would have likely died without the supplies of pet food, and most of them were no longer hunters on their own. Squirrels and rabbits are valuable for human food now, and even they're getting scarce. It's hard to stay upbeat and it smells so bad everywhere. I'm continuing to promote music festivals and plays for entertainment and a distraction from the situation. We just don't hear many people laughing anymore."

Iris asked Henry to meet her out at the farm while her father was busy putting up one of the barricades. He sat with Midnight and rubbed the big dog's head, along both of his sides, over the backbone, and down to the legs. Midnight usually wagged his tail or made some sound of pleasure, but with this ultimate rub, stood still as though he was afraid it would stop if he moved. Henry concentrated on Midnight, anticipating the conversation he did not wish to have.

"How often did you commit these bank robberies?"

He kept looking at the dog as he spoke. "Once or twice a year for several years."

"And this... Community where you live... They couldn't just go out and get jobs to earn money like other people?"

Henry leaned back and looked at Iris, giving her his full at-

Island in the Storm

tention, "I grew up in that world. I didn't invent it. Iris, no amount of me talking about it is going to make it right or make me not guilty of what I did. I can go and tell your father-"

She interrupted, "No. He really likes you. It would break his heart to find this out now when you've been such a good help to him, and to everybody. He needs you right now. He's told me of several things you have done, and ideas of yours that have made a big difference. I'm not going to say anything to my father, but I hate it that you have put me in this position. I... We can't do this to him right now."

Henry rubbed his knees nervously several times as he was looking at Iris. His motion, however, attracted Midnight, who pushed his big head harder on Henry's leg, which caused him to continue to rub the massive dog. Henry said, "Why don't we just try to get through this time for now? I have a good many more things I need to be doing to help, and if, after this is over, if I've not sort of redeemed myself, we can go to your father then." Henry stopped rubbing and moved his hands. Midnight kept his big head on Henry's leg and sighed for him to continue, then let out a loud doggie yawn and walked in a tight circle twice before laying down between them.

Iris watched. "You have become a big part of our lives... of my life. Okay. I don't know how, but I'll try not to think about you and your history for now."

She hesitated. "I heard about how we are working with the people who live north of town, up in Leesburg and all up the Kinchafoonee Creek area."

"Yeah. That worked out well. We're getting most of our chickens from them now. We're also going to get some breeding chickens from them to grow our own stock here closer to town.

Some of their men and women are training with us on the military stuff."

"I'm just wondering how long our luck will last. There really hasn't been any serious fighting yet."

"Not yet."

"You don't think that's going to last?"

"Like you said, we've been lucky."

"I know. I need to find some people who have experience in wound treatment, then I and can set up classes at the hospital for more people to learn how to do that. Maybe the Marine Base or the university can help."

"I hate to say it, but that would be a wise move."

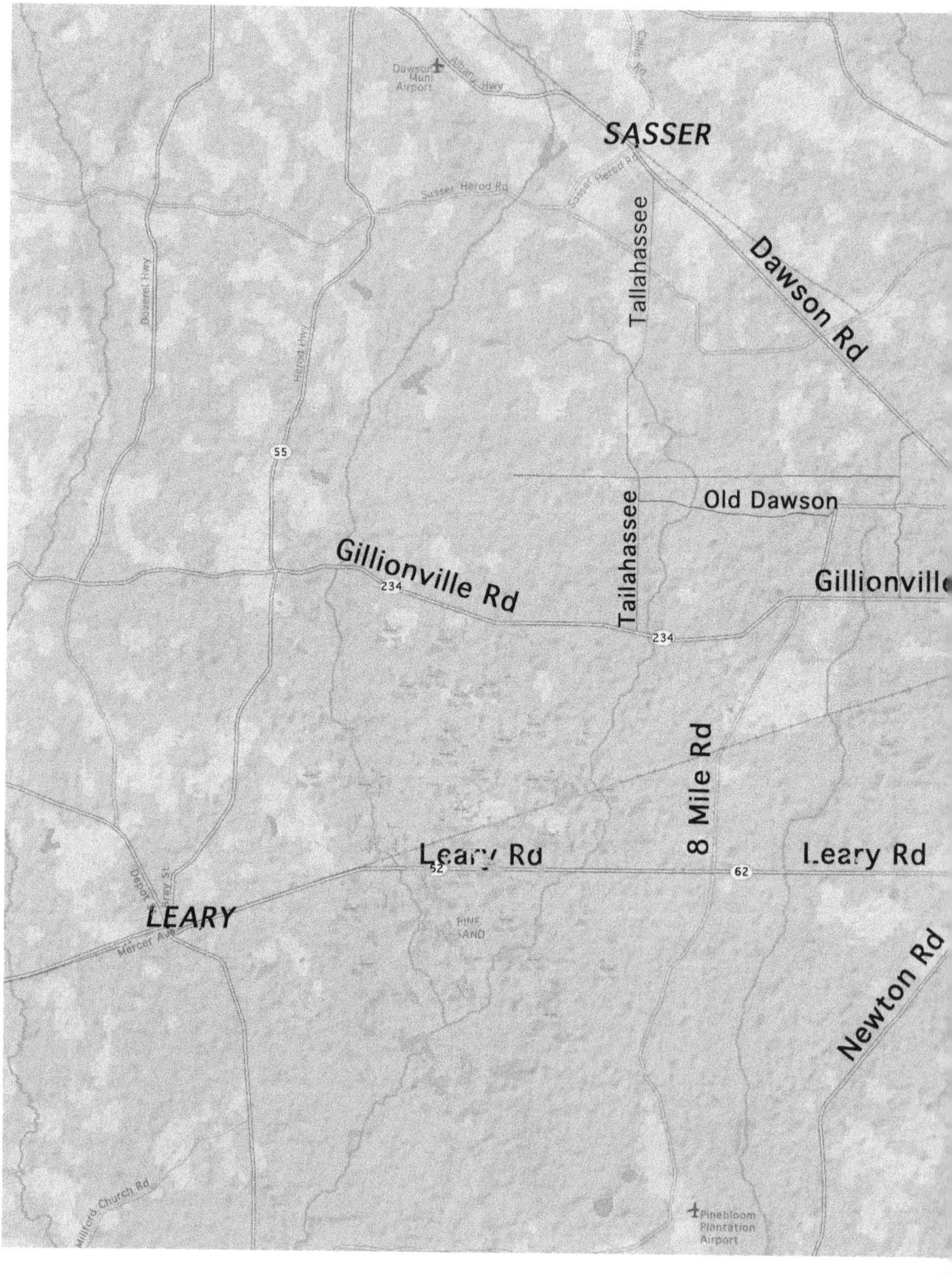

SASSER
Dawson Rd
Tallahassee
Old Dawson
Tallahassee
Gillionville Rd
234
Gillionville
234
55
8 Mile Rd
Leary Rd
52
62
Leary Rd
LEARY
Newton Rd
Sasser Herod Rd
Pinebloom Plantation Airport

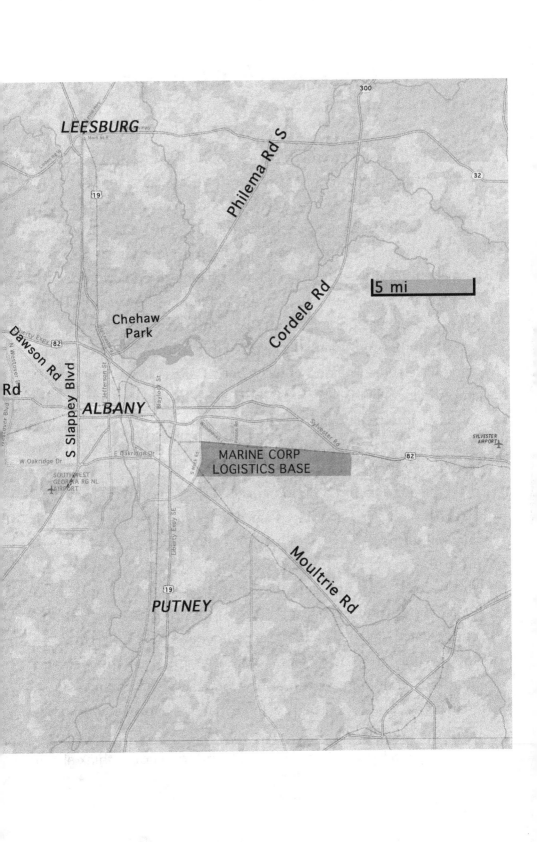

South of Albany

In the early morning hours, twenty miles south of Albany near Putney, three men slowly crawled under the fence, checking for movement or any sign of other people across the large field. It had rained the night before. The ground was still wet and a foggy haze clung to the earth. Through night vision goggles, they could see the structures of a large farm three hundred yards ahead, and planned to circumvent the field using the windbreak trees, other surrounding vegetation, and fences as cover.

Before the crawl, they added bits of twigs and leaves to the ghillie suits obtained at the Marine Base to make them blend into the local landscape even more. Two hours later, as the light of day came to illuminate the area, Henry Graham was in a position in the weeds less than fifty yards from a wide yard set up with benches and stools for a coming meeting.

He continued an imperceptibly slow motion forward until he finally reached a point close enough to hear what was going on as the meeting started. The other two gave him cover from the thicker woods two hundred yards back. He watched the people arrive and settle down into small groups until there were about forty people gathered. Most of them were armed with rifles or shotguns and wore camouflage hunting clothes. As they waited, they drank water from the spigot on the well and snacked on homemade bread the housewives had supplied. A man came out of the house with two others and everyone gathered closer together.

Henry blended into the rough and tried not to think about

Island in the Storm

any of the bugs crawling over him or the dampness from the wet grass. He cleared his mind of extraneous thoughts and focused his attention on what was about to be said so he could report back. Nothing else mattered.

One of the men who had come from the house walked across the field swinging his arms with the self-assurance of someone in charge and stood in front of the others. "'Preciate all you boys coming here today. You two, no… three ladies also. Thought we all should talk about the mess we're in and decide what to do about it." He spat between his teeth to the side, put one leg up on a nearby stump, and leaned over on his knee. "We been doing without a lot of stuff while those folks over toward Albany got lights and all kinds of food to eat. I got family here that's hungry and think it's only right for us to have our fair share of what those folks have. They always did think they were better than us, being here in the country, and now they're showing it off."

There was some muttering in the group, but Henry, listening carefully, could not tell if it was for or against what the man with his foot on the stump was saying.

The man held out his hands and pressed them up and down a few times, which settled down the murmuring. "Now, I'm just saying we got a right to some of that electricity and food or whatever, you know, just enough for us to have some. We can take some horses and a couple of wagons and be over there, get it, and be back in the same day. Two at the most."

Someone from the back of the group said, "I don't know. I don't want to rob no one."

"Yeah," said another, "we might get shot."

The man took his foot down from the stump and stood

taller, stretching his back. He dribbled his hands up and down in the air again to quiet the crowd. "Now hold on. I'm not talking about anyone getting shot or killed. I thought if enough of us went over there, we could just get them to 'volunteer' to give us some stuff. They don't want trouble any more than we do, but the fact remains that all the stores around here are out of food. We don't have any power for no electricity. We gotta do something." He walked into the middle of the pack and looked around the circle. "But I'll tell you what... I'm ready to do what-ever I gotta do to help my family, and that includes taking my gun over there and gettin' what I need." He pulled out a pistol, waved it around in the air, and put it back in his pants.

There was more muttering. This time, more voices were agreeing with what the man who owned the farm was saying. More of the group edged toward the man doing the talking, drawn to him in support, although some still stood over on the side looking doubtful.

The man held up his hands. "I bet if we went over to the Marine Base where they have all those supplies, they'd give us some. We're all Americans here, and if we demanded our fair share, they'd have to cough it up."

There was more muttering from the crowd.

Henry, moving carefully so as not to shake the tall grass, laid his rifle on the ground and slowly stood up. He held his hands out to the side. "Couldn't help but overhear what you folks are talking about."

The bunch turned quickly toward the new voice behind them, most holding their weapons toward him. Many of them looked puzzled at the bulky ghillie suit. Henry slowly reached up to take the hood off the suit to reveal his head. "I'd like to talk to you good people about what you have been saying."

The owner of the farm, who had been doing most of the talking, squinted at Henry, walked to the front of the pack and shouted out toward the stranger, "Who the hell are you sneaking up on us. You look like a damn bush. We ought to shoot you down right here right now."

Henry walked a few paces toward them slowly, still with his hands raised. "Well, I'd appreciate it if you didn't do that 'cause I may be able to help you with what you are talking about, and I don't care to get shot this morning. You can see my hands and I'm not holding a gun of any kind. Besides," he looked all around as though he was searching for something he had lost, "I may not be here alone."

Several of the others in the group now began to look around also, past Henry and toward the woods across a small pasture.

Henry continued to slowly lower his hands, "Now, I come in peace and want to make you an offer to get you what you want in a fairly easy trade. But... If one of you were to take a shot at me, some other people who may be out there in those woods," he turned his head in a jerking motion quickly behind him and then back to the people, "might not take kindly to that. They are hiding like I was, and they're awfully good shots."

The man who owned the farm sneered. "You're full of shit."

"Like I said my friend, I'm just here to talk. Don't mean anyone any harm."

The man pointed at the stranger and leaned back with his head, "You're some kind of nut and you are alone. Let's get him boys." He put his hand on the pistol.

Henry, looking like he was wearing a hanging plant, waved his arms up and down in the air that shook the leaves and twigs on the overstuffed cloth suit, mimicking the calming gesture the owner of the farm had used earlier. "Hold up, guys. Hear me out first. You'd be making a big mistake to rush me."

"Prove it, Mister Bullshit."

"Hold up a minute." Henry took off the rest of the baggy covering and put it on the ground near his feet. He then pointed at an iron bell that was hanging from a nearby barn. "See that bell over there."

"Yeah, so what! What you gonna…"

"Bong." The bell shook from side to side as the sound reverberated through the yard.

"What the hell?" People tensed, squatted, and looked all around in a panic, trying to figure where the shot came from.

Henry spoke to them in a soft, reassuring voice. "No worry. I just had to prove a point. No one means any of you people any harm, but that bell is about the size of your head. Now let me tell you what I came to say." He walked over to the center of the group and stopped where the owner of the farm was standing. "I'm from the people over in Albany, and we want to form a coalition with you for our mutual benefit. Some of you can bring those wagons you were talking about. I'll take you back with me and get you some food and we'll show you how to make electricity. And," he turned around in a semicircle to look at everyone, "you can bring your guns if you want to, if it will make you feel safer."

The man who had been talking still looked skeptical. "How do we know that what you say is not a trap. You might just ambush us on the road."

"We don't have any reason to trap you or do you harm. You were just saying a few minutes ago you didn't have enough food and no electricity. We just want to do business with you. We've been talking to other folks around here and think we've got a chance to develop a steady line of poultry, beef, and pork. We've also got nuts in pecans and peanuts. Our goals are to develop balanced food sources we can all enjoy.

"What we may be short of is something sweet. If you all could grow sugarcane, we can help you get a way to grind and process it. We need the sugar, and the pulp from the stalks is good for livestock. This area might also be a good place for bee-keepers. Besides, we could use your help to raise some crops on a fruit and vegetable farm we started not too far from here, near the River Bend area. You folks could be a big help by using that sawmill you have down by the crossroads with some of the electricity we can rig up. We want to trade you for those things with the stuff you need. We want to form a mutual security agreement with you to protect each other from others who might try to come in here and rob us both. Hell, we've all lived near each other for all of our lives. We have much more reason to band together than to fight."

Several people were shaking their heads affirmatively. One or two were still looking over at the bell, which was slowly stopping its swinging and returning to a position of rest. The man who owned the farm noticed that and realized this meeting had taken a different turn.

Henry continued, "So, if some of you want to learn to be a sniper-scout and sneak around like me, we'll teach you." He stepped back and picked up the suit with various lengths of strips of cloth hanging like a waterfall and tossed it over one shoulder. "So, I'll let you talk among yourselves. I hope a few of you will come on down the road with your wagons and make plans to work together."

Henry took a few steps back toward the edge of the woods, slowly picked up his rifle. and slung it over his shoulder. He turned back to face the group with a more solemn and serious face. "I hope we don't have to fight. We want to work with you and not against you. However, if that is what you choose, we'll be ready." He took a few more steps toward the woods and turned again. "Come on along with the wagons whenever you want to. We'll be watching, and will join you for the trip to get your supplies."

Report from Leslie

Jerico Dozier heard that the team he sent to acquire telephone equipment from the Leslie museum had returned. When he arrived at his office, he was surprised to see that it was filled with several scruffy-looking strangers along with the scouts he had sent. Many of his deputies were also milling around and talking to the scouts. They were filthy and scratched from hiding in briars and blackberry bushes, but had brought back the communications equipment, including a switchboard to connect the hand cracked phones at the various blockades and create a central communications center in Albany. Several people from Leslie came also, and they brought with them some bad news.

The leader of the scouts reported, "Sheriff, we had to hide most of the time nearer to the town. As we got closer, we came across several farms and houses where someone had raided and killed the people. When we finally got to Leslie, most of the place was deserted. It had been ransacked. We smelled death all around. We did, however, find these people who can tell you more. They wanted to come back with us, and they know how to make the telephone equipment work."

The sheriff looked over at the half dozen people who were dirty, ragged and still seemed to be in some state of shock. "One of you tell me what happened."

One woman wiped her hands on her stained dress, stood, and spoke for the others, "Our group here," she nodded at the others, "got away by hiding in the attic. There was an afternoon rainstorm, and when the people who came to tear up our town took shelter, we ran and hid. The rain drops on the tin roofs helped us hide the noise. We could still overhear them as they went through our stuff downstairs, and we were lucky they didn't find us. Some other folks ran off into the woods west toward Smithville."

She looked down at the floor then back up. "They killed some of our neighbors."

"I'm sorry, ma'am. Tell me exactly what happened and what you heard them say."

She spoke softly, so everyone in the cramped office had to keep particularly quiet to hear her. "They came in from the east side of town from the direction of the lake, like you were going out to Daphne Lodge, and just overran everything without any warning. They got everything we had to eat and gathered any food, guns or medicine there was in town. Anybody that resisted, they shot." She pointed to the others. "We compared what we heard later with each other. It started over in Cordele. Seems like they did the same to us as they did to the folks over there. They had just moved over to Lake Blackshear with a whole bunch of people and were going all around the lake robbing houses and raping, taking food, and whatever. Whoever was the boss of these crazy people sent some of them to clean us out, just 'cause we lived over close to the lake."

Her eyes filled with tears and she began to shake. One of the others patted her on her shoulder. She took a deep breath and continued. "They took everything they wanted. It wasn't just the taking of stuff. It was the meanness in how they did it. They humiliated people for the fun of it. Beat them. Raped. There was this evil in them like they wanted to rub our noses in what they were doing to us. Like someone told them to let it all go and hurt us as much as they could." She shook her head. "When any-one resisted, even just a little, they killed them just for fun. They loaded everything they could on some carts and took it all back toward the lake."

She brushed her hair back from her face and spoke in deep breaths. "The folks that hit us... When they went back to the lake to get reconnected with those others... Sounded like they were going to be there til they got into every house or store all around the lake. We heard them talkin' like they were an army of maybe several hundred people, and they said they were mov-ing to take Albany next."

Dozier slapped the table. The woman jumped. "Damn. Oh, sorry, ma'am. This is what we were worried about." He looked at the others from Albany in the room. "This confirms what the man from Leesburg told our border guards and the folks on the boats. Send out a notice that we have to accelerate the training. I want to see the supply people about reinforcing the barricades on the northeast side of town." He looked at the forlorn group from Leslie and then back directly at the woman. "Thank you for coming here and letting us know what happened. I'm so sorry about what went on in your town and what they did to your friends. We can use your help to stop these people. We'll get you some food and a place to stay. We have jobs for you here to help us defend this place." He nodded at one of the deputies. "Get these people some food, clothes, and a place to clean up. After that, take them to set up the telephone equip-ment." He rose and began to leave.

"That's not all." The woman fidgeted. "One of the men said he knew about some kind of radio thing they had set up. The leader of his group was talking to somebody over near Dothan. Seems like they got another small army over there. Anyway, it sounded like their aim, once they finished with Lake Blackshear, was to hit Albany from two directions at once. They kept talking about the Marine Supply Base as their main target and said something about coming by Chehaw."

Island in the Storm

Part IV -
The Apocalypse

Marine Base

Henry met again with Sergeant Sidney at the surplus store just outside the Marine Supply Base. "Sergeant Sidney, is there someone on the base I can meet with to discuss a better situation... About whether we can work together for our mutual security?"

Sidney shook his head. "I'm not sure they would be very receptive. We're sort of on lockdown."

"Look, so far we've stopped two armed groups from pushing their way into Albany. We've got them on our side now, and worked out sharing food and resources. We absorbed that potential threat to the base. Small threat, but we did it. If we had not, those armed people would have eventually found their way here. You need to let your superiors know that we saved them from the embarrassment of confronting and maybe shooting hungry American citizens."

Sidney shook his head again. "Look, I'm low ranking and don't make any decisions. Also, I'd have a hard time explaining to my superiors how we know each other. We're both still at risk if the brass finds out what we've done together."

He thought for a moment. "However, Major Shackelford,

who is in charge of base security, is actually a good woman. I'll tell her what you told me. I think you need to write her a note asking for a meeting and I can get it to her. I know the colonel stonewalled you guys, but she is easier to deal with 'cause she was a combat soldier. She's been in situations where she had to negotiate with the locals for their mutual benefit. She'll like that you helped us out, even though we didn't ask. She may know how to work the colonel and get us involved somehow. He's a supply guy, more by the book. Never been in combat like some of us. Still, there are no guarantees here. As far as I know, we have not received any different orders than to secure the base. Go over there and write the note. She's real straight forward and direct. Just lay it out to her like you would be talking to me. I'll take it back with me and get her reply to your buddy Bobo at the store."

Henry sat down with pen and paper. "Good, and when you talk to her or whoever you see in her office, give an alert that people are coming closer to Albany, big blocks of hundreds of people armed and hungry. We've heard that from more than one source. You guys are going to be tested, and soon. It would be better if we could meet this challenge together, but you all need to be ready nonetheless." He gathered himself and realized that he did use a pen and paper very often, but this was going to be the most important note he had ever written.

Preacher

Sheriff Dozier sat in the warm, stuffy church with his daughter as they had for most of the Sundays of their life, except now, because of the lack of air conditioning, they felt the stifling heat from all the bodies. Someone had found a box of old flat paper fans on sticks that people were swirling back and forth stirring the air. The appalling conditions affected everyone, and today there was a visiting preacher from one of the smaller churches in a nearby town. The regular pastor, without her normal meds, was having trouble breathing and couldn't talk for long periods of time. Visiting pastors took turns preaching in her absence. The visiting preacher today was filled passion, and seemed to take this opportunity in a large church to have a revival that would renew everyone's spirits in the face of all the hardships.

The man rocked back and forth, hanging onto the podium with both hands. His voice boomed through the sanctuary. "Now is the time. The Lord has prophesized, and the Lord will come." He looked around to make sure he had everyone's attention. "Now is the time to give your soul to God and wait for the rapture. Now is the time to repent of your sins and turn it all over to God. Now is the time to prepare. Pack your bags for heaven 'cause the final train is coming."

In a wave from the front to the back of the church, the audience moved like a sloshing ocean as people were now fanning themselves more rapidly with whatever they had in hand. The preacher had begun to sweat, with drops rolling down his forehead and onto his eyebrows, which he swiped with a finger and swatted to the side. From the back of the church, someone motivated by the soaring rhetoric and the emotion tied to the almost athletic movements of the visiting pastor said, "Tell it, preacher!"

He walked back and forth in quick steps on the raised stage at the front of the church. "You can't resist the power of God. Stop giving in to all temptations. Get ready and pray that when the Jesus bus comes by, it'll stop for you.

"Sin has finally caught up with us. Sin has caused the world we knew to fail. We didn't believe enough. We weren't ready to sacrifice enough."

"You tell 'em, preacher! Don't hold back."

In the audience, a little girl started to cry. Her sobs could be heard through the pauses and gasps for air as Pastor Jedidiah Weatherbee reloaded his pitch. The chairs and pews creaked as people shifted uncomfortably on the hardwood.

"I can't say when the last day will come, but you better get ready. I cannot help but wonder why God is punishing us for our sins. We don't have water, electricity, food, or medicine. These are like the plagues in the time of Moses. Is it because we have fallen away from our beliefs? Is it because we have been poor stewards of the land, and degraded the blessed environment our lord gave to us? Is it because we have not respected his distinction of the races and become mongrelized? Is it because we have not followed the commandments in the Bible and have been too lenient with sinners in our court systems? We can't break the commandments and be tempted to kill our fellow man. We just gotta pray for salvation.

"We're gonna look for those answers. We're gonna be saved! We're gonna hold more prayer meetings here every day. I can feel the fires of hell approaching. One thing I do know is that we all got to get down on our knees all the time, every day. I'll be here waiting for you to come. The only thing we have left is salvation. Get some while you can. I say get down on your knees and be ready. There is nothing you can do. Give it all up to the Lord and get ready for the rapture. It's time to lay down with the lambs of God. Don't fight it, 'cause hell's a coming."

He looked down and pointed. "I can see we got our sheriff here with us today. He knows it's a coming. He knows we need to get down on our knees and accept what's coming. He knows there is no need to resist. Come on up here, sheriff, and tell these people how it is. You know the end is coming and you know they need to be ready. These good people need to come here every day from now to Armageddon, from morning til night, and do nothing but pray for forgiveness. Come on up here." He waved his arm for Jerico to come onto the church stage.

Jerico felt uncomfortable with this attention and the request for him to make public statements in church. He shifted in his seat. He thought to himself that the message and style of this revival pastor was very different from what he was used to hearing in church. He sat with a strained expression on his face as the pastor continued to call him up, waving his arm in a circular motion and pulling the stale air toward him to beckon the sheriff. Finally, some of the other people in the church began to whisper to him from the aisles behind or turned to face him from the front, nodding to go on up to join the pastor. At first, Iris held his arm in restraint, then as he shifted his weight to get up, dropped her hand and let him go.

Jerico slowly rose and walked up onto the stage. The pastor stepped aside to offer him the podium. "Come up here as a good Christian man. Testify to these good people that end is here and all they can do is to pray for salvation."

Jerico was finally at the podium and stood uncomfortably for a few moments, looking around the church at people back in the rear of the sanctuary and up in the balcony before speaking. These were people he had known for many years, and now they all looked scared and uncertain.

He paused and touched the Bible resting on the podium. Then he smiled and shook his head side to side at the church audience. "Our visiting pastor reminds me of the old-time fire and brimstone preachers I used to hear when I was a child. Our visiting pastor is calling for the end of days."

There were murmurs in the audience.

He rapped the podium with his knuckle, looking down for a moment at the thick book then back up. "I guess I'm more used to a softer voice coming from the Bible." He patted the book. "I'm more used to hearing about loving each other and the messages of the Beatitudes, and how faith is about confidence and compassion and working toward loving goals. I'm used to the Good Samaritan." He stretched his back, stiff and tired from the long days and stress. "Now, nobody wants to be involved in violence, but the Bible is full of Christians standing up for what is right. People in the Bible stood up to tyranny and slavery and evil. Sometimes that meant fighting. Sometimes that meant dying.

"Our preacher here today may mean well, but he may also need to remember more about what is said the Bible." He let that sink in. There was some rumbling of whispers. "It is true that the Bible is full of despair and trials and tribulations.

"The Israelites were almost always outnumbered, however... Most stories I can remember from the Old Testament were about the Israelites overcoming long odds. Daniel in the Lion's Den, David and Goliath, all those Old Testament battles against superior odds. I remember reading in the New Testament, when the believers were persecuted by the all-powerful Roman army during the time of Christ.

"Those folks in the Bible either had faith or found faith. That's another way of saying gumption, backbone, toughness, courage. They got through their challenges by using their faith. All that stuff, which makes heroes and has moved people forward for years in overcoming the odds, is bound up in faith. I don't care what you call it. I just believe you all need to get some. Now, it is my experience… That no one hates violence more than people whose job it is to carry a gun.

"It's kinda like what is in popular literature. Same as in 'Lord of the Rings,' 'Harry Potter,' 'Narnia,' hell, whoops, 'scuse me folks, even the comic book super heroes and all the other stories of good overcoming evil. Good is outnumbered in the beginning. Good wins by putting aside our differences and working together with other good people and having courage and fortitude. Good didn't just give up.

"If every time someone listened and followed the instruction to 'give it up and prepare to meet thy God,' we'd never have gotten out of the caves."

"If you ask me, and the preacher has asked me… I think the preacher should have said, 'Get up off your ass. Find courage in the Bible, or wherever it is you go to find it, but get some and put your head down and move forward.' Preacher or no preacher, we got work to do. I think I prefer the kind of faith where we have to face adversity and plow through evil. I think it's time we got together, reach out and hold hands together, and then go out together to whip the devil."

The visiting pastor began to make a move toward the podium, but Jerico held out his hand for restraint.

"Sorry, pastor, but you called me up here to hear what I think and that's it. I love the Lord, but I don't think we were put here just to grovel and hope for the best. I think the Lord expects something back from us. The early Christians had to make a tough decision to accept Christ… Even though it meant being thrown to the lions for some of them. It took courage to overcome their fears for something greater. We have the willpower that God gave us and the strength to fight at least some of our own battles. The Bible says there is a time to reap and a time to sow. There is a time to be passive and a time to fight. It also says that God helps those who help themselves. Hell's a poppin and now is the time for us to defend ourselves, and with God's help, we will prevail. I'm asking all of you, help me to help you save this town. Show up. Take on evil. Fight for what you believe in. I think that is what God wants you to do. I'm talking righteous Old Testament whipping ass. Ask for God's help and let's get going. Join me and help the militia. Let's stand together, we've got a town to save."

When he sat back down, the mood of the church had changed. People patted him on the back as he walked to his seat.

Island in the Storm

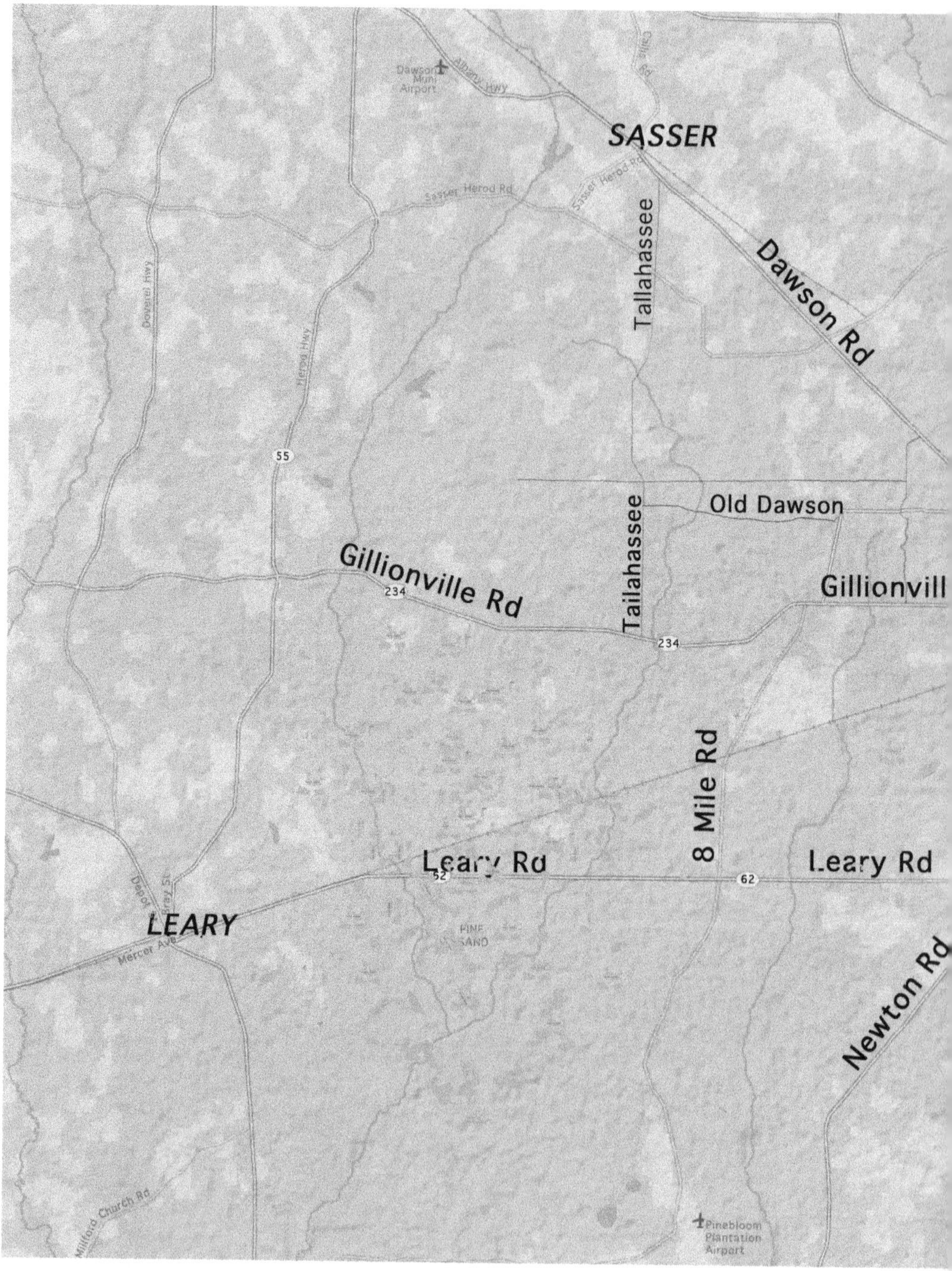

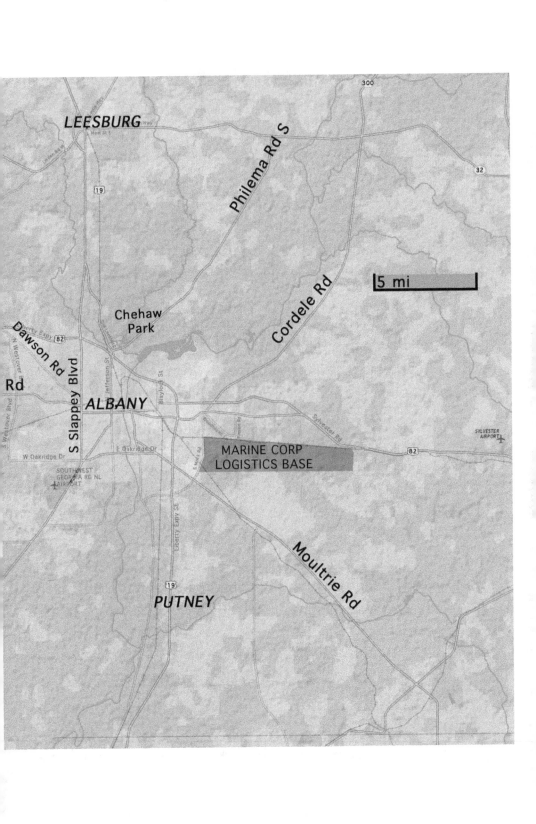

Conflict

Lamar Ballard was smiling broadly as he entered Sheriff Dozier's office. "Jerico, I have some very good news."

"I could use it. Wait. Lamar, you smell funny."

"Yeah. My wife's got me taking sponge baths with the water that's still warm from her cooking. So, I sometimes smell like whatever was in the pot. Today, I think this is eau de peas and carrots."

"Okay. I hope I can get that image out of my mind, but... Good to know. You were saying?"

"Remember several months ago we started the project to develop hothouses and places to grow food during the winter?"

"Yeah. Sort of."

"Well, the construction folks and people from the agricultural extension and colleges and others from the nearby food processing places have all come together, and we have a really good supply of locations that can be used to grow winter food. They've even put together some sort of kits that people at home can use by putting glass or plastic sheets over porches, gazebos or swing sets for home growing. Some of the bigger places even have a system of irrigation in them. I'm feeling really good about what we have put together."

"How about the harvest plans?"

"That's coming along as well. We have a lot of people ready to go into the fields to help. Every neighborhood group will be sending at least a dozen so they can make sure they get a share of the harvest to bring back with them. They tell me some of the first of the crops will be ready in a few weeks. We've set aside a percentage of the crops to be consumed later, and have gathered a big supply of jars and whatever is needed for canning. The foodies are working with some of the cooks from the old restaurants on how to preserve food through the winter months in every way they can imagine."

Dozier leaned back in his chair. "Thanks. That is good news. We've come a long way over the past months, thanks to you bugging the hell out of everybody."

Ballard smiled. "It's been a team effort, and you have certainly done your part bugging people too, including me."

"Well, maybe we will be able to survive, barely, but we can't feed more people than we have now. Even with all those who have died, we're still stretched thin. Wait, what's that noise?"

There was a quick knock, and the door opened as Henry rushed into the meeting with Sheriff Dozier and Mayor Ballard. He steadied himself from being in such a hurry. "I've got three things to report from our scouts, all bad.

"First, that family we heard about, who wanted to join us and bring their animals from the farm over near Whispering Pines Plantation between here and Lake Blackshear, well, when the scouts got there to escort them, the family was gone and so was all the produce and animals. Looks like the big gang that has been camped over at the lake sent some people to get them first. There was blood all over the house. Our people did not hang around to see what else happened. It wasn't safe.

"Second, we sent some scouts to check on that rumor of a small army coming here from the Dothan area. They found some refugees on the road who were headed out of Blakely...

Running away from that band of outlaws who were coming this way. Those people said it was true they were coming here. It's a good thing we already got some products from that White Oak Pastures farm over at Bluffton and the peanut processing place in Blakeley, 'cause they hit Blakely hard and White Oak could also be in their path.

"Our scouts said the people could not tell how many there were in the bunch that attacked them, but it sounded like a lot... More than two hundred and probably lots more. The people our scouts talked to described them as coming in a caravan to loot all the towns on the road headed toward us like a swarm of locusts. Said they were well armed and that it looked like there were lots of people wearing military uniforms in the group.

"Now, last and the most immediate news of danger we got from a woman who lives on the west side of Albany. Earlier, she was attempting to barter a couple of homemade pies over in Sasser when she heard about a gathering of all the men and women who could shoot near Dawson and some places further to the west. The rumblings, which she had to strain to hear, were for a raid on Albany by the collective forces of Dawson, Sasser, and Parrot."

Ballard slapped his knees and stood up. "We'll never be able to stop all of them. We just don't have enough trained militia troops to cover all of those barricades. Plus, we've got to watch all the side streets or they can sneak in behind us."

Henry pointed at a map and continued, "Well sir, I've got scouts monitoring all three of those directions. The biggest bunch of forces are those from Dothan and Cordele. Fortunately, they're still further out. We've got to face the bunch coming from the Dawson area first anyway. Since they are a smaller group,

Island in the Storm

maybe we can stop them in a fight or convince them to join us, like we did with those folks from Leesburg and south of town."

Dozier said, "He's right. We've got to start out west on Dawson Road. We also need to get that force of our best soldiers camped out over on Slappey Drive to be on the alert, and ready to rush as reinforcements to whatever place the attack is coming in."

Ballard nodded. "Makes sense. I'll get the word out. Henry, have your scouts keep an eye out for those coming from the Dawson area. We need to have a good idea when they're going to get here." Ballard continued, "Damn, they've been grinding grain for us. We were trading with them over at the peanut warehouse already."

Dozier nodded. "Yep. Looks like we're gonna find some people that will go back on their word." He looked over at Mayor Ballard. "By the way, you had better get the electrical workers from the power dam at Lake Chehaw ready to come back inside our perimeter on short notice."

Henry mused, "You know guys, I remember my father said there was this fear everyone had in anticipation of a fight just before it started. He said that in the old days, a lot of fighting was about supply and maneuver. It was like if one side could see the other had a better fighting position or more soldiers or could supply themselves better, they'd just pull back and try it another day. Sometimes they would do that until they both got tired and quit. Sometimes they even faked it.

"My daddy said that most sane people will not run into combat knowing they will be killed. If you show the other side that their attack is hopeless, then they might decide that they don't have to fight. Maybe we can show that to some of these people coming toward us."

Ballard asked, "You need to be more specific. What exactly are you suggesting?"

"If we get all the neighborhood militias lined up looking fierce and manning barricades all around, maybe we can bluff some of the people from attacking us just by having a lot of people out there looking tough, even though they may not be good at fighting. Even if they don't have guns, they could hold painted broom handles. We could even get some bigger pipes to stick out, and from a distance, they might look like machine guns."

Ballard smiled. "You might be right."

Jerico Dozier walked over to a map of Southwest Georgia. "Not only that. I've been studying this here." He walked over to the table, put one foot up on the chair, and leaned over on his knee. "From the southwest, we know there is a large group from Dothan coming here through Blakely. We offer them a large civilian community and the Marine Base with all its storehouses of food, gas, and weapons. We're a sugar bowl to those ants.

"They're well-armed, and it's likely there are more of them than there are defenders out at the Marine Depot. Plus, the Radium Springs blue hole is right near there, and that can provide a steady source of fairly clean water."

He tapped the map again. "They'll likely take the south road that will bring them through Leary, in by the airport, and give them a direct shot toward the Marine Base on Oakridge. However, they're limited in their approach because the swamp is on either side of the road, and that will make them come to us bunched up together like they were going through a tunnel. That's our only advantage with them.

"Henry, concentrate on getting your sniper people out to

slow down the Dothan group. Start to hit them as far out on Leary Road as you can. That's our chance."

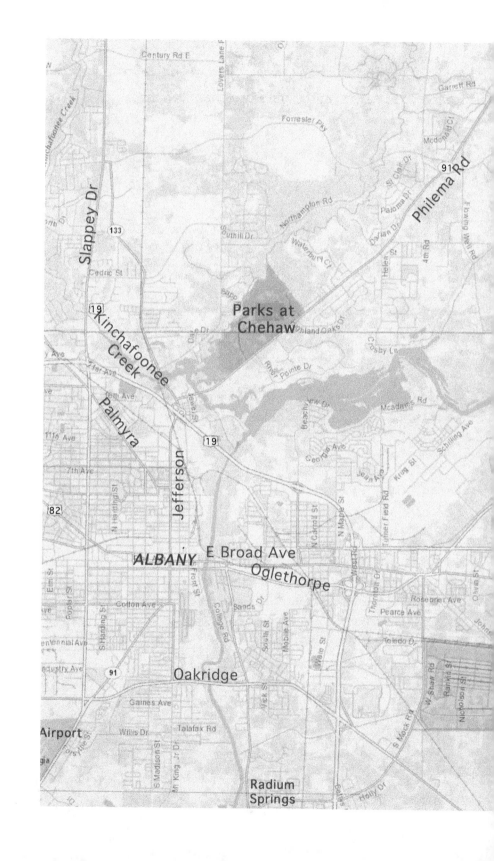

His hand moved over to the upper right side of the map showing the roads from Cordele. "This bunch staging at Lake Blackshear can choose the way they come at us, the time to come at us, and how they collect or divide their forces to come at us in separate ways. They hold all the cards. We need help, and unless the Marines get off their asses, I don't know where it's coming from. We're on a land-based island here in the middle of Southwest Georgia.

"Looks like their plan is to come here, hook up with the Dothan group coming in from the west, likely out near the Proctor and Gamble plant, and take the base. That fits with what the people from Leslie told us."

Ballard walked over to the map and looked. He tapped the map in the two places where the reports of large militias originated. "How are they communicating to coordinate this attack?"

"Don't know that. Maybe they have some kind of walkie-talkie system we don't know about," Henry mused.

Dozier said, "Anyway, we've got to watch for them coming all the time, starting now. That's going to wear down our defenders, who are already weak from hunger."

Ballard pointed. "Like Henry said, Why don't we just flood that area with neighborhood militia when those Cordele people come?"

The sheriff ran his finger over an arc of the U.S. 19 beltway northeast of Albany. "Henry's right. Pile bunches of the neighborhood militias in obvious locations where it looks like we've got every entrance covered. Let's keep the attackers from sneaking in on the side streets, and let people defend their own neighborhoods."

He looked at the map closer and tapped it at the curve of the beltway. "Not there. That's our best line of defense. We must have our best trained troops there to be effective. If a bunch of shoe salesmen and Waffle House cooks run up with shotguns they're just going to get in the way and likely get shot right off the bat. We need to make those Cordele people attack us where it looks like they have the best access, and that's where we 've got to put our best troops. That's here on the beltway.

"I'll send several of the people who have been trained as our mainline militia near the beltway and get them to push some intensive training into those neighborhoods by the hospital and out along Palmyra Road. If the Cordele people think every other avenue is well covered, then they are likely to attack us here." He slapped the map at the curve of the bypass beltway over Jefferson Street. "The neighborhoods near there are the only ones close enough to get to the barricades if we do need help. Okay, anyway, that's for later. For now, let's get over to the barricade out on Dawson Road."

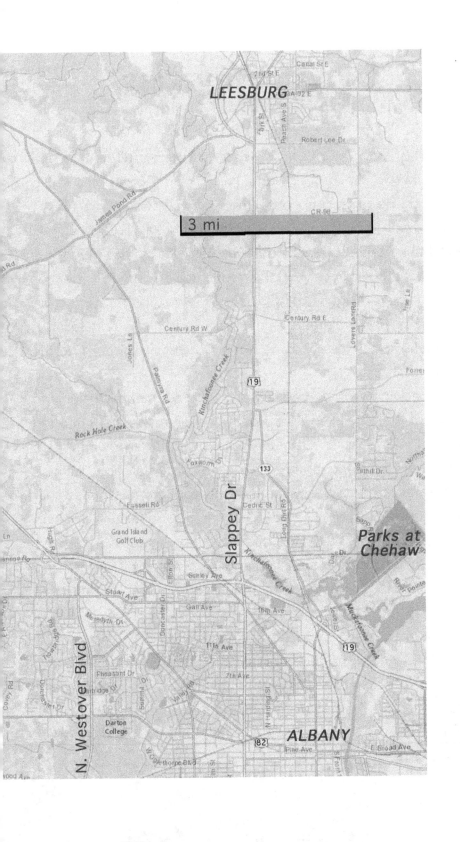

Dawson Invades

The last stray dog in Georgia crept carefully out of the woods low to the ground, one foot, then another, crouching like a cat. He inched up onto the highway separating Albany from Dawson, smelled the air, and looked left and right. He had stayed alive this long not from watching for traffic, which was nonexistent, but by avoiding the gentle voiced human entreaties of "come here doggie." He walked a few steps further across the median and smelled again. There it was, the telltale odor of humans across the road. He turned and slinked back into the woods.

Back down the road toward Albany, Sheriff Dozier and several of the regular soldiers from the main militia were headed toward the bypass on Dawson Road on battery powered golf carts when they encountered a dozen armed people walking purposefully back toward Albany, away from the barricades near the west side beltway. The people were moving fast and looking over their shoulders from the direction they came.

Dozier stopped the cart and held out his arms to stop them. "What's going on? Why aren't you all back at the barricades?"

A man who seemed to be the leader of the group first caught his breath and then pointed. "They're coming! We heard there were several hundred of them heading here now. We can't face that many. All of us from Westgate have been on watch all night and we're tired. You need to fall back to somewhere we can do better against so many."

"Hold up. Did you see these people?"

"No, but a woman who lives on the other side of Faircloth Motors came up and said someone came to her door and told her they were coming… And to run."

"So, no one has seen these hundreds of people, and all you have is a secondhand word from someone we don't know who told a woman that lives nearby. Is that, right?"

"Well, she said the man who told her seemed like he knew what he was talking about, and yeah, he was a stranger. Sheriff, we've been trading off watch duty for three days straight and we're all worn out."

"Yeah. I get that." Dozier spoke up so everyone could hear. "Listen up folks. We've got scouts on down the road back toward Dawson watching for anyone coming. It's more likely the Dawson people sent this man, maybe more than one, to scare us into abandoning the defenses here. We've got some of the cut through roads blocked or being watched, like Oakland and Ledo Roads, but one person could easily slip through the woods and give us false information.

"Our scouts report that all the people who have gotten together over there are still way back near Dawson. Don't believe in any rumors. Trust our scouts to let us know when they are coming. Now, you people go on home and get some rest. We'll need you back here when the time comes. Talk to your neighborhood leaders, and when you're rested, you need to take on a regular shift. Tell everyone to watch for strangers planting rumors or trying to scare us. If we all get jumpy, we won't do our jobs well when they get here." He patted the man on the arm. "Okay, thanks for the report. Go on home."

He turned to a deputy. "Go find Mayor Ballard. Tell him

we need to rotate the barricade watches more frequently. These people are getting tired and worn out. We need all the watches to be shared. We're gonna hold this ground until some other watch teams relieve us. One other thing. Tell the mayor to get his son's drone up here. We need those eyes in the sky to look down the road toward Dawson and see what is really happening. Tell him to bring a laptop or something to show folks the video from the drone. That will get people to calm down here and see that we don't actually have an army on top of us."

The men had built the camouflaged hide in the woods on a curve in the highway leading to Dawson and decorated it with leaves from the surrounding trees. They had a good exit path worked out in case they needed to make a hasty retreat.

After two days, they had a head count of the threat and one person left to tell Henry what they had seen. Neighborhood militia quickly reinforced the other defenses west of the big mall, near the intersection of Dawson Road and the U.S. Highway 82 bypass, in a six hundred-yard-wide ark high on the bypass ramp and also on the road below. This defense was augmented out to the sides with an abatis of interlocked fallen trees with the branches sharpened to points facing the approach of the Dawson group. They also secured nearby access roads entering U.S. 82 with formidable barriers staffed by militia. Then they waited for word of the advancing armed group from the Dawson area.

In the meeting located in the nearby Albany Mall, Henry Graham stood and asked for a chance to speak. He pointed to a spot on a Dougherty County map taped to the wall. "Some of them could come south down Tallahassee Road there, just this side of Sasser, then come back toward us on Old Dawson Road and sneak up behind us. I think we need to try to block them from doing that."

A man jumped up. "You can't do that! It will take away from the barricade. We're shorthanded as it is."

Sheriff Dozier studied the map. "He's right." He pointed at Henry. "Good catch. If we neglect that back road it will leave us vulnerable, but if we staff a barricade, it will also leave us shorthanded. How many people you need?"

Henry shifted his weight. "Well, none from here." He looked over at the group who had been protesting his idea. I didn't plan to take any of you with me. I'll just get some people from out where I live, and maybe some who live out near the intersection of the Tallahassee and Old Dawson Roads."

"But you'll need help to build a barricade."

"I don't plan to do that and doubt we have the time. I'm proposing that I get a small group to hide and surprise them if they come that way. Besides, it's likely they'll send most of the people down Dawson Road directly toward Albany. If they do come our way, maybe there won't be too many for us to handle."

"But what if there is? They'll wipe you out."

"Not if we stay hidden and snipe at them from the woods. We can stop them, turn them around, slow them down, or cut down how many get through. Believe me, a few good shots coming from people who are well-positioned can do a lot of damage. You guys here stack everybody you have behind the barricades and make it look like you got a whole army. Let me take care of the back road."

There were murmurs both pro and con in the large group when Sheriff Dozier spoke. "Sounds good to me. Keep a couple of people with bicycles with you that can ride fast to give us a report of what happens. Whether they get through you or not, either way, we need to know."

When the force from Dawson came the next day, they did split off a smaller group on horseback that turned down Tallahassee Road at Sasser as Henry had predicted. The larger group, mostly walking and naturally moving slower, were pushing supply carts and continued toward Albany at a pace that would bring them to the barricade much later in the day.

Henry told the dozen men and women he had trained to pick good shooting positions, well-hidden and protected. He assumed they would be significantly outnumbered and needed to use hit and run tactics. He had each of them find two or three fallback spots closer to town so if they were routed from the first place, they could move somewhere that was already prepared for them to take up another shooting spot. They had spent the afternoon before and much of the morning getting ready when the scout they had sent down the road toward Sasser came back with the alarm that there were people coming.

Henry and his group were on the east side of Tallahassee Road when they spotted about thirty riders approaching. Other than the two in the front who had their guns out, most other riders had their rifles and shotguns in scabbards to have both hands free to manage the horse. Many had pistols, but those were also in holsters.

Henry had a signal to keep everyone on his team still and ready, but not firing until he gave the word. It was hard for some of the men covered in brush and behind trees not to be impatient as they watched and waited while the riders got closer. One of them whispered, "Henry, we got to shoot them soon as they get past that big tree and we can see 'em all. There are too many of them. We got to even the odds by shooting first."

Henry whispered back. "Be quiet and hold your position. Nobody shoots til I say so. We got to see if there is another way out of this situation."

The same voice as before said, "That's crazy."

"Shhhh."

The riders were almost upon them when Henry spotted someone he knew from buying gas at the man's filing station in Dawson. Henry stood with his gun resting in the crook of his arm and walked slowly onto the road with one hand in the air. He gave a friendly wave to the men and women on horseback and smiled. "Stop! Don't move." Then louder in a friendly voice, "Mike Corley. It's me, Henry Graham." The riders in the lead pointed their guns at Henry and the group reined in just in front of him. Several of the other rides started to pull their guns.

He looked at the riders holding guns. "Be careful guys. You don't want to shoot me, and the rest of you, keep your hands where they are. There are a lot of guns pointed at all of you right now, and most of you will be dead if you try to reach for yours." He then looked at the man he knew. "Mike, you should remember me, I've bought gas at your station and stuff from your store."

The man nodded uncomfortably and shifted in his saddle. "Yeah. I know you, Henry."

"Mike, I want to talk to you or to whoever is in charge of you folks on this road."

Another man riding closer to the front of the pack rode his horse forward to where Henry was standing and spoke. "Mister, you got a lot of guts coming out here by yourself. Now get on back to where you came from and we won't kill you."

Henry to turned to face the man who spoke. "What's your name?"

"You can call me Temp, and just once before we light you up. Now throw down that gun you are carrying and get off this road."

"Temp, like I said, we got a lot of guns pointed at you all and now that I know you are the leader," he spoke louder and pointed at the man, "more of them will be pointed at your head. Simmer down. Let's talk a minute before we all get in a bad place and start shooting at each other and a bunch of us get killed for no reason."

The man leaned back in his saddle, relaxed just a little, and said, "Mister, we got a reason to come here. We're on our way to get some things we need... Some food and stuff that you got over in town. Y'all been holding out on us."

"Fair enough. Let's trade for it. No need to fight when we need each other alive and well more than we need to be shooting at each other. I used to give business to Mike over there, and likely traded with some of you other folks too. Seems like a better way to relate to each other."

"Son, we don't have time to trade. We're in bad need of food and medicine. We're almost out of gas and don't have any electricity."

The gathered horses standing still on the highway next to the woods were attracting an array of flies and other insects. Several horses had relieved themselves and there was a distinct odor in the air. The people on horseback began swatting at the flies. Henry noticed this and spoke to them all in a raised voice,

"Folks, I'd be careful about how you swat at those flies. Please don't get too close to pulling a gun or my people all around here," he made a circle in the air with his free hand, "they might think you are going to shoot someone. That would have a bad result for Mister Temp here." He nodded toward the horseback group's leader.

Temp smirked. "I don't think you got anybody out there and doubt you could hit anything if you did."

Mike Corley spoke up. "Mister Temp, he comes from those swamp people... Always trading in wild boar and gator meat."

After listening to Mike, Temp readjusted himself in his saddle and sniffed, which caused his horse to stomp the ground twice and swish his tail at the flies.

Henry turned back to the man. "Well, Temp, we can help with some of that food and electricity now, today, and do it without shooting at each other. We're also making some more medicine over at the hospital. We've already been trading with some of the folks over at the peanut processing plant in Dawson, even after all this mess started. Right now, you got a bunch of your friends headed down the main highway to get in a fight with a bunch of mine. Let's stop that and all sit down together. We all need to produce what crops and food we can and share it with each other. We've already got people, new friends of ours, up in Leesburg and Smithville, raising chickens and cattle. If everyone around here were to work on raising different kinds of crops, we can all share them and we can all survive. If not, we're all screwed."

"How you pose to do that?"

"You send one of your men on horseback back down this road where you came from to try to catch up with the larger group of your friends that are headed down U.S. 82 to Albany. Tell them to hold up and let's all talk. Then you and maybe one or two others come with me, and we'll ride to where a big fight is going to take place unless we stop it."

"What about the rest of us?"

"The rest of you folks can just hold up here. There is shade over there under those pecan trees and grass and water for the horses. I have some food back over there hidden in the woods to give your folks to eat while we go do what we need to do."

The man thought for a moment and nodded. "That sounds like something we might ought to try."

"Only thing is, your men need to stay put. If they decide to follow on after us, then my people who are watching in the woods will take that as a hostile act. If your people and mine start to shoot at each other, it will kind of undo a situation we're trying to fix. If you have someone you can leave in charge that everyone will follow, that would be a good idea."

Temp gave the order and the horses were unsaddled and put out in a nearby fenced in pecan grove to feed on the grass and undergrowth. The men moved to sit in the shade. The man Henry knew from before, Mike Corley, was put in charge. Henry called for a golf cart to bring the food and water he had planned to use for this temporary peace, and the people from the Dawson area were enthusiastic about enjoying the limited rations instead of getting shot.

Henry kept several shooters hidden in the woods just in case, and then with Temp and two others, he rode down Old Dawson Road to the barricades where U.S. 82 turned into a portion of the loop beltway.

At the barricades, the larger group coming from Dawson,

mostly on foot, had gotten close enough to see the formidable defenses, with people behind walls on the bridge over the highway and blocking the road below. Immediately in front of the barricades on the highway, rolls of barbed wire had been strung across the road. There were also blockades on other nearby side roads leading off U.S. 82 on both sides of the larger highway. They were essentially caught between the ditches in a long "U" shaped chute on the highway with no way off except the way they had come.

Now that they had arrived at the outskirts of Albany, the Dawson group realized they would have a hard time in a direct assault on the fortified positions. Behind the barricades, there were people stacked shoulder to shoulder all around a large semicircle. The Dawson group's only hope was to wait until the horse riders could circle around behind the barrier, then put pressure on them from two directions.

They halted and took up positions on both sides of the highway, finding cover as best they could. When the Albany sheriff began to speak to them, shouting through a cheerleader's megaphone, they stopped and listened to buy time for the horsemen to arrive from the rear.

Both sides sent delegations to talk in the middle of the highway. As they were bouncing back and forth on various demands, several horsemen came from behind the barricades, including Temp and Henry, and the horsemen rode down to join the conversation. When Temp let the others know he had decided to accept the offer to work with Albany instead of fight them, the larger group could see the futility of further aggression and joined in too.

That led to serious discussions on what could be shared

and what was expected from both sides in trying to help each other to survive. By the end of the talks, it was decided to extend a soft perimeter from Albany out to Dawson. They would have better defined free trade inside the perimeter, and could help each other with technology, medical needs, and food.

Some of the Dawson soldiers decided to stay, joining Albany to assist with their more immediate dangers in exchange for additional food and other supplies. They helped to staff the barricade at U.S. 82, which freed up some of the Albany militia members to head over toward Lake Chehaw and the park to meet the threat that was expected any day. The others took some of the chickens and cattle back with them, which the people in Albany had received in trade from the Leesburg and Smithville farms.

In the debriefing for the Dawson Road incident, Mayor Ballard turned to Henry. "Henry, what you did really did save us from a bad fight. We would have won, but likely would have killed a lot of people from Southwest Georgia, including some of our own neighbors. If we can get past these Dothan and Cordele people, we'll be in a good position to hold out from any other attack. After that, we will have good bit of mileage all around as a buffer zone that is friendly and receptive to planting and raising food that can be bartered with others. Maybe then we can finish organizing what we'll plant in the spring, and also make plans for the breeding stock for cattle, pigs, and chickens."

Dozier, who had been standing nearby, was studying the map using his hands and fingers as distance markers to spread from one side to the other. "Henry, the scouts you trained have given us some time." He looked back from one side of Albany to the other, estimating travel times and what obstacles could be put in place to slow the two advancing armies. He walked closer to the map and ran his hand again over the roads leading to Albany from both directions. "We've got to make another run at the Marine Base to get them involved. Let's all three go there tomorrow. Even with all the neighborhood militias and our hardcore forces who are better trained now, we can never stop them if they both get here at the same time. To have any chance, we've got to find a way to delay one of the groups so we can take them on one at the time. Without the support of the Marines, the attack that's heading our way is going to be a disaster for all of us."

Marine Base

The next day, Henry Graham accompanied Mayor Ballard and Sheriff Dozier to visit Colonel Spencer at the U.S. Marine Supply Depot.

As they entered the base commander's office, there were few pleasantries because the earlier meeting had ended rather abruptly, with the colonel not agreeing to any of the requests of the mayor and sheriff. This time, Sheriff Dozier wore his dress uniform in the hopes of giving the briefing a more official tone, and he also brought along a large map of Dougherty County showing sections of adjacent counties. This time too, Colonel Spencer had with him Brumby Shackelford, a female major in charge of base security, and her deputy, Captain Whit Rodriguez, to listen to the briefing.

Shackelford had close cropped hair and wore crisp fatigues showing Marine Corps Combat Air Crew and parachutist wings. She was not a large woman, but looked very fit and had a piercing, no-nonsense look on her angular face. Rodriguez also had on fatigues with jump wings. His sleeves were partially rolled up, exposing muscular forearms. There was a scar on his right cheek that did not look like it had come from shaving.

Henry first asked the colonel's permission, then worked to tape the large map onto the wall. Captain Rodriguez helped the process by grabbing and supporting one side until Henry could get there with the tape. Once that was set up, everyone pulled chairs up near the map.

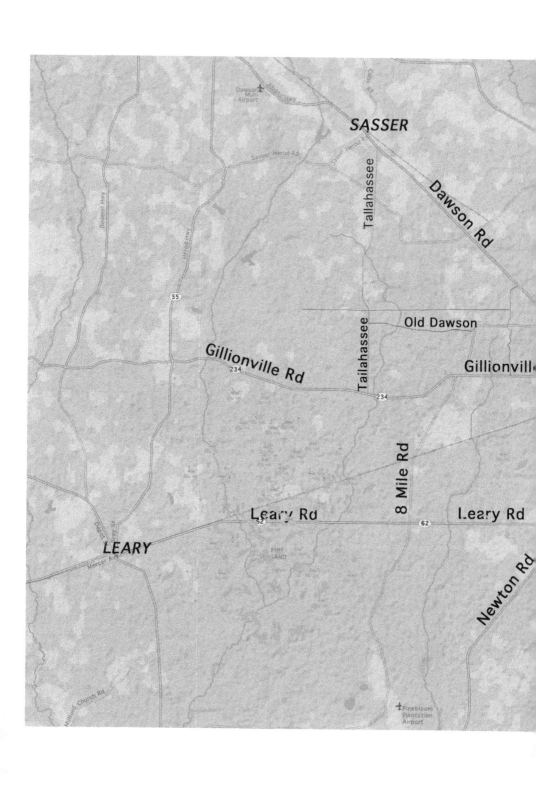

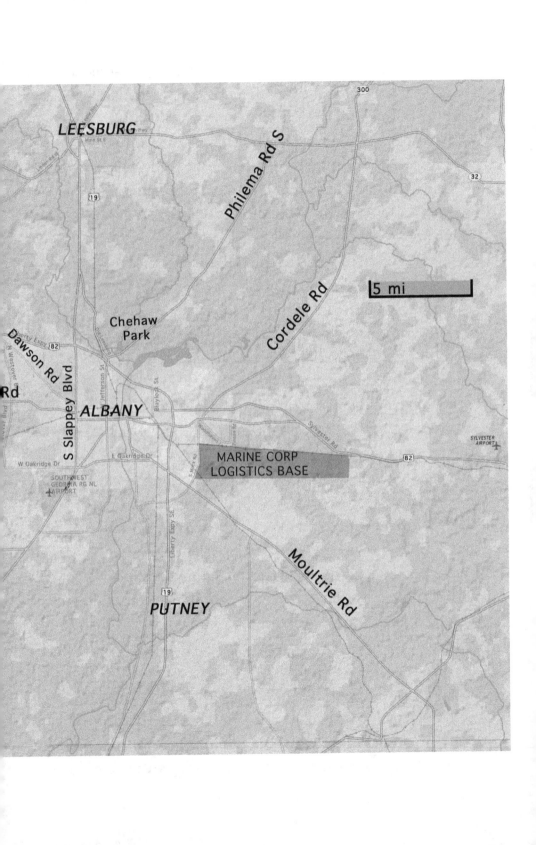

The sheriff took a slow look around at his audience and began, "In the spirit of cooperation for this rather large area under threat, we wish to give you our plans of action and a timetable. After this crisis is over, we would not wish to see anyone criticized for not acting prudently, doing everything they could to face this crisis or carry out their mission... or orders. When I'm done, we'd appreciate any advice you have to offer on how we can improve our plans."

The colonel nodded and gestured toward the map for Dozier to continue. Shackelford and Rodriguez leaned forward to study the map.

"We do not have the resources to repel an attack from every approach and down every avenue into Albany. We do have barricades manned by militia at every major entrance, and will continue to hold those positions as best we can. Because we are defending an interior that is basically a circle, we have a reserve group near the center of the circle that can be sent to reinforce any area under severe threat." He tapped the map at the intersection of Dawson Road and Slappey Drive.

Dozier now exaggerated a little to get the colonel's attention. "Colonel, we have had scouts trained by a former Marine sniper out well over thirty miles in all directions looking for potential trouble. They've managed to infiltrate the perimeter of several threats and we wanted to give you a report that should concern you." He touched the map as he spoke. "We have already stopped large groups coming here from the north, south, and northwest. Initially they were going to come for us, but they were also coming for you. It's likely you could have stopped them, but it would have involved a pretty big fight. We stopped them for you. Now there are more coming. These new threats are from

Island in the Storm

even bigger groups, and that's what I want to show you on the map. We know from what our scouts have overheard that both of these large groups have this Marine Supply Depot as their main target and destination." He gave a summary of Henry's activities and the snipers' reports about the groups from Dothan and Cordele and pointed out their locations and routes on the map.

"Both of these large groups are going to get here about the same time, likely in the next two or three days. Right now, it looks like the group coming from Cordele may attack first coming down Philema Road." He tapped the map. "We have reports that the activities of both groups are somehow being coordinated. All of our main resources will be moved to meet them, and our defenses are prepared accordingly.

"Just in case, we are watching on Leary Road from Dothan with the trained scouts and snipers. Henry here is in charge of the southwestern part of town." He pointed to Henry, who nodded in acknowledgement. "He plans to rely on the snipers to slow down the approach of the people from Dothan until reinforcements can arrive. Once we defeat the group from Cordele, we will redeploy our main forces to meet the threat from Dothan. However, should they be successful in coordinating their arrival at the same time, we will likely not be able to stop one or perhaps either of them."

Dozier walked to the map and pointed out the threat routes again. Then he took out a more detailed map of the east side of Albany and taped it to the wall. This one showed the location of the perimeter highway U.S. 19 near Chehaw Park where they planned to stop the group coming from Cordele near the top of the map, but it also showed where the Marine Base was located near the bottom.

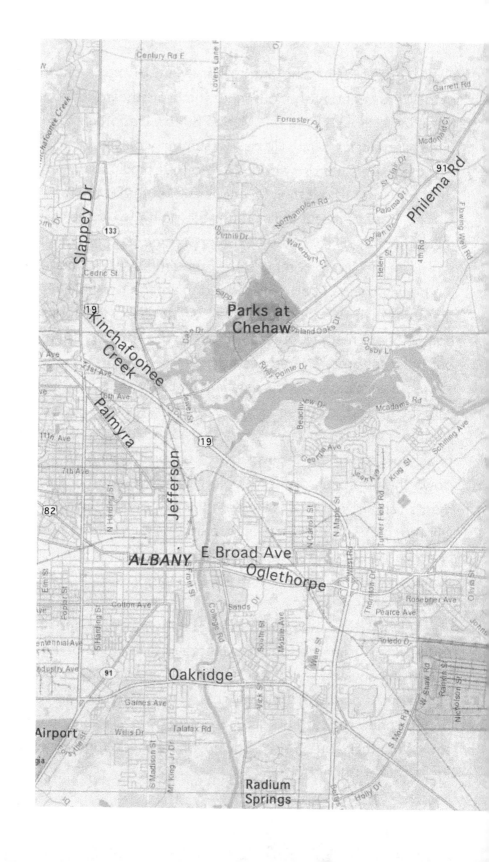

"Now, we plan to meet the group coming from Cordele at the U.S. 19 beltway near Chehaw Park, and that effort will pretty much tap us out in terms of our resources. However, we are concerned that they also could send a smaller force to go around behind us on Highway 82… here. That is the eastern connection to U.S. Highway 19, the beltway around Albany." He pointed to those places and routes on the map. "If that happened, by the time we could shift forces to meet them, it might be too late, and they could already have come down here." He pointed to how U.S. 19 headed south to provide direct access near the Marine Base that would have no buffer defense.

"Colonel, your orders are to defend this base. I'm guessing the orders do not specifically say where you must place your defenders or that you have to stay within the confines of the base to do so. In fact, it might be more prudent to set up an extended perimeter someplace outside the confines of the base, say on the intersection of U.S. 19 and 82." He pointed to the map.

"If someone, such as a detachment of United States Marines, could set up a blocking force on U.S. 19 where it cuts through east and west U.S. 82, and on Broad Avenue, and over here on Oglethorpe." He pointed to those places on the map. "Those positions would be within sight of and within a few blocks of each other, and able to support each other if needed. A fairly small group could defend those crossroads. There is also a direct access back to the base for support or for… redeployment.

"You can defend this base from that advanced position or withdraw into the confines of the base, depending on the tactical needs. After we handle the Cordele people, you can move back closer to the base from that intersection and cover yourself from any attack from the Dothan contingent coming in from the west.

If we can't stop those two groups, they will likely join forces here near the Proctor and Gamble plant." He tapped the map near the intersection of Oakridge and U.S. Highway 19. "It's sound tactics and more prudent than sitting on the base waiting to get hit. It also allows us to do the fighting to cut down on your attackers or even defeat them.

"At best, you might scare them off from any attack on the base or defeat them outright. At a minimum, you could assess their strength and inflict some damage to them from a planned defensive position with a prearranged withdrawal back to the base here. In either case, your exposure to loss would be minimal. We could provide backup for your forces in the form of a neighborhood militia, who would be positioned by you and operate under your orders. That is what we are here to show you today and let you draw your own conclusion as to your actions."

The colonel pointed to the map. "So, we would cover your ass from a back-door attack and also be ready to take on any people from that Dothan group if they got past your snipers and militia-manned barricades out there by the airport. We'd be blocking your butt from two directions."

Dozier looked at the map as though he was seeing this potential for the first time.

"Well, yes I see your point. That would also give you more time to prepare the base here for any eventual attack that was not stopped outside your perimeter. However, we fully plan on being able to shift the main body of our forces to meet the Dothan attack before they get close to your position."

The colonel nodded, stood, and paced back and forth in front of the map. Then he nodded again. He turned to the mayor. "You are mighty quiet today for a man usually so filled with certitude."

"Colonel, I believe the sheriff has stated the position of Albany well, and there is no need for me to add anything to that."

The colonel looked back over at Sheriff Dozier. "Our Marines under Major Shackelford here will agree to block anyone coming at you from the east near the U.S. 19 bypass. However, if those hostiles get past your defenses southwest of Albany by the airport and the threat looks significant, we will move back here to our planed positions of defense with ALL DELIBERATE HASTE.

"However, Sheriff, moving troops under wartime conditions is never easy. Your plan calls for a lot of things to work correctly and in sync. In every historical battle plan I've studied, too many things have to break in your favor and they rarely do. You have limited resources, little practice or equipment, and are being attacked by superior forces from two opposite directions at the same time. To say the least, that's not ideal."

Sheriff Dozier gripped his fist behind his back as he slowly rocked back and forth, forced a smile, and said in a strained voice, "What changes do you suggest for us to make?"

The colonel leaned back. "I'm not sure. I think you have done as well as you can with what you have. You have my admiration for your bravery and my best wishes. Now, we all have a good bit to do to get ready. I suggest we all get to it." He walked to the door, indicating the briefing was over.

Major Shackelford introduced herself again to Sheriff Dozier and Henry. "Once we are all set up in our positions, we need to develop a method of communication. Maybe we can use wireless if we have enough charged batteries to go around or a runner system. From those distances, we should be able to hear the gunfire. Our mutual forces are," she turned to look at the map they had left hanging on the wall, "going to be between two and three miles apart. Important we stay in touch. I'll contact you once we are set up. No offense intended, but I don't think we have the time to work with your militia." She looked at Captain Rodriguez, who stretched his neck by rolling it around and flexed his shoulders as if to get ready for a fight.

As they were leaving, the colonel looked at the sheriff, leaned into him closely, and said, "You are a sneaky son of a bitch. Good luck out there." Then he let out a small smile.

On the drive back to town, Mayor Ballard looked over at Jerico Dozier, who was driving. "Your suggestion that I should let you do the talking seemed to work. Do you think your idea will pan out and they'll join us now?"

Dozier tapped the wood on the steering wheel for luck. "They're Marines. Once they get outside that base and the shooting starts, orders or no orders, they'll be with us."

"Hope you're right. I've got some kind of personality conflict with that man. I just don't understand it."

"Well, you both like to be in charge and to be the main voice in the room. Maybe it got too crowded in his office the last time. Maybe in the future, you should let me talk for you more often, you know, smooth over your rough edges."

"Jerico, sometimes you can be such a pain in the ass. Just drive the car."

After the room cleared, Colonel Spencer pulled out the letter he had received from City Council President Larry Godwin cautioning him about the mayor, tore it into several pieces, and tossed them in the trash basket. He then picked up a plastic bottle lying next to the medical report, tapped a pill into his hand,

and closed the drawer.

Unexpected Trouble

During another meeting the next day, there was a knock on the door. A deputy entered and said urgently to Sheriff Dozier, "Sir, there is a problem and we need you to come with us."

"What is this?" Sheriff Dozier was perturbed at being interrupted from the meeting with a number of the Neighborhood Managers.

"I'm sorry to report this to you, but is seems like this morning, while all of you were over there talking to the new people helping us from Dawson, some of the folks from over near Cordele snuck in and took your daughter, Iris, kind of as a prisoner."

Sheriff Dozier and Henry said at the same time, "What?"

"Yes sir. When she didn't show up for work at the hospital, they sent someone over to your farm to get her and she was gone. They said it looked like there had been a struggle. And there was this note on the kitchen counter." He handed a piece of paper to the sheriff.

The note read, "Sheriff Dozier, I must say, you have a very pretty daughter. Feisty too. She needed encouragement to accept my invitation to come for a visit. If you want to see her again, meet me near the VFW post at six p.m. on the Highway 91 bridge leading toward Chehaw Park."

Henry asked. "There was a big dog on the property?"

The man looked down. "Yes. Sorry to say the dog had been shot. Killed. There was a lot of blood around and some clothing. Looks like the dog chewed up a couple of the kidnappers. The people who came on the sheriff's property to investigate got the local neighborhood folks to take care of the dog's body. I didn't think you'd want to have seen him like they left him there, and we distributed the remains for the neighborhood. That's sort of standard when any pet or stray dies. Sorry."

Henry looked over at Jerico. He felt gut punched, and fought the chill that filled his stomach and went up his back. They both knew Midnight would not have let anyone just come take Iris without a fight. He and Dozier looked at each other and slowly got up from the table.

At six that afternoon, Sheriff Dozier stood on the bridge watching when a large man came out of a nearby VFW lodge and walked slowly, swinging his arms and shoulders with each step, toward the other end of the bridge. The man was enormous, and smiled confidently as though he knew the answer to any potential question.

Dozier spoke first. "Before we go any further, I need to see my daughter."

Rowdy Burdette smiled. "I thought you'd say that." He turned and made a motion to another man standing by the door to the VFW hall. The man went inside, and a moment later, came back out with two other men holding Iris between them. Each man had a grip on one of her elbows. Her hair was ruffled and her dress was smudged in places, but she stood tall and defiant. The man on the bridge looked over at her then back to Dozier. "Okay, she's alive as you can see." He turned back to the men and nodded. They put Iris into a nearby truck and drove off toward Chehaw Park.

As the man turned back to him, Dozier said, "If you do anything to hurt her..."

The big man smiled and gave a false laugh. "Well that's up to you, isn't it? Now you listen up Mister Sheriff. You have til noon tomorrow to tear down that wall over there near the highway and back off. Get away from the other places you have bottled up and start to take them down too. You need to leave big holes so we can pass on through town, and we promise not to hurt anyone. You do that and you get your little girl back. If you don't," he turned to look where the truck was moving rapidly away down the road, "I think I will make your daughter my special pet for a few days before I give her to my men to enjoy." He turned to look back at the sheriff. "I kind of wish you don't cooperate. Hell, we can mow down your little group and go on like we want to do anyway, but it will be easier if you cooperate." He turned and looked back at where the truck taillights had disappeared and the road was beginning to glow in the dimming afternoon sun.

"We'll be watching to see what you do to that half ass construction of a barrier you got going. If I don't see a lot of progress on taking it down tomorrow, I'm gonna send you back her dress. She won't be needing it. You have a good night now." He walked with slow confidence back to the VFW hall where another truck pulled out from behind the building and took him back down the road toward Chehaw.

As Jerico Dozier almost staggered back down the road to where the barricades were being reinforced, several armed men came from the bushes on either side of the bridge where they had been hiding to protect the sheriff. When everyone reached the barricade, Sheriff Dozier relayed the request to the city leaders, including the mayor.

It was quiet for a few moments, then Mayor Ballard said

to Dozier, "You know we can't give in to what they are asking. We've got to resist. If they get in here, they are going to tear up the town whether we fight or not. Our only hope is to resist them. You know I love Iris, but you got to know she is as good as dead. No matter what happens, they will kill her." The others pulled back slightly at this harsh but accurate assessment.

Dozier hesitated for a moment and looked up at Lamar Ballad, who he had known for most of his life. "I hear what you are saying." He took a deep breath. "Do this for me. We have a little time. Before it gets completely dark, I plan to get some people here to start to make some obvious actions at moving some of the bundles, and they can look like they are going to take down the barrier."

"But we can't do..."

Dozier held up his hand. "They'll have people watching. We have over five hundred yards of defenses set up. We can just be moving things from one spot and hiding them behind another, but it will look like we are doing what they ask. I'm hoping that the fake activity will keep them from doing anything to her tonight. Tomorrow morning, I'm going to request another meeting."

"What good can that do?"

"I'm going to ask them for a swap, Iris for me."

Lamar spoke softly to his old friend, "Jerico, that will just get you killed and maybe her as well. Please listen to me..."

Dozier looked around the room at the military leadership. "I'm trying to buy her some time here. Just... agree to do as I ask. We're not going to take anything down from the barricade that cannot be replaced quickly. All the rest of the plans need to go forward. Now, I gotta get out a here. I need to go home."

Henry's Revenge

In the still and quiet of the dark night, Henry, Trey, and two others emerged out of an overgrown crop of bushes halfway between the bridge and the entrance to Chehaw Park where the trucks carrying Iris had entered earlier. They crossed the road quickly and became invisible shadows in the woods that bordered the entrance to the old wild animal park and public campground. They were all dressed in a flat black material that clung to their bodies. Face paint covered any exposed skin so it would not shine in the dark. There was nothing about them to reflect light, snag, or clank.

The other two men were armed with Marine Corps 9mm MP5 submachine guns fitted with silencers. Henry and Trey were carrying Marine Corps SIG Sauer P320 pistols with laser target finders, plus silencers, chambered with the widely popular 9x19 parabellum hollow point cartridges. The bullet flattened on impact to produce a wound almost as lethal as a .45 caliber, but without the extra weight and noise. All four men had night vision goggles courtesy of Henry's Marine Base visit.

The wild animal park had housed four-footed residents who lived in large spaces inside high fence barriers where they could roam freely in the forest. However, without the availability of the special food they needed, and to save them from the pain of starvation, the last of them had been humanely killed and eaten by the people of Albany weeks before.

They stayed on the edge of the forest and away from the cook fires that highlighted the gangs of men eating and drinking alcohol in packs around the many brick pits inside small, open gazebos scattered around the park. There were not too many actual houses or offices there, as it was a family recreation facility. However, in the parking lot of the only large structure, there was considerable activity as thick wood and metal plates were being attached to the front of at least two dozen trucks and carts.

The wide, flat ground of the park otherwise showed limited activity. They waited and watched. Henry counted not more than a hundred people total, and assumed this group was an advance pack that had come here to scout out the best places to attack the Albany defenses, and that they had likely been involved in grabbing Iris. It did not take long for Henry to spot one of the small office structures where a pair of guards shuttled back and forth every couple of hours. Over time, food was carried to the structure by one of the guards.

As the evening progressed, the group, encouraged by the liquor, bedded down. When Henry and his men crossed the road earlier, they had seen several armed guards by the entrance to Chehaw, but back in here, there was no evidence that this big group was worried about intruders. They did not see the large man from the bridge. Perhaps he had gone back over to Lake Blackshear to organize the other attackers. As the night continued, the main activity was the two men shuffling every few hours in and out of the small office they had been observing. As they watched, the most recent pair of guards had to be pushed several times to rouse them from their alcoholic stupor, and they staggered toward the small building to take on their guard duty.

After waiting for another thirty minutes for the camp to settle down, Henry and his friends moved closer to the wooden structure and listened with their ears to the walls. They could hear the murmuring of the two guards. There was a sound coming from one of the other rooms and Henry heard Iris's raised voice asking for help.

"You shut up, bitch, or I'll come back there and shut you up."

"These ropes are hurting me. There cutting off my circulation."

"Tough shit, lady. Now shut up."

Henry positioned the better armed men outside the structure to watch their backs for signs of trouble. There were solid concrete steps up to the entrance, so Henry was not worried about creaking wood or other sounds that might give them away. When the last shift changed, he noticed this current set of guards had just pulled the door open to enter when they approached, so it was not likely to be locked from the inside.

From the sounds of the voices coming through the door, Henry could tell that the two guards were in the first room just inside. As Henry and Trey got ready, they made sure nothing on their clothing or ammunition vest would catch on the doorway when they entered.

Henry had been mourning the death of Midnight and fearful of how Iris was being treated. His anger increased as he and Trey approached the small office and was at a boiling point as he reached the door. He stopped to calm himself, then whispered to the count of three. Trey opened the door and Henry rushed in as quietly as he could. The two guards were playing a card game with their weapons stacked against the wall. Henry pointed his gun at them. Trey followed immediately and closed the door. As Henry heard the door click, he grabbed a cushion to further muffle the noise and shot both of them twice. The "pffft" of the gun firing, even with the suppressor and cushion, sounded loud to Henry in the confined space of the small entrance room. Trey turned off the Coleman lantern and snapped on two dimmer light sticks.

Henry then turned, and with one of the light wands, rushed to the back room and quickly cut the bonds off Iris's writs. He handed her some dark jeans and a black sweater he had gotten from her home earlier when he took Jerico there to rest. "Put these on quickly." When she was dressed, he gave her a dark stocking cap to cover her hair, dark gloves, and rubbed on some of the same face paint he and the other men were using.

He whispered, "Let's go, Puddin'," and pushed her toward the door. By that time, Trey had gathered the guards' weapons and ammunition to take back to the barricades. They had been in the small building less than two minutes, and when they left, all five quickly moved away. The men were in a diamond formation with Iris in the middle. They passed the small groups of soldiers camped and sleeping, quietly reached the shadows, then walked rapidly through the woods that led them to the two-lane road.

Ten minutes later, they were moving carefully on the edge of the road back toward the barricade. About a hundred yards before they reached the bridge, they moved to the other side of the road from the VFW building and slowed their journey. They wanted to be quieter out of additional caution as they were shielded from view by the rough hedge growth along the highway. They were unsure how many of the attackers were still on guard in the building or how alert they might be. As they neared the bridge over Lake Chehaw, Henry flashed a signal with his light to one of his scouts, patiently guarding the other side of the bridge anticipating their return.

Later, Iris was being treated for some scratches and dehydration in a medical tent when Jerico Dozier arrived and rushed to his daughter, grabbing her in a long hug and rocking back and forth. When he opened his eyes, he could see Henry through the tent opening preparing to go to a nearby empty house to catch up on the sleep he had missed during the night.

Dozier walked out of the tent. "Henry... Why didn't you think to tell me about your plan to rescue my daughter?"

Henry thought for a moment. "Sir, I have the greatest respect for you... But... you and people like the mayor tend to talk about everything a lot. This was something that just needed to be done. I was worried it might get out."

"What do you mean?"

"I've been thinking. How did those men know where to find Iris? I kinda think those people out there in the woods have infiltrated one or more of their people into our town. It would be easy for someone to figure out that you and Mayor Ballard have been running things here. Anyone sneaking in could fairly quickly find out a lot about you, where you live, and how important Iris is to you."

"My God, you may be right."

"Not sure, but we shouldn't worry about what we can't control. This situation is not likely going to get any better by waiting. I'm ready to get on with it and kill them, but I'm also wondering how many people we may have let slip into Albany, and if they're enough of them to cause us problems when the shooting starts. Sorry, sir, but now I got to get some sleep."

The sheriff looked back toward the town, "I'm going to get word to the neighborhood militias to look out for strangers. You boys rest. They'll be coming at us when it gets light."

Henry had turned to leave, but with what Jerico said, he stopped and turned back to the sheriff. "I'm not sure."

"What makes you say that?"

"We saw maybe a hundred people over at Chehaw. I'm thinking maybe they'll wait til they have all their people here and ready to come at us before they attack."

Dozier looked toward Chehaw Park and back at Henry. "I see. We'll get that drone back up in the sky at first light to look for them. Maybe we've got another day or two to get ready. After you rest, I'd like you to go over and see about the Dothan situation, and I'll get word to you over there with what the drone tells us."

"Okay, sir. Before I leave, I'll get a couple of the scouts to sneak out in the woods to see what they can find." Mark hesitated. "Sir. I had never, you know, shot anyone before."

Dozier made a sad face, "Me neither. I'm just damn glad you picked this time to start."

Later, Dozier was returning to the medical tent when Mayor Ballard arrived after hearing of the rescue. "Jerico, I'm so glad that this worked out. My prayers have been with Iris and now... And what I said... You know... I..."

"It's okay, Lamar. What you said was the right thing. They would have killed her... or worse. It worked out. That's what counts. Now you need to tell all the neighborhoods to look for any strangers who have recently come among us. In addition to everything else, because they found Iris, I have to wonder if we may have some spies scattered around town. We need to get word to the militias to be on the lookout. Plus, I need to get your son back here to help with the drone. We need more surveillance out there."

As he walked toward a bed to sleep, there was something pulling at Henry. As the adrenaline wound down, his mind was numbing from lack of sleep. He was bone tired, but his head kept going back there, back in the dark. Back to the little house. He had been in danger. He had shot two men. Killed two people. Had to do it. No other way. The blood splattered behind the cushion and on the wall. He did not want to look at them behind the pillow, at what he had done. Had to move on. He was so tired.

Iris was safe. Midnight was dead. He was alive. He had taken lives. Had to do it. He was so tired. There would be more to come tomorrow, or soon. He was now past his earlier doubts and had just killed two men.

Double Pronged Attack

Bubba Gumption and the other scouts Henry had sent to watch for the Dothan army reported that the group had taken over Leary, a small town bypassed by progress, located twenty-five miles from Albany. The scouts said that there were more than two hundred people, many in military uniforms, camped around Leary and occupying the houses. That meant they could be in Albany in less than a day's march. Several people had been killed, and their bodies were thrown in a dumpster where swarms of flies hovered. One foot could be seen sticking out of the top.

The road from Leary to Albany would take the attackers by the airport, and then onto the Marine Base. It was also the road Sheriff Dozier had noticed earlier that cut through the heart of the Chickasawhatchee swamp. This route, although direct, would not offer the approaching army any maneuvering room, as both sides of the narrow road were bordered by marshes featuring watery sink holes and deep bogs.

Inside the Dothan camp, Walter was tired of being a part of the forced march and hated being a part of all the violence. Everything smelled terrible. He had planned to sneak away several times, but when he saw two people shot for trying to leave, he decided to wait and look for a safer time. His cousin had been shot earlier in one of the battles they fought over near Dothan, and he had no idea if he lived. This forced march and the indiscriminate killing was nothing like he had expected. These men were bloodthirsty and crazy vicious.

He tried to stay by himself and volunteer for jobs that kept him away from the rowdy and aggressive types in the camp. This bunch had become solely focused on meeting another group out somewhere to the east and taking over a Marine Base, where they said there was food, gas, and weapons. They weren't accumulating any food to take back home, and he just wanted to get back to his family.

The leadership of Albany continued to implement its defensive plans. Sheriff Dozier directed a wrecking crew to move any rubble left from the places they had disassembled in front of the barricades on the northeast bypass that could provide cover from the people coming to attack them. They completed additional barriers and supplemented those with the stakes and abatis of toppled trees, sharpened and pointed toward the enemy's approach. They urgently continued to train the defenders. When they were finished, there was a six hundred-yard-wide field of fire from the highway on the raised bypass road protected by barricades, and below that, there was another one hundred-fifty yards that required additional defensive structures on Jefferson Street leading into to Albany.

They shut down the Lake Chehaw power plant and took out some parts, so if the invaders captured it, they couldn't make it work. Then they moved any gas-operated portable generators that had been left at the power plant over to the hospital to be used to replace the power they lost. Apartments and homes on the south side of the lake, near the road to Chehaw Park, had been cleared and the residents were sent into town for safety.

At the site of the power plant and the dam, they set up a small defense on a spur of road leading to the dam that was a combination of snipers and some militia in case the people from Cordele came through the nearby neighborhood and found it. A dual purpose of this deployment would be to cover the right flank of the defenders on the bypass highway in case the attackers tried to sneak some people around that side on the water. The boats that came with the people fleeing Cordele were tied at the dock below the dam, ready to take the defenders away in case the marauders broke through.

Behind the lines in a low area protected by a hill, Iris helped the doctors set up a field medical unit to take care of the potential wounded. It was staffed with emergency room personnel. Once the injured were stabilized and triaged, they could be moved a mile down North Jefferson Street to Phoebe Putney hospital for better care.

Elsewhere, Jerico Dozier called in forces from the central neighborhoods to augment the militias at the northeast boundaries of Albany. These troops with limited training supplemented the sparse neighborhood watches in a ninety-degree arc around Albany from the north at U.S. Highway 19, and to the east at U.S. Highway 82. They also filled in the thinly defended areas between the main roads where people could sneak in more easily. Mayor Ballard arranged for additional supplies to be brought to these newly arrived defenders to keep them provided with food and water. The hope was that, although hardly trained and lightly armed, the appearance of many people occupying the full perimeter of the arc would discourage any additional points of attack by the Cordele aggressors. Some of the better trained fighters remained positioned near the intersection of Dawson

Road and Slappey Drive, designated as a reserve to support whichever place the attackers reached first. They were as ready as they could be.

Henry made plans to increase the watch near the swamp for the horde coming at them from Dothan. He sent scouts further out on Leary Road in regular shifts to look for any activity by the approaching army. Earlier, they created sniper nests along the sides of the road, alternating from one side to the other in a zig zag pattern all the way back to the airport. The plan would allow the snipers to harass whoever came down the road from either side in alternating patterns every few hundred yards.

Because the path of the Dothan group would bring them past the Chickasawhatchee Swamp area, Henry moved back into the swamp to be closer to his area of responsibility. This move also enabled him to recruit some of the more reluctant members of the swamp family to join the Albany defenders.

Being back home also gave Henry more time to be with his father, who listened to Henry's description of the plans for the defense of Albany. His father showed new signs of interest. He even rallied enough to go with Henry to see some of the sniper placements and made helpful suggestions on how to improve those positions. Everyone in the swamp picked up on Henry's apprehension, and treated him with respect and deference to his role as one of the new leaders of Albany.

Henry got reports from scouts that confirmed the Cordele group was making more progress on their journey, and would arrive several hours before the Dothan group. He worried there was not enough time to repel the Cordele group and then shift the large company of defenders, on foot from that attack, over seven miles across town, and then be in shape to take on another major assault.

They practiced drills with the local neighborhood militias to fill in the barricades southwest of Albany. However, those defenders first had to be notified to report for the fight, then had to travel often a mile or two to reach the barricades, and this movement was not very effective.

The fact that everyone was weary and malnourished did not help the maneuvers. Henry noticed that many of the defenders here were women, and in South Georgia, it was not uncommon for many women to hunt and shoot. As the time approached for the invaders to come, everyone was doing the best they could, even as their nervous tensions increased.

Early on the morning they expected the attack to start from the Cordele group, Henry received an urgent message to come to the northwest of Albany to join the defenders there. Sheriff Dozier needed Henry to organize sniper teams to take on one or more of those units to slow down their attack. As Henry put on his gear and strapped on extra ammunition, he was pacing back and forth. His father came up to him out of the dim light and touched him. "Henry, what is it?"

Henry nervously told him about the change of plans.

His father patted him on the back. "I've been listening to what's happening. When you leave here, just tell whoever watching the road leading to Dothan to report to me. I can fill in for you. I can assess how things look, how many of them there are, types of weapons, pace of travel, and get word to you. Go on and do your job. I got this covered here. I'll get the snipers to fall back as they shoot so none of them will get hurt. You know that I'm good at that stuff. So, once you get on to where you need to go, I'll move my old hairy self out to a comfortable chair near the road where you can easily find me when you get back. Go on and do your job."

Willis went with Henry as he traveled to the barn and got one of the trucks that still had some remaining gas. "Dad, thank you for covering for me. Make sure the people behind the barricades know how to use the claymore mines in case those Dothan people get here sooner than expected. I'll try to get back to you as soon as I can. Don't do anything to put yourself at risk. You are still not well, and you don't have all your strength."

"Right. Now get the hell out of here. I'll be like a messenger. No risk. I'll just watch what is happening and share that with you."

When Henry left, Willis used a golf cart to reach the barricades near the airport where the militia defenders were spread out across the road. He could tell, after walking around for only a few minutes, that the barricade could be outflanked and bypassed or attacked from behind and if that happened the defenders would be irrelevant. Most were scared of what might be coming at them from the long road ahead. Willis knew courage, and he could see when the mass of soldiers from Dothan gave them a push here, they'd fall back. He gave the militia words of encouragement and left.

Back at the village on the island, he looked around the camp thinking and taking stock of who was left there. Most of the young men and fit women were off with Henry as scouts or were with the military at different points around the city. Others had conveniently disappeared if they did not wish to fight. What was left there were mostly women, young women, and a plan formed in his head. He stood, stretched, and shouted for the first time in several years loud enough for everyone in the compound to hear, "Okay, folks, all of you get over here. Time to go to work!"

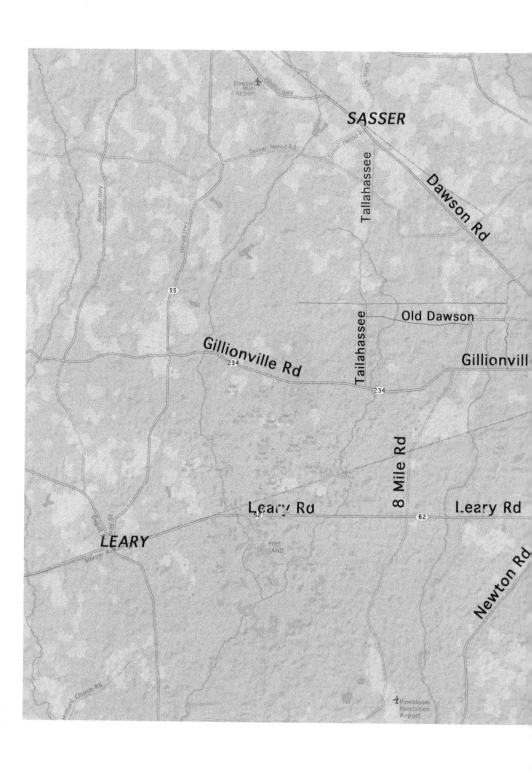

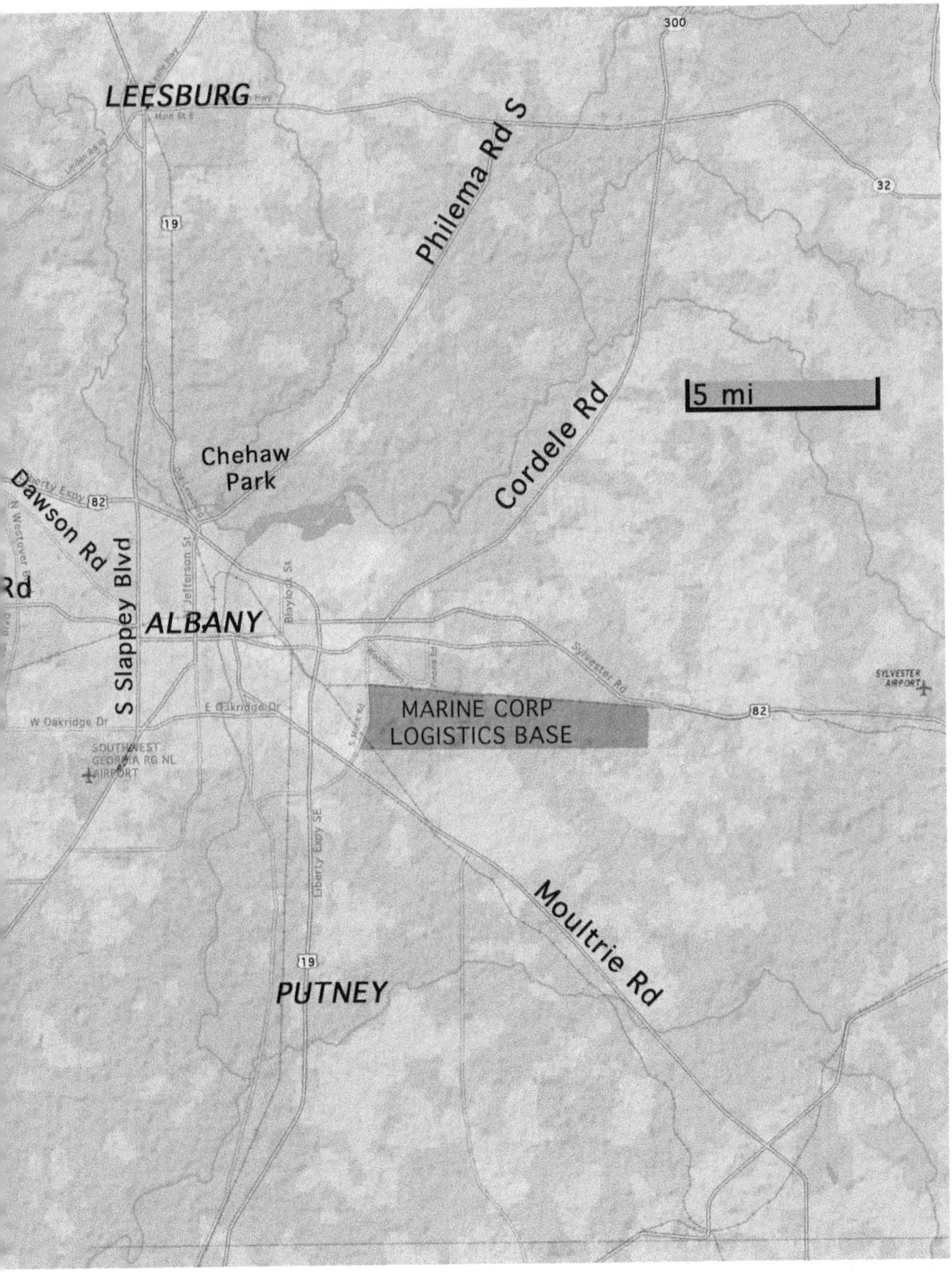
LEESBURG
Philema Rd S
300
32
19
5 mi
Cordele Rd
Chehaw
Park
Dawson Rd
82
Rd
S Slappey Blvd
ALBANY
Jefferson St
Blaylock St
Sylvester Rd
SYLVESTER
AIRPORT
82
MARINE CORP
LOGISTICS BASE
W Oakridge Dr
E Oakridge Dr
SOUTHWEST
GEORGIA RG NL
AIRPORT
Liberty Expy SE
Moultrie Rd
19
PUTNEY

Henry's swamp friend Bubba Gumption and three others were divided into two teams that were the furthest defenders away from Albany, and closest to the approaching Dothan army. They were the point of the spear, and had planned their harassment along both sides of the road leading from Leary to Albany. They would leapfrog each other in sniper attacks on the mass of former soldiers once they began to come down the road.

Finally, at dusk, after milling around for two days and using flashlights to mark their path, the Dothan group gathered together and began to move. The long, straight road leading from those dilapidated buildings toward Albany was accompanied by a railroad running parallel to it, and Bubba correctly assumed that the Dothan soldiers would use both the railway tracks and the road to form two lines heading east. Other than an occasional house or church, heaved up from swamp muck or filled in by truck loads of dirt to give them purchase, the road and the train tracks had no features except that they rose ten to fifteen feet above the swamp floor on both sides. The road was like a two by four lying in the middle of a mud puddle.

Bubba reviewed the situation as he watched. He figured the group of invaders were on a schedule, and that with consistent marching, they would reach Albany the next morning. He relayed this information to Henry. As he watched, he knew that they could slow down this large group by using surprise and well-placed shots. He moved with his partner into position about a hundred fifty yards away from the side of the blacktop. Because of the scattered woods by the road, most of the shooting would be at fairly close range, so as they prepared, both were planning to fire instead of one spotting for the other.

The Dothan troops had scraped together enough gas to

have two supply trucks rolling with the mass of men and women walking in long lines toward Albany. As they began to march in two irregular groups out of Leary toward Albany, almost as soon as they passed the St. Paul Missionary Baptist Church on the edge of town, the marchers noticed the swamp on both sides of the road.

Bubba let them get several hundred yards out of the last remnants of the village and began to take out the trucks. In the dim light, he used his night vision goggles, and with the sniper rifles that had sound and flash suppressors, shot first at the tires, then at the engines, then at the people. At first, the soldiers walking on the road could not tell which direction the shots were coming from, so they reacted by scattering in all directions, diving under the trucks and off both sides of the road into ditches.

After the shooting stopped, they bandaged three of their wounded who had been giving directions, and some of the others helped them return to Leary. Bubba smiled as he remembered Willis Graham saying one of the prime functions of a sniper was to remove the enemy's leadership. Others in the Dothan group found that the supply trucks were disabled, and each person was ordered by the new leaders to take on carrying extra bags and boxes in addition to their personal gear and weapons. With these extra burdens, they walked slower and grumbled more. Bubba and the team across the road watched the captains who were giving orders and marked them in their minds as the next targets.

Bubba let them get several hundred yards further down the road, then he and his partner felled several of the new team leaders with shots to their legs. The group on the road looked toward the dense undergrowth, but with the noise suppressed from the sniper rifles, the several people who were hit had already fallen before anyone noticed they were injured. It was strange because they heard no gunshots. Once again, without knowing where the firing was coming from, the mass of people, fearing for their own safety, leaped in a collective rush down the steep banks and into the murky swamp.

Some of the soldiers from Dothan returned a barrage of gunfire in the general direction of the swamp where they thought the shots had come from, but their efforts were wasted as there was no more fire coming at them. The return shots were randomly spaced along a quarter mile stretch, and their un-aimed bullets dinged in the woods, clipping twigs and small limbs. Two white Ibis birds were flushed by the gunfire and soared gracefully as they slowly climbed over the heads of the men. Their steady, tube-shaped bodies seemed to glide straight ahead like a dart while the birds' white wings with black tips moved in unison, meeting under their bodies as though they were hands clapping.

Walter was covered in cold swamp muck from the ditch where he had jumped, and he felt a bruise to his ribs from the knee of a cypress tree. As the shooting stopped, one of the men who was an officer in his group whispered to get the two other men near him, bandage the wounded as best they could, and take them back to Leary. They were left to their own devices putting together crutches or splints for the wounds. He noticed the supply of bandages they were carrying was limited and wondered how soon they would run out if the sniping continued. However, Walter was happy for the first time in three weeks because soon he would be heading away from the crazy group of marauders, back to safety and on a road that would return him to his family. First chance he had, he would grab all the supplies he could carry from what was left on the road or back in the trucks, put them in a cart, and head for home.

He watched as the rest of them crawled out of the detritus of the steep ditches and took up defensive positions all along the side of the road. Now everyone was more cautious about the use of flashlights. Others moved up the chain of command to assume leadership positions. After monitoring the road and swamp from where the shots seemed to come for another fifteen minutes, the remnants of the Dothan group slowly crept back onto the blacktop, bringing with them fresh cuts, scrapes, bruises, and twisted ankles from their falls, all of which would swell and fester as they continued the journey along the narrow road. Walter watched as they moved slowly into the dark, heading east toward Albany.

The Dothan group became dirty, wet, and disorganized, only to repeat their earlier desperate dive for cover when shots came from the opposite side of the highway from the other team of snipers. The road became a dribble of wounded, with as many people experiencing sprains and disabling injuries from flinging themselves off the high blacktop into the low ditches as from gunshots.

The burden of supplies they were carrying from the trucks also became casualties. They were abandoned after banging into the weary people diving into the swamp and causing additional bumps, bruises, and lacerations. This pattern continued until the anticipation of another ambush led the band to move ever slower. They proceeded cautiously along the straight highway as they approached the place where they assumed yet another attack would come from.

Hours had passed since they began the journey. Each

time they were attacked by the snipers, in addition to the ripping noise of dozens of the Dothan group returning the gunfire, the road was littered with showers of spent shells dinging like wind chimes when they bounced on the hard surface and lay smoking in the moonlight.

Bubba and others moved on prearranged trails and through shallow water from one hide to the next. He thought that Willis Graham's advice to shoot to wound was spot on because caring for the wounded took more people out of the fight. The mass of attackers had slowed down on the road, so they had no trouble keeping ahead of them. Now the total number heading to Albany was reduced by several dozen of the wounded and the caregivers. Their plan was working well until a ricochet caught the woman Bubba was with, and he could see that although it was not a mortal wound, he needed to get her back to the camp on the island for medical treatment.

He patched her wound as best he could, and they moved toward a trail that would take them back toward the island. As he helped her, Bubba thought that this was one of the few times he had been this close to a woman with his arm around her, and she seemed to be appreciative. Then he thought, if all these soldiers make it through and find us, then any thoughts he had of the future with this or any other woman would soon be over.

Across the road, a similar mishap soon ended that team of snipers. One of the men was bitten by a water moccasin as they were moving in the knee-deep water from one hide to another. Those two scouts also decided to go for treatment and moved back two hundred yards to an old game trail they knew would lead them toward the island.

The road leading the Dothan group to Albany was now

wide open. However, rather than being an orderly military force, with its key leaders wounded and stretched back down the road to Leary, the mass that moved toward the town now resembled a well-armed, hungry, angry, frightened mob.

Marines

Captain Rodriguez led a contingent of armored Humvees and two M2 Bradley fighting vehicles roaring out of the gate of the Marine Base. Each Bradley had a 25mm Bushmaster chain gun mounted on its body that could fire more than a hundred rounds per minute, and also a 7.62mm medium machine gun. There were six armed Marines in the carrying sections of each Bradley vehicle packing full gear and extra ammunition. He had the six Humvees in the shop the whole night before making sure everything was ready for action. Unlike Colonel Spencer, who was an expert at logistics and supply, Rodriguez and Shackelford were combat Marines.

Shackelford had stayed on the base as a reserve in case she was needed to come to the rescue with her contingent of two Abrams tanks and more Humvees. They decided it was prudent to hold back the seventy-ton vehicles from running up and down the asphalt highway at fifty miles an hour on spinning steel plates and grinding up the road until they had a better idea of the threat.

She and Rodriguez stayed in close contact, and the advance vehicles were sending back visual as well as audio signals. Rodriguez felt like he was finally being allowed to do what he knew best, and was grateful to be off the base and perhaps headed into action. It had been three years since he had been in combat. Whatever was going to happen to him and his advance team now felt more like a police intervention than real combat, but he felt like the big dog on the block that had finally been released from his chain as he roared north up U.S. Highway 19 with all this firepower.

Colonel Spencer had put on his command face, and had given them strict orders to avoid engaging with the civilians or entering into combat. Rodriguez smiled as he listened to the colonel and thought to himself, "That may work well on paper," but he knew from experience that things happened when you entered a hostile environment on patrol or guard duty. If some people, and it did not matter to Rodriguez if they were American citizens or not, were coming to take their base and try to hurt them or their dependents, it was open season. They arrived and took up strong positions blocking the roads entering Albany from the east.

The Marines were stretched thin and did not have the ground support they really needed, but he felt that for each intersection, the firepower they had allocated would compensate for the lack of personnel. As he looked over the Marines he had handpicked to be with him on this mission, he felt confident the boots he did have on the ground could handle anything that came their way. He made sure the TV relays back to the base were working with Major Shackelford and gave her frequent verbal reports on the situation.

If the bastards tried to push through here, they'd find out what Marines were made of, for sure. He checked each individual vehicle and the Marines deployed around it one more time, then went to back to his position on Broad Avenue between the other strongpoints and waited for sunrise. They were linked. They were locked. They were ready.

Rowdy Burdette looked around at his lieutenants. He had weeded them down to a core group he could trust who all were tough as hell, most of whom had been in the army. He looked over at the man who had just returned. "Okay, what do you have to say for yourself? Tell us why you are back here."

"We went over like you said, near about to Ledo Road, and looked for a place to sneak in behind them."

"Yeah."

"B… But every place when we got close, they had 'em all blocked with these big piles of sticks with pointed ends, that or bales of something blocking the way. We could see lots of people behind the stuff they had barricading the road. It looked like they had turned out too many people for us to get in, and it would have been a hard place to attack. We would have needed more people to take them on and then it would have alerted them that a general attack was coming."

Burdette sneered. "I guess it never occurred to you that if you charged them, then that attack would have pulled more men over there to stop you and away from us. Ah, no matter. We've got the numbers and we've got the firepower. Let 'em spread themselves out. We're gonna concentrate all our forces at one place and plough right through them.

"Besides, we got that other big group coming in from south to get behind these folks. I sent them a message on that ham radio thing to start early. They should be hitting south of Albany soon, and that may draw off some of the folks up on that highway bypass ahead. There's supposed to be more than two hundred of them coming from Dothan and they can push aside any piss-ant militia at a barricade that these locals can come up with. They'll come up and cut in from behind while we're hitting 'em from the front."

"Yeah, Rowdy, and you also sent those others to cut behind them from the other side out to the east and link up with us. We're gonna have them surrounded. Slick as owl shit."

"Yeah. We got them out numbered and out gunned." He thought for a moment more. "We'll need to be prepared to take on more soldiers after we get into Albany."

"What do you mean?"

"We will be the winners… The victors. There'll be lots of people wanting to join us. There are always lots of people waiting to see which side will be on top before committing. That's human nature. We'll have more than enough troops to take on the Marine Base."

He pointed around the room. "All you guys get your teams together. You know where I want you. Give each person all the ammo they can carry. We're gonna smash them hard and keep rolling through that town. By nightfall, we'll be eating at the Marine Base. Those bastards aren't gonna know what hit them."

Dothan Attacks

Dianne, guarding for any intrusive activity coming from Dothan, was parked in a battery powered golf cart along the road next to some brush and under overhanging branches southwest of Albany. This part of the highway had a mixture of higher land along with the swamp, and there was more briar covered forests to the sides. As the day slowly brightened, she could see down the straight road for over a mile and checked every few minutes for signs of motion.

She liked this outdoor job better than working in the munitions factory where she never saw the sun. Back in the dimly lit, makeshift warehouse where she had worked before, every cartridge possible was being made, utilizing every possible shell casing, bullet and primer that could be found. The college science teachers had been conducting experiments to determine which gunpowder charge was the most effective, yet the supply of powder was used sparingly in order to make the maximum number of cartridges. That was important, but it was still a dark and dingy place to work... Not to mention that it might explode. As she swatted away another horsefly, Dianne thought that even with the bugs she had to contend with, working here in the outdoors was a better job than the other one.

Being here on the road also got her out of the exhausting training that was taking place every day. Small bands of neighbors and work associates were becoming more proficient at gathering on short notice, moving with their weapons to some rough barricade, and manning a watch. They were becoming rather good at moving as teams, but to preserve the number of cartridges available, they often made "bang" sounds with their voices when on a charge or repelling imaginary villains. Although this was serious work, most of them remembered childhood games and running around their neighborhoods playacting, and they often collapsed into howls of laughter when someone unexpectedly made the "ah-ah-ah-ah-ah" sound of an imaginary machine gun.

Nonetheless, because of the incessant demands of Sheriff Dozier, they got better. They began to see the value of group cooperation and the importance of taking protective cover. The false hero moments quickly diminished when individuals were, due to their charging about singlehandedly without the appropriate appreciation for danger, suddenly declared dead by their instructors and had to watch from the sidelines or run extra laps around the field.

Some of the militia who, like Dianne, had completed the defense classes were assigned the duty of looking out for trouble. She was pleased to hear the almost indistinguishable low whine of another golf cart coming to relieve her, as it had been a long six hours swatting bugs. She was happy for the cornbread sandwich her relief brought her, and they ate the snack together while she filled her replacement in on the boring morning's non-events.

She started to hand over the powerful binoculars to her replacement when she took one last look. Mmmm. Adjust the focus. Wait. In the distance, looking to the west in the early morning light, the road was side to side full of men. Armed men. She could make out that many seemed to be wearing military uniforms. These people headed her way down the otherwise deserted highway must be the soldiers she had heard about -

coming here all the way from Dothan, Alabama. What the hell? A chill hit her. She looked again. There were so many, she could not count them all. She showed the replacement watcher what she had seen through her binoculars and they both started to sweat. Thankfully, there was a plan for this situation. First, she contacted her commander, then pulled the poster out of its plastic case and set it up on a stick so that when the mass of moving soldiers got here, they could read its message.

They would be politely invited to join the Albany coalition in a pact of mutual trade and defense. If this offer was agreeable to them, they were invited to stop and rest here. Then they were to send forward a small contingent of no more than four representatives to discuss how they might work together, and what they had to trade that would be mutually beneficial. They would signal agreement to this offer by tying a large bed sheet to the tree limb that hung over the road. If they did not do this, then the people of Albany would consider their approach aggressive.

The two women moved both golf carts down the road and watched through the binoculars from another safe spot closer to Albany. The bunch, who looked mostly to be made up of men, stopped and read the sign. Then they threw it down on the road and kept coming. Okay, now this was for real.

The colleague who was there to relieve her kept watching the large group approach and said that she would move back toward town incrementally while continuing to observe the advancing troops. Dianne took off down the road toward town to give the warning. Just ahead, she stopped briefly to give a ride to a chubby man she saw carrying two long, scoped rifles and supporting a woman who had been shot. She took them a couple of miles to a dirt road leading into the swamp and dropped them off.

When she got to the base staging area at the intersection of Eight Mile Road, she found that Henry had gone to the other side of town and that his father, Willis, was there in his place. She had heard rumors that Willis was very experienced, but she also thought he looked rather frail.

She gave him her report and pointed to the map where the mass of soldiers was located back down the narrow highway. He told her to go to the barricade and tell whoever was in charge of the southwest side of Albany by the airport to rally every possible militia person, have them come to staff the barricade, and send warning to Mayor Ballard. "Tell the mayor to send those reserves he has over near the Dawson Road to help the group close to Chehaw."

"But they're coming here. I saw them. Lots of them."

"Yeah, but based on the place you showed me where they are, it may take them a little while longer and maybe we can slow them up some. Those folks over on North Jefferson are likely already seeing some action."

He looked west down the currently empty two-lane road toward Leary. "Tell them once they stop that bunch north of Albany to get back over here as soon as they can. We'll try to hold out here til then." Willis wiped his brow from the morning's rising temperature. He sent the scout back in her golf cart to tell the people at the barricades what to expect, then he looked around at the increasingly bright day. It was going to be another hot one.

As she drove off in the golf cart, she felt that Willis was a man who would be good to his word, and that it was also was likely she would never see him again.

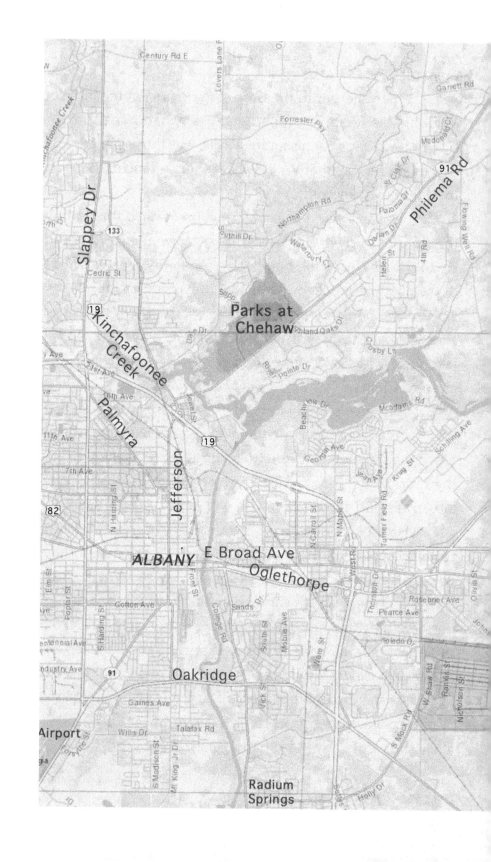

In the glow of early dawn, Jerico Dozier watched the images the drone was sending to the laptop. There was a stream of people and vehicles moving toward them from Chehaw Park under the cover of hanging trees and brush, fed by an even larger group assembling on the highway in front of Chehaw Park. They kept coming out of the trees to stack up in lines on the roadway like runners before a big distance race. More were assembling in front of the barricades on the continuation of Jefferson Street directly north of the large intersection with the beltway. They were disciplined, protected by massive shields, and all of them were slowly headed his way.

As Henry approached the bypass defenses, he could see the medical tents set up on the south side of the expressway. Several stretchers were stacked by the tents along with extra medical supplies. He pulled the truck off Jefferson Street and walked through the maze of tents to find Iris. She and others from the hospital had organized several of these canvas huts staffed with doctors, nurses, and supplies. Where they did not have portable beds, reinforced folding tables were arranged side by side to serve as makeshift operating tables or recovery beds. The lighting was mostly limited to rigged camp lanterns and some battery-operated lights. Since there was no running water, there were large containers of water by each tent. Nearby golf carts were configured with folding tables strapped across the back seat as six-foot beds to carry the wounded from the triage tents to the hospital. These were positioned with the front end pointed toward Jefferson Street, ready to rush patients to the more sophisticated help about a mile away.

When she saw him enter, Iris smiled, still showing the stress of the past several days. She moved quickly to him and looked

Island in the Storm

at him with eyes resigned to day's events ahead. "We're ready here, although I do hope this fight will not happen. My father has been up there all night." She nodded over a slight rise to where the bypass highway circled Albany. "Please, please be careful." Nearby people watched them while making busy movements to restack medicine or bandages, looking for something to do to appear they were not actually intruding on two people's very private conversation.

Henry said, "I have to go. I just wanted to see you. I…"

"I know." She looked deep into his eyes. "I know. Be careful." She touched him lightly on his arm. "I've got to go get some more bandages from the hospital. Maybe they won't attack for a while, or at all. Maybe we can have lunch together in Tift Park soon."

"Maybe." He started to turn then stopped.

She looked with pleading eyes. "Come back if you hear that there will be no fighting. Back to me."

"Henry mumbled, "I'll check back later. I… You take care." He nodded at the others under the canopy and left.

As she watched him leave, she still felt the hands of the men groping all over her when the big man was not watching.

The fear and panic continued to build in Henry as he drove up the ramp in the pickup truck to park behind the barricades on the raised bypass. As he looked out toward the lake, over the scrub bushes and past a small apartment complex from where the attack would be coming from, he could see, even in the dim light, the vacant spaces where the sheriff had taken down structures that might have given cover to the attackers. There were inlets and creek eddies in front of the crescent bypass road, and he felt those would slow down and channel any direct attack onto the paved roadbeds.

Sheriff Dozier had set up a strong defensive position for several hundred yards on the concave curve of the roadbed, with firing positions from the raised highway bypass to offer the shooters a good view from over eighty feet above Jefferson Street. The defenders were a cross-section of Albany old and young, big and little, men and women, black, white and Hispanic and for now, all determined.

The crowded roadway looked down toward the direction from where the attack would come. Several dozen defenders were camped to the sides of the barricades in tents or whatever shelter they could manage. Everyone had their pockets filled with every extra cartridge they could cram in there. Supplies were stacked on the south side of the split highway so they could be quickly shuttled across connecting gaps to the other side, where barricades and firing positions took up much of the roadway.

Below them, and behind the thick bales of plastic spread across the asphalt of North Jefferson Street blocking access to the city, other defenders were taking turns standing watch as they stared into the dark. Henry could see, however, that If the attackers got by this blockade, they would overrun the medical station where he had seen Iris, and then have direct access and be able to take over the city. There was no plan B.

As he walked along the defensive structures, he could see ahead that Jerico Dozier had placed two of the 30. cal. machine guns and the grenade launchers, although with limited ammunition, where they would do the most good. They were distributing ammunition, food, water, and medical supplies to the suspected points of attack, and Dozier's deputies tried their best to group people with similar weapons and ammunition together. As they

Island in the Storm

took turns watching, others tried to rest, curled up on the hard ground.

Henry directed his small team of scouts to hide in the woods, ready to hit the attackers on their flanks or from behind after they had passed. He told them to wait until the shooting started, then to try to pick off any of the opposition's leaders they could distinguish first before causing as much damage as possible to the regular body of the attacking force.

A few minutes later, fresh reports arrived from the last scouts who had been out in the field near Chehaw Park overnight. Their reports indicated new movement of the enemy toward their lines - hundreds of attackers slowly coming in staggered lines toward the barricades as dawn approached. After a last check on his snipers, Henry moved to the point he assumed would be the area of the main attack.

In the dawn's light, they could see a bed sheet tied to a long pole creating a makeshift white flag that waved from behind a low berm less than two hundred yards away. Jerico Dozier acknowledged by clicking a flashlight on and off and waving it in that direction. Several men stood from the bushes and walked toward the barricades.

Dozier looked around. "Mmmm. We don't want them to get too close and see our strength or the disposition of weapons." He pointed to several large men nearby, including Henry. "You guys come with me. Bring your guns. Puff yourselves up and look as badass as you can. This meeting is going to be like a coin toss before the big football game."

They walked forward from the barricades, across the intersection of North Jefferson and Philema Road to the edge of the gravel to meet the others halfway. Both groups stopped about fifteen yards apart.

The tall man who was clearly the leader of the group from Cordele spoke. "Well, Sheriff, I got to hand it to you about sneaking into my camp and taking back your daughter. I sure wish you had waited til I had sampled the goods."

Dozier shrugged his shoulders and let out a sigh. "Before you talk us to death, I'm going to recommend that you take this sorry ass looking group with you and go back to where you came from."

The big man forced a laugh. "Bold talk for a man who may be dead in a few minutes." He looked around at the barricades on the highway then back at the men who stood before him. "Look, Sheriff, we just want to pass. We don't want to hurt you. We just want to have some of what you have. If you let us come in, go on down to the Marine Depot, and take control there, we'll treat you right and just take what we need. We'll share it with you."

Sheriff Dozier smiled at the man. "I could make you the same offer. We'd be glad to share what we've learned and work together, but we're not just laying down. I don't think we need to fight over our future. Better if we work together. Why don't you lay down your guns and send a few people over here to talk? You first."

The big man shifted his weight. "Maybe better for you. I don't think you're gonna forget me using your daughter as a bargaining chip. Mister, we got the troops and we got the weapons and we got the desire. Stand aside or your little bunch here is gonna get yourselves real dead real quick."

Dozier patted each of his hands down like he was dribbling a basketball. "No point in getting all hostile. Now, we'd like to work with you rather than against you. I don't know why you think you have to control us to share what we have."

Rowdy Burdette looked to the men to his left, then to his right, and flexed his shoulders. "That's the way things have always worked, even when we had gas and electricity and internet and all that. The haves always call the shots."

Dozier shook his head. "Not necessarily. In history…"

The man interrupted. "That's not how I see it. No point in bullshitting. You and this bunch of raggedy ass store clerks let us come in or we're gonna roll right over the top of you, and you aren't gonna like it when we do."

"It's not necessary for you to feel that way. I…"

"You're gonna find out how necessary it is." He looked again up at the highway in front of him with the bales and the men behind with their guns. He raised his voice so everyone, even those behind the barricades, could hear. "All you people up there lay down your guns and get out of our way. Or… You can just leave. This fool here," he pointed at Dozier, "don't have enough sense to see that we can kill all of you. If you don't want to die, get on back to your homes and your families and out of our way." Then he looked back at Dozier. "I gave you this chance 'cause we are all Americans here. Take it or you are gonna be dead soon." He half turned and looked back up at the barricades. "Come on boys, we got some killing to do." He started to leave with an intimidating swagger.

Dozier said, "Hey big man!"

The man stopped and said over his shoulder, "What?"

Dozier spoke loudly so many of the attackers he was sure were hiding in the dark bushes and structures of the former golf course could hear, "I sure hope I get the chance to put a bullet in you, but I bet you are the kind of guy who, instead of leading your little group, will hide in the back and let the others do your fighting. I can see that yellow streak there from when you turned your back."

The man hesitated as Dozier spoke, then turned back to face him. "I'll look for you right up there." He pointed to the topmost peak of the highway curve. "I'm coming there to find you and gut you just for fun. You'll see who the coward is then." He turned and continued to walk back toward the VFW hall across the bridge.

Dozier and the small group turned and started to walk back to the barricades. Henry said to the sheriff, "That went well. You've got him scared now."

Dozier shook his head and grumbled, "I just didn't want the son of a bitch to get in the last word, but it looks like he did anyway. Okay, let's get ready." He turned to one of his deputies walking with them. "Did you tell the mayor to get all the neighborhood militias out to watch on the edge of town for any of those people trying to sneak in behind us?"

"Yes sir. That's done and it looks to me like they're watching every road or alley."

When they reached their former positions behind the bales of plastic, Henry learned that his scouts had noticed several new teams of attackers gathering nearby. They also told him the Marines were in place on the highway east of town.

Henry looked down the road toward Chehaw Park and saw, in the early glow of day, the mass of potential attackers gathered behind dozens of vehicles and rolling carts reinforced with steel plates moving slowly up the narrow road toward them. Henry smiled when he realized that the directions he had given one set of his snipers for an ambush put them exactly where they needed to be.

He also noticed that Staff Sergeant Sidney had arrived from the Marines to act as an observer. He showed Henry that he had a walkie-talkie to give updated reports back to Major Shackelford at the base, and to Captain Rodriguez with the Marines at the blocking configuration on the east side of town.

Fight in the Swamp

On Leary Road leading toward the airport, the soldiers from Dothan realized that, because the sniper attacks had slowed them down, they were late for the rendezvous to attack Albany. To make up time, they were trying to jog down the road as best they could when they spotted a golf cart ahead. The occupants of the cart were talking and looking back toward Albany, not in their direction. The soldiers were feeling fortunate that they had gotten within fifty yards of the cart when one of the three young women occupants finally noticed them. She stood, shocked to see them, and the men in the front of the army noticed she was wearing very short gym shorts and a t-shirt. The women rushed to get the slow-moving cart headed away from the soldiers now running full speed in their direction. One of the men shouted loudly, "Come on boys, let's get us some of that chicken meat."

After lumbering for a few hundred yards just ahead of the frenzied gang of men, the cart rumbled off the main highway onto a one-lane dirt path. As the small road narrowed with more potholes, the golf cart, now wobbling and bouncing side to side from one crater to another, could not make much progress as the occupants fearfully watched the men getting closer. Not far down the track, the slow vehicle stopped. The three women got out and took off running at a kind of awkward pace - bumping, staggering, and holding on to each other's arms to keep them steady.

The bumpy, weedy road was fast becoming a narrow, overgrown trail. The soldiers quickly noticed that the golf cart occupants were all attractive young women, unarmed, wearing shorts over their shapely, long legs. They did not notice in the high grass that the women, older girls actually – almost women, were also wearing sturdy running shoes. Just as the soldiers were puzzling this new situation, the fleeing women started squealing and shouting for help as they ran into the woods.

As the pack of soldiers followed, the women scurried down the familiar trail, leaping over stumps and fallen trees, dodging low branches, and keeping just far enough ahead to avoid getting shot or caught by any of the men. Occasionally, they would shout to each other to run faster or to "tell the other girls to get some clothes on."

The trail wandered deeper into lower ground and then into the swamp, dipping into shallow, murky slosh of sometimes ankle or even knee-deep water for fifty yards or more before reemerging on dry land again. The overgrowth of vines and low limbs began to proliferate, and the light dimmed under a thick canopy.

The horde of armed men, unfamiliar with the dense swamp, had many mishaps and tripped, fell, and were injured or got tired, dropping behind only to become strung out on the trail. Many of the slower ones became hopelessly lost as the various small game trails switched, turned, and disappeared into the murky water. However, most of the soldiers, following their leaders, continued confidently ahead gathering scrapes, bruises, and increasing fatigue as they pushed deeper into the swamp to follow the fleeting images of the young women.

The creatures of the forest and the swamp were not familiar with the rush of such dense, noisy traffic. Assuming this intrusion was a threat, startled deer and wild boar hearing the racket of the men and sensing the subtler, swift motion of the women, fled ahead of them and bounded into the side brush, crashing their way through the dense growth.

The women occasionally stopped to catch their breath, always just down a long straight stretch of the path so when they were seen by the gaggle of troopers struggling with their guns and back packs, now feeling heavier with their increasing fatigue in the humidity of the swamp, they would scream and hug each other for a moment, stamping their feet and waving their arms before taking off on the run again. At one of these stops, when the men had spotted them resting, the women split up and took off in different directions. The soldiers stumbling along did the same.

The tiring troopers continued to run in separate groups this way and that for another few exhausting minutes until they noticed that the women were gaining more distance from them. Not having any idea where they were, they decided their best option was to continue after the women on the almost imperceptible trail, and so ploughed on as best they could, making every effort to move even faster.

The women meandered through the familiar zig zag of trails and were now several miles into the heart of the swamp, approaching an area that was the breeding ground for hundreds of alligators. Following another brisk jog, they reconnected with each other on the edge of a deep swamp lake where they were met by friends in silent, battery-powered boats. They were taken over a hundred yards across the dark swamp water, deposited on a patch of land, and left where they could be seen huddling together from across the broad pond.

The flat-bottomed boats moved to the other side of the

Island in the Storm

small island, out of sight but ready to move the women away in case the massive congregation of gators, stirred by the unusual commotion, decided to go after them. There they waited, anticipating the horde of lumbering men splashing into the snappers' sacred breeding grounds.

The men finally caught up and could see from the shore across the large pool of water that all three of the women were now reconnected, soaking wet, and stranded on a small island. Somehow, except for the stragglers who were now scattered all over the swamp, the rest of the soldiers had finally rejoined together in a large band, where they seemed to be far beyond the bewildering trails of this jungle on a quiet shore.

In a mass, they headed toward the women: high stepping into the deepening water, tripping over sunken stumps, falling and splashing, getting up again, and staggering forward. Getting closer to the island, many of the men began to howl and shout with the joy of anticipation as the water began to rise over their heads. After some awkward wading, however, they hit deep water. They now had to try to swim, kicking and flailing while carrying their heavy gear. Compounding this frustration, they were soon confused as they got ever closer to the dry land. The women who had been calmly watching their approach turned and disappeared, walking slowly toward the other side of the island behind a stand of large, ancient cypress trees.

That was the moment the soldiers made the unfortunate discovery that the deeper water surrounding them was not only suddenly filled with outraged alligators, but it was also the breeding grounds for nests of water moccasins coiled in massive balls. Water moccasins, in addition to being one of the most poisonous reptiles alive, are aggressive snakes, and when a lumbering herd of shouting men crashed into their nest containing scores of their friends and family wrapped snugly together for a morning nap, they became quite angry.

The collective screams flushed most of the wildlife within a mile radius, including a roost of buzzards who listened with particular anticipation. In the ensuing annihilation of Dothan's former citizens, the horde of chomping alligators did not seem to mind that some of their breakfast consisted of bites of snake as well as humans, but then again, alligators have never been discriminating gourmands.

One of the shallow draft boats docked on the back side of the island, loaded the women, and took them weaving through the moss laden trees back to their big island home in another part of the swamp. Willis, however, stayed there in the other boat hidden behind the trees of the island listening to the screams and watching the mayhem in the churning water. He mused to himself that in a couple of days, he'd send some people back here in boats with long poles and hooks to fetch any backpacks, ammunition, and weapons they could reuse.

He turned, shook his head, and said to the woman who was operating the boat, "Men are so dumb. We've been getting suckered into this kind of thing since we've been here on this earth. Let's go home before those snakes or one of the gators decide to come over here after us. Remind me when we get home to get some guards posted out on the road to see how many of them come back out of here." He hesitated, looking back for a moment at the convulsing water and the high-pitched howls. "My guess is not many."

Some of the men from Dothan, however, did escape, even after being bitten several times by the water moccasins and alligators, and they wandered through the thick woods disoriented, bleeding, and looking for help until the poison and injuries caused them to collapse in places where they would receive no comfort, and where no one would find their bodies for a very long time.

Others with lesser wounds managed to walk back in the direction they came for a day or more before they too succumbed to the aftermath of their adventures in the swamp, their discomfort amplified by the lack of food or clean water and the fever from infections. The wounded and dying found solace in the nooks and crannies of woods and marshes, and along the road back toward Leary where the buzzards watched and waited for their now full tummies to be ready for another meal.

The Beltway Battle Begins

After the confrontation with the big man from Cordele, Henry and the sheriff regained their positions, and everyone got quiet in nervous anticipation while hunkered behind the barricade. As they reentered, rolls of barbed wire were stretched and secured in front the bales of plastic across Jefferson.

Henry noticed that birds were singing in the early light, and there was now enough glow to distinguish objects and obstacles on the ground in the distance. The morning dew gave a dampness to the surface of the plastic bales and the air, although pregnant with the heat of another late summer's day, smelled of the beginnings of autumn. The peace was short lived. Henry could see the sun would rise behind the men from Cordele as they attacked, and into the eyes of the defenders. These invaders knew what they were doing.

The last of the quiet ended shortly after the big man and his small team disappeared into the scrub bushes across the road. The calm exploded with the shrill sound of gunfire and the thwacks of bullets hitting the plastic bales sounded like hands slapping in the mud, and twinging in ricochets off the concrete and metal of the bridge abutments. From the early morning damp air, the attackers came forward toward the curved defenses of the highway bypass. They emerged from separate intersecting roads and the woods, moving toward the expressway and firing as they leap-frogged from one protection to the other.

The aggressors' advance team at Chehaw had done an

effective job of reconnaissance. The attackers brought their own cover with them in the form of trucks and carts with welded metal and thick wooden plates over the front grills and windows. They would peek out, fire, then pull back behind the shields.

As these modified vehicles broke through the wooded area four hundred yards away from the highway overpass and barricades, they moved forward without significant obstructions over the flat South Georgia landscape. They used the makeshift walls to move closer to the highway and breastworks of the defenders as they pushed or drove the vehicles together in waves, leapfrogging twenty to thirty feet at the time. The attack was made easier by small firing ports cut through some of the welded metal plates over pickup truck grills and wagons.

Peering out through the grey light in the direction of the attack, the Albany defenders reeled from the impact of bullets and several dropped after being shot in the head. Others returned fire, most of them cautiously, barely aiming, just sending bullets back through the firing slots in the general direction of the attack.

The novice soldiers who took more time to aim had a much better chance of hitting someone in the mass of attackers, but the blistering return fire of oncoming bullets all seemed to be converging directly at center of their foreheads. The bullets were dinging and tearing, then smacking into people with dull thuds.

Some of the defenders were grunting and rocking their bodies back and forth in a squat, trying to pick a safer time, flex up, fire, and quickly sink back behind to the protection of the breastworks. Many absorbing the shock of the adrenaline uttered a low, almost constant moan, a primal sound that was a touchstone to keep the horror of impending death away and hold onto a will to fight. Lurch up, shoot, get back down, be amazed you were still alive.

As the battle intensified, Sheriff Dozier moved from one place to the other shouting words of encouragement, organizing teams to remove the dead and wounded so the metallic smell would not infect the others with a fear that could not be overcome. After one of the Neighborhood Managers ran away in terror, Dozier ran back and forth in a crouch motivating the green, innocent defenders to do their best. He could sense where he needed to be to keep the thin cord of courage from breaking. He kept them going.

As the attackers' bullets thwacked into the bales of plastic, the defenders were grateful they did not penetrate, although some were so terrified, they fell into fetal positions and stayed there. Others, prepared by the endless training and exercises over the past months, found their courage over and over to put themselves in the firing slits, selected targets, and shot. Still others screamed and cursed while firing incessantly as the attackers came on.

However, nothing could have prepared the defenders for the horror of the ear-splitting howls, the constant roaring noise, and seeing their neighbors being injured and killed. The .30 caliber machine guns Henry had brought from the Marine Base, fired by unfamiliar operators, roared in response, scattering bullets all over the road. Their firepower kept the attackers mostly at bay.

The fighting soon fell into a stalemate as both sides decreased the shooing to preserve their precious ammunition. Men shook violently as they reloaded their magazines and some continued to emit unearthly hums or moans to keep away the terror.

Sheriff Dozier would come, grab them by the shoulder, and say, "Come on, son. I know you can do this." The attack now came in one steady wave, although still too far away for a rush to the barricades.

Jerico Dozier had recruited a team of volunteers from the neighborhood militia as stretcher bearers. They took the wounded back to the field hospital Iris had organized. Some also pulled the dead away, most with gruesome head injuries, to the other side of the highway and put them under tarps to hide the horrible loss from those still fighting.

Then, as planned, the snipers Henry had placed crawled back up the sides of the lake from their hiding places and gathered under the bridge. Protected by the creek banks and positioned behind attackers, they spread out and began to fire into the attackers' backs. This action surprised and disoriented that section of the assault and made the aggressors take cover, running away from the right flank of the Albany defenders. They left their dead and wounded where they fell.

However, the aggressors soon regrouped, and with superior numbers, counter attacked the snipers and pushed them back. By that time, the sharpshooters, joined from the top of the bridge by the .30 cal. machine guns, had cut into the attack on the east side of the highway and made them too ineffective to mount a frontal attack.

The grenade launchers could hurl explosive projectiles two hundred yards and cripple any attackers where they landed. Even wild shots sent a spray of devastating shrapnel in a fifteen-foot radius and tore chunks out of the wood barriers or cut away at the welds on the metal walls in front of the vehicles. However, the defenders soon ran through the limited ammunition they had, and when it was out, the attackers once again took up their collective movement toward the breastworks.

As the battle raged, Henry heard Sergeant Sidney giving reports on his two-way radio to the Marines at the base, and also to the east where a pack of soldiers was watching their backs. Henry asked Sergeant Sidney if the Marines could bring more ammunition for the machine guns, and Sydney said he'd pass on the request and encourage them to hurry.

That was the good news.

The bad news soon appeared on the back of a long body pickup truck in the form of a mounted .50 caliber machine gun. The attackers had gotten possession of the devastating weapon called the "Ma Deuce" from the truck that stalled on the interstate near Cordele delivering it and other materials to the Marine Base. They now had it swivel mounted in the back of a pickup truck. The truck also had protective metal plates welded on the front over the cab and engine. It rolled across a bridge over the Kinchafoonee Creek on North Jefferson directly north from the defenders and opened fire at about three hundred yards. Adding the power of a .50 caliber machine gun to the battle scale placed a heavy weight on the side of the attackers.

Back Door Threat

About two miles southeast of the increasingly violent action on the bypass road, a band of over a hundred heavily armed men from the Cordele contingent came out of the dim light after a forced night march to Albany and arrived near the intersection of U.S. Highway 82 and the circular bypass. Once they reached the intersection, they planned to turn right onto the U.S. 19 bypass and move north to attack the rear of the Albany defenders.

Earlier they had bypassed the large MillerCoors Brewery surrounded by a blockade of abatis and packed with militia defenders.

A few hundred yards before the intersection, however, they saw another band of local militia behind a hastily thrown together barricade. The attackers fired a collective volley at the barricade that wounded two of the defenders and killed another. After the militia saw such a large and determined group headed in their direction, the defenders quickly ran away, dragging their wounded with them.

More confident now, the attackers headed west toward the bypass and marked places in the neighborhoods along U.S. 82 where they planned to come back later for some serious looting. Their rapid win over the Albany militia made them feel more aggressive, and they quickened their pace just at daybreak.

Once they hooked a right and headed north, the highway would take them directly to where the big fight would take place. If they hurried, they could make that distance in less than an hour. They did not want to be too late to make it a coordinated attack on the defenders and incur the wrath of that Rowdy Burdette man who was in charge.

It was beginning to get lighter as they approached the intersection, and ahead, they could just see U.S. 19 bypass in front on the raised highway with the inviting ramp leading up to the roadbed. So, it would be soon, but… What was that? Squinting, they saw something that looked like vehicles in the road ahead. Although they were walking rapidly in the middle of the highway, they now slowed to a regular pace to determine what it could be. One of the younger members of the group realized that one of the vehicles ahead had the protruding barrel like some kind of a tank. A tank! No. Something else. What the…?

About that time, flares were launched from the collection of vehicles ahead. Once the starbursts lit up the sky, they could see a Bradley fighting vehicle and two Humvee jeeps with machine guns and what looked like small cannons mounted on the back of them, all pointed in their direction. The vehicle lights came on, and behind them were soldiers in helmets and regular military gear. The invaders were now stuck, standing in the middle of the road like a heard of deer in the headlights. This was regular army… No, not the army. This was the, by God, U.S. MARINES! Nobody bargained for this.

Just then a microphone sounded. "Attention all of you people standing there in the middle of the highway, you are facing a detachment of United States Marines, and we have all of you in our gunsights. Do not move or we will open fire. You have two choices, attack us and die, or drop your weapons. If you drop all of your weapons where we can see them, then you will be allowed to turn around and go back where you came from. You have five seconds to decide which it will be." Another volley of flares went up into the sky to augment and replace those now burning and slowly descending around them. It was very bright on the street.

After all that looting over in Cordele, Lake Blackshear, and the other places... After all that marching for days and through the night just to get here... Damn.

"Five... Four... Three..."

The clanking of dropped weapons started like a spring rain, one... then another, with two more, then the noise of a cavalcade of bouncing clanks, clunks, and more clanks. Without waiting for more discussion or an invitation, those in the back of the group turned and started peeling off back down the street, walking at first, then jogging out of the light of the flares, scattering back into the safety of the dark like roaches when a light is turned on in the basement.

In the clean morning air, Captain Rodriguez heard the clatter of small arms fire in the distance that lasted for several minutes. As he listened, the noise was joined by the deeper, throated sound of a rhythmically firing heavier caliber weapon. Rodrigues cocked his head. "Damn, that's the heavy hammer of a .50 cal."

Battle for the Bypass

The devastating .50 caliber machine gun that tore into the defenders behind the plastic bales was fired in short, three-round bursts. With large, powerful slugs, it could penetrate deeply into any protection and carried a savage aftershock. The bullets and their pressure waves shattered and shredded the concrete pilings and bales on the top of the highway where the defenders had, until now, been safely hiding. Because the gun was shaking on the truck springs, its aim was not precise, but where it hit, the effect was catastrophic.

The defenders returned fire, but the heavy machine gun had a steel plate in front of it with just the barrel poking through and their bullets dinged off the protection. Behind the gun's shield, Henry caught a glimpse of the tall man laughing while he blasted them with the gun, throwing shots the size of a man's thumb traveling at a half mile per second.

People began to fall on the defenders' side, and most of those remaining uninjured just hugged the ground. The gun continued to hammer in bursts that chewed up everything in its path, and several defenders began to crawl away weeping. Only the thick plastic bundles could stop it, but even those began to crumble with the pounding. After two or three solid hits, the bindings broke and the bales began to slide apart. The leader of the Cordele group spread the destruction around, often targeting the top of the bridge where he saw that the sheriff had his command center.

As the bales became unstable, the bullets now could

punch through. Not just the .50 cal., now other bullets of lesser size and force could penetrate the weakened defenses. With the defenders hunched down to avoid the hailstorm of projectiles, the attackers crept closer and began to throw pipe bombs. They were not very accurate but when they exploded, the pipe bombs tore huge chunks out of the barrier. Following the bomb throwers, more shooters crept forward to within fifty yards of the barricades, then closer. Now when the bullets hit, bits of the barricade plastic were torn away from the bales and floated in small, thin sheets, drifting in the air and landing like autumn leaves in a gentle breeze.

Henry could hardly distinguish any sounds from the roaring noise, and the others, pressed against whatever protection they could find, heard the pops of gunfire from the sounds of battle through the thickness like cotton in their ears. The noise blended with the screams of fear from their companions, then in a different pitch as the bullets ripped through the barrier to find the soft flesh of the defenders.

Where the shots now hit, there were terrible gashes. Henry could see blood spurting from a chest wound, pulsing with each heartbeat in declining volume. Some of the defenders with panicked faces grabbed their dead or wounded neighbors and rolled behind them using the bodes for extra protection. Some still returned fire back at the attackers, screaming as they fired, seeming to need the indistinguishable whine of "Agggggg" coming animal-like from their throats as a motivation for their flagging courage. With the heavy machine gun blasting into the protective structures, it was a great risk for the defenders to return fire either toward the pickup truck or at the ground forces crawling closer. The battle left indelible scars on everyone.

Jerico still crouched and ran back and forth, directing people to move to where it was safer. A few of the defenders still shot back, mostly without aim, just to send some reply back toward the barrage that was rapidly disintegrating their protection. Some threw the remaining hand grenades, which, for a few minutes, slowed the attackers' progress from rushing forward to where they could have easily jumped the wall.

Preparing a massive charge, now under the covering fire of the big machine gun, the attackers slowly began to creep ever closer to the barricades, pushing the carts and trucks across the highway tarmac. Some now crawled to cut through the barbed wire rolls stretched across the street, and it was clear that they were preparing for a final rush for the barricades.

Henry noticed that most of the impact of the shots was concentrated in the middle of the defenses above and below Jefferson Street that led into town.

This onslaught decimated that area, but toward the extremes of the upper highway on the outer edges, there was little fire. Those defenders, although the least trained and qualified, had better shots at the attackers and could aim their weapons at the sides of the approaching carts and cars. They were able to hold off the attack just enough.

Seeing they were in a hopeless situation, Henry, Trey, and one of Jerico's deputies ran in a crouch for a hundred yards around the far-left side of the barricade, then down the steep flank of the defenses on the Liberty Express bypass. They were bending low, fearing that the attackers might spot them crossing the clearing that led to thick woods at the bottom of the highway.

They ran across the flat surface and crashed into the woods to put them into a firing position against the hammering gun. Vines cut and tripped them as they had to sprint, fall, crawl, get back up, and then sprint again through more than a hundred yards of a thick scrub and briar filled forest. The flanking action seemed to be taking them forever as the big gun continued to sound the rapid bam, bam, bam as it mutilated their friends.

They finally broke free of the brush and could see the back of the truck ahead. Quickly, they maneuvered to get clear shots at the three men serving the big weapon, including the burly leader, still pouring lead into their fellow defenders. Henry said, "Keep shooting at 'em til you're sure their dead." They rapidly pumped a fusillade of bullets toward the pickup truck.

The same moment they shot the big man down, the attackers began their charge in what looked like a wave of almost two hundred opponents screaming and shooting as they ran toward the barricades. Henry and his two companions jumped on the truck and Henry moved the .50 caliber gun to point downward, aiming at the horde of assailants caught between this smashing weapon and the Albany defenders back on the highway behind the disintegrating barricades. Trey helped Henry by feeding the rows of thick cartridges as the deputy watched and defended them from any of the attackers who had noticed them.

Henry began with the attackers rushing to overrun the Albany defenders. The large bullets tore into their flank and rear, cutting down those men in rows. Sometimes a bullet would pass through the flesh of two people before becoming embedded in a third. Some would pass through a body, ricochet off the metal plate in front of the cart, and then pass through again.

Parts of the roadbed became a small stew of blood and tissue. For the attackers, now there was no cover, no hope. The charging wave heading to the barricades moments before was reduced to the bleeding and the dead. Some of the attackers turned and fired at the truck, and above the noise of the firing, Henry could hear pings like small bells ringing as the bullets gonged the metal protection. He felt the sharp sting of metal from ricochets.

He saw the deputy jerk and fall, then Trey grunt and stagger as at last the bullets fired from the attackers reached them on the truck bed. Trey managed to wrap something around his arm and continued to feed the gun with one hand. After a few moments of continual firing, they realized they had run out of ammunition. The back of the truck was ankle deep in spent brass shells. Henry saw blood dripping, and noticed he had a dozen dings on his arms and face caused by bits of flying metal that had bounced off the truck's armored plates. He wiped away the blood dripping into his eyes as he helped Trey feed another long, heavy belt of ammunition into the gun.

The desperate attackers turned and ran to seek protection away from the impact of the 50 cal. However, the defenders who had been huddled on the roadbed of the bypass now realized that Henry had control of the large machine gun, and they joined in, rising and pouring a new barrage of fire down onto the men from Cordele. Henry, with a new belt of cartridges, swung the big gun around to join them.

It was too much to take. All along the battle line, the army that had come from Cordele, fearful of being shot from behind or by the Albany defenders before them, broke and ran as fast as they could back toward the bridge leading to Chehaw.

When the firing slowed, Henry helped Trey rebandage his arm and found that the truck, protected by a steel plate, although with two flat tires shot out in the in front, still had a working motor. He drove it wobbling toward the bridge to join their colleagues who had witnessed the rescue. By the time they reached the barricades, they could see survivors were stepping around the dead to tend to the wounded.

At the same time, new defenders arrived at the bypass barricades from the reserves on Slappey Drive and the neighborhood of Rawson Circle. Many of the bypass defenders had been shot in the head and were dead. Those that were wounded were moved to treatment, and those positions were filled with the new arrivals. The uninjured who had withstood the barrage of the heavy machine gun were told to rest.

The Marines Have Landed

Henry parked, helped Trey get down off the back of the truck, and sat him by the road under the bridge until he could find some help. He stepped around the dead attackers and went up the bank to see about the main area of defense on the top of the bridge. As he reached the top of the barricade, he saw that Bubba had arrived, and was making his way onto the upper highway driving the other swamp truck. He quickly filled Henry in on what his father had done to stop the attack from the west, and how the remaining soldiers were being chased back home. Most of them, once they learned what had happened to the others in the swamp, had thrown down their heavy weapons and packs to run back toward Alabama.

Henry asked Sergeant Sidney to direct a group to stand watch in case their enemies tried to return. He told one of the militia leaders to reload all the weapons they could find to be ready for another attack. Sidney sent a final message through the communications gear, picked up his weapon, and immediately took charge of organizing the defenses.

As Henry looked around, he could see dead and wounded everywhere. He asked Bubba to shuttle the wounded defenders to the hospital in his truck since Henry's had been riddled with bullets and was unusable.

Survivors were taking some of the walking wounded down for medical care. Henry directed others to apply makeshift bandages, then lift those who could not walk onto stretchers and into Bubba's truck. They also used golf carts to carry them down to the triage tents and moved the dead across the highway to put them under a tarpaulin.

Once Bubba's truck was almost full of the wounded, Henry showed him where to find Trey and take him to the medical tent. Several Humvee jeeps arrived with Captain Rodriguez, who shouted, "We're going to give you a hand. We heard the shooting and then heard it stop." He saw Sergeant Sidney and shouted, "Open this blockade and let us through. We'll make sure those people are gone."

Sergeant Sidney, Henry, and some of the defenders moved aside several of the shattered bales of plastic, and the captain roared through with four Humvees, two armed with MK 19 Grenade launchers that could fire forty grenades a minute over fifteen hundred yards, and two with M134 six-barrel mini guns that could spew two thousand rounds a minute over a half mile. Shortly after the jeeps burst through, bouncing over the bodies of the wounded and the dead attackers, they heard explosions and a burr of the mini guns that chased any remaining invaders back toward Lake Blackshear. Captain Rodriguez returned, and they used one of his jeeps to shuttle the rest of the wounded to the triage station or to the hospital a mile away. That was when Henry saw Iris.

Death

As the noise of shouting and rushing about continued and an occasional last few shots were heard in the distance, the wounded continued to be moved to care. Henry now left that task to others as he rushed over to Iris and her father.

She held her father's head in her lap and leaned over to shield him from the glare of the rising sun. One of the massive .50 caliber bullets had torn through a stack of trays embedded in a plastic bundle. By the time the bullet, now almost spent, hit Jerico, scores of plastic shards had penetrated his body. As his life literally was leaking from him through the tatters of his stomach and chest, his face was unscarred and peaceful, serene even, as his eyes searched from her face to the area he could see surrounding him. The shock from his wounds had blocked most of the pain but left his mind confused. Iris shed large, silent tears as she tried to hold her face stoically. She tried not to alarm him but was unable to restrain the finality she could see in his wounds.

When she saw Henry with the nicks and blood smeared on his face, she took in a sharp breath. He knelt by her and felt the noise and horror of the action dim, becoming muted outside the momentary umbrella of care covering the three of them.

As Jerico's eyes found Henry, he tried to speak as a shot of pain hit him.

Henry lightly touched Jerico's hand as he too leaned over him, then he held it firm. "You did it. You set us up to win this fight."

A slight smile came over Jerico's face as he turned his

head back to his daughter hovering over him. He sharply grimaced with another passing bolt of pain, and a distant look came into his eyes, a realization of his limited future. He struggled in the effort to speak again to Iris. "You look so much like your mother in this light." He took in a breath with some difficulty, still looking at his daughter. Then he looked back over at Henry, still kneeling over him and holding his hand, and Jerico Dozier's face frowned with a puzzled look, temporarily disoriented with the shock. "You cut yourself."

A man rushed up to grab Henry by the shoulder and half whispered. "We held them off and they's gone. They stopped all the other bad guys from trying to get in. We safe for now."

The man's words had pulled Henry back from the bubble of compassion into the fray, the greater chaos and noise returned to his consciousness and he looked at the man. "Get everyone supplied with more ammunition. Set up watches on the main roads and stay sharp."

As he was giving the orders, he felt the hand go slack. He looked back down at Jerico and noticed that his eyes had shut. Henry slumped, then reached over and gently touched Iris on her shoulder and squeezed. "I'll get some guys to take him to your house and prepare the grave."

In the distance, they could hear rapid gunfire and explosions as the Marines were chasing the final group of attackers from their Chehaw Park camp. Iris watched more Marine vehicles and solders arrive in silence, her hands on her lap, covered in her father's blood.

Marines

Henry was directing people to gather anything from the dead attackers they could use in the future - clothes, weapons, shoes, belts, backpacks ... when Marine Major Brumby Shackelford joined Captain Rodriguez and he directed her to Henry, who everyone now looked to as their new leader. Shackelford was all business as she looked from the dead sheriff and his weeping daughter to Henry. "We're here now. We scared off a big group back down on the road to Sylvester and they went back east. I don't think they'll return. However, we kept some people there blocking that road. Now we're here to help."

Henry looked around at the carnage. "What changed your mind? I thought when we were back at the base, your colonel said..."

The major held up her hand. "He changed his mind." She looked around at what the Albany militia had done, what it had cost, and scraped her boot back where it was in a puddle of blood coming from Sheriff Dozier. "He's not a bad man, but he was never in combat. When we got outside the base and saw what you were facing, and that you were protecting us instead of the other way around... Well, that's not how Marines operate. I called him on the radio and explained how it was out here. We're with you now."

As the last of the wounded were being put on stretchers to be moved to the triage tents or the hospital, the major gathered her troops and the Humvees and said to Henry, "We're going to take a run out toward where you said they camped at

Chehaw and then on toward Lake Blackshear. I want to make sure they're gone."

"Thank you, Major, but one thing."

"What?"

Henry looked around at the bodies and the people treating the last of the wounded. "This is hard, but we don't have the food or medicine to take in any prisoners or to treat any of them out there who are wounded. We can barely take care of our own. Don't bring any of them back here."

The major thought for a moment, nodded, and said, "Got it."

Seventy-two of the Albany defenders died, including the deputy who had been on the truck with Henry securing the big gun, and all of them were buried and honored in services over the next few days. In the cleanup over the next week, they found two hundred and fifty-seven dead attackers northeast of town, including the big man who was the leader and had caused so much carnage between the interstate highway and Albany.

Willis Graham

Henry stood quietly at the Battle for Albany memorial site. Earlier, the crowd had slowly dispersed after the ceremony where Mayor Ballard had dedicated a plaque to Sheriff Dozier next to one for Willis Graham. He discussed Willis's military career and described him as a man of great courage, and finished the service with a moving statement about his exploits in the swamp to defeat the group from Dothan. He also acknowledged Henry's presence in the audience and gave him credit for his own brave actions.

Near the end of his comments, the mayor announced that electricity generated by the waterwheels on the river had provided enough energy to relight sections of downtown and several buildings in the riverfront area. He said he had a special message for any other outlaws who wanted to come to Albany and cause trouble. He then hit a button, and the music of Ray Charles once again began to blast from the speakers surrounding his statue with the song lyrics, "Hit the road Jack, and don't you come back no more, no more, no more, no more!"

The crowd erupted into cheers and applause and began singing the song along with the recording. Henry noticed that someone had made a carving of a cat nursing some kittens as well as two puppies and placed it there near the memorial site like an offering.

Ballard came up to Henry after the service. Now the music was playing, "Georgia, Georgia, no peace I find. Just an old sweet song keeps Georgia on my mind."

He stopped and stood by him. "I meant what I said about your old man. He saved us from that Dothan group. I don't think we all appreciated him or told him so enough back when it happened."

Henry nodded. "He always gave out more than he got back, at least that was true with me." He looked over at the sign and laughed. "Anyhow, the town giving him that marker for everybody to see is about the last thing he'd have expected. Makes me wish I could tell him now that he's gone. Thanks for doing it."

The mayor looked over at the twin monuments. "They both deserved it."

Henry snapped his fingers. "Oh, congratulations on your election to another term."

"Thanks. This will be my last. We've got things stabilized, and it's time for me to back off and let others do the job. It's been hard and I need a break. I'm staying for this term because before I retire, I want to set up a financial system that rewards people for what they do. Sort of like money used to be. Been working on it with the economics professors and some folks who used to be at the banks. It won't be perfect, but will be a start at a real economy, not just trading things back and forth."

"Well, the election system you set up seems to work."

"Yes. We've sent a team out to restart elections and cooperate with other towns. That will be for the best. What we need now are good managers to make the things we've put in place run more efficiently. I'm also gonna work with some others to support people who need extra assistance. We're calling ourselves, 'Helping Hands.' We're gonna work with kids who are slow in school, people who are sick, and people who just need someone to, you know, give them a hand."

"That sounds like a great idea."

Ballard clapped Henry on the shoulder. "How's Iris coming along. I missed her today. You know, she's been…"

"Yeah. These past few months have put some bark on her."

"Well, let me know if I can help. We've finally got enough going on to set up some charitable support. Maybe she can help with that? At least we're making more medicine now in the labs. That ought to make her happy. Everybody liked her idea to get a traveling medicine wagon to go out and once a week circuit ride the outer perimeter to provide basic healthcare. It will help solidify our relationships with those small towns. They're working on how to manage the resources and put it together."

"Thanks, I'll tell her that and ask about the charity stuff. Might be good for her. You've been kind to us both."

The mayor looked over at the markers again and took in a deep breath. "Jerico Dozier was about my best friend."

"I know." Henry returned the gesture by patting him on the shoulder as he turned and left.

As Henry walked away, he remembered his father looking up at him while lying on his cot shortly before he died. His father had always been able to read his moods. Willis leaned up on one elbow. "Maybe we need to talk about what happened," he said.

Henry nodded. "Yeah. I thought you might help me sort through some things. I think I'm in a kind of shock." Henry bent forward and rubbed his temples with both hands. "I keep seeing all the blood, hearing the screams, and I'm having trouble sleeping. I get these aftershocks, like tremors from the explosions and bullets whacking into the barricades. It's like I'm getting more scared now that it's over than I was when it was happening. I miss all the people who are gone. Was it like this for you back when you were in the war?"

His father drank some water from a nearby jar and sat up, slow with pain, on the side of the bed so he could look Henry in the eye at the same level. "I know about those feelings you have. This thing out near Chehaw was a shock to everyone. That kind of violence all of a sudden hittin' everyone is something y'all will never get over. It's the worst thing a human can experience."

He paused and took a deep breath. "When you were are coming up, I wanted to make you strong and tough. That's what I knew. It worked. You are strong and tough, but you are also smart enough not to get stuck on that. That macho stuff can be phony, and you saw through it and measured that against the times you really needed to be gentle. That's why you feel what you feel. That's the best part of you. Maybe you got that from your mother. You got to care to be really strong. You are better at that than I was."

"But Dad..."

Willis waved his hand. "You tell the others, don't try to make sense of any of it. Not what you did. Not what anyone else did. It just happened and you've got to move on. There is no explaining war and combat. You can't think it through. If you dwell in it, it will eat you."

Henry frowned. "But the new people I've been around and gotten to know in town were so different from those people who attacked us."

"The people weren't different, the leaders were. There was human nature and leadership on both sides. Some people are reasonable and have good intentions and others with dominant voices can move them in a bad direction. Been like that always, I guess. People who had the qualities that folks wanted to follow were born to be leaders. Your Sheriff Dozier was one. I see it in you. Leadership is a burden to carry, but if you have those qualities, it is better to do it well than to shirk it and have some half-ass bullshit artist come in that can take over. Just don't let them try to make you into something you're not."

Two Years Later

Henry came into the house and patted Gator, the mixed breed puppy they had gotten from a farm over near Dawson. Gator returned to Iris, drawn by smell as she prepared part of the rattlesnake she planned to cook with some garden vegetables. "Here," she tossed Henry a bundle of snake, "How about smoking that so we can have it later?"

He set the package down on the counter by the door. She noticed that he hesitated and asked, "So, how did the meeting go?"

Henry took a deep breath. "They finally made it official and turned over the sheriff's job to Major Sheffield."

Iris leaned on the counter. "So, she's got pop's job. Bitch. You never should have let her get it." Because rubber and elastic were gone, she picked up a piece of twine and tied her hair back with quick, determined motions.

Henry watched her movements and said, "It was the mayor and the council's place to make that call."

"You have influence. You could have said something. You should have taken it."

"I'm not a manager. She's got those skills and experiences."

"She's a bureaucrat who sent over all these rules to the hospital about how she is telling us to run things. She does not have a clue what we need to do. My father would never had done that."

"I thought that was just about security for the meds. Safety and stuff..."

"We don't need her to tell us that."

"Iris, we both know it was not her fault the Marines were slow to come."

"She's still always been such a stuck up, prim b..."

"You're gonna have to work with her. She's... still rather... official. At any rate, when you go back to work tomorrow, you'll find that she'll be sending over more of the supplies from the base to the hospital."

"She and the other military have been getting too bossy."

"Don't forget they are doing a good job of protecting the perimeter and expanding the boundaries. Everybody's working well with them now. The council thought it was past time to let them take over more of the logistics, as well as security. Since Colonel Spencer died of his cancer six months ago, she's been using the Marines to do most of the patrolling and training anyway. Our militia and the Marines have been working closer together, and there are really no barriers between us and them anymore. They've been supporting our people going out and negotiating agreements with other towns. The number of people in the militia is winding down and they've turned into more of a group to help people than to be like the military or the police. She will be better at maintaining order and all that stuff. I've got all I can do with the scouts."

"I still don't trust her." She put one hand on the counter. "Our baby sure is taking his or her time." She leaned into the counter and used the leverage to stretch her back. "What other good news you got?"

"We're going to make another train car haul up toward Columbus. They're getting everybody and the horses lined up to make the push Thursday morning. Some people are loading the cars now with trading stuff and making plans on how to organize the supplies they'll be bringing back from up there. Gonna use the new barter currency with the textile mills in Columbus, where they've got a warehouse full of bolts of cloth and some ready-made clothing. They'll also be bringing back goods from the harvest along the tracks. Folks over there had it worse than we did. Town population is down almost fifty percent. Some from fighting, but mostly starvation. They said the smell from Atlanta is still winding down."

"Okay. I really don't want to hear about all that. It's upsetting."

"Yeah. Sorry. Ah, next month, we're also going to get some stuff from up at Butler, where they have that big solar farm. Those folks have electricity to power the equipment for sawmills, lathes, weaving, and welding. It's about the only place that's growing in size 'cause they have jobs. They are making things people need and can't get anywhere else."

"Well, I just hope we can get more medical supplies from over at Fort Benning like I asked for."

Gator was now jumping on the side of the counter where Henry left the snake meat. Henry pulled off a small piece and threw it out in the yard and Gator rushed to snag it.

"Oh, and Bubba found some more gear and a few guns in the woods going out toward Dothan." Henry laughed. "Amazing how some of that stuff is still showing up after all this time. He was out there with two of the women from town he was supposed to be training. Trey said the women really looked glad to be back in town with the stuff."

"He still creepy?"

"He just never developed social skills with the ladies. Oh, I forgot. Bubba heard a rumor from somebody he met on the road that a new U.S. government was forming, and they were trying to reestablish power grids. Said this bunch was setting priorities to send the new power they could generate to places when it was available. They were going to start with industries like medicine, food, and clothing."

Iris put down the damp dish cloth. "I'll believe that when the air conditioning comes back on and some fancy dressed person rides up here in a gas-powered car to tell us we have to pay taxes again."

"Well, I'm not holding my breath either."

"Mmmm. So, Sheffield has the sheriff's job but you're hanging onto the sniper-scouts?"

"Yeah. They've got a different mission. We're still going on trips even further out to see what's there and who might be friendly... or not. Those farms out on the edges that have the land to grow more food are doing well under the barter system, but they're also the most vulnerable without anybody else around them."

"Did you stop by to check on the markers for your father and mine?"

"Yeah, over near the Ray Charles statue. Actually, it was Shackelford that got some people to clean up the weeds around them. I didn't have to say anything. I think they'd have liked the signs near each other."

She was looking out the window at Gator and dried her hands on her pants. "Maybe so. Didn't think they knew each other all that well." She pointed. "When you take that snake to smoke it in the box you made, start the fire to cook this part here and put on the big pot of water to heat." Iris handed him the bit of snake she had rubbed with some sorrel leaves in a container to grill outside with sliced peppers and onions.

Henry looked down, swallowed, and let out a sigh. "I did wrong by my father. I used to say he didn't want to come to dinner with you and your dad, but I never invited him. I thought he was so rough that maybe he'd run you off. I got too hung up on you and your dad and neglected my own. Never told him I was sorry for that."

Iris let her shoulders relax a little. "I'm guessing from what I remember about him, he knew that. You two seemed close. He loved you no matter what and wouldn't have held it against you." She smiled. "Maybe I enticed you too much."

"Maybe. I was sure gone on you, but I was still a jerk to him."

"Yeah. I can still see that in you sometimes." She threw the wet towel at him.

He caught it in one hand and laid it on the counter. "Well, you were quite a distraction."

She smiled slyly and rubbed the bulge in her stomach. "Still could be if you'd get that snake smoked."

He gave her a glance, then looked out in the yard. "Well, here lately you've been telling me that you are an old, married, pregnant lady."

"Not so old." She smiled again with her head crooked to the side.

She watched him leave and saw where the afternoon sun highlighted the scars on his face caused by the bits of metal from ricochet slugs dinging off the truck. His skin never filled in, but left little indentions and some ugly scars on Henry's forehead and cheek. She'd seen kids stare at him on the street.

Just as well. The horror of the beltway battle should never be forgotten or repeated. The roar of the noise from the bullets and explosions, the screams and seeing the blood, and her father never left her. If Henry was the battered poster child to keep that from happing again, it was okay with her.

Henry noticed the day lilies and spring roses returning along the fence leading to the road as he set the snake up on the small metal smoker bin. He was thinking about how much Iris had changed as he watched her putter through the kitchen window. She lost her innocence, and now all her actions had a hard-edged determination. The goodness of her character had not changed, but the compassion with which she saw things and expressed herself had diminished. He wondered if having the baby would soften her again.

Henry missed the sweetness she had before, but recognized a change in almost everyone. Yet, he thought, everyone had not been kidnapped, threatened, manhandled and had her dog killed trying to save her. Everyone had not had their father die in their arms from his stomach and chest being ripped open. Still, he missed that innocence in her and in them all. He had learned, at last, that his father had been right. At night, and sometimes when he least expected it, the dreams came.

End

Other books by Jay Beck
you may wish to read

Jay Beck's most recent book, *Casting Stones*, was awarded the best historical fiction written in

Georgia by an independent Writer for 2019.

Reader comments on *Casting Stones*

"I found this book to be gripping both for its intrigue related to the Greek election but also for the understory of the ancient statues of the Greek gods. Jay's background inside of a presidential election comes through the pages as you feel the reality of what he writes. Heartily recommend the book!"

"This is an interesting, extremely well-written historical novel about a young American political consultant advising a presidential campaign in Greece in the 1980's. The story is filled with political espionage and intrigue, well-developed characters, and fascinating descriptions of both Ancient Greek history and modern-day Greece. It's also the story of the behind-the-scenes battle between the United States and the Soviet Union to influence the political and economic future of Greece before the fall of the Soviet Union in 1991. I highly recommend the book."

"The author takes his incredible gift of storytelling, adds wit, suspense, and political expertise, and the result is another good book. I'm impressed with the way he takes his extraordinary professional experiences and weaves them into a narrative that is both compelling fact and fiction. I recommend this book and can't wait until the author's next book is out."

In reading this book, you become totally involved in the characters. The descriptions of them in their many circumstances make you keenly aware of the dangerous time it was during the 1985 election in Greece not only for Mark Young but for the author as well. Reading about the treasures of Greece, Maria Beckett, a truly brilliant, passionate patriot and especially the author's brilliant writing is a must-read for everyone.

"Wow – this was an amazing book!!! Jay Beck's writing keeps the reader totally engrossed in the story!!! This is a historical novel – so as well as being a good story, you might just learn a little history while you are at it!!!"

"The story is set in Greece during the 1985 elections. The story is written in the perspective of Mark Young – who is a political consultant. The story tells a lot of the battle between the United States and the Soviet Union – in regards to the Greek election. I don't write spoilers – BUT, I will warn you that once you get into this story, that you will have a hard time putting the book down until you reach the ending. (I would be awake all hours of the night reading!)"

"You can count the truly riveting novels on campaigns and politics on one hand. But John Beck, with his hands-on knowledge of American consultants abroad, has produced another great read, following a previous story on a campaign in Panama. This time the action is set in Greece in the mid-eighties and the U.S. and the U.S.S.R. are both 'meddling' in tough and devious ways. And, again, Beck has a 'femme fatale' as a key player in the action, a Greek woman who may be the most interesting character (in my view) In the book.

His prior book, *Panama's Rusty Lock,* reached number two on Amazon in Central and South American category

2020 historical fiction Finalist for the Manhattan Book Awards.

Reader comments on
Panama's Rusty Lock

"Page-turning! Panama's Rusty Lock is interesting and intriguing. Jay Beck really is an insider that can communicate a story. Descriptions that are very vivid - a must read. Thank you, Jay, for showcasing the Panamanian story that has not been told in such a lively fashion. It is compelling to me and everyone else that I know that has read it. Modern history well written."

"As a history major in college, this book was impressive in its scope and the author's personal knowledge of actually being involved in the history as it was being made is an incredible read. Five stars seems inadequate. I give it 10."

"Best book I have read in many years. Don't miss it!"

"As someone who has never given Panama much thought at all, I didn't expect to be very engaged here. Jay Beck managed to yank me out of the comfort of my home and into a climate of political unrest and corruption. The unsettling accounts of the drug trade in the area was by far my favorite part, and I will be seeking out books on that subject in the future. Panama's Rusty Lock will appeal to those who love their drama mixed with politics."

"I absolutely love historical fiction and non-fiction books, and it seems like they have come together in Panama's Rusty Lock: A Novel."

"I would highly recommend it, especially to lovers of historical fiction."

"Panama's Rusty Lock is a fascinating backstory of the 1984 Presidential election in Panama, the country's first free political election in 16 years. The author, Jay Beck, takes the reader on a deep dive into the machinations of multiple, and warring, political entities during the campaign and, in the process, reveals a land rife with corruption, drug trafficking, fraud, CIA sponsored wars, abuses of power, and endless spying. Jay Beck, who worked in Panama on this campaign, captures the essence and exposes the underbelly of this landmark political event. Highly recommend."

"I absolutely love historical fiction and non-fiction books and it seems like they have come together in Panama's Rusty Lock: A Novel. I learned quite a bit about Panama and the world around it - something I hadn't really read about before. Usually, when we think of historical fiction, we think of wartime novels, but that certainly isn't the case here. The unrest and corruption felt hauntingly real and I appreciate that, no sugarcoating, but no overdramatization as well. Certainly a great read for anyone who wants to know more about Panama's history or anyone who just wants a great story. Note that there are some elements of drug culture for those that are sensitive to it."

CPSIA information can be obtained
at www.ICGtesting.com
Printed in the USA
JSHW030309200121
10882JS00001B/1

9 781736 119006